PUFFIN BOOKS

The Angel Stone

Livi Michael is the author of four books for
adults and the bestselling series of books about Frank
the hamster, for younger children. Her award-winning
book for teenagers, *The Whispering Road*, has received
much critical acclaim. She has two sons and
lives near Manchester.

LIVI MICHAEL

The Angel Stone

PUFFIN

PUFFIN BOOKS

Published by the Penguin Group
Penguin Books Ltd, 80 Strand, London WC2R ORL, England
Penguin Group (USA) Inc., 375 Hudson Street, New York, New York 10014, USA
Penguin Group (Canada), 90 Eglinton Avenue East, Suite 700, Toronto, Ontario, Canada M4P 2Y3
(a division of Pearson Penguin Canada Inc.)
Penguin Ireland, 25 St Stephen's Green, Dublin 2, Ireland (a division of Penguin Books Ltd)
Penguin Group (Australia), 250 Camberwell Road, Camberwell, Victoria 3124, Australia
(a division of Pearson Australia Group Pty Ltd)
Penguin Books India Pvt Ltd, 11 Community Centre, Panchsheel Park, New Delhi – 110 017, India
Penguin Group (NZ), cnr Airborne and Rosedale Roads, Albany, Auckland 1310, New Zealand
(a division of Pearson New Zealand Ltd)
Penguin Books (South Africa) (Pty) Ltd, 24 Sturdee Avenue, Rosebank, Johannesburg 2196, South Africa

Penguin Books Ltd, Registered Offices: 80 Strand, London WC2R ORL, England

penguin.com

Published 2006
1

Set in Bembo 11.5/14.5 pt
Typeset by Palimpsest Book Production Limited, Grangemouth, Stirlingshire
Made and printed in England by Clays Ltd, St Ives plc

British Library Cataloguing in Publication Data
A CIP catalogue record for this book is available from the British Library

ISBN-13: 978-0-141-31923-0
ISBN-10: 0-141-31923-2

To my father, who has had constant faith in this project.

Acknowledgements

Many people have helped the development of this novel. My thanks to the librarians of Chetham's Library, Michael Powell and Fergus Wilde, to Carol Davies for several consultations and advice, and to Ian Hunton, for advice on technicalities and technical support.

And a special thank you to my agent, Philippa Milnes-Smith, and my editor, Pippa le Quesne, for their tireless support and efforts above and beyond the call of duty!

Contents

Inside the Crypt

Beneath the steps dividing choir from nave
a narrow stair drops downward to the crypt,
a vaulted cavern, reeking of the grave
both damp and sulphurous, like candles dipped
in oily water. Points of fiery light
hang in the gloom beyond the studded door.
A switch is tripped; there's nothing strange in sight
but pillared shadows on the muddy floor.

You will not see him, here among your friends,
nor hear him, though the silence is complete.
He's always standing where your vision ends,
no ragged breath, nor furtive scrape of feet.
He has no place in time, no fixed estate.
Your future is his past. He's never late.

Simon Wood

Here, Now

Manchester, Present Day

Slowly the spinning sensation stopped and the darkness returned. Kate could feel tiles beneath her feet, and smell a cold, night smell. Where was she now? she thought. *When* was she?

She seemed to be sitting on a wooden bench. When she groped along the bench her fingers closed on something metallic. The torch.

Kate switched it on. Its pale beam fell on the Angel Stone with its sand-coloured carving. The Angel Stone. Something she could recognize. The one thing that had survived the centuries unchanged. She took a deep breath. She was here again, back in the cathedral, just as if nothing had happened. There was the choir screen, there the video monitor. The door to the crypt lay closed and still. What was she supposed to do now?

I'm here, all right? she said silently. *What happens now?*
Nothing.

Darkness and silence. Kate listened as hard as she could, clutching the torch with both hands, but she could only hear the whispering of trees outside. She felt as though the universe had collapsed around her, yet everything was unchanged. She remained where she was, waiting for the world to settle into something she could comprehend.

It is only in the darkness that we find out who we really are.

Someone had said that to her, but she couldn't remember who.

Suddenly Kate turned the torch off. She forced herself to sit in absolute darkness for a while, and when she became aware of how tightly she was gripping it, made her fingers relax.

'That's better,' said a voice further along the bench.

Kate almost dropped the torch. She fumbled for it wildly, then switched it on, swinging the light round. The old man flung his arm up to shield his eyes.

'Careful,' he said. 'My eyes aren't what they were.'

Then he smiled, as though he had said something funny. Kate moved sharply away from the bench and kept the light on him. The beam travelled over the long, silver hair and the black cap. He wore a dark, dusty cloak that fell to the floor in folds round his feet.

'Wh-who are you?' she said, when she could speak. 'What are you doing here?'

What am I doing here? she might have added, but didn't.

'Good questions,' the man said. 'But turn the light off, please. I can't see you.'

'I can see you, though,' Kate said. She moved to the front of him slowly, still keeping the beam directed on his face like a camera. The old man raised his sleeve and Kate's light fell on the dark cloth. She could see the weft of the wool, and a small thread that had come unravelled, but his face was shrouded in darkness.

'Are you afraid of the dark?' he enquired mildly. Kate didn't respond. She kept the torch trained on him, trying to see over his arm. But she could only see the skull cap above and the silver beard below.

'You won't learn anything, if you are,' he said.

Kate's foot kicked against the wooden bench and the torch-light slipped, but she adjusted it again quickly.

'Your generation knows nothing of the dark,' the man continued. 'And so you know nothing. Don't you remember me telling you that it is only in the darkness that we find out who we really are?'

He raised his other hand and Kate's torch went out.

She thought she heard herself screaming, '*NO!*' and she clicked the switch desperately, but nothing happened.

'I'm sorry,' the voice went on, 'but I really can't talk to you with that thing glaring in my eyes.'

Kate stood in the absolute darkness, and all sense of who she was fell away from her. She wanted to run, but had no idea where to. She had questions to ask, but could only hear the blood pounding in her ears.

'Now,' said the man. 'What is it that you wanted to know?'

Kate groped for the reassuring solidity of the bench.

'I want to know where my father is,' she said.

And as she said it, she felt a burst of grief and longing so pure that she feared it would choke her. Why had he left her? she thought.

'Do you remember,' the man said, 'that I once showed you a star?'

And suddenly Kate did remember seeing a prick of ice-cold light through a window. She had been there with this old man. The Warden. She remembered him now. They had looked at it through a thin sheet of tin with holes punched in it, which the Warden had slid up and down a wooden rod, explaining the nature of the star's orbit. At the same time she remembered her father trying to explain to her about time, using a piece of paper and a needle.

'Different worlds, Kit,' the Warden said. 'Each of them revealing more fully the celestial plan. Have you never wondered about that mystery, Kit? Have you no questions of your own?'

'Why do you keep calling me Kit?' Kate said. 'Where's the boy? Where's –' but she could not bring herself to think about the spirit. 'What have you done with him?' she said.

The Warden smiled sadly. 'I sent him on a journey,' he said.

Kate felt a pang of fear. 'A journey?' she said. 'Where to?'

The Warden did not reply.

'You mean you killed him,' she said.

'Killed?' the Warden's voice was thoughtful. 'That's one way of looking at it.'

'How many ways are there?' Kate said sharply. The Warden's voice was melancholy. 'You'd be surprised,' he said. Kate felt a spark of rage.

'You did kill him, didn't you?' she cried. 'But why? What did he ever do to you?' and to her horror she felt tears welling in her eyes. Angrily she dashed them away.

The Warden rose, and in the dim light from the windows she could see him moving his hands in distress. He came towards her.

'Kit – Kate,' he said. 'Don't be afraid, please. I will explain – I will try to explain.'

He placed a hand on her arm. She started to pull away from him, but he put his hand over hers. His voice was gentle. 'Come with me,' he said, and Kate's protest died away. To her surprise, she allowed herself to be led through the small arched doorway on the north side of the cathedral.

There in the doorway, she paused. To the right of the

cathedral, the great modern structure that was Urbis glowed with a greenish light and sporadic traffic moved along Corporation Street. Neon lights flashed and street lamps lit the road with an electric glare. Even the massed clouds glowed orange.

To the left of Urbis and a little way ahead, lay all the inns of Long Millgate, exactly as they were four hundred years ago.

There was a yellowish, wintry light. The wind blew flakes of snow and vegetable matter along the street. Kate could hear the noise of the river. She looked, bewildered, from one world to the other. Try as she might, she could not see the point at which the sky, or time, changed.

'It's all here,' she said aloud, wonderingly. 'All of it here, now.'

Simeon

I

2nd October 1604

Simeon's head nodded with the rocking of the cart and finally flew up after a particularly hard jolt. His mother's arm tightened round him.

'Manchester,' said the wagoner, and he spat neatly over the bridge into the water. He was a man of few words and much chewing. Simeon would have liked to ask him what he was chewing, but whenever he thought of speaking, his mother sensed it and squeezed his arm, warning him to be silent.

But now the wagoner seemed inclined to talk.

'See that church?' he said. 'Warden's a wizard.'

He glanced sideways at Simeon's mother as he said this, and she looked quickly away. Ahead of them there was a huge church surrounded by a cluster of buildings. All day layers of dense cloud had threatened rain, but now an orange sun pierced the layers, kindling the windows of the church, and the stone of the steeple glowed.

'A black wizard, aye,' the wagoner went on. 'Some say you can see him flying from the steeple like a black crow at sunset. Others say he roams the streets at night in the form of a great black dog.'

Simeon felt his mother squeezing his arm.

'So you'll have to be careful here,' the wagoner went on. 'Mind your Ps and Qs.'

Simeon didn't know what that meant, but his mother gave him a warning look.

'You don't want him turning you into summat nasty.'

'We will not trouble him,' Simeon's mother said, since the wagoner seemed to require an answer.

'But maybe he'll trouble you,' said the wagoner, and Simeon's mother was silent.

Simeon didn't like the wagoner. He had told his mother so as they had climbed in and she had hushed him violently. They had trudged for more than twenty miles and it was the first lift they had been offered. Now the wagoner flicked the reins and the horse hauled them slowly over the bridge that led across the river to the town.

Part way over the bridge, a hoarse, desperate voice startled them.

'Water!'

Simeon jumped so violently he nearly fell off the cart.

'Water!' cried the voice. 'For mercy's sake!'

Simeon looked all around, but he couldn't see where the voice might be coming from. The wagoner cackled.

'It's a magic bridge, this,' he said, winking broadly at Simeon.

'Water!' cried the voice again.

'Water!' cried Simeon, in exactly the same tone.

'Eh, that's good,' said the wagoner. 'You ought to put him in one of them travelling shows.'

But Simeon was hanging out of the wagon, leaning towards the sound of the voice.

'Simeon!' his mother said, pulling him back in. 'Where's it coming from?' she asked the wagoner, and he jerked his head towards a curious building in the middle of the bridge.

'A little chapel,' he said. 'Built a long time ago. No one

uses it now. But at the bottom there's a cellar for them that need teaching a lesson.'

He clicked the horse on past the stone chapel and the voice went on calling to them.

'Water!'

'There's water all round you, if you look,' the wagoner called back, and Simeon could see that the building dropped below the side of the bridge, where it hung, suspended, over the foaming river. He half stood again, craning backwards towards the voice.

'Will they let him out?' he whispered in the old language.

His mother said nothing, but pulled him back down, wrapping the blue blanket that they used as a cover at night more firmly round him.

'Hush, Simeon,' she said in a low voice.

'You don't want to worry yourself about such as him,' said the wagoner. 'He'll have been caught thieving, or missing church. You'll most likely see him in the stocks tomorrow.'

Simeon said nothing then, but watched the thick folds of the wagoner's neck as he leant forward to encourage the horse up the hill. He could feel a trembling start in the pit of his stomach and spread outwards into his limbs. He tried to concentrate on his mother, on her thin fingers clasping his arm and the strands of auburn hair whipping into his face.

A little way from the church, the wagoner stopped his horse.

'This is as far as I go,' he said. 'You'd best get out here.'

He got out himself and looped the reins round the branch of a tree, then held out his hand to Simeon's mother. 'Payment,' he said.

Simeon's mother clutched at the slipping blanket. 'I have no money,' she said.

'I didn't suppose you had,' said the wagoner.

Simeon's mother hesitated, then let go of the blanket and took the wagoner's hand. Simeon caught at her other hand, but she pulled away from him.

'Wait here,' she said, touching his face. 'I won't be long.'

She stood poised for a moment on the wagon, then jumped lightly down. Simeon stared after them as the wagoner led his mother into a copse of trees and bushes.

When his mother left him, he didn't know what to do. He pressed his hands down on his trembling knees. He could smell this new town, for each town they came to had its own smell. This one smelt of refuse burning on smoky middens, and something else that he would come to know as the smell of wet wool, stretched out in the fields to dry. Though it was evening there was a great noise: carts loading and unloading, men shouting, children crying and women calling to them. The smell of people rose, sharp and distinctive as the smell of cows. Simeon could hear the ring of a blacksmith's hammer, a dog barking and the rolling of barrels. Then suddenly the church bells rang out, a whole peal followed by a single bell chiming. Simeon spread out his fingers, one for each chime, against the ragged material of his trousers. This was the way his mother had taught him to count, but he always lost track before he got to five.

A bird flew down from the steeple, wheeling slowly, and landed on the branch almost level with Simeon's head. So close, Simeon could see that its feathers were not all black, but blue-green in places, and its eye a round, hard orange. It jerked its head from one side to another, then gave a hoarse call. Simeon blinked rapidly, remembering what the wagoner had said about the Warden. The bird came closer and he could see the ridges inside the bony beak, the thin, flickering tongue. Then it spread its wings and rose, flapping, above him.

Something in Simeon's head shifted with the lifting of the bird. He could feel the tilt and balance in his own skull, and he swayed lightly as the bird flew away. He stood up in the wagon, craning forward, but he couldn't see it any more. That was something he wanted to know. 'Where do the birds go, Mam?' he was always asking. 'Where do they go?'

As if in answer, there was a sudden rustling in the branches behind him and Simeon's mother emerged from them. She seemed out of breath and distracted. She hurried round the side of the wagon, holding her hand out to Simeon and gazing up at him with the urgent look he knew well.

'Run!' she said.

2

Simeon leapt from the wagon and dropped on all fours into the mud. He could run fast, faster than his mother with her long skirt, and soon he was pulling her along a ginnel that led between two high walls, into the streets of the town. The wagoner was coming and in Simeon's mind he was grunting and snorting like a great beast; he could feel his hot, reeking breath on the back of his neck.

But at the end of the ginnel he forgot all about the wagoner. There were so many people: people carrying water, washing, baskets of cut herbs. The houses were built so close together, with the first storey jutting out, that people on opposite sides of the street could reach out and touch. A woman sat in the doorway of one of them, spinning. A cart rolled slowly, impossibly, along the narrow street, taking barrels to an alehouse; there was a butcher's shop with great carcasses hanging from iron hooks, bellies open, ribs exposed, dogs gathering hungrily around.

Simeon and his mother dodged and weaved among the mass of people. Simeon didn't like it, so many strangers pressing and jostling, but he knew it was the best way to disappear, for they had done it many times before. They pushed their way along the sloping street, following the faint but definite sound of music, past an apothecary's shop with coloured jars in the window. Further down, a bellman went past ringing his bell and calling out the hour, then two men in college robes, also ringing a bell and calling out, 'Alms for the poor, alms for the poor.'

Simeon hoped they would find something to eat soon, and then they could leave this noisy, stinking town and sleep in the woods as usual. He could feel sleep stealing up on him, even in this hectic place. Beyond all the noise he thought he could hear the soft call of the woods with their secret, creeping life, nosing and burrowing and crawling to rest among the roots of trees and the undergrowth. His eyes drooped and he moved with the rhythm of the people around him, who had blurred into one many-headed beast. Then they turned a corner and his mother stopped.

'There you are!' said the wagoner. Simeon's eyes flew open and his mother gripped his hand tightly. The wagoner was looking at Simeon's mother with an ugly expression, and behind him stood the night watchman, with his lantern and long axe.

Simeon's mother fell back a step or two. He could feel her fear through her fingers.

'These are the ones I were telling you about,' the wagoner said, still looking at Simeon's mother. 'I know that strangers have to be reported to you.'

'We don't take in beggars,' the night watchman said.

'They're not beggars,' the wagoner said. 'They're with me.'

Simeon's mother looked at him quickly, then away. The night watchman jerked his head towards her.

'Is she with child?' he said.

'No,' said Simeon's mother quickly, for she knew that no parish wanted an extra mouth to feed. The night watchman glared at them through narrowed eyes. Simeon looked at the gleam of the long axe and wondered how far they would get if they ran. In one town his mother had been whipped through the streets, and they had been chased from another by the hue and cry.

'Do you have anywhere to stay?' the night watchman asked.

'They're coming with me,' said the wagoner, before Simeon's mother could answer. He held out his hand to her and Simeon's mother hesitated, then got in the wagon. Simeon climbed in after her and the wagoner untied the horse, which was tethered to a railing.

'Very well then, go,' the night watchman said. 'But don't let the Beadle catch you begging. He'll have you whipped!'

The wagoner said nothing to this, but flicked his reins, and his horse set off with a feeble, protesting whicker.

The noise of the town increased as they moved slowly along the street. Simeon could see men drawing up the boards of their shops, a milkmaid carrying brimming pails. A tiny boy in a thin shirt ran in front of them, and his mother called after him shrilly, 'Joachim! Joachim!' Bigger carts than the wagoner's blocked the highway near the market and the drivers saluted each other. Finally they pulled into a long street of houses that were all a different size and shape and leaning as though propping one another up. Someone emptied slops from a window, narrowly missing them.

Then the wagoner pulled up his horse and looked at Simeon's mother with a peculiar expression on his face.

'All right, lady,' he said. 'Hand it back.'

Simeon's mother looked down, away from him. Simeon looked at the wagoner, mystified.

'Hand it back, Mistress,' he said. 'Or I'll call the night watchman again.'

Simeon's mother still wouldn't look at him, but in a sudden swift movement, she withdrew a leather purse and placed it on the seat. Clutching Simeon's hand, she leapt down with him into the miry street.

'Think yourselves lucky!' the wagoner said, flicking the reins so that the horse moved after them. 'They call this place Hanging Ditch!' He passed them and sludge from the wagon wheels flew up and spattered Simeon's mother's skirts.

A football whizzed by and one of the young lads looked at them with a jeering face. Simeon's mother squeezed his hand. 'Let's go,' she whispered.

Some of the houses had the sign of the hand outside, which meant that ale was brewed there. Simeon's mother knocked at the side door of one of these, for she dared not go in alone, and when a serving woman came out she curtseyed quickly.

'God save you, Mistress,' she said. 'God bless you and your family –'

'Clear off!' the woman said, slamming the door.

'Mistress,' Simeon's mother said at the next house. 'I am a good worker, a tireless worker and we do not need money, only a little food and somewhere to stay.' But she backed off hurriedly as the woman called her dogs.

'You have a kind face, Mistress,' she said at a third place, sinking down in a curtsey and peering earnestly upwards. 'A lucky face. I can tell your fortune from your face.'

'Witchcraft!' the woman said, and she made the sign of the evil eye.

'No witchcraft, Mistress, but a gift from God,' his mother

said, clutching Simeon's hand and hurrying back into the street.

More than an hour later, the main streets were clearing, but they still hadn't found a place to take them in. They trudged past alehouses that were all more or less in a state of disrepair. The smell of mutton and ale wafted out, reminding Simeon how hungry he was. He had to wait while his mother went inside one after another and quickly returned, looking tired and pinched. Simeon didn't like the inns anyway. The sour, stale, fatty smell sickened him, despite his hunger, and the shouting and laughter from inside deafened him. He kept asking his mother if they could leave now, but his mother only shook her head. She seemed determined to stay in the town.

'You again!' one man shouted. 'Where are you off to, eh?' and an old woman in a doorway spat as they passed.

'Come home with me, pretty lady,' said an old man, ragged and covered in sores, and two boys in an alleyway sniggered. A fine rain started and Simeon's mother pulled the blue cloth over their heads.

'I don't like it here,' Simeon said, but his mother wouldn't answer.

'*Daya,*' he said, touching her face, 'Let's go,' but his mother only shook her head and said he must speak English here.

They carried on past more houses that had the sign of the hand outside. From one there was the sound of shouting and singing, from another several men rolled out, kicking and punching. A crowd of men burst out of the doorway with them, shouting them on. Simeon and his mother darted backwards, into the shadow of the nearest alley. A woman ran out of a side door past them and elbowed her way through the heaving crowd.

'Shift your pockmarked arses!' she cried. And seizing a barrel that stood by the door, she dashed water all over the two fighting men, who rolled away from one another to much laughter and jeering from the crowd.

The woman, who was small and round, but fierce, grabbed one of them and gave him a great kick.

'Clear off home!' she told him, then rounded on the others.

'That goes for you lot as well! You should be ashamed of yourselves. As if we're not in enough trouble!'

She went on at them like this for several minutes. Some of the men laughed and jeered at her, but one by one they backed off, complaining.

'See, now I'll have to get more water!' the woman said. 'And I'll bet the pump's closed,' and she picked up the barrel and hurried towards the market square.

Simeon's mother glanced at him and clutched his hand, and they followed the woman, for no reason that Simeon could think of, other than that they didn't know what else to do.

The marketplace was empty now, except for a man propping up fleshboards against some rough wooden stalls, and an old man pushing a broom slowly through the rubbish, which was blowing around. In the centre of the square there was a tall stone column and next to this a wooden stand with a ladder. On top of this the stocks were fixed. Simeon's eyes slid away from these. He had seen too many people punished there.

Pigeons flew down from the gables to peck at the rubbish. Simeon felt a pricking in his shoulders, and his arms lifted like wings. Then he heard the woman's voice.

'Go on,' she said. 'You've not closed yet.'

'You know the rules,' a man's voice answered. 'Only as much water in one vessel as one woman can carry.'

'Well, I'm a woman,' the woman said. 'And I can carry more than that. Go on, fill it up.'

'You've already been once,' said the man.

Simeon's mother walked quickly towards the voices, which were coming from the next street. Where this street met the market square, there was a water pump and a man standing guard. In front of him was the small, round woman, plump as a bird, with strands of light brown hair escaping from her cap.

'Am I not a woman?' she said playfully, and the man, who was very young, not much older than Simeon, looked uncomfortable.

'It's my job, Mistress,' he began, but she turned away from him as Simeon's mother approached. The woman had a small, pointed face and a squint in one eye, though her eyes were not quite crossed. She stood with her head jutting forward, as though expecting trouble.

Simeon's mother stood at a decent distance, with her head bowed. The young man looked her up and down, but she did not look at him.

'God save you, Mistress,' she said.

'And yourselves,' said the woman, looking at Simeon, who was wheeling his arms now, watching the birds.

'My boy is thirsty,' his mother said.

'We don't want beggars here,' said the young man at once.

'Oh, forget about your job for once, can't you, Jonathan?'

said the woman, and she unhooked a metal cup with a long handle from her apron. 'Give the lad a drink.'

Jonathan looked as though he might argue, then he sighed and pressed the handle of the pump. Water flowed into the metal cup, and the woman held it out to Simeon, who drank noisily, then passed the cup to his mother, who finished off the water and wiped her mouth.

'Have you got somewhere to stay?' said the woman and Simeon's mother shook her head.

'Beggars, I told you,' said Jonathan in a low voice. 'We've been warned against them.'

'I can work,' said Simeon's mother quickly.

'Of course you can,' said the woman. 'And the boy too – is he your son?'

Simeon's mother nodded as Simeon ran at the nearest birds, scattering them.

'Simple, is he?' the woman said, and Simeon's mother stiffened.

'He is a good son,' she began.

'Oh aye, they always are,' said the woman. 'He looks a fine, strong lad. Big enough to carry some water. So don't argue,' she said, as Jonathan opened his mouth. There's two women now and a big, strong boy. Get it filled.'

'You'll be looking for Mistress Butterworth's,' she said to Simeon's mother, 'if you want a bed for the night and work in the morning. Which is where I'm heading. If Master Jonathan will get a move on.'

Jonathan looked very put out as he filled the vessel. He muttered something about the Lord's rule, but the woman ignored him.

'Can you carry this?' she said to Simeon as he returned.

In the past year Simeon had grown tall and strong. He

was taller than his mother now. He took hold of the barrel, then braced himself and swung it up. It was heavy, almost too heavy, but he would never admit it.

I don't know what the constable will say,' Jonathan grumbled. The woman's face turned hard.

'And I don't know what your master will say when he hears what you get up to in the taverns,' she said, and Jonathan blushed furiously, opened his mouth, then shut it again.

'Follow me,' the woman said, and she trotted swiftly across the square, Simeon staggering after. 'My name is Mistress Barlow, but I'm known as Susan. What are your names?'

'Mistress – Peploe,' said Simeon's mother as Simeon caught up with them. It was not a name she had given before and she touched him lightly to make him remember. 'Marie. And this is my boy, Simeon,' she said. Susan flashed him a quick, friendly smile.

'He's like my youngest brother,' she said. 'How old is he? Twelve? Thirteen?'

Marie nodded.

'He's growing tall, isn't he?' Susan added. 'All arms and legs. Well, I'm sure we'll find work for him to do. Here, give that to me,' and she took the barrel from Simeon, despite its weight and her size, and they went back into the street they had just walked along, and immediately the noise grew louder.

'Long Millgate,' she panted.

Crowds of men were stumbling from one inn to another, singing. Susan ducked and weaved round them, speaking all the time in a breathless voice.

'You'd best let me do the talking when we get there

– Mistress Butterworth's been out of temper lately – she's up for a fine at the Court Leet – but the other maid, Peggy – she's off now – with child and having a bad time of it – so God knows there's work enough if you're willing – and at least the boy can lift a barrel – All right, mistress?' she said to the old woman who had spat at them before. She sat on her doorstep with her chin in her hand and did not acknowledge the greeting, but went on staring at nothing in particular and mumbling to herself.

Then Susan stopped outside the house where they had first seen her. It was the most dilapidated building of all, shorter than the buildings on either side, and a hot, greasy smell wafted out. Part of the gable end seemed to have fallen in and the windows consisted of tiny leaded panes, several of which seemed to be broken or missing. Smoke billowed thickly from a lopsided chimney and there was the sound of raucous singing from inside.

'Mistress Butterworth's,' she announced.

3

Susan led them through a doorway so low that it scuffed the top of Simeon's head as he passed. Instantly all was darkness, smoke and noise. Simeon held on to his mother's hand as they pushed through jostling bodies. The floor felt slippery beneath his feet. Susan elbowed her way through, shouting, 'Out of the road!' and 'Keep your hands to yourself!'

What light there was in the room came from a great fire on the far wall and two lamps in a window recess. Flakes of soot fell into the fire and smoke blew out, and since everyone appeared to be smoking, the whole room was wreathed in a thick fug. One man stood on a table singing 'Percy of Northumberland'. It was a well-known song and several other people joined in. Susan took them through a further doorway and down a step that Simeon stumbled over, into the kitchen, where another fire blazed. Spattered pans hung round it and a big iron pot hung over the flames. Susan set the barrel of water down and gave the pot a quick stir with a wooden ladle.

'I'll just fetch the mistress,' she said. 'Sit you down.'

Simeon looked at his mother. There were a lot of questions he wanted to ask, mainly about food, but she just shook her head briefly and carried on nodding and tapping her foot in time to the music. Neither of them sat.

Simeon was just beginning to think he would sit down, when he heard a voice.

'Well, you took your time,' it said. It was a rough voice, as deep as a man's, but when Simeon looked up, a massive figure of a woman filled the doorway. She wore a blue skirt and kirtle, tied round the middle with a thick rope, from which dangled a huge bunch of keys. She wore no cap, and black hair hung about her face. Through the mass of hair Simeon could just make out two black eyes, staring. Susan followed her into the room, looking like a sparrow next to a great, fat goose, Simeon thought, and when she was a few steps away from them, the woman stopped abruptly.

'Who's this?' she said to Susan, without taking her eyes off Simeon and Marie.

'New staff for you. This is Mistress Peploe,' Simeon's mother sank down in a deep curtsey, 'and her son, Simeon.'

Marie tugged at Simeon's hand until he remembered to lower his head. But the woman seemed unimpressed. 'Hrrummph!' she said.

A voice called from the other room, 'Has all the ale run dry?' and Mistress Butterworth turned and bellowed so loudly that all the pots rattled.

'Hold your horses, can't you? I've only got one pair of hands!' Then she turned to Susan.

'Get 'em out,' she said and turned to go back into the alehouse.

'Hold on a minute,' Susan said. 'They're here to help.'

'Help themselves to my food,' the woman said.

'Mistress Butterworth,' said Susan, bridling. 'We've been run off our feet all week. Don't tell me there's no work going!'

27

And a man's voice called out again, 'What kind of an ale-wife are you that can't serve ale?'

'The kind that'll shove that tankard where the sun don't shine,' shouted Mistress Butterworth, and she heaved her great bulk over the threshold, jerking her head in the direction of Simeon and his mother.

'They'd better be gone by the time I'm back!'

Simeon's mother made a movement as though they would leave, but Susan caught hold of a large, greasy apron. 'Here,' she said. 'Tie this on.'

'But – your mistress,' said Simeon's mother.

'Never mind her!' Susan said. 'I've wore my legs down to stumps this week, doing the work of three. If she imagines I'm keeping that up, she's got another thing coming. Here, you!' she said to Simeon. 'Can you ladle stew into them bowls?'

Simeon looked at his mother, who nodded, and Susan passed him another apron.

'You come with me,' she said to Simeon's mother, and together they disappeared into the crowded room.

Simeon was very hungry. He stood staring after them for a moment, then picked up a bowl and the ladle. He tried to sip some of the stew from it, but it was too hot. Tentatively he stirred the globules of grease around. Then he spooned some of the lumpy liquid into the bowl. One ladle almost filled it and some slopped over the side. He wiped this with his finger, sucking it. Then Susan reappeared.

'Not that much,' she said to him. 'See, I'll show you.' And she tipped half a ladle into an empty bowl, then taking another ladle, topped it up with a little water. Simeon looked at her.

'Cools it down,' she said and winked at him, then left, carrying three bowls at once.

'Cut that bread, will you,' she said when she came back again. 'Not so thick,' she added, and showed him how to cut the loaf thinly and put half a slice into the bowl with the stew.

Simeon went on cutting bread and ladling stew into bowls while Susan and his mother dashed back and forth, carrying them. He helped himself to stew and bread while no one was looking and managed not to cut his fingers. When the bowls came back empty, Susan merely wiped round them with a crust of bread and passed them to Simeon to fill again, and when the stew ran low, she topped it up with water from the barrel.

Once Mistress Butterworth appeared in the doorway and stared at him, and Simeon wiped his mouth just in time.

'You still here?' she barked.

Simeon didn't know what to say to this. Mistress Butterworth glared at Simeon's mother, who appeared behind her with Susan.

'Is she pregnant?' she asked, just like the night watchman.

'She look pregnant?' Susan said, because Simeon's mother was as thin as a wand. 'Any of us looks pregnant, it's you,' Susan muttered, glancing at Mistress Butterworth's great, round belly.

'I'm not feeding no bairns,' Mistress Butterworth said, glaring at Simeon as Marie followed Susan back into the ale-room. 'Here, you,' she said to him. 'Come here.'

She vanished through a little door at the far side of the kitchen, and Simeon could hear much huffing and cursing. Then the door flew open again.

'Give us a hand, can't you?' she snapped.

Simeon dropped the ladle, which clattered to the floor, and hurried over. Mistress Butterworth was dragging a barrel up the cellar steps. Simeon tried and failed to squeeze past her. Then she retreated a little way down the steps and stood behind the barrel, glowering up at him. Bending down, Simeon grasped the barrel with both hands. It was heavy, but he was strong. His mother always said he didn't know his own strength. He tugged upwards and the barrel lifted, banging and clattering against the door frame. Mistress Butterworth looked as if she might say something surly, then merely pushed past him. 'In there,' she said. Simeon heaved the barrel towards the doorway of the alehouse.

'Leave it!' she barked, and he set it down. Mistress Butterworth pushed it further in with her foot, then went in herself. She didn't come back. After a moment Simeon picked up the ladle from the stone floor, wiped it on his trousers, and went on serving the stew. His mother ran past and touched his arm lightly, to show that she was pleased with him.

A little later, there was a commotion in the inn, and Susan appeared at the kitchen door.

'Black Jack of Ancoats,' she said in a low voice to Simeon's mother, who was helping Simeon to carve up the last of the bread. 'He's trouble, he is – don't you serve him. I'll deal with him.'

Simeon looked at his mother and she touched his arm to show that she wasn't afraid, then carried two more bowls through. Immediately there was a burst of laughter. Simeon dropped the ladle into the stew and hurried to the door.

A rough-bearded man stood with his back to the fire. He wore a black scarf tied round his head like a pirate, and he stood with two or three others, but a space had cleared around them. He looked about, as if searching for someone to pick on.

'Why, it's Master Henshaw,' he said, looking at an older man with scanty hair. Haven't you worn your knees out yet, praying in your secret chapel?' and when the old man didn't respond, he said, 'And Robert Capper – have you still got a priest in that hole?'

A younger man looked as though he would answer, but another held him back.

'Mistress Butterworth!' cried Black Jack. 'Your inn is full of papists!'

Mistress Butterworth pushed past him roughly, carrying a wooden tray.

'As if you cared, you Godless tinker,' she said, and when Black Jack and his companions only laughed, she said, 'Any of you start stirring it in here and you're out – do you hear me?'

Black Jack and his friends made appreciative noises, but they took the ale from the tray and sat at the table nearest the fire. Black Jack produced knucklebones from a pouch and they began to play, bouncing a small black ball on the floor, while some people watched and others turned away.

Susan hurried towards Simeon, and he stepped back quickly into the kitchen.

'Where are the bowls?' she said. 'Come on, hurry up!'

Simeon wished his mother was there, but she seemed to have vanished in the crowded inn. He scalded his fingers rescuing the ladle, which had fallen into the stew, and Susan tutted at him and wiped the handle with a filthy cloth. Then he ran out of bowls, and Susan took down a loaf of hard, stale bread and showed him how to cut a slab from that and use it as a plate for the stew. This kept him busy, but whenever Susan went back into the ale-room, he followed her to the door, trying to catch sight of his mother. At last she came back into the kitchen and he caught hold of her apron, but she pulled away from him.

'I have work to do,' she said, smiling and frowning at him at the same time. Simeon hurried after her to watch from the doorway. Susan was serving Black Jack, but his mother walked by them and as she passed, one of them put his arm round her waist.

'What's this, then?' he roared. 'A new maid?'

Simeon's mother, still holding bowls of stew, tried to twist away, but Black Jack stood up and tweaked at the cap Susan had given her. 'Take your cap off, Pretty,' he said.

Simeon started forward, then looked all around for a weapon. All he could see was the knife on the table. His mother had told him never to pick up a knife. *It will be used against you,* she had said. Simeon's fingers hovered above the knife for a moment only, then closed again and he ran into the crowded room.

'Put her down,' Susan was saying. 'You don't know where she's been.'

'Aye, but I know where I'd like to take her,' the man said.

Simeon's mother twisted away from him strongly. All her pretty auburn hair fell round her shoulders. She held her hand out for her cap, but Black Jack held it out of reach. Simeon knew that if they caused trouble at the inn, they would be thrown out, but he ran forward anyway. But before he could reach the fire, Mistress Butterworth's massive form blocked out the light. She delivered a ringing blow on the ear to the man who held Simeon's mother.

'Has there not been enough trouble in this house without

you starting?' she thundered. 'I'll not serve troublemakers. Either sit down or clear off!' and when the man looked as though he might hit back, she barked out, 'Sit – if you want some ale!'

The man sat, muttering, and Marie snatched her cap back from Black Jack. Mistress Butterworth turned to her, and Simeon thought she would be ordered from the inn, but just then someone called out, 'The minstrels are here!' and the crowd shuffled, making room, and three men made their way to the fire, carrying their instruments.

'A song!' bellowed Black Jack, and he and all his men drummed their fists on the table. Simeon's mother replaced her cap, then stood very straight and still as one by one the minstrels began to play. Her pale face was yellowish in the firelight and strands of hair escaped the cap and tumbled down. The lute player nodded at her, and there was a kind of challenge in his eyes. Marie hesitated, then began to sing in a low, husky voice, just as she had sung with Simeon countless times, in marketplaces and inns, or the hall of some great lord.

'I'll sing you one-oh,' she sang with the minstrel.

'Green grow the rushes-oh.'

As she sang, the inn grew quiet. Simeon could see all the watching faces. Part way through, someone took out a wooden pipe and played it with the lute, tabor and whistle.

'Two, two the lily-white boys,

'Clothed all in green-oh.'

Simeon gazed at his mother as she sang, and Black Jack watched her also, with his snake's eyes. A brightness seemed to spread from her into the rest of the room, and by the end of the song everyone had joined in.

'One is one and all alone, and ever more shall be so . . .'

When she had finished, people called for another song, but Mistress Butterworth said, 'Enough! Would you keep my staff from their work all night?'

And so Simeon knew that his mother had won and they would stay.

4

Simeon thought that the night would never end.

'When do they go?' he asked his mother, meaning the customers.

'We stay open till we're shut!' Mistress Butterworth said. And in fact the inn didn't close until the very last person had staggered out of it, singing. And when Simeon looked, there were still two or three unconscious on the alehouse floor.

'I'm not carrying them out,' Mistress Butterworth said, kicking one of them, who barely stirred. 'They'll make their own way out in the morning.'

Susan took Simeon to a tiny garret at the top of a dark stairway, hardly bigger than a cupboard. The handrail was broken and two of the stairs were rotten.

'No wandering!' Mistress Butterworth bellowed after them. 'I'll not have him raiding my cupboards at night.'

'Take no notice,' Susan whispered. 'She's got to go to the Court Leet tomorrow and she'll be fined, for sure. That's why she's in such a foul mood.'

Simeon didn't know what a Court Leet was, and he didn't ask. He stared around the tiny room as Susan spread sackcloth on a wooden ledge. There were boxes stuffed with cloth and plates, old jars that smelt funny and a crate of apples. Where would his mother sleep?

'Your mother's sleeping in my room, with me,' Susan said, as though she had heard him, though he had not spoken aloud. 'I'll show you, if you like.' She reached up and stuffed some rags into the tiny, broken window in the ceiling. 'Best not go wandering around on your own after dark, though, eh?' she said, brushing past him as she left the room. 'State of these stairs.'

Simeon had no intention of wandering around in the dark, but it was the first time in all his life that he hadn't slept with his mother. Six stairs separated the garret from the room his mother was to share with Susan. This was hardly any bigger, but there was a straw mattress on the floor that was big enough for two. His mother was bending over it, and she saw him and straightened. Simeon hurried to her and she touched his face.

'Simeon,' she said. 'You have your own room now.'

She smiled at him encouragingly, but her face looked worn. Simeon's stomach clenched.

'With you,' he said to her in Romany, but she shook her head slightly and replied in English, 'You'll be fine.'

'Course he will,' said Susan heartily. 'Big boy like him. You can't go sleeping in your mam's room all your life, you know.'

Simeon stared at the floor. His mother picked up the blue blanket they had used as a cover in the woods.

'Come,' she said, and led him by the hand back to the garret room. She rolled up his blue blanket and placed it at the top end of the wooden ledge.

'Sleep,' she said, touching his hair. Simeon rolled over and pressed his face into the wool. It smelt of his mother, which was some comfort, but the night before him seemed huge.

36

His mother stayed with him, smoothing his hair, whispering a story about Squirrel, Prince of the Forest, who was so cunning that only the gypsy could get the better of him. And Simeon remembered when he had caught a squirrel and they had eaten it, and it was very good. Then his mother sang him a song, in her low, sweet voice, about the last of the gypsies, *riginzi*, (remember), and when she thought he had finally fallen asleep, she tiptoed away.

As soon as she had gone, Simeon sat up. He stared into the impenetrable darkness, which was nothing like the darkness of forest or field. Cautiously he extended his hand, feeling his way round the walls of the room, so that he would know the dark through his fingers. He felt round all the boxes until his fingers found the apples. They were brownish and rotten, the last of the autumn crop, only suitable for pickling or making cider. Mistress Butterworth had said that he wasn't to touch them, but Susan said he could have one or two if he liked. He ate one now, including the bitter, browning flesh and the core and stalk, leaving nothing, then he stared at the sloping roof, where Susan had stuffed the window with rags, but still a cold draught came through, and the noise of the town, that never seemed to fade entirely. He could hear the night watchmen ringing their handbells on the hour; the sound of barges unloading and people passing to empty their privy barrels into the river; horses whickering; pigs grunting and squealing; dogs barking and a few drunks out later than they should be, singing.

Somewhere, beyond all these noises, the forest beckoned. He could climb through the window and escape over the roofs of the houses, to the trees. But he would never leave without his mother.

The room was cold and he had no candle. Cautiously, Simeon stood up and pressed the door with his fingertips. It creaked open and he paused for a moment, holding his breath. Even at this distance he could hear Susan's hefty snores and Mistress Butterworth coughing on the landing below. She had a room all to herself, with a fire, and there were two other rooms on the same floor where guests could sleep. Beneath them was the kitchen with its small cellar, and the ale-room.

Simeon padded down the stairs, remembering which two were rotten. He had learnt to move quietly through the forest, where there were wolves and bears and hunters, without snapping a single twig. He stood outside his mother's door, listening to Susan snoring. He longed to creep in beside his mother, but since Susan was in the same bed he didn't think she would be too pleased. Instead he pressed his fingers up against the door and sank down quietly. In the morning, his mother found him propped up against it, stiff and cold, and she held him for a long time. Susan nearly fell over them both.

'What's this?' she said, but Simeon's mother didn't answer. Susan stepped past them, muttering to herself. When she returned she was carrying a basin of water.

'Best get washed and ready,' she said. 'Mistress Butterworth's at the Court Leet today, so we're in charge.'

5

Mistress Butterworth pulled the clogs from the feet of a Flemish weaver, who was still lying on the alehouse floor, and handed them to Simeon.

'You'll need these,' she said. Simeon stared at her, not understanding that he should put them on, until she gave a great snort.

'Look at the gormless loon – they're for your feet – not your hands!' she said.

Simeon had never worn shoes in his life and his feet were hard as leather. But he put the clogs on and clopped awkwardly across the floor to Susan.

'Don't take any notice of her,' Susan whispered. 'She's just been fined. "Keeping an unruly house," they said. She'll be in a foul mood all week.'

And to Simeon's mother she added. 'They say the Warden was driven out of the building. Every time he appears there's a riot.'

Simeon's mother seemed surprised by this. 'But isn't the Warden in charge of the church and school?' she asked. 'Surely the people cannot drive him out?'

'He's supposed to be, aye,' Susan said, lifting a barrel. 'But he's too busy with his charms and incantations. Selling his soul to the Devil. They say he's over a hundred years old. I don't pay any attention to the rumours, but –'

Simeon didn't hear any more. He was too busy concentrating on his clogs, which seemed to want to walk a different way from his feet.

Mistress Butterworth was serving ale as usual, to those people who had filtered out of the Court Leet. Her great laugh rang out in the alehouse, but in the kitchen she was, as Susan had predicted, in a terrible mood, and twice boxed Simeon's ears.

She shouted at him for forgetting to bring up the barrels from the cellar, then while he brought them up, the grains of barley roasting in the outhouse scorched and she shouted again.

'Get a move on, can't you?' she thundered, and Simeon stood uncertainly, wondering what a *move* was, and how you got one on. She said other things to him that he didn't understand, such as, 'Hold your horses,' when he ran past her into the yard, and Simeon looked, but he couldn't see any horses.

'Look at all that bread,' she said later that day, when there had been few customers. 'It'll all have to go.' So Simeon ate as much as he could and threw the rest on to the midden for the pig. But when Mistress Butterworth came back, she stared at him as though he had lost his mind.

'I meant it'll all have to go to the *customers*!' she roared, and she shouted at him for a long time, so that he stopped listening to the words and could only see the shapes coming from her mouth. This drove her to a frenzy and she called him the village idiot and raised her ladle to him, but his mother pulled him away.

'I do not beat him,' she said, and Mistress Butterworth

launched into a tirade at Simeon's mother instead, until Susan interrupted.

'Give over, can't you?' she said. 'Give your tongue a rest, your eyes are watering!'

She was the only one who dared to speak to Mistress Butterworth like that and Mistress Butterworth seemed lost for words. She glared at Susan murderously for a moment, then back at Simeon, but all she said was, 'Go fetch the pig.'

Simeon liked the pig, who was called Matilda. She was a brown-black colour, lop-eared, with bristles along her spine and a very bad-tempered expression on her face. Let out of her pen, she rushed about the yard, squealing and nosing in the midden for fallen apples. But when he held an apple she pushed her warm snout into his hand. That morning he had taken her with Susan to the swineherd, who took all the pigs of the town to pasture on Collyhurst Common, and now he had to collect her again.

Simeon ran past all the alehouses of Long Millgate. The street was unusually quiet, except for the college men, ringing their bell and asking for alms for the poor, and a single cart unloading.

Where Long Millgate crossed Toad Lane he heard the swineherd's horn and all the grunting and squeaking and jostling of hundreds of pigs as they made their way back into town. He hurried away from the streets so that he could collect Matilda while she was still free to run about snuffling.

The swineherd, who was hardly any older than Simeon himself, merely nodded as Matilda left the thrusting herd, and blew his horn again to tell the people of the town to collect their pigs. Simeon thought it would be a fine job to be a swineherd. He prodded Matilda gently with the stick he'd been given, but she ignored him, turning over twigs and small stones with her nose. He could see the dark shapes of beech nuts gathering in her mind as she nosed through the mud and dirt. He prodded her again, harder, and she set off at a run.

Simeon didn't like to beat the pig too hard, but he had to chase her quite quickly or she would run about the streets of the town, which was forbidden. He trotted after her, tapping her on the rear with the stick. Sometimes she stopped suddenly and he almost fell over her, then she would nudge him on with her snout.

As they turned back on to Long Millgate, Simeon was stopped by the sight of a column of people walking as though in procession. They were dressed in black, though some of them wore armour and iron helmets, and they were singing a psalm. Their leader went from door to door, banging like a constable and calling out, 'Look you to the Lord's Day!' and 'It is the Sabbath already – the Sabbath has begun!'

And when they passed a drunken man, staggering from one side of the street to the other, one of the armoured men dragged him to his knees, and the leader, a short, pale man as thin as a whippet, barked at him, 'Do you know the Lord's Prayer? Can you say it? What is the Seventh Commandment?'

But the drunken man's head only lolled back foolishly and his mouth hung open, so that eventually the short man let him go with a snort of disgust.

'These people are doomed,' he said.

Simeon hung back, holding Matilda by one of her lop ears, as the procession crossed the street. He pressed himself into a doorway as the man looked back along it with his pale, pale eyes, and felt his knees tremble. If they stopped him, he would not know what to do. But the man only went on knocking on the doors of alehouses.

'Remember the Sabbath Day!' he shouted.

And all his followers cried, 'Amen!'

As soon as the strange procession crossed into Hanging Ditch, Simeon ran all the way to Mistress Butterworth's, in case it had called there.

'They'd be sorry if they did,' said Mistress Butterworth, when Simeon described what he'd seen.

'It's a disgrace, that's what,' Susan said. 'Why can't folk get on with their own lives?'

'Why would they,' Simeon's mother said, her back turned, 'when they can destroy other people's?'

'God's Army, they call them,' Susan said, and Mistress Butterworth snorted exactly like her pig. 'They say that their leader, Robert Downe, gives sermons in the woods and fields.'

'Trees'll listen, maybe,' said Mistress Butterworth, biting a leg of chicken. 'No one else will.'

Susan shook her head. She told them she'd had a visit recently from Mother Orton the prophetess, whom some called witch because of the cats she kept and because of the long strands of hair from her chin. Mother Orton used to be the Wise Woman in her own village, but now she lived in a hut by Collyhurst Common. People feared her, but still consulted her about the weather or their sweethearts. And when she came to your door for food, it was unwise to turn her away.

'She told me Martyn would make himself free in twelve months' time,' she said a little smugly. Martyn was a tanner's

43

apprentice, but his master was too mean to let him marry. 'And that we would have three children.'

'You'd best hurry, then,' Mistress Butterworth commented. 'You'll be too old for that soon.'

Susan glared at her, then said, 'Anyway, she was called to Mistress Tupper's house, you know – the mercer's wife? Her youngest son's been ill. He took a fit before church and screamed that he wouldn't go. And when Robert Downe and his lot heard about it, they had the poor lad tied to his bed for a week, and they all stood round it chanting and blowing vinegar up his nose to drive the Devil out.'

'Sight of that lot'd drive anything out,' Mistress Butterworth said, chewing the bone.

'They'll drive us out, if they come here,' Susan said, and Mistress Butterworth replied that she'd like to see them try.

Simeon's mother remained silent, her hair falling over her face, but Simeon knew she was distressed. He wanted to comfort her, but Mistress Butterworth did not like his displays of affection.

'Give over fondling,' she would say, or, 'Put him down, you don't know where he's been.'

But now he could sense his mother's worry, and when Mistress Butterworth went upstairs, and Susan to the hens in the yard, he said, '*Daya*, let's leave.'

He spoke in the Romany tongue, that he wasn't supposed to use any more, and his mother looked at him sharply, but said nothing.

'Why are we staying?'

'Where would we go?'

'Anywhere,' Simeon said, spreading his arms wide as though to hold all the forests and rivers and mountains, the roads they had travelled, the things they had seen. But his mother's face looked stricken and worn.

'Simeon, I'm tired,' she said.

Susan came back in from the yard.

'Not a single egg,' she said, then looked at them curiously. 'What were you saying?' she asked. 'What are them words?'

Marie shot Simeon a quick, despairing look, but he said, 'Romany.'

Susan sat down, wiping her hands on her apron. 'Are you two really gypsies?' she said. 'You're not dark – at least, the lad's darker than you are, but – we used to have gypsies in our village and some of them were black as pitch.'

Simeon's mother looked at her for a long moment, then lowered her gaze.

'My father was Irish,' she said. 'He came to this country in a year of famine, looking for work . . .'

Little by little, with interruptions from Simeon, she told their tale. Her father and sister had died of hunger in a ditch and she had sat beside them as the rain fell, waiting for them to wake up. Then the gypsies had passed in their coloured wagons and taken pity on her, though she was a *hedgemumper* – a non-gypsy traveller. She had been taken into Rosa's wagon. Rosa called herself Queen of the Gypsies. She could tell fortunes and cure sickness, even sickness of the heart. She had eleven daughters and a son called Tobin, who was a little older than Marie. At that time, Marie was not yet five years old.

The gypsy life was hard, especially for the women, who worked like slaves, chopping wood; making clothes; cooking anything edible they could find; looking after the children and animals, the elderly and sick and making things to peddle at village fairs. The winters were hardest of all, when they were driven from one village to another, for no parish wanted them.

Marie and Tobin became inseparable, and she learnt from him to track animals soundlessly through the forest; to climb trees, or hide, holding her breath for more than a minute at a time underwater; to charm birds from trees and rabbits and moles from their holes. From Rosa she learnt to dance and sing, to cook and sew, tell fortunes and make gypsy charms.

Then came the time when the gypsies all headed north, for the King of Scotland had promised them their own land. They had camped in the forests outside Edinburgh, and in the morning, Marie had heard a rustling in the bushes. She had followed it quietly, thinking of food, further and further into the forest, but however far she went, she could not find the creature that was making the noise. At last she realized how far she had wandered, and hurried back, looking for signs of where she had trodden before: a snapped twig or bent blades of grass. But when finally she stumbled back into the clearing, she fell down in terror. For there, hanging from every tree, were the gypsies she had known and loved: Rosa and her eleven daughters and their husbands, and even their children. And in the last tree of all hung Tobin, his hands tied behind him, the front of his trousers stained.

Marie lay on the rough ground, unable to get up. But then the snow started to fall, though it was April, and the spirit of Rosa stepped down from the tree. She raised Marie up and pressed a hand to her stomach; Marie could see the jagged line round her throat.

'He is the last of my line,' she said, and for the first time

Marie knew she was carrying Simeon. She fell to her knees and retched until her stomach griped with agony, then slowly she stood up. She could not bring herself to look at the terrible bodies, to ask how it had happened. Dazed and freezing, she made her way southwards, out of the woods. Whenever she doubted which way to go, the spirit of Rosa was there, and when she knocked at a door Rosa had led her to, they gave her food.

Spring and summer passed and the weather worsened again. When it was nearly her time, Rosa led her to a barn. There, in the depths of agony, she saw not only Rosa, but Tobin smiling at her. They were with her when she bit through the cord and wiped Simeon clean and fed him. Then slowly the months passed and she could not see Rosa any more. There was only Simeon and Marie.

Susan and Simeon sat in silence as Marie finished her tale. Simeon could feel his mother's sadness, that welled up like deep water in the hole through which her memories flowed. Susan took a long breath.

'Eee, that's sad,' she said, and sighed again. Then she said, 'I didn't know you could tell fortunes. Will you tell mine?'

Simeon's mother managed a smile. 'It is not always good to know,' she said.

'Well, I'm not worried,' Susan said. 'What do you use – salt?'

Marie shook her head. After a moment she told Simeon to fetch water in a bowl. 'Have you a coin?' she said to Susan, and she tied it up in muslin, then sank it in the bowl. After a while she untied it and the muslin floated upwards. Then all three of them peered into the bowl, but Simeon could only see the reflection of their heads in the candlelit water.

'I see a house,' Simeon's mother said. 'It is this house. Martyn is here.'

'Come to marry me,' Susan said, but Simeon's mother shook her head.

'He is leaving,' she said. 'And you will not go with him. You – drive him away.'

She pushed the bowl away from her, then shook her head as though to clear it.

'Well, I don't like the sound of that,' Susan said. 'Why would I drive him away?'

When Simeon's mother said nothing, Susan stood up, pouring more water from the jug into the cooking pot, and Simeon could see that she was put out.

'Perhaps it's not my future you're seeing, eh?' she said, sitting down again, and before Simeon's mother could speak, she went on, 'What about Simeon – can you see his?'

'No,' said Simeon's mother, too quickly.

'Oh, go on,' said Susan, but Simeon knew she wouldn't; he had asked her before.

'You cannot see properly when you are too close to the person,' his mother said.

'Oh, well,' said Susan, yawning hugely. 'It's getting late. And it's church in the morning.'

Simeon's mother looked at her.

'We'll have to go,' Susan said. 'If Mistress is fined again, she'll end up in stocks.'

6

In the morning, as Susan had predicted, Mistress Butterworth told them they all had to go to church.

Simeon's mother looked down at the pot she was scrubbing and said she'd rather not.

'I weren't asking if you wanted to,' Mistress Butterworth said. 'I'll not pay another fine!'

'It's all right,' Susan said, squeezing Simeon's mother's arm. 'You don't have to take Communion. We can slip out before that and start serving the ale.'

Churches were dangerous places, Simeon's mother always said. People were marked out by their attendance and non-attendance, by how much piety they showed. The eyes of the town's rulers were on them: the magistrates and Borough Reeve, the Byelawmen and constables and Beadle. If they went to church, they could no longer pretend they were just passing through the town.

But not to attend church was a sin and a crime, the crime being treason, for since the old King had introduced the new Church it was a treasonable offence not to go. There were fines, and those who could not pay the fines were whipped. Then if they still refused to go, they could be sent to the New Fleet Prison, everything they owned taken from them, and beaten and starved until they agreed to take Communion.

'You're not a papist, are you?' Susan asked in a whisper, but Simeon's mother shook her head.

'I am not of any faith,' she said.

Susan looked at her strangely, but all she said was, 'Well then, it shouldn't matter.'

Simeon wondered if his mother would refuse to go. He hoped she would, because that would mean they would have to move on.

'Yes, we will go,' she said, nodding as though she had come to some major decision. Then she looked at Simeon and smiled. They would hurry back, she told him, because Sunday was the busiest day at the inn, and after church everyone wanted ale. She took off her apron as she said this and wound up her hair in a scarf with a determined expression on her face, so that Simeon could not see her thoughts.

At eight, the church bells began to ring and all the people of the town began to drift in twos and threes, then sixes and sevens, then larger and still larger groups, from Dean's Gate and Toad Lane, Withy Grove, Market Stead Lane and Smithy Door, towards the great church. Services were held all day, Susan said, because there were more than three thousand people in the town, and big as it was, the church would not hold them all. At the gates, the poorer people waited while the rich filed in: the Lords Mosley and Radcliffe, with their great households, the Earl of Derby from his home in Alport Park; Sir Samuel and Lady Tippings with their big family; Ralph Hulme with his. Then came the burgesses and town officials, then the wealthy wool and linen drapers, who each had their own pew, the merchants and shopkeepers and innkeepers. Mistress Butterworth came towards the end of these, with Susan and Simeon's mother following her and Simeon shuffling after them in his woollen smock and clogs. Behind them came all the poorer families of the town: the shepherds and shearers, dyers and swineherds and pot boys, then the paupers. They all had to stand round the periphery of the church at the back. It was smelly and crowded, with everyone jostling for position, and Simeon could hardly see.

He had been to church only two or three times in his life, and this was the biggest church he had ever seen, high-vaulted and double-aisled, with great windows of coloured glass portraying angels and demons. In the centre of each was a picture of the Virgin, holding her child with a sweet and tender expression like Simeon's mother. Susan saw him looking and whispered that images of the Virgin were now forbidden, but because it was the old King's grandmother who had put them in, they had been left alone. 'So we're lucky, eh?' she nudged Simeon. 'Still got all our fine glass and ornaments.'

Simeon didn't answer, for he was looking upwards. He had seen, high up in the roof of the church, two rows of stone angels, each one carrying a golden instrument, and each with their wings half spread, as though about to fly down from the roof.

Then the Warden came in, dressed all in black with a wooden staff. There was muttering from the crowd and Simeon shrank behind Susan.

'Don't worry,' Susan told him. 'He'll not try his magic here. Though they do say,' she added, 'that he comes and goes from the church and no one sees how. He's just here one minute,' she snapped her fingers, 'and gone the next.'

Behind the Warden came the choir and Fellows of the church, and they all sat behind an ornate wooden screen, so that they could not be seen by the congregation, which made Simeon feel a little better. Then the boys from the grammar school came in with the High Master and Usher, and sat in their pews. Finally the constables came in, dragging four recusants from the prison, who looked battered and bruised, and they had to kneel in chains between the altar and the pews.

The altar was a wooden table and the curate stood before this in a plain black cassock, and he read to them all from a prayer book in English, not Latin.

Wedged as he was between two pot boys from different inns, his mother and Susan, Simeon couldn't see much, so he gazed upwards at the angels, who looked as if they were playing with the choir. When the people in front of him shifted a little, he could see that a different preacher stood at the lectern.

It was the man Simeon had seen the night before, leading his army of followers through the town. He stood, glaring down at the congregation, as though he would read from the great Bible, then he snapped the Bible shut, walked away from the lectern and began to pace up and down in front of them. He wore no helmet this time, nor hat or priestly robes, just plain black day clothes, and his head was shaven. He was so thin that his Adam's apple stood out in his throat like an egg that might hatch.

'In this town there are many gateways to Hell,' he said, glaring at the recusants. 'And each of you has been led there by the wiles of the Serpent – yea! Even unto doorways that open directly on to the fiery pit! Look around you!' he cried, nodding fiercely, and Simeon looked all around, but he couldn't see any burning doorways.

'Will not a filthy inn draw a hundred people sooner

than an hour's tolling of a church bell? These chapels of
Satan need no bells. You are drawn to them like pigs in a
byre. And what do you find there? Your inns and taverns
are stuffed full of vagabonds and thieves! Those who are
sick with sores go there to amuse themselves and infect
others. Sores on their bodies, yea – and sores on their souls.
There is but one text. I say to you,' he said, punching one
fist into the other palm. 'Keep – holy – the – Sabbath –
Day. Observe the Sabbath and ye shall thrive in the Lord's
house. And the Christian Sabbath,' he said, glaring at them
all, 'begins on the Saturday eve.'

The congregation stirred and shuffled and there were
some murmurings of dissent. This was not the usual
sermon, the preacher being one of the radical Puritans of
the Salford Hundred. But his followers were with him and
they cried, 'Amen!' at the end of each declamation. He
left his lectern, as the crowd protested, and began walking
among them. He was so short that he could not be seen,
but his voice rang out clearly.

'As for your other pastimes and amusements – what are
they but the Devil's own entertainment? Your football is
more fighting than recreation – a bloody and murdering
practice! The Devil squats over you while you break your
bones! And cockfights – where you waste your money on
bets, watching birds wound one another to death with
their beaks – what are they but sacrifices on the altar of
the Evil One?'

There were some cries of 'Leave it out!' and 'Go preach
in your own parish!' but the preacher's followers cried
loudly, 'Praise be to God!'

'A manly countenance you have charged with brutish
affections!' the preacher cried, and everyone began muttering

and looking around to see where he was. 'You have given the use of your tongue to ungodly talk, your desire to uncleanness, your senses to wickedness, your honour to shame, your days unto vanities and your life unto death. Your belly is your God, your end destruction. I love you in the Lord and therefore I speak so plain.'

Simeon gazed upwards at the stone angels in the roof. He thought he could see the stone mouths moving. They were mouthing words to him that he could not hear.

Now the preacher moved further into the congregation, shaking their hands as though he was one of them, and calling out texts from the Bible.

'Ezekiel 34, "the good shepherd watcheth after his sheep"; John 10:11, "I am the good shepherd and the good shepherd giveth his life for his sheep"; John 10:16, "other sheep I have, which are not of this fold, them also I must bring, and there shall be one fold and one shepherd".'

'Mam,' said Simeon loudly into the pause, 'what are the angels saying?'

The people near to him stirred and sniggered, and the preacher looked round sharply for the source of the interruption, then began to push his way towards Simeon, shaking the hands of shepherds and carpenters as he passed.

'If all the world were flowing water,' he said, gazing earnestly into the face of Aelfred the shearer, 'and every year one drop should be diminished, the sea should all be dry before the godly man shall cease to live in the Lord. I am a minister of Christ and I have sworn to tell the truth. If you do not believe me, you do Him wrong.'

Simeon craned his neck, but the stone angels were still and silent now.

'The angels have stopped speaking now,' he said sadly. Susan drew in her breath sharply as the preacher approached, and his mother said, 'Hush!'

'For God's sake,' muttered Mistress Butterworth. 'Shut the brat up,' and Simeon's mother squeezed his hand tightly so that Simeon knew he had to be silent. And suddenly, there before them, was the preacher. He took in Simeon's mother's stained, colourful dress, and Mistress Butterworth's big, gaudy hat, and his nostrils flared as though assailed by the smell of brimstone.

'They are clothed in finery,' he said in a hoarse voice, 'but shall be dressed in rags.'

His gaze lingered on Simeon's mother, who kept her own eyes lowered and gripped Simeon's fingers. The preacher looked as though he would say something else, but the words died in his throat. Then suddenly recovering himself, he turned away and began to make his way back to the altar.

'The Devil is among you always,' said the preacher, returning to the lectern and glaring at the congregation. 'He is before you now in the form of those who would take you away from the one true church and lead you to damnation!'

He pointed at the kneeling recusants. 'See that you root them out – every man look to his neighbour, for here among you is the Serpent!'

The congregation shifted restlessly as the sermon drew to a close. They did not like this preacher, but they feared him. He had been known to visit people in their homes and interrogate them for signs of papistry. Since he had come to the parish, more people than ever had been thrown into the New Fleet Prison.

When at last the preacher finished, the Warden rose and there was a different murmur. He stood at the other lectern and began to read to them from the new Bible.

He stood in front of an ancient stone on which there was a carving of an angel. The stone was so far away that Simeon could hardly see it, yet suddenly it appeared to be outlined in white fire.

'Mam, Mam,' Simeon said in a loud whisper. 'The angel's on fire!'

This time everyone turned and looked, muttering. Mistress Butterworth glared at Simeon and the Warden paused, looking for the source of the disturbance, but he couldn't see Simeon in the crowd. After a moment he went on reading. Simeon's mother's fingernails were digging into Simeon's hand and he knew she was afraid, but he couldn't help himself. Behind the Warden the angel spread its wings and a great darkness opened, like the darkness of a starless night. Simeon felt a trembling spread upwards through his limbs and his bones felt weak, like water. His tongue loosened and he felt as though he would cry aloud, but suddenly the Warden stopped reading and stepped down from the lectern. Behind him the angel shrank back into the stone. Simeon breathed hoarsely. His mother clutched him and Susan looked at them both in consternation. But it was time for the final prayer before Communion, and the curate stood at the altar again. He had to raise his voice, stuttering a little, before the people made their way forward, bowing their heads.

Those who did not want Communion made their way through the great doors, pushing and jostling, yet a space cleared round Simeon and his mother, and when they were outside people muttered and moved away.

'What do you think you're doing, you?' hissed Mistress Butterworth.

Simeon's mother ignored her. 'Who is the preacher?' she asked Susan.

'Which one?' said Susan. 'The ranting one's Robert Downe, and the one with the stammer's Matthew Palmer. Is he all right?' she asked, nodding at Simeon.

'He's fine,' said his mother. 'It was the lack of air, that's all – he couldn't breathe.'

'I'll stop him breathing,' said Mistress Butterworth, 'if he shows me up like that again.' And she stumped off in the direction of Long Millgate. Susan took Simeon's mother's arm.

'Come on,' she said. 'Let them stare.' And they followed Mistress Butterworth out of the church grounds. Simeon held on to his mother's hand. There was a flickering at the edges of his vision, as if one world was shifting rapidly into another, but he couldn't understand what he was seeing. A great weariness settled on him like dust.

'What are you looking at?' said Susan to one woman who was poorly dressed, and the woman looked quickly away. 'I don't know, Simeon,' she said in a lower voice. 'For a quiet lad, you know how to draw attention to yourself.'

But she put an arm round his shoulders as they joined the crowd of people who were heading towards the inns of Long Millgate.

7

Matthew Palmer lit the candles and the church was filled with pools of light and shadow. It was almost time for the evening service, when the boys would proceed along the aisles of the church to each of the old chantry chapels, saying the *deus misereatur* and *de profundis* for the souls of those who had left money to the church and school. His hands shook a little, for the Puritans would be there and he knew what they thought of such practices. He was especially afraid of their preacher Robert Downe. *The dead are already damned or saved, regardless of your prayers,* he would say. *You do but corrupt the souls of your congregation by clinging to such popish practices. In our church they are already banned,* and so on.

Matthew Palmer shivered because it was chilly in the great church, and because, in less than an hour's time, he would be required to sit and eat with Robert Downe and his Army. He could imagine few things worse than eating with that joyless crew, who wore mourning clothes and wept as they ate, flogging themselves before and after until flecks of blood flew in the food. But they had required his presence especially, which meant that they wanted to discuss further changes to the church and its services. They did not like the windows, they had said, and Matthew Palmer loved the windows, each of which told a story. But in the centre of each of them was an image of the Blessed Virgin, which of course they objected to. There were few churches in England that had such windows left, or chantry chapels. The story was legendary in the parish of how, in the days of the old king, Henry VIII, soldiers had arrived to smash the windows and chantries, the altar and images of Mary. They had entered the church on horseback, but the old priest had stood his ground and went on saying the prayers.

'Who is it that you pray for?' the leader had asked, and when he had been told, 'The Lady Margaret Beaufort, grandmother to the King,' he had stopped short, and after a fierce consultation with his men, they had ridden away again. And so the church was left intact, though they had to replace the stone altar with a wooden table.

But now the Puritans would have the walls and windows whitewashed and shutters put up. They would have no sung services, only prayers spoken in English. They would add to the confusion that already existed in men's hearts. For the old ways did not die easily and men still went in secret to the Purgatory fields on Hallows' Eve, to light fires and say prayers for their beloved dead, to spare them just one day from the pains of Purgatory.

He lit the final candle and stood gazing at the reflections in the chantry plates. What would he say to the interrogations of Robert Downe, he wondered, for few could stand up to him. The man was a born inquisitor.

When he turned away from the candle, he was startled by the figure of a woman, her head draped in a coloured cloth from which auburn hair escaped. She moved forward, seeing that she had disturbed him.

'Father,' she said.

'Wh – who – what is it?' he managed.

'I need to speak with you.'

Matthew Palmer looked quickly over one shoulder, then the other, and stepped forward.

'I-I-I c-cannot take Confession,' he said, for he had been asked to do this before, but the woman shook her head.

'No, no,' she said. 'It is about my son,' but she stopped and seemed not to know how to go on.

'Has he – f-fallen into sin?'

'No, Father, he – I want him to sing in the choir.'

Matthew Palmer was considerably astonished. 'In the choir?'

The woman nodded. There was a look of distress on her face. Matthew Palmer looked from her to the great shadows of the nave. Was someone there, listening?

'The b-boys of the choir are from the – from the s-s-school,' he said, and the woman nodded again. 'He c-cannot just join the c-choir,' he explained.

But she said, 'No, father – I want him to go to the school.'

Matthew Palmer did not know how to say this, but women from her station in life did not normally send their boys to the grammar school. 'The – the s-school is not m-m-my affair,' he said.

'But he can sing, Father.'

'Sing?'

'Like an angel from Heaven.' She caught at the sleeve of his cassock, and once again the curate looked anxiously out into the church, certain he had seen a movement. The woman was speaking again in low, hurried tones.

'My son – he is not like other boys. I cannot send him to be an apprentice – there are no apprenticeships for him.

But he can *sing*, Father – he has this one great gift.'

'Is that a vagrant begging?'

Robert Downe's harsh voice rang throughout the nave and Matthew Palmer's heart sank like a stone as he came into view. 'What do you want, dole money? The proper place for beggars is outside the church gates!'

The woman let go of the curate's sleeve. 'I am no beggar, sir.'

Robert Downe eyed the woman, his gaze travelling up and down her fantastical, coloured clothes.

'I saw you earlier, at the morning service,' he said softly. 'What do you want?'

The woman started to speak, but Matthew Palmer said, 'It is a s–spiritual m–matter.'

The preacher pounced. 'A spiritual matter, eh? Come on then, let us hear it!'

He walked round the woman as he spoke, and she stood very still, with downcast eyes. 'You are from the inns, are you not?' he said suddenly.

'Yes, sir,' the woman said.

'Which one?'

A look of anxiety crossed the woman's face, but she said, 'Mistress Butterworth's, sir, near the bakehouse.'

The preacher looked blank for a minute, then he said, 'I know it – it is a lawless, unruly house.'

And when neither of them answered this, he said, 'Well, we do not hold our spiritual affairs in secret here, we tell them all, before the Assembly. That way there is no place for secret shame.'

'Th–that is wh–what I c–c–counselled,' the curate said, stuttering so badly he could hardly speak. 'I s–s–said sh–she could c–c–come to the n–next Assembly.'

'Did you so,' said the preacher, barely disguising his contempt for the curate. 'Well then –'

But before he could launch into a sermon, Matthew Palmer took the woman's arm.

'I will see her out,' he said, without a single stutter, and he steered her firmly away from the chantry and along the aisle of the church to the main door. He said nothing, and to his relief neither did she, for the echoes would have magnified their voices, but when they reached the door she pulled her arm away and looked up at him beseechingly.

'If you would just hear him sing,' she said.

Matthew Palmer spoke in a low, nervous voice.

'You must f-forget this f-f-f-foolishness,' he said. 'There is no p-place for v-virtuoso singing in this church. Soon there m-may be no p-p-place for s-singing at all.'

He lifted his hand as the woman tried to speak.

'Go,' he said. 'If you are d-determined to get your b-boy into the school, you m-must see the High M-m-master. Or the Warden. Th-that is all.'

He would not say any more, though there was something in the woman's gaze that tore at him, something like a wounded animal, trapped. She looked at him, and he held her gaze, then swiftly she turned and hurried away, her clothes like a bright flag in the fading light.

8

Simeon waited for his mother to come home. She had slipped out between serving dishes, saying that she had an errand to run and would not be long. But that was ages ago. Simeon had crept into her bedroom and stuck his head out of the window. He watched the women coming back from the town pump carrying water, the drover with his cart, the street cleaner pushing his broom slowly, painfully. The two college men began their usual rounds. Evening shadows lengthened and still she hadn't returned. Any minute now Mistress Butterworth would call for him, her voice loud and harsh like a cawing bird, but he couldn't rest until he knew where his mother was.

Suddenly he heard voices below. Simeon recognized one voice and the black headscarf. It was Black Jack with one of his friends. Simeon ducked quickly back from the window. Black Jack had been in the alehouse all afternoon and had kept asking Simeon's mother to dance for him. Simeon loved to see her dance, leaping on to the tables and clapping her hands. Her face lit up and she smiled to herself mysteriously as if no one else was there, but he didn't like the way the men looked when she lifted her skirts. And in particular he didn't like Black Jack. There was something hard and cold shining in him, like a pewter plate. Simeon pressed himself against the window frame, listening.

'You like her, then,' the friend said.

And Black Jack's voice answered, 'Aye, she'll do.'

'You think she'll go with you, though?'

Black Jack murmured something that Simeon couldn't hear and there was a low, unpleasant laugh.

Then Simeon saw his mother hurrying from the direction of the church. His heart tightened as he watched her, the bright movement that was almost a dance in itself.

Black Jack's voice said, 'Go now,' and he retreated into the shadow of the nearest alley. As Simeon's mother passed, he stepped out and caught her. Simeon heard her '*Oh*,' of surprise as Black Jack pulled her into the alley. He leant so far out of the window that he almost fell, trying to see what was going on. He heard low voices, Black Jack's and a murmur of protest from his mother. She pulled away from him into the street, but as Simeon watched, Black Jack grabbed her and kissed her, then she tore away and hurried into the inn.

Simeon stood very still, his heart thudding. He heard Mistress Butterworth calling for him and still he didn't move, until her footsteps came clumping up the stairs.

'Drat the boy! Where is he?'

Then he slipped out of his mother's room and pushed past Mistress Butterworth quite roughly on the landing.

All that evening there was no time to talk to his mother. The inn got more and more crowded, the customers more and more drunk. Simeon's mother danced for them and sang, and in between she hurried in and out of the kitchen, her face thin and drawn. Simeon carved the bread, dished out stew, washed pots. He was clumsier than usual, and more and more of the stew spilt, until Mistress Butterworth ordered him to scrub the floor. Then he had to bring barrels up from the cellar and fetch water from the pump. A fight broke out at the inn, though it was no worse than usual, and Mistress Butterworth threw everyone out, but when it had finished, they all piled back in again.

From the kitchen door, Simeon watched Black Jack getting drunker and drunker with his mates. He demanded one song after another from Simeon's mother and pulled Susan on to his knee as she went past. Susan pushed him away, giggling. Simeon's face burned with hatred as he watched the man, the grey-black hair escaping from his headscarf, the stubble on his chin, the darker hair where his shirt fell open and the tattooed rose on the back of each of his hands. But to Simeon's relief, Black Jack and his cronies left well before closing time.

Gradually the inn cleared, for the next day there would be a market and an early start for everyone. Simeon's mother came into the kitchen, winding up her hair into her cap. She gave Simeon a worn smile, but Simeon did not smile back.

'What did he say to you?' he asked in the old language.

'Who?' said his mother in English, still winding up her hair.

'Phew! That room stinks!' said Susan, hurrying by. 'Give us a hand will you – them tables'll have to be scrubbed.'

Simeon's mother picked up a cloth, but Simeon caught her sleeve.

'I saw you!' he said, in English this time.

Simeon's mother looked startled, then wary. She knew what he meant.

'In the ale-room?'

'No – the street.'

For a moment Simeon thought she would tell him off for spying on her, but all she said was, 'Nothing – that he does not say to other serving maids.'

Simeon knew she was lying, and it hurt him worse than if he'd been beaten.

She made as if to go again, but Simeon said, 'I don't like him.'

'Oh, Simeon,' his mother said in a sigh. She wouldn't look at him, but her face was troubled. 'He said nothing – he just wanted to make sure that I would sing for him, that's all.'

No! Simeon wanted to shout, but he couldn't. 'Don't go away,' he whispered.

Now Simeon's mother did look at him. She touched his face and pressed his hand to her cheek. He was taller than her now. 'Simeon,' she said softly. 'I will never leave you.'

And the muscles in his face and chest untightened a little, for now he knew that she was telling the truth.

9

On market day the whole town seemed crammed into the market square. There were fifty or more butchers' stalls and fleshboards packed into Smithy Door that led down to the river. The heads of pigs and sheep and cows hung overhead, tripe spilt on to the cobbles so that they were slippery with offal, and Simeon could hardly get past for the bumping and jostling. But his mother wove her way through, carrying a basket on her head, to the fishmongers' stalls near the river, then the stall with live geese, and Simeon hurried after her as fast as he could.

There were pedlars selling amulets of dried toads and rabbits' feet to ward off plague. There was a man offering to cut hair, trim beards, or pull out sore teeth. The last of the autumn apples were piled in dusty heaps at one end of the market square, together with turnips and cabbages. Then there were the stalls selling woodware, besoms and straw hats, or bales of wool. Women sat on baskets, the baskets in front of them filled with duck eggs and geese eggs, and chickens and doves were crammed into yet more baskets, and there was a panicked rustling as they tried to flap their wings. The market-lookers and ale-conners were out testing the produce, and Byelawmen circled the outskirts of the market, looking for those who would sell their produce unlawfully, without paying rent. Through all of this the Beadle moved with his painted staff and coat of yellow kersey with its forty-eight silver buttons, whipping the poor devils who were tied to the whipping post, for he got fourpence for each one. And one of the dyers' apprentices was manacled to the stocks and there was plenty of refuse around for throwing.

Simeon didn't like the market. He got nervous when so many eyes were on his mother. He expected someone, Byelawman or Beadle, to challenge their right to be there and maybe take his mother away. He kept losing sight of her in the crowd, and was relieved to see her again, balancing her basket on top of her coloured headscarf and making her way towards Susan, who was haggling over the price of a pot.

'Are we right, then?' Susan said cheerfully, and Simeon helped them to carry all the goods, as they made their way back to the inn.

But when they got back to Mistress Butterworth's, several people were standing outside the inn, looking at a notice that had been nailed to the door.

'Can't anyone here read?' Mistress Butterworth demanded, as Susan pushed her way through, but Susan couldn't and neither could Simeon, or his mother.

'Take it to the High Master's house,' someone towards the back of the crowd suggested.

'No, the night watchman,' said someone else. 'He's a man of letters.'

And sure enough, the night watchman, whose name was Roger Twist, turned the corner from Toad Lane on to Long Millgate and stopped abruptly when he saw the crowd. He was a burly man with a purple nose and was a regular customer at the inn.

Mistress Butterworth elbowed her way towards him, brandishing the notice.

'Here, you!' she said. 'What's this?'

Roger Twist took the notice from her and started to read silently, but moving his lips to the words. His brow creased and furrowed as he read and he shook his head.

'Well?' demanded Mistress Butterworth. 'What does it say?'

Roger Twist seemed reluctant to tell her. 'It's an official notice,' he began.

'I can see that,' said Mistress Butterworth. 'What's it about?'

'It's from that preacher chap – Robert Downe,' said Roger Twist, and when Mistress Butterworth snorted, he said, 'Calm yourself, Mistress, there's no point getting worked up.'

'Just read it,' said Mistress Butterworth.

Roger Twist sighed and shook his head again. 'It's all nonsense,' he began, then, catching the look in Mistress Butterworth's eye, he started to read.

'"In this year of Our Lord sixteen hundred and four, on this day of Grace –"'

'Get on with it!' snapped Mistress Butterworth.

'"– notice is hereby given that the said inn or bawdy house, belonging to the said proprietor Mistress Alys Butterworth, shall be prohibited from opening its doors and serving ale or other strong liquor, or food of any kind, to any persons from sundown on the Saturday evening throughout the hours of Sunday, this being the Sabbath, and the Lord's Day." Then there's that bit from the Bible about keeping holy the Sabbath Day,' he added, looking up.

There were cries of 'Shame!' and Mistress Butterworth looked like a bull about to charge.

'*What* did you say?' she demanded.

'Not me, Mistress,' said Roger Twist. 'I have nothing to do with it – nor anyone I know,' he went on, scanning the page for signs of the Lord's seal. 'This is definitely the work of that preacher – see, here is his signature.'

'Give it here,' said Mistress Butterworth, and she snatched the notice from Roger Twist, scanning it herself just as though she could read. Then she opened her mouth and a stream of language so foul spilt out of it that most of the crowd stepped back muttering, and even Roger Twist went pale.

'Is he trying to shut me down?' she thundered. 'Well? Is he?'

'Nay, Mistress,' Roger Twist began. 'He doesn't have the authority.'

'I'll give him authority!' bellowed Mistress Butterworth. 'Let him come here and tell me himself, the weak-kneed, lily-livered, son of a pock-faced –'

'Mistress Butterworth,' implored Roger Twist, trembling. 'Calm yourself – you don't know who's listening –'

But Mistress Butterworth was beside herself. 'I hope they're all listening!' she roared. 'And watching too. See! This is what I think of your notice!' And she tore the paper into tiny shreds. There was a half-hearted cheer from the crowd, but most of them had already started to disperse. Simeon's mother stood behind Susan, her fingers pressed to her mouth. Simeon touched her sleeve, but she wouldn't look at him. He could sense how worried she was.

'That's right – clear off, all of you!' bellowed Mistress Butterworth. 'Look to your own affairs! You don't think this'll stop here, do you? It won't be long before he comes looking for you – and you're all too milk-faced to stand up to him.'

She shook Susan off, who was trying to pull her inside.

'Go your way – and tell everyone you meet that Mistress Butterworth is open for business as usual!' she roared. 'And plans to be so all week and every week – *and* on the Sabbath Day – *especially* on the Sabbath!'

Then she finally allowed herself to be dragged inside the inn by Susan.

For most of that day the inn was quiet and no one dared approach Mistress Butterworth. Simeon's mother looked worried, her face strained as she chopped up the meat she had bought. Simeon couldn't understand why they were still there. They had never spent so long in one place before.

'Can't we leave now?' he asked his mother when he got the chance, but she only shook her head and told him to take the scraps out for the pig.

'Why are we still here?' he asked her as she prepared the stew, but she would only say again that she was tired of moving on.

Simeon could see that she was tired. Something in her that had always pressed her on and kept her going through even the hardest winter, seemed to have gone. When he looked at her he saw the image of a bird that had fallen from the sky, and he felt a pang of fear.

'When will we leave?' he said to her as she carried the warming pan upstairs to Mistress Butterworth's room.

'Not now, Simeon,' she said.

'But when?'

His mother sighed as she laid the pan by the hearth and

started to make up the fire. 'I do not know,' she said in a low voice, and there was a long pause.

'I do not want to leave,' she said, finally. Simeon made a sudden movement and knocked against the chair that stood by the bed. That was what he was like here, because nothing seemed to fit. In the forest he could move like a deer, or fox, but here he could not move for breaking or spilling things, or knocking them over. His mother rose and caught his arm, then touched his face.

'It will not be for ever,' she said. 'Just for a little while.'

Simeon stared at her, but there was a sudden racket downstairs and the sound of many people entering the inn. A man called out for ale. Black Jack and his cronies had arrived.

10

Wherever Simeon's mother went, men always looked at her. She was not yet old, because she'd had Simeon when she was little older than he was now. They watched her when she went about the town in the coloured dress that she would not give up because Rosa, Simeon's grandmother, had made it for her. The blacksmith called out to her as she passed, 'Hey, pretty lady, where are you going today?' and one of the minstrels sang after her, '*Oh, mistress mine, where are you roaming?*' Whenever she went into a shop, the shopkeeper would ask her questions, about where she had come from, had she come with the Flemish weavers and was she staying long, and did she want any company? But she would only smile her fleeting smile over her shoulder, and when the smile passed, her face seemed more wintry than before. When she went to market, a little space would clear around her. The wives of the town would stand apart from her and jog their men if they caught them looking. Soon she preferred to stay in the alehouse and let Simeon run errands about the town.

His day began early, when there was only a pale wash of light in the sky, but the roosters were crowing and the first fires smoking. He had to collect the eggs from the henhouse, though the hens had almost stopped laying, then take Matilda to the swineherd. When he got back, his mother and Susan had prepared the dough and Simeon had to take it to the common oven to be baked, then run on other errands, to the mercer's for pepper and nutmeg, or ribbon for one of Mistress Butterworth's hats, the cobbler's or the knife-grinder's or the chandler's. He had to dodge the blacksmith's mastiff, which should have been chained but never was, and the rude apprentices who shouted after him and sometimes threw stones.

There was so much to see and hear and smell – the acrid smell of woad from the dyers' workshops; the strange chanting of the Flemish weavers; the croft by the river, where sheets of wool were pegged out to dry and billowed in the wind like blue sails – that he often forgot what he was supposed to do, and was frequently in trouble.

Whenever possible, he loved to run down to the river to watch the barges unloading. The river stank from the tanning workshops that lined its banks. A smoky vapour rose from the surface and mingled with the smoke of the town that came from the chimneys and the middens and the blacksmith's forge. When the sun shone through the smoke like the yolk of an egg gently cooking, all the colours turned hazy and the light quivered, and solid surfaces took on the vagueness of a dream. If he stood very still and silent as a heron, he could hear other noises and movements through all the powerful music of the town, the little, furtive movements of settling birds and mice rustling through grass. He could imagine he was still in the forest, where the sunlight slipped over dappled leaves, but then he had to go back to Mistress Butterworth's, and all too often he had forgotten what he had been sent out for in the first place. Then Mistress Butterworth shouted at him and said he was as much use as teats on a cockerel, but when she threatened to beat him, Susan stood between them.

'I'll sort him out,' she said, winking at Simeon's mother and pulling Simeon into the yard. She held the long beater they used for beating the straw mattresses and mouthed, 'Make a noise!' at Simeon, whacking it against the mattress she had dragged downstairs.

Obediently, Simeon cried loudly and they laughed together, holding their hands over their mouths in case Mistress Butterworth should hear.

Simeon's mother got on very well with Susan; Simeon could hear them laughing as they swept the guest rooms and he wondered if that was why his mother wanted to stay. She had never had a friend before.

Susan had a sweetheart: Martyn Rigby. He was apprenticed to Bill the Tanner, who was as mean as a flint and would not let him finish his apprenticeship to marry. He kept saying that Martyn owed him for food and drink and clothing, and it was to be hoped that Martyn would outlive his master, Susan said, because the list of what he owed got longer by the day.

She talked about him all the time. He was younger than she was and a bit slow, she said, with ears like a sheep, and he stank like a dead cow, but he was a grand kisser. And she talked about her family: six brothers and sisters, both parents dead, the youngest boy living with her married sister near Burnley. Susan talked a lot, but she rarely asked questions, which suited Simeon's mother fine.

The days shifted quickly, but Simeon still felt that he was waiting for his real life to return. When he went to bed he lay down listening, until the murmur of people's voices, their thoughts and dreams, drove out the whispering of the forest and the rustling of leaves.

By the end of the week the inn was busier than it had ever been. Saturday came and the inn stayed open far into the night. There was singing and fighting, at least four people were knocked unconscious and lay in their own vomit, and still Mistress Butterworth did not throw anyone out.

'I'll show them po-faced Bible-banging lepers,' she said. 'Free ale after midnight!' and the drinking and fighting went on. Even Simeon had to serve in the alehouse, which he did not like to do, for some of the boys from the grammar school were there and they called him 'Butterworth's loon' and tried to trip him up and make him look foolish.

At last even the most determined reveller made his way home, singing. It was well past two in the morning when Susan, Simeon and his mother hauled themselves upstairs and collapsed on their beds. Simeon was too tired even to think of the forest, he sank instantly into a deep, exhausted sleep. He dreamt that he was lying underwater, because his mother had told him to wait. Men were out looking for them: he could hear the thumping sound of many feet marching by on the banks of the river. Then his mother's hand reached down.

'Simeon,' she said, 'Simeon, wake up!' and she shook his shoulder.

Simeon opened his eyes, immediately alert. His mother was there, pressing a finger to her lips. It was time, Simeon thought. Time for them to go at last. He rose quickly and followed his mother down the stairs.

'What the bloody Hell's going on?' said Mistress

Butterworth, appearing at the doorway to her room in a dishevelled state. 'What's that racket?'

'You'd better come and look,' said Susan, who was already up, standing by the window in her shawl. Mistress Butterworth wrapped her own shawl more tightly round her and pushed past Susan, growling. As they followed her into the room, Simeon's mother motioned to him to be quiet.

Surrounding the inn was a party of Puritans, dressed all in black with their severe collars and tall hats. Some had fallen on their knees in the mire of Long Millgate, all were praying. Simeon looked, but he couldn't see the preacher Robert Downe. Instead, a man Susan said called himself 'Smite-the-unholy' was reading aloud to them from the Bible.

' "And I saw a beast rise up out of the sea, having seven heads and ten horns, and upon the horns, ten crowns," ' he intoned, his sparse grey beard quivering as he spoke.

Mistress Butterworth stuck her great, shaggy head out of the window. '*Oi!* You lot! What kind of time do you call this?'

But Smite-the-unholy only raised an accusing finger in her direction. ' "Awake, awake O Zion! Put on thy beautiful garments O Jerusalem, for the Day of the Lord is at Hand!" '

And all his followers cried, 'Amen!'

Mistress Butterworth ducked back inside, eyes blazing. 'I'll give him *beautiful garments!*' she said. 'Fetch the pisspots!'

Simeon stepped out of the way as Susan hurried past, and Mistress Butterworth bellowed out of the window again.

'Get your grimy arses away from my door, you dunghill rats!'

'"And thou, Jezebel, most profane, most wicked, the day is come when thy iniquity shall be brought to an end,"' Smite-the-unholy yelled back at her. '"Thou shalt be cast into the bottomless pit; thy body shall lie in the streets for the vultures to pick at and the dogs to gnaw!"'

'Pick at this, Greybeard,' Mistress Butterworth roared, and she flung the contents of the chamber pot at him, scoring a direct hit.

Smite-the-unholy stood gasping and drenched.

'Purple whore!' he shrieked. 'You will be devoured by the Beast! Thy children and thy children's children will be devoured by the worm that gnaws thee, even to the fifth generation!'

Mistress Butterworth laughed down at him.

'Stow it, Grandpa,' she said. 'You're only here because your wife won't have you!'

Susan pulled at her shawl, to drag her away from the window.

'Leave it!' she said. 'Ignore them. They'll soon get fed up.'

But the chanting Puritans showed no sign of getting fed up.

'"Woe unto him that buildeth his house by unrighteousness and his chambers by wrong!"' yelled Smite-the-unholy.

And his followers cried out, 'Praise be to God!'

Then Roger Twist, the night watchman, appeared, ringing his bell. 'Four in the morning,' he boomed, 'and all's well.'

He stopped at the sight of the crowd.

'Four in the morning!' cried Mistress Butterworth, scandalized. 'That's it!'

And she ran down the stairs, her steps thundering through the inn, pausing only to grab the carving knife from the kitchen table. Then she burst out of the door and felled the preacher with a great blow. Smite-the-unholy sank to his knees in the mud and several of the assembled group started forward, but before they could reach her Mistress Butterworth seized the old man by the beard and began hacking through it with the knife. Smite-the-unholy howled and shrieked.

'Get you and your band of God-blasted maggots away from my door!' she hissed. 'Or something else'll be cut off!'

And she brandished the knife at those followers who tried to stop her, but Roger Twist lunged towards her shouting, 'Eh! What's going on?'

'I'm teaching this weasel here some manners!' said Mistress Butterworth, still wielding the knife so that Smite-the-unholy's followers fell back and yet more fell to their knees in prayer.

'Come on now – drop the knife,' said Roger Twist. 'Move it along, all of you – you've had your fun.'

'This is the Lord's work,' cried one of the women, and Simeon recognized her as Freegift Fletcher. 'We are in deadly earnest!'

'And you'll be earnestly dead if I have to call out the constables!' shouted Roger Twist. 'Fancy a shift in the New Fleet, do you?'

The assembled group fell back, muttering.

'And you, Mistress!' said Roger Twist. 'I've told you already – *drop the knife!*'

Reluctantly Mistress Butterworth dropped the knife and Smite-the-unholy's beard at the same time.

He doubled over, retching. 'Spawn of Satan,' he gasped, and Mistress Butterworth aimed a savage kick at his behind.

'Did you hear them?' she said to Roger Twist as Smite-the-unholy was helped away by his followers. 'I know what this is about – they want to close my inn.'

'Well, it's a pity they've got nothing better to do,' said Roger Twist, who was a good customer. 'Come on, you,' he said, chivvying the crowd. 'Clear off, or I'll have you up at the next Assizes.'

Smite-the-unholy backed off, crying querulously, '"He flattereth himself in his iniquity until his pride shall be cut down! We shall break the pride of the lofty –"'

'Oh, go grow your beard!' said Mistress Butterworth, turning her back on them all and re-entering the inn. 'Right!' she said, once inside. 'Who's for breakfast?'

Simeon and his mother hurried nervously to put water on to boil. Mistress Butterworth, however, was in a great good humour. Susan put a tall pot on her head in imitation of the preacher, and Mistress Butterworth's great gusts and bellows of laughter could be heard throughout the inn.

It was Sunday, but Mistress Butterworth told them that no one had to go to church. All day the church bells rang and people piled in after the services, and by the end of the day the inn was packed and heaving and Mistress Butterworth told her story again and again.

All day long a feeling of worry gathered in Simeon's skull, as though the claws of some great bird were closing round it. He dropped an urn of milk and scorched the meat on the spit, and cut his own finger with the bread knife, until he was ordered into the backyard with the pig. He could tell from his mother's face that she was worried too, though he hardly had time to speak to her, the inn was so busy. It cleared early, however, for the next day was market day again, and Simeon's mother told him to go up to bed – she would do the remainder of his work for him.

But he had hardly rested his head when there was a terrific thudding on the front door. He leapt out of bed and almost fell down the stairs in his hurry to get to his mother.

Thud – THUD – *THUD*!

'What in Christ's name's going on?' shouted Mistress Butterworth, flinging the door open. Halfway down the last flight of stairs, Simeon could see a figure on horseback in the street.

'Mistress Butterworth!' it declaimed in a loud voice. 'Come out of your stinking pit!'

'Get the Hell away from my door!' thundered Mistress Butterworth. 'Susan – fetch the constables!'

But before Susan, looking white and scared, could move, two men in armour burst in. They flung a rope round Mistress Butterworth and began to haul her into the street.

'Susan!' she yelled. '*Susan!*'

And Susan set about the nearest man with the pan she used for warming the beds. It clanged uselessly against his armour. 'Help – fire!' she screamed, because all around them men were lighting turfs in the street.

Simeon had a dazed feeling as though he had fallen asleep in his room and was dreaming. He stumbled out into the street after Susan. All around him there were more men in armour, with drawn swords and helmets flashing in the flames. Others had fallen to their knees, praying in the street. The man that Mistress Butterworth had so rudely sent on his way, Smite-the-unholy, was reading aloud from a prayer book.

'"Strike thine enemies, O Lord, blast them with the flames of thy truth . . ."'

Mistress Butterworth was dragged to her knees in the mire of Long Millgate. The man on horseback dismounted and Simeon could see it was Robert Downe.

'Mistress Butterworth,' he thundered, 'you are charged with defiling the Sabbath, and spreading corruption through the streets of this town. What have you to say for yourself?'

Mistress Butterworth spat fully in the man's face. The man raised his metal fist and swung it at her. Mistress Butterworth's face crumpled bloodily and Susan screamed.

'Whore of Babylon!' he hissed. 'Too long have you spawned your filth on these streets!' He raised his voice. 'The wrath of the Lord shall visit the servants of Satan!' he boomed.

And those kneeling all around cried, 'Amen!'

Simeon's face smarted from the blow given to Mistress Butterworth and his eyes watered freely so that everything became a blur. Some men ran to fight the flames and others struck out at them with swords. Robert Downe wrenched Mistress Butterworth's head back and Simeon could see her face streaming blood by the light of the fires. His flesh shrank as the preacher drew a knife, and Susan screamed '*No!*' again, but was thrust back against the wall of the inn.

In regular, rhythmical thrusts, the preacher began cutting the hair from Mistress Butterworth's head. It fell in great tufts to the street, leaving bloody patches on her scalp.

'Thus does the Lord lay low his enemies!' he cried in a voice that was shaking with fervour. 'As Satan lifts thee up, so shall the Lord cast thee down!'

As the last tuft of hair fell, the armoured men began dragging Mistress Butterworth along the street, while others ran to light more fires. Mistress Butterworth's gown caught fire as she was dragged and scraped over the cobbles. By this time a great crowd of people had gathered, and they surged along the street after them, some shouting abuse, others screaming, and Simeon was caught up in the press. Behind him he heard his mother shouting his name but he couldn't break free. The crowd surged to the marketplace where the whipping post and stocks stood, and beyond there to the ducking pool that stood in Lord Radcliffe's grounds.

By the time she hit the pool, Mistress Butterworth's body was a sheet of flame. The men holding the ropes waded in with her and held her under, while all the Puritans stood chanting with the preacher and Robert Downe lifted his voice.

'By fire and water shall you be purged!' he bellowed.

And his followers cried, 'Amen!'

Mistress Butterworth surfaced, spluttering, and was dragged under again. Simeon could feel the pressure in his own lungs. He wanted to cry out, but it was as though they would burst.

Behind them, in Radcliffe Hall, lights flared, but the preacher continued, 'Root out the evil in your midst! If thine eye offend thee – pluck it out! And let not any witch or servant of Satan live, for the Day of the Lord is here!'

'What the Devil's going on?' shouted Lord Radcliffe, standing half dressed at the gate to his house. The crowd fell silent as Mistress Butterworth surfaced again, no longer struggling, and Susan ran forward.

'Be vigilant, all of you,' cried the preacher, lifting his sword. 'For the Devil has many disguises. He speaks through your enemies and your friends – yea, even through your families!'

'I asked you a question!' cried Lord Radcliffe, striding away from his gate and drawing his sword. The preacher did not move.

'Shrink not from accusing thy neighbour, nor thy wife! Speak out, for the flesh can be mortified, but the damned soul lives in eternal torment!'

'Either get out of my grounds now,' thundered Lord Radcliffe, 'or I'll set my men on you! What do you think you are doing?'

'The Lord's work, sir,' said the preacher, turning at last. 'And it is long overdue.'

Mistress Butterworth's body was dragged to the side of the pool and several people ran forward, wrapping it in sheets.

'You do exceed your duty, sir,' said Lord Radcliffe in a low, furious voice. 'The Borough Reeve shall hear of this.'

The preacher ignored him, leading his horse towards the pool.

'Our work here is done,' he cried. 'But let all of you take this lesson to heart and beware!'

Then he led his horse away from the ducking pool, and all his followers fell in behind him, walking in a long line back towards the marketplace.

'Look what you've done!' Susan screamed after them. 'I hope you're proud of yourselves!'

But they did not turn round, or give any sign that they had heard.

Lord Radcliffe pushed his way through the crowd that now surrounded Mistress Butterworth.

'Who is it?' he demanded, and when someone told him he asked, 'Is she alive?'

He bent forward over the crumpled heap that was Mistress Butterworth.

'She is alive,' he said. 'Just barely. Who is with this woman?'

'I am,' Susan said, her face stained with smoke and tears.

'Can she be taken and cared for?'

'I don't know, sir,' Susan said. 'They were trying to burn down the inn.'

Lord Radcliffe cursed softly. But then Simeon saw his mother at last, pushing her way towards him. She reached him and clasped him tightly. 'They have put out the fire,' she said to Susan.

'Fetch a cart,' Lord Radcliffe said to his manservant, who ran off obediently. 'Now get back, all of you,' he said to the restless crowd. 'This is neither the time nor the place for a gathering. Go back to your homes.'

The townsfolk fell back, muttering, as the cart arrived. Mistress Butterworth's body, still wrapped in sheets, was lifted on to it. Simeon could see the burnt stubble that was her hair, and smell the scorched flesh. Susan climbed in the cart with her and after a moment, Simeon and his mother climbed in too. People fell silent, watching them, as the cart pulled through the crowd, their faces sullen, fearful or angry. Susan sat cradling Mistress Butterworth's damaged head; Simeon's mother folded her arms tightly round her son, and he could feel the trembling spread from her limbs to his own.

12

Mistress Butterworth stayed in her room with the shutters closed. Susan rubbed lard into her burns and sent Simeon out gathering nettles to make tea, which she said was good for burnt flesh. The door to the ale-room was kept shut because the room itself had been so damaged by smoke and flame, and when visitors came to see how Mistress Butterworth was, or to ask questions, they sat in the blackened kitchen with Susan, sipping her bitter brew.

Simeon looked after Matilda as usual and helped his mother scrub the smoke stains from the landing and her bedroom, but there was no money left for running errands now that the inn was closed. His mother chopped up the last of the meat she had bought at the market into a stew, and Simeon kept a small amount of ale brewing in case there should be any customers, but few people called by, apart from the Beadle.

He sat in the smoke-stained kitchen in his coat of yellow kersey and propped his whip and staff against the wall.

'It's a terrible thing that's happened, terrible,' the Beadle said, taking a long slurp from the pewter pot.

'Well, do something about it then,' Susan said, pushing the hair out of her eyes. The Beadle shook his head and sighed. 'These fanatics – what can you do with them?' he said. 'I've always said the middle road was best. A man of peace, I am.'

Simeon eyed the whip.

'Are you telling me you can't do anything about it?' Susan said, while Simeon slunk out. He did not want to stay in the same room as the Beadle, though later he heard Susan giving him the sharp edge of her tongue.

'Lay low?' she said. 'Is that the best you can do? While we've got no money coming in and there's rates to pay, and tithing – not to mention food. How are we supposed to manage?'

The Beadle said something that Simeon couldn't quite hear, then Susan's voice rose shrilly again.

'Suppose they close all the inns down and then start on the shops? Why would they need officers of the law when they can take the law into their own hands? Why would they need a Beadle?'

Simeon could hear the Beadle now, backing on to the landing.

'Oh, I don't think it'll come to that,' he said. 'Folk'll still want whipping.'

Susan drew a deep breath. It had come to a fine pass, she said, when madmen from outside the town could ride roughshod over the folk in it, and not one of the officials could lift a hand to help. What were they paying rates for, she asked, if not for some protection?

The Beadle looked a bit dazed by this outburst, and edged towards the door.

'Well, I take your point, I do indeed,' he said. 'But there's no reason to make a fuss just yet. I'll have to be going now,' he said hastily, before Susan could start again. But I'll put all your points to the Borough Reeve – he's the man you want. He'll have them all up before the Court Leet – you mark my words. He's the man you want.'

And he hurried off before Susan could point out that the next Court Leet was in April, nearly six months away.

Then, when the Borough Reeve finally came with his lawyer, Susan nearly got herself arrested for raising her voice to them both. They asked a lot of questions, but seemed to think it was Mistress Butterworth's fault for keeping an unruly house. And the lawyer was firmly on the side of the Puritans.

'We have to establish,' he said, 'the extent to which the attack was provoked.'

That was when Susan raised her voice, until the Borough Reeve threatened her with the stocks and a good whipping. Their claims were being investigated, he said, which was more than they deserved, given the character of the establishment.

And in the meantime, his lawyer added, they should do nothing, go about their business, stay out of trouble. They could do worse, he had said, than to present a respectable face to the town. And they should all attend church.

'The church?' Susan said. 'Where that madman preaches?'

'If you stay away, you do but add fuel to his fire.'

Susan expelled a savage breath, but the Borough Reeve took his hand away from his long chin and said, 'Enough of this. Our business is finished. I am sorry for what has happened and I wish your mistress a speedy recovery. But she has been a regular at the Court Leet for the last few sessions. She does not help herself.'

A series of expressions flitted across Susan's face, but when she spoke at last it was in a low, even voice.

'Does that mean,' she said, 'that we cannot open the inn?'

For the first time the Borough Reeve looked un-comfortable.

'It is best to leave things as they are for now,' he said. 'while your mistress recovers. Things should return to normal after Christmas.'

Susan was speechless. After Christmas!

'You may see us out,' the lawyer said.

Susan had no choice but to drop a curtsey and show them to the door. When she came back into the kitchen she sank down heavily at the table and sat for a moment, hunched in despair.

'Well, that's it,' she said. 'We'd best start selling the stock.'

13

The next day his mother told Simeon they were going to church.

'Why?' he asked, wondering if it was Sunday, although he hadn't heard the bells ring. His mother told him not to ask questions, but to put on his smock.

It was late afternoon and there was a flitter of starlings against the reddening sky. As they approached the church, Simeon could hear the choir singing. They entered quietly as the choir stopped and slipped into a pew. The Choirmaster stood at the lectern, lecturing them all, then he waved a hand.

'That will have to do,' he said. 'Go on, then, go.'

Simeon shrank back in his seat as the choir left in a disorderly rabble. Then his mother tugged at his sleeve and he rose from his seat and followed her to the front of the church. It seemed different now, without the congregation, the roof as high as the sky and hung in shade. He craned his neck, looking for the stone angels up above, while his mother spoke to the Choirmaster.

'To sing for me?' he said. 'Why?'

'Will you hear him sing?' his mother asked. Simeon didn't understand. His mother had told him he was not to sing at Mistress Butterworth's.

'This is not a theatre, Mistress,' the Choirmaster said, snapping his psalter shut. He stepped down from the lectern, towards them. Simeon's mother twisted the rags of her skirt. 'Only hear him sing,' she said, in a soft, pleading tone, but the Choirmaster turned away.

'Choir practice is over,' he said.

'Let the boy sing,' said a voice from the nave, making Simeon jump. It was the Warden, stepping forward from the shadows. His voice echoed strangely in Simeon's mind.

'We are not auditioning here,' the Choirmaster said.

'You are the Choirmaster, are you not?' said the Warden.

Simeon stared at him. The Warden had lifted his hat and a black skull cap sat on his silver hair. Beneath this, his eyes glittered strangely and a shadow formed behind him. There was his own shadow, cast by the candlelight, and the shadow of something else, a little to one side.

'I don't know why you are here, Mistress,' the Choirmaster said. 'I don't know what you have heard, but the choir is not open to auditions. All places are filled.'

'You think there is no room for improvement?' the Warden said, coming forward until he stood in front of the stone on which the angel was carved. 'I have just listened to some of the worst singing I can remember hearing. Perhaps you should start again with new choristers.'

When the Warden spoke, the words echoed in Simeon's mind as though two people were speaking, though maybe it was only the echoes in the church. The shadow that stood to the left of him reached the Angel Stone, and the stone glowed suddenly with an angry light. At the same time Simeon could hear music playing. He looked upwards again and thought he saw the stone angels bending towards him with their instruments.

The Choirmaster sighed.

'What will the boy sing?' he said.

Simeon swayed in time to the angels' music.

'Simeon,' his mother warned him. 'He will sing the *Agnus Dei*.'

The Choirmaster moved towards the organ. But the words to a different music were tumbling through Simeon's head, and before the Choirmaster could start to play, he began to sing.

'I'll sing you one-oh

'Green grow the rushes-oh.'

It was the song his mother had sung so often in the alehouse, and as he sang it, all the angels began to play, and Simeon's voice arced upwards to meet the instruments.

'One is one and all alone and ever more shall be so.'

'Simeon,' his mother pleaded, and there was an edge of desperation in her voice, but the Warden raised a hand.

'Enough,' he said.

The Choirmaster stood down from the organ. 'Where did he learn to sing like that?' he said.

'He didn't learn,' said Simeon's mother.

'But – how does he follow the music?'

'He can always follow.'

'Wait a minute,' the Choirmaster said. He returned to the organ, pulled out the pedal, and played a note. 'Sing it back to me,' he said.

Simeon wasn't listening. He was waiting for the angels to play again, but his mother touched his shoulder and he heard the note. He reproduced exactly the harsh sound of the organ, feeling it reverberate in his chest.

'Simeon!' his mother said, and she sang the note to him; then he understood and sang it back to her. The

93

Choirmaster began to play simple phrases at first and then more complicated ones. Simeon understood that the organ was singing to him, and he sang back to it, and then they sang together, as if it were a game. Higher and higher the notes climbed and Simeon's voice climbed with them, arching upwards to the vault of the church.

The Choirmaster stopped playing, and sat back. The Warden stared at Simeon with glittering eyes, and his mother stood with her hand pressed to her mouth. Simeon could not see whether she was happy or sad.

'Well, I think we've established,' the Warden said, 'that the boy can sing.'

Simeon stared at his mother's face, wondering if he had done something wrong, but the Warden was speaking again.

'Perhaps you had better present him to the High Master,' he said. His voice had changed now and there was only one person speaking. Simeon looked, but he couldn't see the shadow. He could hear the music again and he moved his fingers as though playing along with it. Then his mother caught his fluttering hands and sat down with him in a pew. He gazed into her eyes, which had green-gold lights in them, like the forest.

Then the Warden stood in front of them, and cleared his throat.

'You serve at one of the inns of Long Millgate, do you not?'

Simeon's mother went on looking at Simeon, but she nodded.

'Is that where you live?'

'It is, sir,' Simeon's mother said. 'But the inn has been closed by the Puritans.'

She spoke to the Warden, but she was looking at Simeon. It was as though she was asking something from him, something like forgiveness. The Warden leant forward.

'How old is your son, Mistress?'

'Nearly thirteen,' his mother answered. Then they heard another, harsh voice towards the back of the church.

'And I have already said that the school is not in need of new pupils!'

A man appeared with the Choirmaster. He had a heavy, mottled face, and it sat on a large white ruff like a pudding on a plate.

'What is all this?' he asked.

Simeon stopped listening. He always found it hard to understand what a stranger was saying. Only as he grew to know someone, and like them, did their words make any sense to him. And then sometimes, he could hear not only their words, but their thoughts. This man was angry, he could see that much, and he could see the hard, jagged shapes of words. But his accent was strange. Simeon would not look at him. He looked around instead for the angels.

'Will the angels play again?' he asked his mother, but she only pressed a finger to his lips.

The angry man asked only one question of Simeon's mother.

'He will be thirteen after Christmas,' she answered him, and the man snorted. But the Warden spoke to him in his double voice and it was full of menace, and then the angry man started to shout. Simeon's mother kept her arms round him as the man walked away; then the Warden turned to them and Simeon shrank back.

'What is your name?' he asked.

'Simeon,' his mother said for him. 'Simeon Peploe.'

'Well, Simeon Peploe,' said the Warden. 'How would you like to start school here on Monday morning?'

Simeon shook his head, staring. Light from the Angel Stone flickered around the edges of the Warden, and his double shadow appeared.

'He will be here,' his mother said quickly. 'Thank you, sir,' and she caught the Warden's hand and kissed the ring on his finger. Then she pulled Simeon from his seat before he could say anything and together they left the church. When he glanced back, the Warden was watching them, and Simeon thought he could see, against a shaft of sunlight on the old man's cloak, the pressure of black wings beating down.

14

More than an hour later, Simeon and his mother were still walking through the streets of the town. Simeon could not believe what she was trying to tell him. He kicked a stone against a wall.

'I don't want to,' he said.

'Simeon,' said his mother. 'There is no place for us here.'

They had wound in and out of the streets of the town in the darkening light, and had come finally to Withy Grove, where the willows, shorn of leaves, dipped and swung their branches like great brooms in the breeze. Facing them, the Seven Stars Inn looked out over open fields. It was cold, but in the depths of misery, Simeon could only feel the cold place inside.

'I don't want to,' he repeated.

His mother took his hand. She led him to a low stone wall and perched on it. He sat down with her and she unwrapped the woollen shawl from her shoulders and draped it round them both. It was the same shawl she had carried him in as a baby.

For a long time they sat in silence, his mother having exhausted all arguments. Simeon could feel what warmth there was from her body seeping into his, and smell the scent of her: the smell of ale from the inn, and lavender from the water in which she rinsed her hair. He was aware of the familiar, slightly acrid smell that was all her own, that he had known all his life, all the days and nights they had spent together, in open fields and woodland, sharing the same worn blanket. He could not imagine what he would do without that smell.

After a long time, his mother spoke.

'All our lives we've been on the run,' she said. 'Wandering like beggars from one town to another, always driven away. It is no life,' she said, raising a hand as Simeon started to speak. 'It's not the life I want for you. You're nearly thirteen – the age when all grown boys leave home and learn a trade. But what trade can you learn, Simeon?' she said, and her voice was shaking. 'What can you do? You can *sing*.'

Simeon was silent. They had always sung together, he was thinking.

'If you go to that school,' she said, 'you will learn to read and write. You will learn to speak properly, like a gentleman, and use a sword. You will be taken care of for at least the next two years. And when you've finished, there'll be a place for you, Simeon, some kind of work you can do.'

'No,' Simeon said. Inside his head he was shouting. His mother gave a sigh that shook her whole body.

'You know what happens to vagrants,' she said, and a vivid image of the bodies of the gypsies swaying in the clearing flared in Simeon's mind, though at that time he hadn't even been born. A shudder passed from his mother's body to his.

'I won't leave,' she said. 'I'll find work at one of the other inns and visit you every day. I'll earn money to keep you there. It is our chance, Simeon, our chance to lead a different kind of life.'

'No!' Simeon said. He stood up, letting the shawl flap round his mother.

'You don't want me,' he said. 'You don't want me with you any more.'

'Oh, *Simeon!*' his mother said, and she slapped the wall behind her with both palms. 'Everything I do is for you. But it's not enough, Simeon, it's not enough any more.'

And her face crumpled and she began to cry.

Simeon stared at her. His mother's shoulders shook beneath the thin wool of the shawl and her hair hung over her face like a straggly curtain, but she made no sound. She hardly ever cried, not even that one, terrible time when she had been whipped. Fear tugged at him. His mother bent forward and something in the movement seemed utterly wretched. He reached out a hand awkwardly and smoothed her hair. 'Don't cry,' he whispered. A great sob burst from his mother and she fell into his arms. He could feel the thinness of her body shaking against his, and her despair. Tears started in his own eyes.

'Who will look after Matilda?' he asked.

His mother looked up, pushing her hair back. 'I will,' she whispered, then her face crumpled again. 'I'll visit you every day!' she told him, but Simeon wasn't crying now. He remembered the time when they had stood in a field together and there was a mass of stars, so low and bright he thought he could touch them. And he had spread his arms wide and it seemed that within their stretch he could encompass the whole sky.

Look, Daya, he had said, *I'm holding the sky up!*

And his mother had stood a little way from him and

stretched her own arms out. *No,* she had said, *I am.*

And they had run round the field with their arms spread out and it had seemed as though between them they could hold the whole sky.

'Don't cry,' he said into her hair. '*Daya*, don't cry.'

Slowly his mother stopped crying and they hung on to one another. The wind whipped his mother's hair into his eyes and nose, but he hung on, his mind full of thoughts of the school, with its strange uniform and even stranger books that he could not read, His mind dwelt on the boys who had come into the inn and tried to get Simeon out of the kitchen so that they could laugh at him. And worse than this, more frightening than all of them, was the gaunt figure of the Warden, with his double shadow.

But this was his mother; he would do anything for her. He shut his eyes tightly and buried his face in her hair.

As they clung together, the door of the inn opened and a group of men came out. Simeon's mother straightened slowly, pulling away from him and wiping her eyes. One of the men came over.

'Well,' he said. 'Here's a pretty sight.'

It was Black Jack. Simeon stepped away from him, scowling, but his mother managed a smile.

'I've not seen you recently,' Black Jack said, looking Simeon's mother up and down, 'but you're looking better than ever.'

Simeon's mother wrapped the blanket more closely round her shoulders.

'You heard about the inn?' she said.

Black Jack's face changed. 'Aye,' he said. 'A curse on all Puritans.' He lifted his voice and shouted, 'A pox on the

Puritans! They should be driven out of town with their own whips! Hung by their own hair shirts!'

Simeon's mother laughed a little, nervously, then took Simeon's arm.

'Where are you going?' asked Black Jack.

'To draw water for Mistress Butterworth,' said Simeon's mother.

'Then let me accompany you,' Black Jack said. 'A pretty lady should not have to carry water alone.'

Simeon's mother hesitated and Simeon glared at Black Jack.

'Besides,' continued Black Jack, 'I want to pay my respects to Mistress Butterworth. The whole town knows she has been badly used.'

He fell into step beside Simeon's mother, taking her other arm.

'I'll join you later,' he called to his friends, who stood grinning on the steps of the inn.

For a time Simeon kept pace with them, clinging to his mother's arm in a determined way. Gently but firmly, however, Black Jack steered Simeon's mother away from him, and as they crossed the road, he stepped between them. Simeon fell back, watching his mother. She seemed a different person now, looking up at Black Jack and laughing, smoothing her hair. Simeon didn't think his jokes were so funny, but she evidently did. She hadn't noticed that Simeon was no longer walking with them. He fell further and further behind, until the shadow from the schoolmaster's house fell between them and across Simeon's heart, for it seemed to him that she had already left.

15

The weekend passed like a dark dream. Simeon helped his mother to sell the best linen and the pewter plates at the market. On Saturday Susan found work in the wash house, and Simeon's mother in one of the other inns. She could not sleep there, she said, and there was no room for Simeon. Susan spoke to him with a false brightness, about what a fine gentleman he would become at the school. Simeon said nothing to this, but stared at his bread and meat. Only once did he beg his mother not to send him to the school, but she got annoyed with him and told him he was a man now. Then she cried a little and clung to him, then quickly hurried away.

On Sunday, Mistress Butterworth's relatives came and took her away in a cart. Susan said she would sleep in Mistress Butterworth's room that night, and Simeon's mother took him into her room. They lay together in the old way, tucked into one another, and Simeon stayed awake for a long time, feeling the imprint of her body against his. He knew his mother wasn't sleeping either, but she was wrapped in silence. They had often been silent together, of course, but in this silence he was alone.

In the morning, instead of going to market, Simeon's mother made him wash his face. She scrubbed at his hands with a cloth, and tugged a comb through his unruly hair. Simeon looked for some sign in her face that she was grieving, but her face, though strained, seemed turned in on itself, and he could not read the expression in her eyes.

'When will I see you?' he said, and he buried his face in her neck.

'Simeon,' she said, rocking him. Then she put her hands on his shoulders, pushing him away.

'Every Saturday afternoon, you will be off school, and you can come to me. Every Sunday you will see me in church, I promise. Look at me, Simeon,' she said as he shook his head, and Simeon looked at her with eyes full of misery.

'What do you see?'

It was a question she had asked him before and he knew the answer.

'I see myself,' he said, looking into the shining surface of her eyes. For most of his life, that had been the only mirror he had known.

'You are in my eyes,' she said, 'and I am in yours.'

Then she took him by the hand and led him downstairs, and Susan hugged him and told him what a grand lad he had become. Then hand in hand, they crossed Long Millgate, passing the old woman who sat in the doorway mumbling, and the mother who cried out 'Joachim?' looking for her son, and then they came to the gates of the school and Simeon's mother rang the bell.

One of the Fellows came to the gates and asked them their business. Simeon did not like the way he looked at his mother, but she only curtseyed and said they had been told to come by the Warden. The man looked as though he would send them away, but thought better of it.

'Wait here,' he said, and Simeon waited, clutching his mother's hand, for women were not supposed to go further than the gate. A door opened and Simeon felt a great fear clamouring inside, like the panicked rustling of the birds he had seen crammed into wicker baskets in the market. But it was not the Warden who appeared, but the High Master, looking vastly displeased. As he approached them, Simeon made a sudden movement as though he would run away, but his mother gripped his hand tightly and looked at him with imploring eyes.

'You are a man,' her eyes said. So Simeon stayed where he was, as the High Master gazed at them both severely. Simeon's mother started to explain, but he raised a hand.

'I will take him now,' he said, and he lifted himself on to his toes, then lowered himself again. Simeon pressed his hand to the gate as his mother walked away. She did not look back, and fear seeped into the empty space in his heart.

Dust

Manchester, Present Day

Two bikes threaded their way through the traffic on Deansgate, which was entirely static. Then sirens erupted and there was chaos, as two police cars, an ambulance and a fire engine attempted to make their way through. Cars, buses and trucks edged on to pavements or into side streets, pedestrians crammed themselves into shop doorways. Kate took a chance, dodging and weaving through four lanes of disrupted traffic. She was already late.

Someone in the cathedral had decided it was time for Manchester to commemorate its pre-industrial history and had got together with local history groups, Theatre in Education and Manchester Museums, to devise a project for inner city schools.

'It'll look good on your CV,' her personal adviser Judith had told her. 'You might get off Special Report.'

'No way,' Kate had said and Judith had raised an eyebrow.

'Don't you *want* to get off Special Report?' she had asked. Kate had glowered. She did, of course, want to get off Special Report, as it meant that Social Services were watching her, waiting for a chance to take her away from her dad.

'Can you sing?' Judith had asked and Kate had glowered even more.

'I'm not doing no solos,' she warned and Judith had sighed.

'Well, I don't suppose you'll have to,' she said. 'You can choose what you want to do – filming, technical support. I just think it'd be good for you to, well – get involved. It might compensate for all the times you've been off school.'

'All half-term?' Kate said. 'Every day?'

But Judith had merely closed Kate's file, and looked at her.

School had finished now, but she was still expected to be at the cathedral for the preliminary meeting. She had gone home, changed, got temporarily distracted by the mess in the kitchen and by the fact that her father wasn't in and she didn't know where he was. She had left him a note and set off at a swift pace for the city centre.

Kate jogged past the visitor centre and entered the cathedral by the main door. Instantly the noise of Manchester faded. Rays of light with dust motes in them streamed through the vast windows, and a banner proclaiming the *Year of Plague, 1605*, was strung between two pillars. A large group of students was sitting on the chairs towards the front of the nave, where there was an altar and a carved wooden screen. A short woman with spiky grey hair was speaking to them. Kate spotted Babs and Nolly from her class towards the back and made her way towards them.

'Sorry,' she said, as she nudged someone's chair, and 'Sorry,' again as she kicked someone else's bag. The project leader, Karin, paused for a moment to let her sit down. Babs looked up, smiling briefly, and passed Kate a sheaf of notes and a name tag, which Kate pinned reluctantly to the front of her T-shirt.

'So you see,' Karin said, 'we don't have exact figures, but

roughly half the population died. Think of that. Half of all the people you know.'

Kate kicked the chair in front of her rhythmically.

'That's half our class,' Nolly whispered.

'Well, so long as it was you,' Kate said.

Nolly never responded to thrusts like this.

'Yeah, but you'd miss me though, right?' he said.

Kate ignored him. She couldn't help being mean to Nolly – everyone was. It didn't stop him hanging around where he wasn't wanted.

'Rioting broke out,' Karin went on, 'law and order broke down. People tried to escape, but they were forbidden to leave the town.'

She looked at the sullen, uninterested faces.

'Come outside for a moment,' she said. Rows of faces stared at her dully. 'Come on,' she said. 'All of you – outside.'

There was much sighing and mumbling and scraping of chairs as people pressed forward. Karin led them through the north door of the cathedral. Kate pulled her thin jacket more tightly round her as the wind blew right through it.

'All right,' said Karin. 'What can you see?'

The immense glass structure of the new museum, Urbis, shone with a cold light, like ice. Traffic hauled itself slowly along Corporation Street, held up by the temporary traffic lights. To the right of the cathedral were the expensive shops of the Triangle, ahead was Victoria Station. A row of fountains jetted into the air at the bottom of the grassy area between the cathedral and the station.

'I want you to get a feel of how small Manchester was in 1605,' Karin said. 'Almost nothing you can see now was here then. There was the cathedral, which was just a church, and the college, then known as the Manchester Free Grammar School. No, not Chetham's,' she said, indicating the tall, red building facing Urbis. 'That was built later. The college building was the old manor house behind – if you walk down there you'll see a plaque on the wall saying Long Millgate – that was a street four hundred years ago, full of inns. Deansgate was where it is now, and the river curved round the side of the cathedral, which was just the parish church. On the south side of the church there was the market square, and Market Stead Lane. That was more or less it. Manchester was a village then, not a city, but two or three thousand people were crammed into these few streets.'

'Miss, what about the shops?' Babs asked.

'Karin,' Karin corrected her. 'They were mainly on Market Stead Lane and Smithy Door, which ran from the church to the market square. Now – what do you notice that the church hasn't got?'

Silence. Kate stared up at the griffins and gargoyles above the door.

'Come on,' Karin said. 'What kind of things go on in a village church?'

'Weddings, Miss,' someone said.

'Yes, and?'

'Funerals?' said Babs.

'That's right,' said Karin. 'At one time there must have been a graveyard. In fact, we know there was, because the graves got so overloaded at the time of plague that bodies had to be buried in the fields. But no one knows what happened to the graveyard. At a guess, it was probably where the Triangle shops are now. Why do you think it's not here any more?'

No one knew. Kate fiddled with her name tag. She wondered how many of the kids were voluntarily giving up their half-term break, and how many, like Kate, had been drafted in. Probably only Babs was genuinely enthusiastic.

'Well – what is Manchester famous for?' Karin asked. 'It's doing it now,' she added.

'Raining?' Nolly said, and indeed a fine, cutting rain had begun.

'*Raining*,' said Karin. 'And what happens when enough rain falls on rivers – they overflow – that's right. And there's flooding. So that's why Manchester no longer has a proper graveyard, or crypt. Much of this area has been built over the original Manchester.

'Well, you don't seem very excited,' she went on, when this failed to elicit a response. 'Can't you see what it must have been like?'

'It's freezing, Miss,' one of the girls commented, and several voices agreed.

'Yes, OK,' Karin said in a resigned tone. 'Back inside. I want you to meet some of the people who'll be working with you.'

Everyone filed back in, past the posters showing what the church and surrounding area would have looked like then.

'Right, everyone,' Karin said, and she introduced them to Danny, a short, stocky man with wiry black hair, who would work with them on the technical side, and Zoë, a sculptress with long dreadlocks, who would be making a series of figures from clay; Leah the candle-maker and Alf who would help one group to create a stained-glass window, portraying scenes from the Year of Plague.

'Hopefully you'll all get a chance to work on at least two activities,' Karin said. 'But for now, we've put you in groups according to the activities you specified on your forms.'

She read out the names of the different groups. Kate hadn't filled in a form, but she had been put in a group with Babs and

Nolly. Of the three pupils from Kate's class, only Babs had volunteered, but then she volunteered for everything. Nolly had been drafted in for failing all his SATS, Kate because of persistent truanting. They were in Group B with three white kids from Lower Broughton, who sat further along the row, snickering and whispering. Thus far they hadn't spoken to Kate, Babs or Nolly at all.

Danny clapped his hands.

'OK, Groups A and B come with me, please.'

Kate shuffled to the front with the rest of her group. Only Babs looked keen.

'Right,' Danny said. 'We're going to be creating a PowerPoint presentation on the Year of Plague.'

Danny explained that they would make a video in which they would talk about the plague from the perspectives of different characters.

'We need actors and narrators,' he said, handing a sheaf of scripts to Group A. 'So you'll have to sort out who does what between you. And anyone who isn't being filmed can help with the lighting and sound.'

Babs stepped forward eagerly to hand out the scripts.

'Take them away and look at them, and you can tell me tomorrow who's doing what,' Danny said. 'Now, who doesn't want to be involved in either acting or narrating?'

A girl from Group A raised a hand. Kate hunched her shoulders. She didn't want to be filmed.

'So I take it you're more interested in the technical side,' said Danny.

Kate shrugged.

'Well, er – Kate,' he said, reading her name tag, 'I'd like everyone to have a go at different aspects of the filming process, OK?'

Before Kate could answer, Karin called for all the groups to come together.

Part of the project was to make sure that all the kids from different inner-city schools mixed together, though now as they gathered round Karin they still stood in separate clusters. Group A stood ostentatiously apart from Group B, and Kate, Nolly and Babs stood a little way from the white kids in their group, Lorna, Stefan and Danielle. Stefan was thin and coffee-coloured, dressed like a scally. Lorna and Danielle were spotty, shifty-eyed and mean-looking. Danielle kept messing with her hair, which was streaked in many colours.

Karin told them that the real work would begin tomorrow and cont. ue through half-term. There was some moaning at this, because tomorrow was Saturday.

Karin held her hand up. 'There might be a television crew here at the end of the week,' she said. 'Possibly *Newsround* and certainly *Look North West* will be interested in doing a feature. So we want everything to be underway when they arrive.'

There was a more enthusiastic response this time.

'Will we be interviewed?' one of the lads wanted to know.

'Possibly,' Karin said, running a hand through her spiky hair. 'You might want to consider choosing a spokesperson from each group. But remember –' she said, as an excited babble of voices broke out, 'all this is conditional on you turning up every day, between 9.30 a.m. and 1 p.m. We will be reporting back to your various schools at the end of the project, and registers will be taken.'

Just like school, Kate thought.

'All right,' said Karin. 'Now those of you interested in singing, come forward.

'We want to make a soundtrack, for the PowerPoint presentation,' she continued, as no one moved. 'Just some music from the time. You don't have to sing on your own.'

Babs got up, then Stefan and Lorna. Kate hung back as more and more students went to the front. She didn't want to sing, or be on TV. She remained half hidden behind one of the great cathedral pillars, reading the notes she'd been given, while everyone else gathered round Karin.

The cathedral was bigger than any church she had ever been in, double-aisled, with an ornate wooden screen, behind which, her notes said, the choir sat. Kate slipped into the choir stalls, looking at the carved wood of the misericords. There was a fox teaching two cubs to read and monkeys stealing clothes from a sleeping pedlar. She pulled one of the seats down and sat on it as the singing began. Someone had made marks on the armrest and she got up again to have a look.

WLC, 1604, the letters read. Kate traced them with her finger. She thought of all the boys who would have sung from these choir stalls, or sat there bored, carving their names surreptitiously with a knife. Strange to think that kids then were no different from kids today.

'I'll sing you one-oh,' the students sang.

'Green grow the rushes-oh.'

Kate felt suddenly that all this had happened before, but that was nonsense, she had never been here before. She felt as though all the different eyes, of griffins and gargoyles and carved faces were watching her. She stood up and stepped away from them hurriedly, back into the nave.

All of the north side had been rebuilt after the bombing in the Second World War, her notes said, and the bombing itself was commemorated in the Fire Window at the eastern end, which glowed with a flame-coloured light. Up in the roof, the evening sun glinted on the golden instruments of fourteen stone angels.

It was peaceful, at any rate. A homeless person sat at the back, near the stall where an old woman handed out brochures to visitors, and the verger moved quietly through the small chapels at the side of the nave. Kate moved to a seat several rows back and looked at the altar.

A woman sat a few rows ahead of her, caught in a beam of light from the window, like a projection. Kate hadn't noticed her before. Sunshine glinted on her auburn hair, but what really caught Kate's attention were her clothes. She seemed to be wearing a blanket of faded blue cloth, and beneath this a long skirt, which would once have been brightly coloured, but now it was pale and stained.

One of the players, Kate thought, assuming she must belong to the project.

But then the woman turned and looked directly at her, and Kate's heart fluttered wildly. Then she blinked and rubbed her eyes and the woman was gone.

Seeing things now, Kate told herself. It was the light in the cathedral, hazy and full of dust, and all this historical talk. But she could have sworn there was blood on the woman's blanket.

Suddenly Kate knew she had to get home. She didn't know where the feeling came from, but it pulsed in her urgently, like a heartbeat. She got up, scraping her chair back roughly and left the cathedral unnoticed. As she turned the corner on to Deansgate, her strides lengthened into a run.

Master Kit Morley

I

4th October 1604

Joseph Pryor, the youngest boy in the Manchester Free
Grammar School, twisted and turned in his cot. He was
not yet seven and he missed his mother, whom he had been
told he would not see again, because she was something
terrible, called a papist. He slept in the dormitory for the
younger boys, though one of the older boys always slept in
there as well, to make sure they said their prayers and got
to bed. There were twelve beds, called cots, end to end, but
even though all the other children were there, Joseph was
very afraid of the dark. He spent much of his time trying to
disguise the fact that he wet the bed, though from the smell
of the room, he did not think he was the only one.

Joseph stiffened as he heard footsteps along the corridor
outside, then breathed again as they went away. He was
frightened of every noise, and there were many. But most
particularly he was frightened of the Warden, whom
everyone knew was really the Devil.

'He pads along the corridors in the shape of a huge
black dog,' the older boys had told him. 'And his eyes are
as big as saucers and they glow with the fires of Hell. He
snuffles along the edges of the door, trying to get in. But
so long as you're asleep and you've said your prayers, he
can't get in.'

Joseph tried to speak, but his voice would only come out in a squeak. 'S-suppose you can't get to sleep?' he had asked.

'Then he comes for you,' the biggest boy, called William Chubb, told him and Joseph had stared at him as though he was drowning.

'But good boys always get to sleep,' one of the other boys had put in and Joseph Pryor felt worse than ever. For he said every prayer he could remember twice over and still he could not sleep. He had been caned once in class for falling asleep and once in church for yawning, but as soon as he got into bed, he felt wide awake. And when he did fall into a shallow, intermittent sleep, he wet the bed, which was partly because he was too frightened to get up in the dark and use the pot. Yet he prayed all the time: he had prayed to God to make him good and to remove the stain of his parents from his soul. He had even promised to try to forget his mother, though that prayer made hot tears fall on to his blanket. And he prayed every day that the Warden would not notice him, or come for him at night. He could not be good, because if he was good, then God would hear his prayers.

There was another movement outside and Joseph Pryor went rigid again, his heart pounding, but it was only the creak of ancient joinery, as though the old house was grinding its teeth. On every side he could hear the sound of rough breathing that told him all the other boys were asleep, and if he didn't sleep soon, it would be time to wake up and sit through more long, appalling lessons that he did not understand. He half sat up in bed and looked over to where the oldest boy lay.

'Kit,' he whispered; then louder, 'Kit?'

The older boy stirred. 'Kit?' Joseph said again.

'What?' mumbled Kit.

'Are you asleep?'

'Yes.'

'Oh,' said Joseph, and Kit sighed. Turning over he asked, 'What is it?'

'I can't sleep.'

'Say your prayers.'

'I've said them all. Twice.'

Kit groaned inwardly. But he knew what it was like. He too had been younger than the other boys when he had been taken from his mother. He too had come from a Catholic family and had never seen his mother again. And he too had had the nightmares; sometimes he still had them, though he was nearly fourteen.

'I will say them with you,' he said, and after a moment more of lying in the warm place in his bed, he pushed the cover back and got up, trying not to swear as he banged his foot. He sat on the edge of Joseph Pryor's bed and the small boy curled into him. Kit pressed the younger boy's hands together in prayer and kept his own closed over them.

'If you sleep like this, the Devil cannot hurt you,' he whispered, and Joseph nodded, his eyes wide. Kit said the prayer that all the small ones said and Joseph said it with him.

'I pray the Lord my soul to keep . . .'

Then they said the *Nunc Dimittis* together and finally, feeling the pressure of Kit's body next to his and the warmth of his hands round his own, Joseph's head nodded forward. Carefully, Kit eased himself away from the sleeping child.

The next day Joseph rose at six, feeling much better for his sleep, and followed the other boys down to prayers.

It will be all right, he told himself, vastly encouraged by the fact that he had, after all, slept. So long as he kept his head down and no one noticed him.

After an hour's prayer, it was time for breakfast, which took place in the Great Hall. This was an oak-panelled room, lit by burning torches. There were two tables for the boys and a long table for the Master and Usher and Fellows. On his first day, Joseph had been stunned by the noise. Twenty-two boys ate meat with a knife, scooping up the juices with a spoon. There was a large notice on the wall:

Sup not loud of thy pottage.
Belch near no one's face with a corrupt fumiosity.
Scratch not thy head at the table, nor spit you.
Dip not thy meat in the salt, but take it with a knife.
Eat small morsels of meat, drink softly, soft like a beast
    in the field.
Wipe thy mouth on a napkin, not the tablecloth.
Blow not thy nose on the napkin.

Joseph could not read this, but one of the older boys had recited it to him. They seemed to take great pride in breaking most of the rules straight away, particularly the ones about belching and spitting, and no one told them off, because the Masters were doing the same thing. Joseph Pryor kept his head down and said his prayers with the others before and after food. Then he helped to clear the pots away and did not drop a single one.

Today will be a good day, he told himself.

But it was after breakfast that the blow fell. The Usher, Master Gringold, a tall, thin man with a crooked, melancholy nose, told him to take the Warden's breakfast to his room. He had to repeat this twice before Joseph understood him, then ask why the boy was staring at him like a frightened rabbit. Kit half rose from his seat.

'I will go,' he said.

'You will not,' said the Usher. 'I did not ask you.'

'Well?' he said to Joseph, who had turned as pale as a pudding cloth. One of the older boys tittered, and Joseph turned suddenly, without a word, and trotted as quickly as he could towards the kitchen. He could not run so quickly with the tray, and each step he took felt like the tolling of a bell.

Today will be a good day, he reminded himself, but it was like a small, frightened squeak in his mind. As he approached the stone stairway that led to the Warden's room, he tried to pray, but he had forgotten how, and he stared up at the gargoyles in dismay, because if he couldn't pray, then the Devil would surely appear. He could leave the tray at the foot of the stairs, but then he would be caned. Sweating, he began to climb, and when he came to the arched doorway of the Warden's room, he gave a timid knock.

No answer.

Relief washed over Joseph Pryor as he realized he could simply leave the tray there.

I knocked, he would say, *and no one answered.*

But as he bent down to leave the tray, the door swung open suddenly, silently. Joseph's heart began to hammer and pound. His gaze travelled up the Warden's long black robes, fearful of what he would see. But the Warden only looked distracted. He wore a skull cap that the older boys said concealed his horns. Joseph pressed his lips together to stop himself whimpering, and backed away.

'What is it?' the Warden said irritably, and Joseph pointed to his food.

'Well?' barked the Warden, and Joseph stared at him blankly.

'Pick it up, lad – pick it up!'

Tears stung the back of Joseph's eyes as he crept forward, and his palms were sweating as he picked up the tray. When the Warden took it from him he scuttled away again immediately.

'Hoy – you there – what's your name?' the Warden snapped after him, and Joseph paused in terror, then looked over his shoulder.

'J-Joseph P-Pryor,' he managed to say, and the Warden stepped towards him.

'You know Master Morley?' he asked.

Kit? thought Joseph, and he nodded warily.

'Tell him I want to see him.'

'Well?' he said again, as Joseph failed to move. 'You may go. *Go!*' he snapped suddenly, and Joseph turned tail and ran, as though the hounds of Hell were after him.

2

When Joseph returned to the Great Hall, only a few of the older lads were left, playing dice before church, which of course was strictly forbidden. Joseph's stomach clenched all over again, since he was afraid of the older boys, apart from Kit, who was sitting at one end of the table, watching the game.

Will Chubb was playing Michael Langley, but as Joseph approached nervously, he said, without looking up, 'What is that, drawing near?'

Nathaniel Parker, a sly-faced boy with slanting eyes, replied, 'An incubus!'

But Michael Langley said, 'No, it is only Master Pryor, but horribly changed,' and they all made noises of horror and disgust, so that Joseph looked around fearfully, and started to sweat.

Then Ben Hewitt said, 'Oh, Joseph, Joseph, what has he done to you?' in such mournful tones that Joseph thought he might start to cry.

'Leave the lad alone,' Kit protested.

But Parker had risen and placed his hands round Joseph's forehead, pretending to feel for bumps. 'Yes – I thought so,' he said, 'the horns are growing,' and Joseph's hand flew to his forehead and the older boys laughed.

'What is it, Joseph?' Kit asked, and Will Chubb said,

'Lost his tongue – that's one of the first signs.'

Kit ignored him. 'Have you got a message?' he persisted and Joseph nodded.

'Do we have to guess?' said Chubb.

At last Joseph managed to speak.

'He – he wants you to go to him – he wants to see you,' he stuttered, going very pink.

'Who does – the Beadle?' said Chubb, grinning round, but Joseph could never bring himself to say the Warden's name.

'The Warden?' coaxed Kit, and Joseph nodded. Tears came into his eyes and all the boys made sepulchral noises. Chubb whistled.

'It's your turn now,' he said, looking at Kit, who seemed disconcerted. 'He's had Pryor here as his snack, now he wants a main course.'

'He wants to see me now?' asked Kit, and Joseph hung his head.

'Hold on to your crucifix,' said Langley.

'Don't eat or drink anything in that room,' said Hewitt.

'Don't touch anything while you are there,' said Parker.

'I will walk with you,' said Chubb, as Kit reluctantly stood. 'If you are not back in half an hour, I will come for you.'

'Stay near the door,' Langley called after them. 'If he starts anything, you can run away!'

'And if he starts chanting in tongues,' said Parker, 'use your sword.'

'Look out for the magic wand,' said Hewitt.

'What are you?' said Kit, over his shoulder. 'A bunch of serving maids?'

'Speaking of serving maids,' said Chubb, as they left, 'there is a new one at Mistress Butterworth's. Worth checking out, I hear. Not young, but pretty. We thought we might go there later to take a look. Are you coming?'

'Maybe,' said Kit distractedly. He did not like the inns as much as the other boys and only went when he couldn't get out of it, but Chubb, who already at fourteen had dark bristles on his face and a voice too deep for the choir, always wanted to go.

'You'll need a drink when he's finished with you,' Chubb said as they crossed the courtyard. 'That's if he lets you go. But don't worry, I'll call for you and say the Usher requires you for sword practice.'

'What, on a Sunday?' said Kit.

'You don't think he cares what day it is, do you?' said Chubb, 'or even knows? Such things don't exist, where he comes from.'

Kit opened the door.

'Don't worry,' Chubb said, 'he'll have to let you out for church, or the Choirmaster will want to know why.'

Kit shook his head and closed the door on his friend. He did not share the same dark fear of the Warden that the other boys professed to have. But he couldn't help wondering, as he walked up the stairs, what exactly the Warden did want with him and how he might get out of it. Yesterday he had been sent to summon the Warden to the Court Leet, and the Warden had looked at him oddly then. And the room had smelt funny: pungent and smoky.

There was a notice pinned to the door of the Warden's room.

Do not disturb, it read.

Kit read it twice. He raised a hand towards the door knocker, then lowered it again. He should leave now, he thought, before the Warden realized he was there. He hesitated for a moment, then tapped softly on the Warden's door. Maybe he wouldn't hear him, Kit thought, but before he could turn, the door opened.

'Ah, Kit,' the Warden said. 'I see you are admiring my notice. But it does not apply to you.'

Kit said nothing. The Warden looked at him ironically.

'Well, don't just stand there,' he said. 'Come in, come in,' and wishing that he had left sooner, Kit followed him into the room.

3

'Look closely in the glass,' said the Warden, Dr Dee. 'What do you see?'

'I see myself,' said Kit. 'What should I see?'

An impatient look crossed the Warden's face, then as if he had become aware that the boy was studying him in the mirror, he stood to one side. Kit continued to stare at himself, wondering what all this was about. He had hardly ever seen his reflection before. In the High Master's house there was a single mirror that reflected a blurred, distorted image, but this one was pure and clean, like looking into a still lake. He wondered where the Warden had got it from. Such mirrors as this cost a small fortune, he knew. He pushed his fair hair out of his eyes and studied himself more closely. Was this his mother's face? he wondered. His nurse had once told him he was the image of his mother.

Behind him, the Warden crossed the room to where the tallest mirror stood, draped in red cloth.

'How about this one?' he said, and reluctantly, Kit moved to his side, and with a flourish like that of a showman in a travelling fair, Dr Dee removed the cloth.

'What do you see now?' he asked.

'Myself, again.'

'Look closer,' said the Warden.

Kit looked, and shook his head.

'Draw your sword,' the Warden commanded.

Kit drew his sword, and against his will gave a faint gasp. For the figure in the mirror drew its sword on the opposite side. The Warden watched him closely as he parried and thrust. It was as if he was engaging with an opponent in the mirror. Kit knew that he was expected to say something, so he kept quiet, sheathing his sword.

'Now this one,' said the Warden, uncovering a third mirror. There, in the depths of the darkened glass, the figure of Kit hung suspended, upside down.

'You see?' the Warden said.

Kit closed his eyes, remembering that the Devil used many tricks to ensnare souls; then he opened them again, looking at the Warden.

'What is this?' he said, and the Warden covered the mirror again.

'The science of optics, my dear boy,' he said, 'which reveals aspects of the known world hitherto unseen. And aspects of the hidden world. Look.'

He crossed to the table and withdrew another cloth, revealing a large stone, black and polished. Kit stepped forward warily.

'Look well, beyond the surface,' the Warden said.

Kit stared into the polished stone, seeing nothing but the image of himself and the Warden, the right way up this time. 'How many mirrors have you got?' he asked.

'You have seen them all,' the Warden replied. 'Hush now and concentrate.'

Kit looked. The Warden stood too near, he thought. He could smell the perfumed oil in his beard. Then, as if in response to Kit's unspoken thought, the Warden withdrew and busied himself with his papers.

Kit wasn't sure what he should do. His gaze travelled over the other items on the Warden's desk: a globe encircled by the celestial spheres, a compass and quadrant, a set of tables with mathematical figures.

Terrible rumours surrounded the Warden – that he kept the heads of corpses in his room and drank their blood. Kit could see the room reflected in the stone, but he could see nothing incriminating. It was lined with books by Boethius, Copernicus and Paracelsus. The *Malleus Maleficorum* stood next to Menghi's *Fustis Daemonum,* and Copernicus's *De Revolutionibus Orbium Coelestium*. He had never seen so many books before. *How much did this lot cost?* he wondered.

The Warden still said nothing. The back of Kit's neck began to ache, and he considered stepping away, but the Warden began to speak.

'"There are more things in Heaven and earth . . ."' he quoted, standing behind Kit, '"than are dreamt of in your philosophy." Worlds undreamt of, different planes, dimensions, levels of reality man has never previously perceived. There is a higher knowledge, Kit, than any brought to us in books, and at last, by means of science, man is ready to receive it direct.'

Kit felt his shoulders tense.

'The pursuit of knowledge is the road to damnation,' he said bravely.

'Who told you that – Master Gringold?' said the Warden, with barely concealed contempt. 'Yes, that is what he would say. That is what they teach boys.'

Kit watched him warily. The Warden had addressed

him by his first name, when the other Masters called him Master Morley. Kit wasn't sure what he thought about this. The Warden seemed to be assuming a kind of intimacy.

'The Bible says it,' he ventured.

'Ah, the Bible,' said the Warden, with an unreadable expression on his face. 'The Tree of Knowledge that caused the calamitous Fall.' He pressed his fingers together. 'But what if there were other books, Kit – books as sacred as *Genesis* – that teach a different lesson? Books that were never included in the Bible?'

Kit wondered if the Warden was trying to trap him. 'What books?' he said.

'Books that teach to the contrary, that God designed man to be his ultimate equal, higher than the angels and yet more free. Books that teach the path to wisdom, that were wisely kept from common men. I say wisely, for these are dangerous books, Kit.'

Kit could feel his heart thudding. He knew the penalty for heresy.

'Angelic wisdom is encoded in these books,' the Warden said.

Kit shook his head to clear it, for the Warden had lit a scented candle. *Stay near the door,* Langley had said.

'Why are you telling me this?' Kit asked, stepping back from the stone.

Dr Dee turned away. 'I cannot explain it all to you now,' he said. 'But what I am offering is the chance to study – Knowledge – the kind of Knowledge that is available to few men. My knowledge, Kit. I am offering you my Knowledge.'

Kit wished he could stop the hammering of his heart. What would the High Master say? And the other boys?

But there was something that the High Master and the other boys knew nothing about. The secret that Kit had kept as long as he could remember, which woke him, sweating, at night. Was it possible that in all this heretical knowledge there was something that might help Kit?

'Well?' said the Warden. 'It would mean perhaps a few hours' extra study every week.'

Kit found his tongue. 'I do not know,' he said. 'I study already, many hours.'

The Warden closed his eyes. He was not pleased.

'Do you see that tapestry?' he said, and Kit started at the change of subject. He looked towards the tapestry, which fell from ceiling to floor. On it there was a unicorn and an angel.

'Lift it,' the Warden said.

Wondering why he was simply doing as he was told, Kit lifted it. Beneath, there was the same oak panelling as in the rest of the room.

'Put your hand up and a little to the left.'

Kit put his hand up.

'Press the panel,' said the Warden.

Kit pressed the panel. It gave. With a start of surprise, Kit realized he was looking at a doorway. *A priest hole*, he thought, staring into the darkness. He had heard of such places before, where rich Catholics hid their priests in times of persecution.

'Open it,' the Warden said.

Kit looked back at him, but the Warden sat unmoving, the tips of his fingers pressed to his mouth, dark eyes glittering at him. Kit pushed the door, which swung open silently. There was only darkness beyond.

'Do you see a stairway?' the Warden said.

'No,' said Kit.

'It is there, nonetheless,' said the Warden. 'Feel with your fingers a little way and you will find the handrail.'

Kit groped inside the doorway with his hand. *This is it, now,* he thought. The part where the Warden thrust him down the stairs and slammed the door behind him. Was this how he got his corpses?

'Step in further,' the Warden said.

How long before anyone looked for him? And if they found him, what would he say? 'Well, a famous Black Magician told me to get in a dark cupboard, so I did.'

'Further,' said the Warden. To Kit's horror, he was right behind him. Kit's hand went to his sword, but the Warden only said, 'Your eyes will get used to the darkness,' in a mild tone.

Kit's feet found the first step of the stairway.

'See where it takes you,' the Warden said. 'And then return. Be quick.'

He went back into his room and Kit turned sharply, expecting him to slam the door behind, but he left it ajar.

Muttering curses under his breath, Kit began to grope his way down the stairs. The stairway wound round and steeply down. Kit's eyes slowly adjusted to the darkness and there was a faint light coming from somewhere. Despite his fear, he was curious. Soon he could hear the noise of the river. Where the stair ended, he could see a grid above him and a kind of ledge to enable him to climb out. He stood on the ledge and pushed upwards. The grid gave easily.

The roar of the river filled his ears as he climbed out and the light was dazzling. He stood on the bank, blinking in surprise. Next to him was the old scullery door that no one used any more. Only the scullery maid would still come along this path.

Before anyone could see him, Kit lowered himself back through the grid, pulling it across once he was through. Moments later, he stood in the Warden's room.

'Two and a half minutes,' the Warden said. 'There will be times when I require you to come to our meetings in secret and leave again the same way. At other times I will send for you. What do you think?'

'Are there more of those passages?' Kit said. 'Is that how you get to the church?'

For he had remembered how the Warden had appeared and disappeared in church on more than one occasion, and everyone had thought it part of his evil magic.

But the Warden only smiled.

'Enough,' he said. 'Are you interested in my proposition or not? It will have to be our secret.'

More secrets, Kit thought.

But the Warden continued, 'The High Master need only know that I am offering you extra tuition in mathematics, in preparation for Oxford. What do you say?'

'I don't know,' Kit said. 'I will think about it.'

The Warden sighed. 'Try to contain your enthusiasm, boy,' he said. 'I am offering you extra tuition in mathematics and astronomy, as well as other, more secret arts. Do you not wish to learn? Have you never wondered about the secrets and mysteries of the world?'

Kit's face burnt suddenly with the urge to tell his own secret and the Warden stared at him curiously.

'Well?' he said, but Kit was silent. 'I will send for you tomorrow, after lessons,' he went on, gathering the papers on his desk.

Kit opened his mouth to speak, but at that precise moment, there was a tapping on the door. The Warden frowned.

'Who is it?' he said, and Chubb's deep voice came through the door.

'Master Chubb, sir. If you please, sir, it is time for the choir to enter church.'

The Warden frowned again, then nodded.

'You may go,' he said to Kit, and turned back to his papers. Then, when Kit failed to move, he said, 'Go – what keeps you?' and without a word, Kit left the room.

4

'Well, go on then,' said Chubb, as they ran into the forecourt.

'What?'

'Tell us what the old wizard wanted you for.' And when Kit said nothing, he said, 'I came to rescue you, didn't I? Before he turned you into something even the cook wouldn't put in the stew.'

Kit looked at him. William Chubb was a thickset boy with a swarthy complexion. He had no interest in lessons, but excelled at all kinds of sport, especially boxing. They had started at the school together as small boys, both feeling very alone, and had remained friends when others their age had left. But Will would have no understanding of what the Warden was offering, none at all, and less of Kit's great secret. And he would not leave Kit alone until he told.

'It was nothing,' Kit said finally. 'He was only offering me the chance for more mathematical study.'

Will's mouth dropped open. '*More* maths? Twenty hours a week not enough for them? I hope you told him what to do.'

'I suppose it is for the Exhibitions,' said Kit.

'You never told him you would?' exclaimed the older

boy. 'As if there isn't enough to do already – extra choir practice, extra Greek – I never see you as it is,' he nudged Kit. 'I told you my girl in the taverns has another put aside for you.'

Kit was saved from having to answer this by the appearance of the Choirmaster, who stood at the entrance to the church, looking around distractedly.

'Ah, there you are, Master Morley,' he said. 'You keep us waiting. I shall have to report you if you are late again.'

Kit hurried forward to join the rest of the choir in the porch, while Chubb, whose voice had already broken, looked smug and joined the other scholars who were forming a queue outside the school.

The choir filed in together and sat behind the wooden screen. Kit's fingers searched automatically for the carving that Will had made with his knife on the armrest between their two seats. *WLC, 1604*, it read. That was where he used to sit, next to Kit, until his voice had broken and he was able to leave the choir.

'Never mind, Kit,' he had said, 'I'm sure your voice will break one day.'

Chubb was only a couple of months older than Kit and he was always teasing him about his smooth face and slight build. Even so, Kit missed him being in the choir, for they used to pass notes and chew tobacco that was sent to Chubb by his parents. And now Kit had to sit next to Charles Leigh, brother to the Choirmaster.

The Fellows filed in after the boys and took their seats. Last of all came the Warden. Kit turned his head and would not look at him, but even when he wasn't looking, he felt that the Warden's gaze was on him, like a slight heat on the side of his face. Yet when he glanced back, the Warden was not looking his way at all. His eyes were lowered, as if he was praying.

Kit tried to concentrate on the misericords, which were carved into stories. In one of them a woman scolded a man for breaking a cooking pot, and in another three men played backgammon. A fox carrying a big stick taught two cubs to read and a monkey knelt over a swaddling babe. They were very old, these carvings, and Kit had come to know them through his fingers, all the days he had sat in various seats behind this choir screen. If he didn't look at them directly, he could sense the life in them moving. A wild man fought a dragon, a hunter disembowelled a stag, and more monkeys stole the clothes from a sleeping pedlar.

The church was full and the animal stench of the congregation penetrated even behind the screen. The new preacher from Salford conducted the first service. He was a short, unprepossessing man, who wore no priestly vestments and walked among the congregation so that he could not be seen. Kit tried to pay attention, for he would be examined on the sermon the next day, but his mind kept drifting to what the Warden had said and what it might mean. He already had several extra hours of study for the Exhibition at Oxford and extra sword practice, for the King had decreed that all scholars should be proficient with a sword. It was all right for Chubb, whose parents would pay, but the school would have to pay forty pounds for Kit's Exhibition, so the High Master was determined that Kit should pass.

As if conscious that Kit was thinking of him, the Warden's gaze met Kit's as he rose to read his part of the service. His eyes glittered ironically, as if he knew what was in Kit's mind, and as he made his way out of the stalls, he inclined his head very slightly, as if to say, *I will see you soon.*

Not if I see you first, Kit thought, though if the Warden sent for him, he would have to go.

Finally it was Communion, and the choir also rose, though it was known that the preacher from Salford disapproved of this and would ban all singing if he could. It would not be a great loss to ban this choir, Kit thought, since they were not very good. Amos Turner, who had sung in the choir for more than sixty years, was deaf and finished every line long after everyone else. Charles Leigh, a large, sleepy man as unlike his wiry brother as it was possible to be, was actually snoring, his immense shoulders hunched over his psalter.

Then, after Communion, the congregation filed out, the bells rang and the next congregation filed in. All that day, the church services progressed. Candle flames waved in air like the movement in a forest. Every now and then, a spindle of wax from a guttering candle fell into the brass holder with a bell-like note that merged with the droning of wind in the distant vaulting, and the voices of the congregation brushed echoes from the roof. A greenish light glazed the windows and the congregation was now illuminated, now dark. Their breath rose in a smoky vapour, like the breath of beasts in a stall.

After the final service Kit's head was aching and he had a low, dragging sensation in his stomach. He knew what that meant, but there was no one here he could tell. He managed to escape Chubb and made his way back to the dormitory and lay on his bed. But he had hardly started reading *A Short Introduction to Grammar,* when Chubb burst in.

'What are you doing?' he exclaimed. 'We're going to the inns!'

'Well go,' said Kit. 'I'm not stopping you.'

'Aren't you coming?'

'I have a headache,' Kit began.

'Yes – from all this reading!' Chubb said. 'A pint of ale will cure you.'

'I've no time,' said Kit. 'I have to catch up on my study somehow.' He glanced sourly at Chubb as he said this, for Chubb had no need to study at all.

'Well, a night out will do you no harm,' Chubb said. 'Whatever that ranting preacher says – don't tell me you've been listening to the sermon again.'

'Well, since I am to be examined on it tomorrow,' Kit pointed out.

'Come now,' said Chubb, 'you could make all that stuff up.'

He did a passable imitation of the preacher's broad accent. '"I bring you glad tidings of great joy. You are all damned except for me." Well, I'd rather be in Hell than any Heaven with him in it. What are you reading now?' he said, sitting on the edge of Kit's bed, and he groaned aloud when Kit showed him.

'The road to Hell is paved with rhetoric,' he said. 'I can't believe you'd rather lie here reading about forty-eight parts of speech, than come with us to the inns. Have you got a girl beneath this bed?'

'Two, actually,' said Kit.

'Aha, one for me!'

'We were waiting for you to leave.'

Chubb grinned, then began to bounce on the bed. 'Sorry, girls,' he said. 'Don't mind me.'

Kit shook his head, smiling reluctantly. At one point, he and Chubb had been best friends – brothers, almost,

Chubb had said. But Chubb's parents had money and the difference between him and Kit was increasingly apparent. Chubb was never punished, no matter what he did, and in any group he had to be the leader. But he bore Kit a kind of respect, because he was the only boy to beat him at sword fighting, and sometimes, like now, the old friendship between them returned.

'Come on now,' Chubb said, 'get up,' and he made as if to snatch the book, but Kit held it out of reach. 'Maybe tomorrow,' he replied.

Chubb shook his head and told Kit he was a sad case, but finally he left. Kit lay on his bed, staring at the wall. When the Warden sent for him, Kit would tell him that he had no time for extra study. Yet if he didn't tell someone his secret, Kit would have to go up to Oxford or Cambridge, to study either law or theology, still bearing his terrible burden.

The book lay open on his chest, forgotten. He would choose law, rather than theology. There was no place for a former Catholic to study theology. Anyway, if that new preacher was anything to go by, he did not like what was happening to the Church. But to practise law cost money and Kit had none. What were his alternatives? He could become like the Usher, and stay at a school like this one. That was the worst prospect of all, Kit thought. He had better jump in the river now.

Kit fell at last into an uneasy sleep and was only wakened by the return of Chubb, Langley, Parker and Hewitt, who were all drunk and falling over themselves.

'You should have come with us, Kit,' Hewitt said. 'We had a good time.'

'I can tell,' Kit said.

'That new maid is worth a visit,' said Parker. 'Sings – and dances too!'

Kit hushed Hewitt as he started to sing.

'She's older than I thought,' Chubb said, climbing into bed. 'She has a great loon of a son, as old as us.'

'She was flirting with me,' said Langley, and the others jeered.

Finally they were all in bed and Kit pulled the covers over his head, but Chubb, who was in the next bed, said in a low voice, 'I hope your girls were good – mine was.'

Kit ignored him, but Chubb seemed in a mood to talk.

'People say the new maid came fresh from the woods,' he said. 'Living wild and free as a gypsy. Never been in a town before.'

'People will say anything,' said Kit.

'No, but she is different,' Chubb said. 'I'd like to take her into the woods!'

'Calm yourself,' said Kit. 'Say your prayers.'

'You say them for me,' said Chubb. 'I have better things to think about.'

But he was silent then and soon Kit heard him snore, while Kit lay wide awake now, wondering what it would be like to live wild in the woods.

The next day began with prayers at 6 a.m. The bell rang and all the boys got up, bleary and cursing. Hewitt had to be pulled from his bed by the feet. There was breakfast of cold meat and potatoes swimming in a pale gravy, then the boys went to their classroom, where they were examined on what they had learnt from the lessons in church, and Chubb was reprimanded for answering in English, for Latin was the official language of the school.

'You are not in the fields now,' the High Master said.

'The preacher spoke English,' said Chubb. 'If it is good enough for a man of God, sir, I thought it must be good enough for me.'

The High Master glared at him and some of the boys looked fearful, as if they thought he would be beaten. But Kit could have told them that this would not happen. Chubb, whose father was rich enough to buy the school, was never beaten. Only last week he had led a group of the younger ones into the town, breaking into gardens and stealing the fruit from orchards, and all the boys had been beaten except for Chubb.

'Since you were paying such attention to the new preacher,' the High Master said, 'perhaps you can tell us what he said in his sermon.'

And Chubb, who hadn't listened at all, said, 'Of course, sir. He said that it is already decided before we are born that most of us shall go to Hell. Though I must say, sir, that it hardly seems fair. Do you think it fair, sir?'

The High Master ignored the question.

'And what is Hell?' he asked, glaring round at them all, and without waiting for an answer, he carried on. 'Hell is a dark and foul-smelling prison. The walls of that prison are four thousand miles thick, and the damned are heaped there without number, bound and helpless in the eternal flame. Imagine that,' he said, his eyes beginning to bulge. 'Imagine what it is like to burn your finger in a candle flame, then imagine that pain magnified a thousandfold, through every part of your body. Can you feel what it is like to burn?' he went on, pacing now. 'To be scorched by eternal flame as the blessed martyrs were scorched for their faith? The blood seethes and boils in the veins, the brains boil in the skull, the heart glows and bursts in the breast and the tender eyes flame like molten balls. At least the misery of the martyrs ended in eternal bliss, whereas the damned suffer without release, until the end of time.'

Several of the younger boys looked as if they wished they had not eaten their breakfasts. The High Master took a long pinch of snuff. Rows of youthful faces looked at him mournfully. He nodded.

'We will say our Catechism,' he said, and the Usher rose and began walking round the room just like the High Master, but with a little hop between the placing down of one foot and another.

' "What is your only comfort in life and in death?" '

' "That I am not alone, but belong, body and soul, to my saviour," ' the boys chorused.

After the Catechism, the boys separated into different classrooms. The younger boys were taught by the Usher and the older boys went with the High Master. They filed past two of the poorer scholars, Monks and Peveril, who sat at the entrance to either classroom, writing the boys' names in the registers with long quills. *They might as well have a board round their necks saying 'Poor'*, Kit thought. Chubb, who was rich, could do anything he liked. Monks and Peveril, who were not, could do the work of the school.

The High Master lingered in the Great Hall, talking to one of the Fellows, and Chubb strode up and down the classroom, imitating him.

'The Manchester Free Grammar School is a dark and foul-smelling prison,' he began, making his eyes bulge just like the Master. 'It would smell better, if the kitchen staff could cook. The walls of this prison are four thousand miles thick,' he went on. 'And there are many bricks. How

145

many bricks would it take to build a wall four thousand miles thick, Morley?' he said to Kit, who laughed with the rest, though quietly, for the Master was coming. He knew that Chubb despised this Master, whose family had once worked for his own, but privately Kit thought him better than the previous one, who used to line up the boys on cold mornings and beat them all to keep himself warm.

Soon they all heard the heavy tread of the High Master along the corridor. Chubb slipped back behind his desk and lessons began.

The morning lessons ended at eleven, except for Kit, who had to study Greek for a further hour until he could join the rest of the boys for lunch. Then, from 1 p.m., the older boys studied the histories of Caesar and Livy, and learnt the poems of Horace by heart. At 5 p.m. there was a further meal, and then the boys were free, apart from Kit and Chubb, who had to practise swordplay with the Usher.

Hugh Gringold was a tall, spindly man with limp hair and a mournful face, but a surprisingly good swordsman.

Kit had forgotten about sword practice and was trying to catch up on his Greek translation, when Parker was sent for him.

'Ah the *late* Master Morley,' the Usher said, in his nasal voice, and held up a hand as Kit started to apologize.

'No time,' he said. 'Take your places, gentlemen.'

Kit and Chubb took off their cloaks and drew their swords. They began to circle each other, under the watchful eyes of the Usher, whose job it was to prepare them for a display when the Lord of the Manor came to visit next month. It was by order of the King that each school should train its scholars in archery and the sword, since the standard throughout the country was so poor, he had said, that he could only raise an army of peasants. Kit and Chubb excelled at both sports. Kit was lighter, but more agile, disarming his opponents with lightning moves. Chubb was very strong for a boy of his age and fought without fear. They would display their skills along with the finest in the country at Oxford and Cambridge early in the new year.

Chubb made the first thrust and Kit parried it rather awkwardly. The Usher narrowed his eyes. The boy was going through the motions as though preoccupied. He missed two of Chubb's thrusts.

'In a real fight, you would be dead now,' he told Kit. 'You are not wearing clogs and neither do you have a wooden arm. Use it!'

At last something clicked in Kit. The Usher saw the moment it happened. He stepped back, smiling; it was like hearing music, or watching the natural flight of a bird.

But they were interrupted by the arrival of the curate.

Matthew Palmer seemed very out of breath.

'I have just s-seen the W-Warden,' he panted. 'K-Kit is to g-go to him immediately.'

'What *again*?' said Chubb, and Kit lowered his sword, aware of the gaze of the Usher.

'What does he want?' Master Gringold said.

'Extra tuition, sir,' Chubb said promptly. 'Isn't that right? Kit is to learn the art of necromancy.'

The Usher's face changed and the curate paled.

'Mathematics, actually,' Kit said, wondering how it was that Chubb, who wasted no time on thinking, could guess so sharply.

'Well, I hope he has asked the High Master,' the Usher said. 'It is hardly convenient.'

When Kit did not answer this, he said. 'Oh, go on then. We will make up the time later.'

'I will call for you,' Chubb shouted after him as Kit turned and made his way across the forecourt, conscious that they were all watching him. The Warden should have sent for him in secret, he thought, and then he could have used the secret stair.

5

The Warden stood with his back to Kit, facing the bookshelves. He brought out an immense tome.

'Today we will study the Enochian alphabet,' he said. 'There are two thousand, four hundred and one letters, set out in ninety-eight tables.'

Kit's mouth fell open.

'It is the angelic alphabet,' the Warden went on reverently. 'The one spoken to Adam, before the Fall. Adam knew two languages: one to communicate the knowledge of God to his descendants, and a lesser one for everyday usage – eating, washing and so forth. The lesser one was dispersed into a thousand tongues in the Tower of Babel – into all the languages on earth. But into the other language was inscribed the wisdom of Heaven. All of which,' he said, patting the enormous book, 'is set out here, for you.'

He looked at Kit to see whether he understood.

'Close your mouth, boy,' he said. 'Before a bird flies in.'

Kit closed his mouth.

As if this wasn't bad enough, there were the names of all the angels to remember, in all the separate spheres of Heaven, and the different names of God, spelled out in forty-two characters. Then there were the arts of *Gematria*, *Notarikon* and *Temurah*, in which the words of the Bible were given numbers that equalled the sum of their letters, and then the letters were transposed to make new ones that revealed the hidden meaning of a sentence. In these sentences, the Warden told Kit, they would find the secret Will of God.

'It may not be easy,' he said unnecessarily, 'but this is the most valuable knowledge you will ever learn, the greatest undertaking of your life.'

Or a complete waste of time, Kit thought, but he said nothing.

The Warden looked at him quizzically. 'Well, boy?' he said.

Kit thought hard. Mostly he was thinking how he could possibly get out of this one, but it was hard to concentrate with the Warden's eyes boring into him.

'I – am already learning Latin,' he said faintly, 'and Greek.'

The Warden nodded. 'That's good. You should also learn Hebrew – we'll see if we can fit that in.'

Kit had a sudden vision of himself still coming to this room when he was as old as the Warden.

'You do not have to learn it all in one week,' the Warden said. Then seeing the expression on Kit's face, he added, 'Look at you – all this knowledge handed to you – cutting out years of study, and what are you thinking? I'll have no time for the cockfights, or the bear pits –'

'No, actually,' Kit said, but the Warden was in full spate. 'No student today knows the meaning of scholarship. Twenty hours a day I put in,' he said, lowering his gaze towards Kit. 'Twenty hours for all of the best years of my life. For years I kept a cockerel in my room, so that it would crow and wake me. What do you know of study? Who is worthy of this knowledge today? You are not worthy – I can see it in your face. Unless you value this knowledge more than your own life, you are wasting your time and mine. You should leave and leave now.'

This should have been Kit's chance, but somehow, with the Warden glaring down at him, he couldn't bring himself to go. After a long moment, he bent his head over the book and the Warden expelled a sigh and sat down as though already weary. Only once did Kit venture a comment, after trying and failing to create a sentence from the word 'revelation' translated into the Enochian alphabet.

'Why would God go to such lengths?' he said, fretfully. 'Why not make it plain?'

'Because of the Fall, boy,' the Warden said in exasperation, as though this was obvious, and Kit had to listen to a lecture on the destiny of Man, working his way back from Ignorance to Bliss.

'I thought ignorance was bliss,' Kit muttered, then coloured swiftly as he realized the Warden had heard. He wondered if he would beat him, but the Warden only regarded him shrewdly. Then he pushed away his chair.

'Come here,' he said, and reluctantly, Kit rose. They stood together by the window. It was a clear evening and Kit could see a crescent moon and the outline of the full moon, which was in darkness.

'The new moon, with the old moon in her arms,' the Warden said, but Kit was looking towards the rooftops of Long Millgate, where his friends would be in the taverns.

The Warden took something out of a drawer. It was a metal cylinder with a glass at one end, and he showed Kit how to look through it.

Kit looked and drew in his breath sharply. It took him

a moment to realize that what he was looking at was the world of Long Millgate, much bigger and nearer. The Warden tilted the glass for him, and he was looking at the enormous, blurred brightness of the moon passing swiftly in front of him. He moved the glass away, and the moon hung far and still in the distance.

'"We do but look through a glass darkly,"' the Warden said.'Change the glass and the world changes, or new worlds appear. God has granted us this ability, to invent new ways of seeing. To make up for our own, limited eyes.'

He took the telescope from Kit and trained it on another part of the sky.'Look at that star,' he said. Kit looked. It was like a prick of pure, ice-cold light, blurred at the edges.

'Venus,' the Warden said. He took a different instrument from his desk. It was a thin sheet of tin attached to a wooden rod, and it had tiny holes in it that looked as though they had been made with a needle. The Warden slid it up and down the wooden rod.'Can you find the star through one of the holes?' he said.

Kit fiddled with the tin while the Warden propped the rod up on the window ledge to keep it still. At last Kit could see a point of light through one of the pinpricks in the tin, and the Warden explained how, by measuring the time it took for the planet to move from one pinprick to another, you could measure almost everything about it: the nature of its orbit, the angle of declination from the ecliptic.

It was simple, but brilliant. Kit could hardly take it all in. But what he understood clearly as he listened was that the Warden was no common scholar. His intelligence and learning shone far more brightly than that of any of the other teachers. What was he doing here, Kit thought, where people feared or despised him? But the Warden had turned back to the window.

'Down here, all is chaos and distraction,' he said, 'but up there,' nodding at the sky, 'all is order and harmony. Different worlds, Kit,' he said, 'each of them revealing more fully the celestial plan. Have you never wondered about that mystery, Kit? Do you have no questions of your own?'

Kit burnt suddenly, fierce and bright as the star, with the desire to ask his question. If anyone could help him, the Warden could, he thought. But the Warden seemed to have forgotten he was there. He remained staring out of the window and when Kit looked at him, he saw that the Warden's mouth was moving silently, as though he was speaking to someone or something Kit couldn't see. Kit felt a chill of fear in his stomach, but just then there was a knock on the door and Chubb's voice came through it.

'Master Chubb, sir, come to collect Master Morley for evening prayer.'

The Warden glanced at Kit sharply as though he suspected that some private arrangement had been made with Chubb, but all he said was, 'Do not come tomorrow. We will leave it now until Friday, after your lessons. Use the secret passage.'

Kit had forgotten that he had meant to tell the Warden that he would not be coming back at all. He bowed hastily and clumsily, though the Warden was no longer looking, and hurried from the room.

6

The rest of the week was divided between prayers and lessons, Scripture and fasting.

On Friday the boys fasted all day, and there were examinations in everything they had learnt that week. They had to answer questions at the front of the class and if they got them wrong, the ferule, a long stick with a rounded end, was taken out.

Also on Fridays fines and punishments were handed out. Michael Langley was whipped for drinking the Communion wine, Nathaniel Parker for saying, 'Jesus, Joseph and Mary,' as an oath.

At teatime, Kit sat with the others at the long table, eating his meat.

'Are you coming out with us tonight, Kit?' Ben Hewitt asked.

Kit shook his head.

'Of course not. Kit has other appointments to keep,' Chubb commented drily.

Kit wished that Chubb was not so good at guessing what was going on. He would never be able to keep his meetings with the Warden secret.

'What is he teaching you?' asked Langley. 'Have you raised any corpses yet?'

'Does he speak to them?' Parker wanted to know. 'Is it true that he keeps human heads in jars?'

Kit opened his mouth to say that there was nothing like that in the Warden's room, then closed it again. It was best to say nothing.

'We are studying maths,' he said firmly, and there was a chorus of jeers.

'Is that what he calls it?'

'Are you counting the heads?'

'I vote,' said Parker, 'that we should follow him and listen outside the door!'

'What?' said Chubb, 'and miss all the fun of the inns?'

He caught hold of Joseph Pryor's jacket as he passed and ordered him to fetch more bread. 'It's a pity you aren't more sociable, Kit,' he said. 'By the time you get round to visiting the inns, the Puritans will have shut them all. And there will be no Warden any more,' he added. 'That mad preacher will run this school. We'll all be on bread and water and in bed by six.'

'I would rather have the Wizard Warden than Ranting Rob,' Langley said.

'Better the Devil you know, eh, Kit?' said Chubb.

Kit stood up. 'I have to see the Choirmaster in church,' he said. 'You can follow me if you like.'

And he left the room, hoping that they would not take it into their heads to come after him. He crossed the square as if he was going to church, then glanced round swiftly and doubled back on himself, following the path that led round the back of the college buildings to the river.

At first he could not find the grid in the fading light; then he found the door to the old scullery and there in front of it was the grid. He knelt down in the muddy grass and tugged it up, wondering why on earth he was playing this game. But tonight might be the night that he finally asked the Warden for his help.

He followed the stair in darkness to the panelled door, then his heart gave a great lurch as the Warden cried aloud.

'Where are you?'

Kit stared into the darkness in alarm. If there was someone else with the Warden, then surely he would not want Kit to appear by the secret entrance. Yet he had told him to come.

Silence.

Kit thought he heard someone muttering, then silence again. His heart thumped uncomfortably. Why had the Warden shouted? If he had company, why could Kit hear nothing now? If Kit interrupted them, he would give away the secret door. If the Warden was alone, he must be shouting at the wall. Kit didn't know which was worse. He hesitated and considered leaving, then raised his hand and knocked timidly on the wooden panel.

He heard the Warden swear, then ask, 'Who is it?'

'Kit, sir,' he answered. 'You said to come for my lesson.'

There was another protracted silence, then Kit heard the tapestry being pushed to one side. 'Come in,' the Warden said, and Kit pushed the panel and entered the room.

The Warden's study was a mess, with papers scattered all over it, but there was no one else there. He was hastily pulling the rug back in place.

'Is everything all right?' Kit asked, nervously. 'Are you – are you well?'

But the Warden seemed distracted. He picked up his

books, then put them down again, then stood staring into the middle of the room. Kit had the growing feeling that he shouldn't have come.

'Sir?' he said finally.

At the same time the Warden announced, 'The mirrors,' in a definite tone, 'today we will look at the mirrors.'

Kit's heart sank. He didn't understand what he was supposed to see in the mirrors and he didn't care. But the Warden was already uncovering them and wheeling the tall one forward, the one in which Kit had thrust at himself as though fighting with an opponent.

'Now, boy,' he breathed, 'let us see what you can see.'

But the peculiarity of the mirrors had lost their enchantment for Kit. 'I see myself,' he said dully.

'Keep looking,' the Warden said. 'Try to let your mind clear and your eyes relax. Let the mirror reveal to you its secrets.'

Kit glared at himself, pushing back his hair with his fingers. 'I see nothing,' he said.

The Warden stood behind Kit, placing his hands on his shoulders. 'Look well into the glass,' he said, then stopped. His words died away into a kind of rattle in his throat. Kit glanced at him in the mirror in surprise. The Warden didn't move, but Kit could feel him squeezing his shoulders. Then he felt something brushing his cheek and he rubbed it.

'I still can't see anything,' he said, but the Warden was silent, staring into the glass with uncanny eyes. For a moment the thought crossed Kit's mind that maybe the Warden could see something else in Kit, the thing he kept hidden, but that the mirror might reveal. He made a movement away from the glass, but the Warden was still squeezing his shoulders. Kit lifted his arms and dropped them again. He would bluff it out, he thought.

'I don't know what I'm looking for,' he said.

'Can you see nothing in the glass?' the Warden asked tremulously. Kit thought of asking him what *he* could see, but his nerve failed him. He shrugged his shoulders in as casual a way as he could manage. 'Nothing at all,' he said.

'Get you gone!' cried the Warden hoarsely, frightening Kit.

'Pardon?' Kit managed to say, but he had the eerie feeling that the Warden was not speaking to him. Then he had the sudden sensation of something brushing lightly over his face and hair, like cobwebs, and he pulled away.

'Have we finished now?' he asked, but the Warden was still staring into the mirror.

'What is it?' said Kit, for the Warden had gone deathly pale.

'I said leave,' he replied in a low, strangled voice.

Then all at once, he seized a phial of water from his desk and flung it at the mirror. Kit watched in dismay as the water spattered over the blank surface.

'What is it?' he cried again. 'Did – did you see something?'

The Warden sat down, shaking in his chair. Kit very much wanted to run away, but he couldn't just leave him like this.

'Are you all right?' he asked in a hushed voice. The Warden covered his face briefly with his hands. 'It is nothing,' he said eventually. 'You had better go.'

Kit opened his mouth to ask one of the many questions

crowding into his mind, but the Warden waved a hand at him.

'Go,' he repeated; then as Kit failed to move, he shouted angrily. 'I said *go!*'

And Kit fled.

7

All that weekend, Kit thought about the Warden. He thought about him when he was doing his translations of Virgil and Ovid, and when he sang in the choir and the new preacher ranted on. He had not made an appointment to go again, and even if the Warden sent for him, Kit did not want to go. Everything the other boys said about him was true, he thought. The Warden was a Black Magician, and he probably had brought a curse upon the town. Kit would tell him nothing.

The business of the school went on as usual. Each chorister was paid fourpence a day for singing, though the Choirmaster said they were not worth it and he would speak to the High Master about stopping the allowance. Kit did not see how it could be stopped, for out of this allowance they had to pay for quills and books, including a commonplace book in which they wrote learned phrases and proverbs, quotes and vocabulary.

In addition he had to pay a penny each morning for Peveril or Monks to write his name in the school register, and a fee called cockpenny which went for the Usher to keep the cocks for cockfighting on Saturdays. So he had little enough money left for the inns, though Chubb, who had plenty, was always urging him to go. He was generous with Kit and shared his books with him, but Kit did not always want to be indebted to him. Neither was it wise to refuse him all the time, so when on Saturday Kit's cockerel won, he did go out to the inns and get drunk with the others.

The rest of the time he played stoolball with the younger lads, or handball with Langley or Parker. He got out of football, when the lads ran riot with the apprentices through the streets of the town, because of his extra Greek practice, and he was glad afterwards, because four windows were broken and the constables came to the school.

On Monday morning there was no inspection by the Warden. He sent a message to say that he was sick, and Kit thought uneasily of the state in which he had left him, but felt relieved that now he would probably not send for Kit.

Then that lunchtime, the news broke that the Puritans had closed an alehouse. Langley and Parker had slipped out with Chubb at eleven for a pint of ale and seen the ruins of Mistress Butterworth's inn.

'What do you mean, closed it down?' Kit asked.

'Not *closed* it down, *burnt* it down,' Chubb said, stabbing his meat with a knife.

'And burnt her too,' said Parker. 'I heard she's dying!'

'She'll not die,' Chubb said. 'She's too tough, that one. Pickled in her own ale,' and he told them the story he had heard.

'Who knows how many more inns they will close,' Langley said, and Hewitt wondered what had happened to the pretty maid.

'Perhaps she will go back to the woods,' he said, and Parker suggested they should go after her, but Chubb was not amused.

'He is nothing but a peasant, this preacher,' he said. 'He should be herding swine in Salford,' and he stopped Joseph Pryor as he ran past and ordered him to fetch his tobacco.

The rest of that week, the atmosphere in school subtly changed. The High Master seemed distracted and had many meetings with the Fellows. Rumours were rife that the new preacher would be asked to teach at the school, because he had the support of the Bishop of Chester. Chubb said he would rather hang him first.

'At least we're getting out soon,' he said to Kit. 'I for one have outgrown this place.'

For once Kit agreed with him. Much as he dreaded university, he too felt that he'd had enough of the school. He kept his head down and helped the younger boys to learn their alphabet, in between translating Greek and putting in extra sword practice. He was determined more than ever now to do well at his Exhibition. It seemed that the Warden too was keeping a low profile and he did not send for Kit.

But the following Monday, Kit opened the doors of the school and there was the High Master.

'Master Morley,' he said. 'Here is a new boy. Take him to the Usher.'

He stood to one side, revealing an awkward, gangling boy who stared at Kit with great, dark eyes and looked frankly terrified.

'You will show him round the school,' the High Master said, speaking even more peremptorily than usual. 'You can be his guide for the first weeks: introduce him to the other boys and so on.'

Kit took in the displeasure in the High Master's tone,

the shabbiness of the boy. He wore a woollen smock, all stained down the front, and tattered breeches. He had wooden clogs on his feet like the Flemish weavers wore and they were covered in dust and mud from the street. He looked as though he should be herding pigs.

'He cannot read,' the High Master said, as if the words tasted bad in his mouth. 'It will be your duty to teach him his alphabet and to tell him the ways of the school. He is to stay with you at all times when you are not studying. When you are busy, he can study with the youngest boys.'

More duties.

Kit waited for the Master to introduce the boy properly, but he only rose once on to his toes and sank down again, nodded, said, 'Well then,' shut his mouth tightly and stalked away. Kit stared at the boy and the boy stared back.

'What is your name?' Kit asked after a pause, and the boy mumbled something he couldn't hear.

'What?'

'Simeon,' the boy said. He had a curiously vacant look, almost glazed, like an animal in a falcon's claws. The other boys would destroy him. Kit sighed. Doubtless it would be his job to protect him as well.

'You had better follow me,' he said, turning. Stumbling awkwardly in his clogs, the boy followed. Kit remembered how he had felt in his first weeks of school. But he had been only seven, recently bereft of his mother. How old was this boy? He was a little taller than Kit, but seemed much younger. When Kit had started school he could already read. It was not usual to take boys in unless they knew their alphabet at least. And the High Master didn't want him, that much was certain. But then he hadn't wanted Kit either.

Kit paused outside the room where the younger boys were saying their Catechism to the Usher. He looked Simeon up and down.

'Are those your only clothes?' he asked. The boy looked terrified again at being spoken to, but nodded. Kit thought. He didn't want to introduce him to the other boys looking as though he had just slept in a stable. There was a store cupboard where some spare clothes were kept for the boys who got muddy, or who had just grown out of clothes that could be passed on. Perhaps he could get him some decent garments first.

'Follow me,' he said again.

They were in luck. In the store cupboard they found a set of clothes that Chubb had grown out of recently: doublet, jerkin, hose, all in the school's navy, and a white shirt and ruff belonging to Kit. Since Chubb was the biggest boy in the school, his clothes would probably fit.

'You can put these on for now,' he said, and the boy stared at him, then right there in the corridor began to strip off his smock.

'Not *here,*' Kit hissed and pulled him into the library. He watched as the boy pulled off his ragged shirt. He was very thin, all his ribs stuck out. He had thick, brown hair that turned auburn in the light from the window, a brown face and dark, dark eyes. He fumbled with the buttons and hooks as though he had never used them before.

'Here,' Kit said finally, 'let me.' And the new boy stood passive, like an infant, while Kit did up the hooks and eyes on his shirt and doublet, and tugged the blue hose up his legs. Try as they might, however, they could not get the shoes to fit. Simeon had long, bony feet, widely splayed.

'You'll have to put your own back on,' Kit said at last,

losing patience. The boy hesitated, then put his clogs on again. They looked decidedly odd with the rest of his outfit. Nevertheless, Kit decided, it was the best he could do.

'Now we can meet the Usher,' he said, and still speechless, the boy followed him back along the corridor.

'That is where we eat,' Kit said, pointing to the main hall. 'School starts at seven each morning in winter, and six in summer. We have breakfast at nine. At eleven we finish for the morning, and at noon we eat again. And then at five, when lessons end, we have our evening meal before going to the dormitories, where we sleep.'

The boy said nothing to all this, but kept looking over his shoulder at the door which led outside.

'This is where the Usher teaches the younger boys,' Kit said, wondering briefly if Simeon was embarrassed to be classed with the youngest pupils.

But his face gave away nothing except fear.

They stood outside the door of the classroom, which was now silent apart from the sound of scratching quills.

'I must go to my lessons now,' Kit said to Simeon. 'But I will meet you here at eleven. Do you have any money?'

The boy shook his head, looking even more afraid.

'You must have money for your books,' Kit said. 'And a penny for the boy who writes your name in the register.'

He waited, but the boy said nothing. Kit shrugged. It was not his business, after all.

After a moment he knocked at the door and Master Gringold told him to enter. The boy stared at Kit for a moment longer, then hung his head and went into the classroom.

All the rest of that morning Kit worried. He worried about how he was ever going to fit all his extra study in, and the practice with the sword. He wondered how long it would be before the Warden sent for him again. He had not even started to learn the Enochian tables. And now he had this new burden of Simeon. His head ached as he struggled to translate the passage from Seneca about the crises and victories in Roman history. Then at eleven he went back to the primary room and waited while the small boys came out, pushing and jostling. Simeon stood inside with the Usher, who looked up as Kit approached.

'The boy knows nothing,' he said, as though Simeon wasn't there. 'Not even his Catechism. We will have to send to the petty school for a hornbook. You will have to give up an hour each morning to teaching him the alphabet.'

Kit nodded, looking down at his feet. He would have liked to ask how he was to make up that extra hour, but the Usher, like the Master, did not seem to be in a very good mood.

'You may go,' he said, and when neither boy moved, he repeated the order. 'Well – go!'

This was the moment Kit dreaded. He led Simeon out along the corridor that led to the courtyard. The new boy tried to slip his hand into Kit's as they went, and horrified, Kit pulled away. Some of the boys were already playing stoolball, using long bats and a stool as a wicket. Two more were playing handball against the wall of the library. Kit couldn't see Will Chubb, but he knew where he would be. He took Simeon round the corner to the back of the school which faced the river, where the boys were not supposed to go. Chubb lay sprawled on the low wall, smoking a pipe. Hewitt, Langley and Parker were with him, and he sat up as Kit approached.

'Who's this?' he asked, looking Simeon up and down.

There was a gleam of recognition in his eyes. Simeon hung his head and hunched his shoulders, as a broad grin spread across the older boy's face.

'Butterworth's loon!' he said.

8

'Are we taking in pot boys now?' Chubb said to Kit later that day. They were having tea in the Great Hall and Simeon stood over them, setting out the wooden bowls. It had quickly been established that he had no money and could not write the names of the boys in the register, so he had been given jobs to do. He had poured water into the silver ewers that were set out for the boys to dip their fingers in before eating, and now he was serving the stew. There were potatoes as usual, swimming in a brownish liquid, with some meat and a chunk of bread.

'At least you're well trained for this, eh, pot boy?' Chubb said, raising his voice, but if Simeon had heard him, he gave no sign. Chubb spat his tobacco into Simeon's dish as he sat down and the other boys sniggered, then laughed more loudly as Simeon started to eat.

'For God's sake, Chubb,' Kit muttered.

'What – are you his nursemaid now?' said Chubb, stuffing meat and bread into his mouth. 'Nursemaid to a pot boy? You'll do well at Oxford. Anyway,' he said, as Kit started to speak, 'I dare say it's all the same, where he comes from. I heard all the floor sweepings went into the stew at Mistress Butterworth's.'

Simeon ate steadily, ignoring this, which was just as

well, Kit thought. Then, when he cleared away the dishes, Chubb stuck his foot out and Simeon went flying, and true to form, the Master told Simeon off rather than Chubb.

'Help him to clear up this mess,' the High Master said to Kit. 'Then you may as well give him his first lesson in the library.'

Kit stared at the High Master's retreating back as the other boys fell about and Chubb choked on his ale.

'You are the pot boy's pot boy,' he spluttered. Kit was suddenly furiously angry, but there was nothing for it but to help Simeon wipe the tables free of gravy and sweep the floor. Then they borrowed a hornbook from Joseph Pryor, and went to sit in the library.

Kit summoned all his patience, but he couldn't help getting aggravated when Simeon just couldn't see the difference between the letters. When Kit traced them for him he simply stared at Kit, as if he was looking for something that he could not find.

'Look at the book, not at me,' Kit said, and when Simeon went on staring, he said, 'What is it?'

Simeon lowered his eyes. Then he looked over his shoulder, towards the door.

'Can I go now?' he asked.

'Go?' said Kit. 'Go where?'

Simeon looked at Kit in surprise. 'Mother,' he said, as if Kit should have known.

'Don't you understand?' Kit said, exasperated. 'You don't live with your mother any more. You live here. This is your home.'

Simeon gave him a look of such blank incomprehension that the words died away on Kit's lips. He remembered vividly being seven years old, grappling with the idea that this place was his new home. He didn't want to think about that. Yet it wasn't the same and Kit struggled to put his finger on the difference. It was as though Simeon had no concept of home. If you looked inside him, Kit thought with a sudden leap of imagination, you would only see dark forest, stretching endlessly on.

The next half-hour stretched endlessly on, as Kit tried to compare the shapes of the letters to the shapes of birds or beasts, and Simeon shifted about, knocking the quill from Kit's hand, banging his knees on the table and scratching himself. At last, Parker knocked on the door.

'Time for evening prayer,' he said, smirking.

Kit rose and Simeon got up with him. He seemed now to be mirroring Kit's moves, even when Kit ran a hand through his hair. Kit thought of speaking to him about this, but then decided he couldn't be bothered.

The boys proceeded in pairs to the church and inevitably Kit was paired with Simeon, who tried to hold his hand again. Kit tugged it away more viciously than he intended. 'Keep your hands behind you!' he said.

There was a mass of leaden clouds in the sky and wind whipped the yellow leaves in the courtyard into flurries. Kit stared at the ground, preoccupied with his own problems, and was only jolted out of his thoughts when Simeon broke out of line, running towards Long Millgate.

'What —?' said the High Master.

The Usher, who had been dealing with Simeon's inability to sit still all day, said, 'Where is he going *now*?'

The High Master's face darkened. 'Chubb, Parker!' he rapped out and, like arrows, the two boys shot after Simeon.

Kit's heart sank. He should have held his hand after all, he thought.

Unaware that he was being chased, Simeon stopped dead, looking in confusion along the street, and Kit knew he was looking for his mother.

'Got you!' said Chubb, seizing Simeon's jerkin, but with a wild, twisting movement, Simeon broke free. Parker snatched at him, but he veered towards the church. The Usher and several boys ran into the alley beside the church, blocking it off. Simeon hesitated only for a moment, then leapt upwards into the branches of a tree.

To the delight of those standing closest to him, the High Master swore, then strode towards the tree, waving his stick. He beat it against the trunk.

'Come down at once!' he ordered, then stared upwards in confusion, for the boy was no longer there.

'Where is he?' he shouted.

'There – there!' cried the boys.

Simeon had leapt from the branches of one tree to another. The yew trees kept their needles, so that it was hard to see him, and they grew close to the church itself. When he came to the tree that was closest to the church, Simeon paused. Some of the boys were already climbing the yew after him, despite the shouts of the High Master. However, before they could reach him, Simeon leapt suddenly for the sculpted architrave round the church windows and began climbing the wall like a spider.

'Stop him!' cried the High Master, and all the boys started chanting. This was the most exciting thing that had ever happened in their nightly procession to the church.

Simeon hauled himself upwards, using the stone griffins and gargoyles as levers, towards the carved cornice that decorated the lowest edge of the church roof.

The High Master was purple with rage. This was heresy,

or blasphemy at least. And if the boy made it to the roof, how would they ever get him down?

There was a shout from the watching boys as Simeon hauled himself over the edge of the roof and ran along it. But there was only a sheer drop on the other side, down to the banks of the river.

'Get him down!' howled the High Master, as Simeon ran backwards and forwards, looking for a way to escape.

Kit hung back, hoping he would not be told to go after Simeon, and stared upwards with the other boys. It was hard to see in the dark. Beyond the river there were the great woods of Alport Park, where the Lord's men hunted. He knew that if Simeon made his way there he would be lost to them, for he would be at home in the forest as none of the town-dwellers were. But it was more likely that he would be killed by the fall. He watched as Simeon ran along the roof of one of the side chapels, gazing towards the main roof, then suddenly shrieked, a high-pitched, lonely sound that made Kit shudder.

The High Master looked round, and his gaze fell on Kit.

'You there,' he barked, and Kit's heart sank even further. 'Do something!'

Kit stepped forward.

'I think he will come down, sir, but we will have to stop shouting.'

The High Master glared at him. 'Can you get him down?'

'I don't know, sir – I think he doesn't like all the noise.'

The High Master turned to the assembled boys.

'*Quiet!*' he thundered, and they all stopped chanting. 'Well?' he said to Kit.

Kit hesitated for a moment. There were buttresses at the corners of the building that were sculpted into a kind of ledge towards the bottom. With the Usher's help, he climbed on to the ledge at the corner nearest to Simeon, then a little higher. But he could not climb as well as Simeon, and when he reached the next foothold, he had to stop.

'Simeon?' he called.

No answer.

'Simeon,' Kit tried again. 'You can't stay there. Your – your mother isn't up there – she's down here.'

There was a scuffling noise from the roof, then at last a shaggy head looked over the cornice. 'Mother,' it said.

'She's waiting for you, Simeon,' said Kit. 'She doesn't know where you are.'

Simeon paused, looking again towards the woods. Kit understood that he would jump over the edge if he had to, and his heart shifted a little, for he recognized that urge. It was what he had felt when sword fighting, the urge he had never named, that the Usher had said would make him a great swordsman. Simeon was feeling it now. He had passed all the usual considerations of saving his own skin.

'Simeon,' he called softly. 'Come back. Your mother does not want you to go.'

At last Simeon seemed to be listening. 'Mother,' he said again.

Kit shifted his grip slightly, sweating. 'Yes, your mother,' he said. 'If you come down now you will see her again, I promise. But not if you run away. You must come down if you want to see her.'

And he went on like this, talking to Simeon, and it was almost like talking to himself as a young boy. And finally Simeon swung one leg over the cornice and began his descent. Thankfully Kit slipped to the ground.

He found himself admiring Simeon's skill as the boy swiftly descended after him. The High Master, though, was merely incensed. He grabbed Simeon as soon as he hit the ground and began beating him with the stick. Kit flinched as Simeon howled. There were none of the usual formalities that attended beatings, which were usually performed in the Great Hall on Fridays. The High Master was simply flogging Simeon for all he was worth, and the other boys stood round watching, with eager, fearful faces.

Finally the High Master paused, hat askew.

'Take him away,' he rapped. 'Lock him in the cupboard,' and Chubb and Parker hurried to do as they were told. Simeon was locked in the school's cupboard for failing to understand that he could not leave the procession.

Two hours later, Kit was told he could let him out. It was entirely dark in the cupboard, and cramped. Simeon was crouched with his limbs folded into unnatural angles, and all the light in his eyes had died.

'Mother,' he said.

Kit sighed. 'You have to sleep with the rest of us,' he said, and he led Simeon to the dormitory, finally allowing him to hold his hand, for he was afraid that Simeon would try to run away again.

9

It was Kit's duty to sleep in the younger boys' dormitory again, and Simeon also slept there, since there was an extra bed. He seemed not to have lain on a bed before and tried to lie on the floor beside it at first, but Kit told him sharply to get up.

'You must say your prayers,' he told him, and when Simeon just looked at him uncomprehending, he made him kneel down with the rest and repeat after Kit:

'O my God . . .'

'*O my God . . .*'

'I am heartily sorry . . .'

'*I am heartily sorry . . .*'

'For having offended thee . . .'

'*For having offended thee . . .*'

Simeon stumbled over the words and did not get up when everyone had finished, but remained staring around at the door and window. Kit could tell this would be a long night.

'Now lie on the bed,' he said, and straight away Simeon lay, fully clothed and in his clogs, on top of the bed, until Kit made him get up again and turn back the sheets. Then he had to quieten the little boys, who were all laughing.

'You must stay in your bed,' Kit said, wondering in

despair if Simeon even knew what he meant, but Simeon nodded and lay still, staring at Kit, until Kit turned away from him and pulled his own sheets up.

But in the morning there was a furore.

'Get off me!' Joseph Pryor cried shrilly, and Kit turned to see him struggling from beneath Simeon, who was crouched over him.

'What are you doing on his bed?' Kit said.

Joseph cried, 'He has pissed on it!'

Everyone around them woke up, and watched in horror and delight as Joseph ran for the Matron.

'What's going on?' Kit asked in despair.

Simeon replied, 'He – was crying.'

Kit closed his eyes briefly.

'I told you, you are not allowed to leave your bed,' he said, for Simeon had broken a cardinal rule, but did not seem to understand this.

'Black dog, black dog!' he cried in a whimper that was exactly like Joseph's own, and the other boys all laughed between their fingers. Kit thought he understood what had happened. Joseph must have had another of his nightmares and Simeon probably tried to comfort him. One or both of them may have wet the bed. He didn't know about Simeon, but he knew Joseph did it regularly, though the little boy would not admit it.

Matron came with a face, as Chubb put it, like a shovel, and spoke sharply to Simeon, who didn't listen at all.

'Black dog, black dog,' he whimpered in a tearful voice, pointing at Joseph, who went pale, then very pink.

'Liar!' he shouted, almost crying again, and Matron said that was enough. She told Simeon that she would not report him this time, since it was his first night, but he would have to clean up the mess in the room. Kit ushered the smaller boys down to prayers, thinking that would be the least of his problems, for it would be all over the school that Simeon had got into bed with a younger boy and wet it.

At breaktime the older boys teased Simeon unmercifully and stood round him in a circle chanting 'pig-boy' and 'piss-boy' at him.

Then Parker said, 'Look – is that your mother?' and Kit had to catch Simeon before he ran off again.

'Leave it, Parker,' Kit said, as all the boys laughed.

But Chubb said, 'It can't be his mother – she'll be long gone by now.'

'*No!*' Simeon cried, astonishing them all, and he launched himself at Chubb. This was a mistake, as Kit could have told him, since Chubb was the best boxer in the school, but he was taken by surprise as Simeon bowled into him, and soon the other boys closed round them, chanting, '*Fight!*' '*What* is going on here?' demanded the Usher, pushing his way through. Kit helped him to haul Simeon off Chubb, whose face was bleeding.

'That dunghill rat bit me!' he said, and he jabbed his fingers into Simeon's chest. 'You will be sorry for this!'

Once more, Simeon tried to make a break for it, but the Usher barred his way.

'You must shake hands!' the Usher demanded, then swore as Simeon clawed him.

'The cupboard!' he roared to Kit and, with a pang of sympathy, Kit helped him to bundle Simeon back into the cupboard. They may as well leave him there, Kit thought, as the Usher ordered the other boys to disperse, for all the good his schooling would do him.

'Let him calm down before lessons,' the Usher said, straightening his robe.

'Yes, sir,' said Kit. Then he added, 'Sir – why is he here?' But from the look on the Usher's face, Kit could tell that he was as baffled as Kit.

Later that day, though, Kit found out. He was told to take Simeon from the cupboard to the church, where the Choirmaster waited for him. And for the first time, Kit heard Simeon sing. He repeated the phrases the Choirmaster sang to him and his voice soared upwards to the angels in the roof. Kit stared at him, astonished at the purity of the notes, and the Choirmaster closed his eyes and shook his head.

'How is it possible?' he wondered aloud. 'How is it you can hold a note so long?'

Simeon didn't answer. He looked up at the angels in the roof of the nave.

'Look at me,' the Choirmaster said, and Simeon looked. 'Watch my finger and hold the note until I tell you.'

He sounded the note and Simeon reproduced it in a tone of chilling purity, that went on, and on. Kit waited for the Choirmaster to lower his finger, but he kept it raised, an incredulous smile breaking over his face.

'Like sustained light,' he said, as the note drew finally to a quivering close, and he felt Simeon's chest and ribs as if searching for his secret.

'I have never taught a boy who could hold a phrase so long,' he said to Kit. 'And I have taught many, many boys. Too many boys. Where did you learn to hold your breath?' he asked Simeon, and Simeon hung his head and mumbled something about swimming underwater.

'Underwater?' said the Choirmaster.

'For fish,' said Simeon, looking up at last. 'Or when the men came,' he said, and Kit had a sudden image of the deep silence of water and the greenish light where the sun shimmered through.

But Robert Leigh did not want to know about the details of the boy's life, which he was sure were sordid enough. He was too enchanted by Simeon's voice to enquire further. He made him sing the *Agnus Dei* with Kit, and their two voices blended and separated again, like oil in water.

However, his singing did not make life in the school any easier for Simeon. All that week things got worse. The older boys tripped him up on the stairs as he went past, or bumped into him when he was carrying the mop and bucket, so that the contents spilt over the floor. They followed him when he was told to clean the church, trampling mud over the places he had mopped, until Matthew Palmer intervened.

'Have you n-nothing b-better to do, M-M-Master Ch-Chubb?' he said.

'N-n-no, s-s-sir,' Chubb said innocently, as his friends sniggered.

Kit stood up for Simeon on occasion and was kind to him in private, but he was treading a difficult line between his friends and the new boy he was supposed to protect. Most of the time he just tried to steer him out of their way, but this was not easy, since they all had to attend prayers, sleep and eat together. Twice he had to untie Simeon from his bed, so that he could get to his lessons.

The one thing he could say for Simeon was that he did not complain or cry.

'They are not so bad, really,' he said inadequately, as they rescued Simeon's jacket from the close-stool, where the chamber pots were emptied. He searched for something positive to say. 'It is just that you do not know them yet. When you get to know them, you will see that they are just like me.'

'Not like you,' Simeon said. He so rarely said anything that Kit had to ask him to repeat this.

Then he said, 'Yes, they are like me and I am like them.'

'No,' Simeon said definitely.

Kit felt annoyed. 'How do you know what I'm like?' he said.

Simeon stared at him, then said, 'You are like a moth that changes colour on the bark of a tree.'

It was the longest sentence he had ever uttered. Kit knew the kind of moth he meant – he had seen them on the trees near his old home. They changed colour according to their background. He stared at Simeon, wondering how much he could see, but before he could speak, the bell rang to summon them to their different classes.

IO

Towards the end of that long, terrible week, the Warden finally sent for Kit.

Kit barely stopped himself from groaning aloud. He had done none of the extra work, and as the days had passed, had felt a hope flaring in him, that the Warden might have given up on the idea. And when the Warden missed the usual school inspection again, sending a message to say that he was sick, Kit had hoped that he might not, after all, have to explain that he didn't want the extra lessons.

Now he trudged up the narrow stair to Dr Dee's room. The notice was still pinned to the door, but Kit knew he could not simply go away again.

'Come in,' said the Warden, when he knocked.

Kit opened the door. Inside, the room was dark and stuffy, and a kind of smoke that smelt of the burning of many herbs hung in the air. The Warden had apparently just got out of bed and had flung his robe on over his nightgown. Kit stared at him. He looked terrible: yellowish and haggard, with a bright, feverish light in his eyes.

'Come,' he said in a hoarse, throaty voice. 'Let me look at you.'

Kit didn't want to go any closer than he had to. The

Warden smelt stale, like old age. He pressed his bony fingers beneath Kit's chin and tilted his face upwards, looking into his eyes. After a moment, Kit pulled away.

'I have not had much time –' he began.

'Never mind that now,' the Warden said hoarsely. 'Tell me about yourself.'

'What?' said Kit, considerably surprised. No one in the school ever asked anyone else about themselves. It was an unspoken rule, though mysteriously, somehow, everyone seemed to know.

'Your parents,' said the Warden, sitting down and indicating that Kit should do the same. Kit remained standing.

'My parents are dead, sir,' he said stiffly.

The Warden nodded as though this was what he had expected. 'They were Catholic, were they not?'

Kit stiffened further. What was this, some kind of religious inquisition?

'I was brought to the school,' he said, 'in order to be trained in the true faith.'

The Warden's mouth twisted into what might have been a smile. 'Very right and proper. And who brought you here?'

These were things that Kit preferred not to think about. But he answered, 'It was the former Master, sir, William Chadderton. And Mr Carter.'

The Warden nodded.

'And have you no legal guardian?'

'The school is my guardian, sir.'

Dr Dee nodded again. 'Did your mother and father have no relatives?'

Kit shook his head, wondering what this was about. It

brought back painful memories. He had been not quite seven years old when he had been taken from his mother and put on Oliver Carter's horse, and they had galloped all the way to the school, a distance of more than twenty miles. All his life he would remember the smell of that galloping horse.

The Warden was looking at him intently.

'Neither my mother nor my father had any brothers or sisters,' Kit said.

'Ah,' said the Warden, and he pressed the tips of his fingers together, still gazing at Kit.

'Is that all, sir?' Kit asked, staring back.

The Warden rose and walked round Kit, first one way then the other. He lifted a lock of Kit's hair. It was as though he was smelling it.

'Do you know what the Great Rite is, Kit?' murmured.

All at once, Kit knew he did not want to be in that with Dr Dee. The Warden's eyes were huge and black, a a peculiar smell came from him. Kit backed away.

'I have to go,' he said.

'Oh, not yet,' said the Warden, still in that same soft voice that didn't sound quite like his.

Kit moved away. He thought he had turned, but somehow he was still facing the Warden.

'We've not finished yet, Kit.'

And Kit found that he couldn't move. His tongue seemed stuck to the roof of his mouth and sweat broke out on his forehead. The Warden took one step towards him, then another. Kit struggled to break free. The Warden smiled.

'It is a ritual that has to be done at a certain time,' he

said. 'Preferably at the dark of the moon. Do you know when that is, Kit?'

All at once, Kit found his voice.

'I don't want to know about rituals! I've had enough! I don't want to come here any more!'

The Warden stood very close to him, and Kit was almost overpowered by the smell.

'Is there something you are not telling me, Kit?'

Kit stared into the fathomless black eyes. *How does he know?* he thought, then, *Does he know?*

'Some secret sorrow, perhaps,' the Warden murmured. 'A burden you cannot share.'

He knows, Kit thought and involuntarily his hand moved to his face.

'I can help you unlock that secret,' said the Warden, and felt a great yearning in his heart. 'We can work together, Kit. A sorrow shared is a sorrow halved. But you must work with me, Kit. I cannot work alone.'

'Yes,' Kit said. He felt almost faint with relief. Abruptly the Warden turned away.

'The dark of the moon is next week,' he said. 'I will send for you and you will come to the church at midnight. Do you understand?'

'Yes,' Kit said again.

'That is all,' the Warden said. 'You may go.'

At last, Kit found that he could move. He hurried to the door, almost knocking over the Warden's chair, and fumbled at the handle. He blundered outside, taking great gasps of air. He felt as though something terrible and unclean had happened, but beneath his horror, as he hurried down the stairs, was the conviction that the

Warden knew about his problem and would come up with the solution. Kit could not run away now, because more than anything, he needed to know what he had to do.

11

Kit could hear the chanting as he made his way across the forecourt and his heart sank. *What now?* he thought. He followed the sound halfway up the stairs to the top corridor, where he could see that all the boys were standing round Simeon in a jostling crowd.

'Give it up, pig-boy,' Chubb said, and one of the other boys pushed him.

'Hand it over now!'

'Thieves have their noses slit.'

'And their ears cut off.'

'Brooke,' said Chubb, 'pass me your dagger.'

Kit closed his eyes. First the Warden, now this. He had the ignoble urge to sneak away, to pretend it wasn't happening. It was not fair, he thought. Why was it always up to him?

'If he won't talk,' said Parker, 'we can test him in the river.'

Kit opened his eyes, just as Simeon was thrust down the stairs towards him. He fell awkwardly, cracking his head on the stone wall, but Kit took the brunt of his weight.

'What's going on?' he asked.

Chubb leapt down the stairs.

'This arsewipe has taken my dagger.'

The two boys stood on either side of Simeon, who had sunk down on a step between them.

'Know that for a fact, do you?' Kit said.

'I do,' said Chubb. 'And we are going to get it back.'

'Does it take so many of you?' Kit said, taking hold of Simeon and helping him up.

'Leave it, Morley,' said one of the boys.

'You leave him,' said Kit.

'Is he your pet?' said Chubb.

'Have you asked him if he has taken it?'

'We're asking him now,' said Chubb, and he booted Simeon, who scrambled behind Kit. The other boys surged down the stairs.

'Stop!' cried Kit, and he spoke the words that he knew for certain were social death. 'I will fetch the Master.'

Chubb's face registered disbelief, then scorn. 'You would *tell*?' he said.

Kit did not answer.

'Perhaps we should tip you both in the river,' Chubb said, and there was a chorus of agreement. Kit and Chubb stared at one another.

'It does not become you,' Chubb said, 'to turn traitor.'

'It does not become you,' said Kit, 'to turn coward.'

Chubb's eyes widened, then he put up his fists in a boxing stance.

'We will see who is the coward,' he said, and the other boys pressed them down the stairs to the bottom corridor, where they cleared a space.

'Fight!' one of them said, then they all chanted, 'Fight, fight, fight!'

Kit knew Chubb could always beat him at boxing. But he put up his fists because there was nothing else he could do. When the first blow landed he felt the blood spurt from his nose.

'B–b–b–boys!' cried Matthew Palmer. 'What is going on here?'

He pushed his way through the crowd. 'F–f–fighting?' he said. 'In s–school time?'

He took in the sight of Simeon cowering and Kit's bleeding nose.

'What is this about?' he said.

Kit wiped his nose and said nothing. Chubb said nothing either, since the boys were not supposed to keep daggers in the first place. Matthew Palmer was reminded vividly of his own schooldays. He could tell he would get no answer.

'Have you no l–lessons to go to?'

Gradually the knot of boys loosened, muttering.

'I w–will not go to the M–M–Master this time,' the curate said. 'But let me not c–catch you again.'

The other boys drifted away, leaving Kit, Chubb and Simeon.

'Sh–shake hands,' said Matthew Palmer.

Reluctantly, Kit and Chubb shook hands, not looking at one another.

'Right,' said Matthew Palmer. B–back to your l–lessons.'

Chubb turned immediately and went into the classroom. Simeon remained where he was. Timidly, he raised a hand to Kit's face.

'Nose –' he said. Kit moved away.

'I know,' he said, pressing his sleeve to it.

'Bleeding.'

'It'll be fine.'

'Pinch it – look.'

Kit struck Simeon's hand away. 'Leave it!'

Simeon fell back, then he said, 'Blood, here?' He lifted his chin.

Kit looked. 'No,' he said.

'Blood in my mouth – look,' he stuck out his tongue. Kit didn't want to look at Simeon's tongue. He stared round the corridor in despair.

'My tooth hurts,' Simeon said.

'Stop going on about it.'

'I didn't take the dagger.'

Kit sighed. 'I know,' he said. Then he pressed a hand to Simeon's shoulder, turning him round. 'Go to your lesson,' he said.

'Traitor,' Chubb hissed as Kit passed through the door to his own lesson. Kit dodged his foot, which was stuck out so that he would fall over it, and sat at his desk. When he started to write, Chubb spilt ink as though by accident over Kit's work, and when Kit was told to bring out his Greek translation, he discovered that all the pages were torn and the High Master reprimanded him sharply.

'You will miss your evening meal and come to my office to write it out again,' he said.

Kit returned to his seat, ignoring Chubb's smirking face. He did not mind as much as Chubb would like him to, because at least if he was in the Master's study he would be saved the trouble of avoiding the other boys. Or rescuing Simeon. He thought briefly about Simeon, then remembered that he had to go to the church for an extra session with the Choirmaster, and relaxed just a little. He would keep going somehow, he thought, until the Warden came up with a solution to Kit's problem. One that would hopefully take him a long way from the school.

12

Kit sat with George Stursaker, the High Master, again. He had been translating part of the *Iliad* all week. Master Stursaker leant back in his chair and closed his eyes, for he had just eaten a huge meal in front of Kit. His breathing became rougher and more rhythmic. Kit glanced at him sourly and wondered if it would be safe yet to sneak away. Then he rubbed the back of his neck and applied himself to the translation once more.

The passage was quite an exciting one. The opposing sides, Greek and Trojan, had met in battle and Agamemnon was face to face with a Trojan warrior.

Iphidamas stabbed Agamemnon on the belt . . . (there was a phrase Kit could not translate) *keeping the grip on his spear, but he failed to pierce the glittering belt . . . Agamemnon gripped the shaft, and pulling it towards him with the fury of a lion, dragged it out of the man's grasp. Then with his sword he hit him on the neck and brought him to earth . . .*

Kit stared at the words, wondering what it would be like to be in actual combat on a battlefield. He had practised swordplay often enough, but had never had to fight for his life. When it came to it, would he be brave enough to stand his ground or would he turn and run, as Hector had run from the incensed Achilles?

It was Kit's greatest fear that he would not be brave. He was a good swordsman, the Usher was always telling him so, but anyone could be overtaken by panic when the moment came to face death. That was what made the difference between a warrior and a hero.

The High Master slumped in his chair, Kit stared vacantly out of the window and both were startled by a rapping on the door.

Parker's voice said, 'Kit is required for sword practice.'

Kit looked at the High Master, who sat up and assumed an alert expression.

'Very well,' he said. 'That will do for now.'

Kit hurried from the room before Master Stursaker could change his mind. He barely glanced at Parker, who was saying something to which Kit didn't listen. He reached the main door to the courtyard and opened it, feeling the air, which was sharp with rain.

And there before him stood Chubb with the rest of his gang.

Kit looked round, but there was no sight of the Usher. Chubb grinned. He had taken off his jerkin and rolled up his shirtsleeves.

'Time to settle our differences,' he said. 'Swords or fists?'

'What is this?' said Kit.

'A chance to prove yourself,' said Chubb. Kit's heart leapt nervously.

'I don't need to prove myself to you,' he said, turning to leave. Immediately Chubb's sword was at his throat.

'Come now, Kit,' he said. 'We have a quarrel to settle.'

'The quarrel is in your head, not mine.'

Chubb gave him a look of mock incredulity. 'Are you refusing to fight?'

Kit stared at the faces of the boys who had until recently, been his friends. Nothing much had happened since the ripping of his Greek translation and he had hoped it would all die down, or pass like the ill wind it was. But now, here they were. Some were grinning, others eager and intent. Not one of them was on Kit's side and they were not going to let him back out.

'Fight among yourselves,' Kit said, and tried to go again, but the point of the blade quivered against his chest.

'Not turning coward, are you, Kit?' said Chubb.

Beneath his apprehension, Kit felt a spark of rage. *This is it*, he thought, and he felt a dull surprise that the situation had presented itself so quickly. He swallowed hard, hoping that no one would notice his fear.

'Have it your own way,' he said, throwing off his jerkin and drawing his sword.

The other boys backed away from them, forming a circle as the two opponents crossed swords. Chubb grinned his wolfish grin, which faded as Kit thrust. He just managed to parry in time, but fell back, startled by the ferocity of Kit's attack.

Then Chubb regained ground, and the two boys went round and round, swords flashing. Kit leapt on to a low wall, then Chubb thrust him off and bounded down some steps. Kit flicked the hair back from his eyes and followed. This was unlike any practice. Chubb had stopped grinning; Kit felt a white-hot rage. He ignored the other boys, who were chanting for Chubb. Years of anger boiled up in him. Near the surface it was fury at all the petty meanness and taunting of the past week; at the impositions of the High Master and his barely veiled contempt; at the extra, unwanted responsibilities for Simeon and the strange, unpleasant behaviour of the Warden.

Beneath the surface it was older and more terrible.

Round and round the courtyard the two boys leapt and ran, thrusting and parrying. Kit never took his gaze from Chubb's eyes. In them he could see arrogant pride, then the first flicker of doubt. Kit knew he was gaining ground. He felt, not excitement, but a cold, malevolent pleasure. His arm was not as strong as Chubb's, but he was faster and more skilled. The watching boys fell silent.

But Chubb had too much at stake to allow himself to be beaten. The moment came swiftly, almost too swiftly to be seen. Chubb slipped on a wet stone, Kit stood over him, waiting, and in the lightning pause, Chubb lunged upwards and twisted his sword. Kit felt a fierce pain in his side and he crumpled to the floor.

A shout went up from the onlooking boys. Kit sensed, rather than saw, them withdrawing fast, and heard someone cry, 'Run!'

Kit felt curiously light-headed. He clutched the sharp pain beneath his ribs. Blood leaked through his fingers. Was this what it felt like to die?

He raised his head and looked round. A blackness gathered behind his eyes, but he could see the doorway that led to the Warden's room. Gritting his teeth, he tried to pull himself over the stone flags.

The pain of movement was almost too much. Kit slumped and shut his eyes. Wasn't this what he had always wanted? In the darkness there was peace. A way out of all his problems.

Against his will, his body struggled to survive. His arm moved and his breath caught on the pain between his ribs. His leg kicked feebly, then pushed and inch by inch, Kit crawled across the ground, towards the Warden's door.

Another Trick of the Light

Manchester, Present Day

Kate's pace increased as she rounded the corner past the row of shops with their metallic shutters pulled down and the waste ground where kids were jumping on the roof of a car. She ran through the narrow passage on to the Phoenix Estate. She could run fast but her breath caught on the stitch in her side.

Outside her house, which was one of a row of maisonettes, there was a group of kids kicking a football up against her front door. Kate felt a spark of rage.

'Stay away from my house!' she shouted, pushing past. The door was locked, which was a good sign, at least. Kate didn't knock, in case her father was still asleep, but fumbled with the key she kept on a string round her neck, aware of all the watching faces, wondering if one of the gang would try to jump her as her back was turned.

'Dad?' she shouted as she entered the hallway.

There was no answer and Kate ran upstairs to his room. Her father's bedroom was a tip. Books and clothes scattered, crumpled tissues, papers, cans of beer. The bedcovers had been pulled back, which was his version of making the bed ('airing it' he always said) and the wardrobe door was open. Nothing else in the house seemed to have been touched, although there was a bowl of half-eaten cereal in the fridge.

She had to run into the kitchen twice before she saw the envelope propped up against the radio. It contained a few ten-pound notes and some change, and a note to her in scrawling, shaky handwriting.

My dear Kate, it read.

I am going away for a few days. I know you will be a good girl and take care of yourself. It is better for you if you don't know where I am. Maybe you can stay overnight with friends. This is all the money I have, but I am going to try to send some more.

There was a smudged mark, then:

I am so sorry.
I love you,
Your father.

Kate stared at the note. She could hear a whistling noise inside her head.

Going away for a few days?

Where to?

Her father had never left her before.

He had come in late, of course, many times, and she had stayed up late waiting for him, worrying. But some time in the early hours he would always roll in, half dressed and singing, and she would put him to bed.

She stared at the note again, uncomprehending. Then, pointlessly, she ran through the house once more. 'Dad – Dad!' she called.

All the rooms were empty.

Feeling sick, Kate returned to the kitchen. There were

greasy pots everywhere: on the table, in the sink. That was one of the things she had meant to do this half-term – get to grips with the house. Now she screwed the note up and flung it at the wall, kicked a chair, and slammed a cupboard door shut.

Friends? she thought angrily. *What friends?*

She picked up the note again and sat down at the table.

It is better for you if you don't know where I am.

Why? Kate thought. Why was it better? Then she gazed, unseeing, at the wall. This was not the first time her father had been in trouble. Her heart pounded and her palms began to sweat. What was she supposed to do? She couldn't let anyone know she was here on her own – that would bring Social Services in. That meant that she couldn't start asking if anyone had seen her dad.

Suddenly Kate felt furiously angry. She wanted to scream and shout, to trash the house. But she would be the one who had to clean it up.

Kate closed her eyes. When she opened them again, she reached for the envelope and counted the money. Nearly sixty quid and she had thirty of her own, saved up from a paper round. She looked in the fridge. There was some bacon, and half a loaf, an opened bottle of milk. In the cupboard there was cereal and biscuits. Only because she shopped. But she could manage for food at the moment.

In fact, she would be all right here for several days, unless . . .

Unless people turned up, looking for her dad.

Kate pushed her hair back with her fingers, pressing them into her skull. She couldn't afford to get scared now. She should be getting her head together and thinking of a plan.

Where could she start? She wanted to phone someone,

though she did not know who. Their own phone had been cut off and, unlike everyone she knew, Kate did not possess a mobile. Anyway, there was no one to phone.

Kate stood up abruptly, pushing the chair back. She needed some air. She needed to sort her thoughts out and decide what she had to do.

Kate left the house, making sure the door shut properly behind her, and walked past the kids, who were on skateboards now. She wondered if they knew anything. But she would never ask. She crossed the square and went through a narrow passage. The fine rain had continued, but this hadn't stopped some other kids throwing fireworks at one another across the waste ground. Kate dug her hands into her pockets, and headed towards the shops, trying to look as if she had somewhere to go.

The kids on the waste ground called out at her as she walked past, but she ignored them, digging her hands into her pockets and kicking a stone across the pavement. She felt calmer now that she was outside, though a little hollow. Her father would be back, she thought. He had done this disappearing act before, though not for long, and he didn't usually leave a note. But she felt sure that he would come in that night, completely unaware of the trouble he'd caused.

'Ah, Kate!' he would say. 'My beautiful daughter!'

The best thing she could do was to try to keep things normal, not let anyone know he'd gone, turn up at the cathedral project as usual. She couldn't afford to be reported for failing to attend.

The light had faded, and the freezing drizzle soaked through her clothes. Kate retraced her steps to the square where she lived, preoccupied with her thoughts. Only when a bird called did she look up and see the woman, crossing the square towards her from the other direction, head down, the blue blanket pulled over her hair and shoulders. Kate recognized her instantly from the cathedral and her heart beat faster, though she didn't know why. What was the woman doing here?

Just as she thought this, the woman vanished. Kate blinked, her vision shifted, and the square was as it had been, the skateboarders now standing about aimlessly. She looked round, but there was no sign of the woman. *A trick of the light*, she thought as she reached the door of her house. *Another trick of the light.*

The Warden

I

3rd October 1604

In the dark surface of the stone, a single candle flame was reflected. Fire in the stone, infinitely deep and far away. The stone was obsidian, polished so that its black surface shone like a mirror. Its property was to make that which was near seem far away, and to bring distant things near. It had come all the way from Mexico and had cost a small fortune.

The censer swung lightly on its chains, releasing the bitter perfume of camphor, ambergris and myrrh. Dr Dee had almost run out of myrrh. It was expensive, and where was he to get a further supply in this God-forsaken hole? He had already sold off his jewels and most of the pewter plate.

He breathed deeply. He must not allow himself to be distracted. He adjusted the stone on the silk cloth and continued to kneel in front of it, murmuring the invocation that corresponded to the Nineteenth Seal.

Now all he had to do was wait. Once he had waited for seven hours, murmuring the invocations in Latin, Hebrew and in Enochian, the tongue of angels, and still nothing had happened. If only he could find a skilled scryer, someone who could *see* the angels. But that thought too was a distraction. He returned his attention to the stone, eyelids half closed, breathing settling into the slow rhythm that was necessary for trance.

The candle burnt low. He had told the Fellows of the college that he needed more light for his studies and they had responded ungraciously, as usual, that what with the roof of the church needing repair and an additional window tax, he was lucky to have been given any candles at all. He had supplemented the two they had given him with his own, smaller candles, and it was one of these now that guttered and went out.

He did not move to relight it, but the thought of it disturbed him like an itch. What was happening to his ability to concentrate? He was getting old, his mind wandering. Each time he performed the rituals it seemed to take more effort for less result. His joints were too stiff for kneeling, his feet subject to cramp on the cold stone floor. What would happen to his life's work as age overcame him?

Feeling defeated, he hauled himself stiffly on to his chair and sat, still gazing into the stone. Another hour passed. Far away, it seemed, he could hear the chanting of the clerks. His shoulders and hips ached, but it was as if he was losing the will to move. That at least was a good sign. A stillness crept over him, up his neck and into the muscles of his face. Gradually his head nodded forward.

In the heart of the stone, the light began to flicker and change. The dark surface rippled like water, into a shape resembling eyes, or the round 'o' of a mouth, swiftly disappearing again. Then a pattern of fingertips pressed from within the stone and caused the surface to alter and bulge. Dr Dee shifted in his sleep and mumbled. He began to dream. He was standing in front of the stone. He thought he could make out a robed form and the outline of folded wings glowing with a dull sheen like that of pewter. In his dream, Dr Dee gripped the edges of the stone and leant towards it. There was a face that he could almost see, though he could not make out any features. Then it spoke and the Warden's mind filled dizzyingly with blue-grey light, but try as he might, he could not make out the words.

'What – ?' he said aloud in his sleep. 'What – ?'

Another candle flickered and went out near the sleeping form of the Warden. The dark surface of the stone shimmered again like liquid, and this time the fingers pressing against it became more clearly visible, and then the surface of the stone gave. In one fluid movement, the hand protruded from the stone, fingers searching along the wood of the desk. They were stubby, with blackened nails and a scar across the knuckles. They reached the sleeve of Dr Dee's robe and grew still. Dr Dee's arm twitched in his sleep and at last he heard the words that the angel was saying.

The Son of Darkness cometh.

The image of the angel flickered and billowed, as if caught up in a great wind. The fingers tugged Dr Dee's sleeve lightly, then moved to where his beard lay across his arm.

In his dream, Dr Dee gripped the sides of the obsidian even harder.

'But what must we do?' he cried.

The fingers twitched his beard playfully, then moved higher, pinching his nostrils together so that he could not breathe. At the same time, someone knocked at the door. Dr Dee awoke, snorting, and the hand instantly withdrew, back into the polished stone.

2

Dr Dee stared round, bewildered, as the knocking continued. He had a cramping pain in his right side where his kidney had once inflamed and caused him such agony that he thought it would kill him; the joint of his big toe was complaining, and there was a taste like ashes in his mouth. *The taste of death,* he thought, and at once began to move stiffly round his room, slapping himself to get his circulation going.

Only a dream, he told himself, picking up the inkstand. Once again he had fallen asleep, when he was trying to fall into a trance.

The soft but persistent knocking continued. He drew a sudden breath, gathering his papers together and expelled his breath slowly. The knocking came again, *tap-tap-tap.*

Muttering curses, Dr Dee took up the candle and opened the door. There stood one of the boys of the college, holding a candle of his own.

'What is it?' snapped the Warden. Sometimes, if he was intimidating enough, the intruder would simply withdraw. But this one only blinked.

'If you please, sir,' he said, 'Mr Carter wishes to know if you will join us for breakfast.'

'For breakfast?' said the Warden, as incredulously as if

he had been asked to stand on his head. Was it that time already? Surely he hadn't slept all through the early hours? He restrained himself from a sharp response, thinking suddenly that he recognized the messenger. He raised his candle towards the boy's face, but instead of retreating, as so many of them would, he stood his ground. He was tall and fair-haired, the lines of his face strong and clear. It was one of the boys from the choir, a promising lad he had noticed before when considering his need for an assistant. One day, he had thought, he would show the lad his room, his books, talk to him about his work and see if there was any corresponding light in his eye. One day, but not today.

'Tell Mr Carter,' he said testily, 'that I shall breakfast here, in my room,' and he began to close the door. The lad stepped forward.

'Mr Carter said to say that he is sure you will not have forgotten that the Court Leet is to take place in one hour.'

In fact Dr Dee had forgotten all about it. He closed his eyes. The Court Leet. Perhaps the most tiresome of the many events at which his presence was required. He opened his eyes and glared at the boy, who did not shrink back as most of them would, thinking him the Antichrist, but returned his stare with one almost equally stern.

'What is your name, boy?' he said.

'Kit Morley, sir.'

'Well, Kit,' said Dr Dee. 'Tell Mr Carter that I will be down soon.'

The boy bowed as minimally as would still be polite and retreated along the corridor. Dr Dee stared after him reflectively for a moment, then went back into his room. He checked the date in his almanac. Yes, there it was, 3 October

1604. How could he have forgotten? The Court Leet was a twice-yearly event at which all the petty grievances of the town were aired. It would drag on all day. He would have to put away his magical equipment.

At the far side of the room there was a tapestry hanging on the wall. It was his own, the Fellows disapproved of all ornamentation. Behind it there was a panel in the wood, hidden among the other panels, but when pressed hard enough it gave into a space in which a priest might hide, and beyond this there was a stairway. The Warden, used to hidden entrances and exits, had discovered this in one of his thorough searches. An escape route. It had proved useful to him before when he had not wanted to be disturbed. He could hardly believe it had not been discovered. But the Fellows, unlike the Warden, were ignorant of stagecraft and magic, a good deal of which depended on simple mechanics like the hidden door.

Dr Dee put his stone, the wax tablet and the carved table into the space behind the door. He picked up his books, the *Liber Mysteriorum,* and Trithemius's *Stenographica,* and was about to replace them on the shelves, when he paused. Surely in one of these there was an analysis of instructive dreams? Forgetting about breakfast, he sat down at his desk and began turning the heavy pages.

He hadn't got very far when there was another rapping at the door. Dr Dee ignored it, as he always ignored the first knock, in the hope that whoever it was would go away. But whoever it was knocked again.

Dr Dee sighed with infinite exasperation. Then, restraining himself, he opened the door. There stood that stuttering fool Matthew Palmer, one of the curates. He could not meet the Warden's glare, but looked all round nervously, as though trying to see into the room.

'Well?' said the Warden quietly.

'M-Mr C-Carter said,' the curate began, and paused.

'Yes?' said the Warden, and the curate quailed.

'M-m-m,' he tried, then started again. 'The-the Court Leet,' he managed.

'I know about the Court Leet,' said the Warden in the same, dangerously low voice.

Matthew Palmer shuffled backwards into the wall. He could hardly bring himself to relay the message. He blinked several times, but the words would hardly come.

'M-Mr Carter says that if you – if you f-f-fail to attend there will be a f-f-fine – and – and it will be t-taken f-from your p-p-pay.'

There. He had said it. He stood gasping and blinking owlishly.

Dr Dee felt torn between outrage that Carter had sent this lackey with his insulting message, and awareness that he could not afford any more fines.

'Tell Mr Carter,' he said finally, 'that if he wishes to threaten me, he must come here himself.'

Matthew Palmer looked more terrified than ever.

'Oh, I-I-I d-don't th-think –'

'That is apparent,' said the Warden, and he shut the door.

There was a long pause, during which he heard no footsteps. Matthew Palmer was evidently not sure what to do, but eventually the Warden heard him retreating along the corridor. Dr Dee put on his cloak and hat and stood by the window, waiting. It was now broad daylight, but a fine drizzle fell into the courtyard. From his window he could see the pink stone of the college buildings, the yellow stone of the church, the black and white buildings that led into the noise and squalor of Long Millgate.

Today he would sit through all the wearying business of the town, all the petty quarrels and complaints about wandering pigs and neighbours pouring their chamber pots out of their windows when someone they didn't like was passing.

'Pigs and privies!' he had snapped at Oliver Carter the last time they had spoken. 'You have brought me, a scholar from Cambridge, to this backwater, where I must deal with pigs and privies!'

Where was Oliver Carter anyway?

Dr Dee shuffled the papers on his desk, which were petitions from the townsfolk, imploring him to intervene by magical means, in their misfortunes. 'My sheep have wandered,' 'Someone has wounded my cattle,' 'Will I marry?' 'Will my child survive?' There were dozens of them each week: poor people promising him their savings, apparently undeterred by the fact that he did not respond. For he dared not be seen practising magic. He could not earn money by practising the one art he knew.

A little over a year ago, before Queen Elizabeth died, he had still had hope. She had found him a house when he had returned from abroad, impoverished after all his dealings with the barbarian Kelly. Then she had found him this position. Which was hardly ideal, but better than the workhouse, and only a temporary measure, she had assured him. He remembered her saying those exact words the last time he had seen her. She had been dressed magnificently as usual and her eyes glittered in the white mask of her face. But her teeth were rotten, so that she would not smile, and he had thought, as he bent over her hand, that he could smell something unhealthy and stale in her. The smell of loneliness, perhaps. The young girl he had first tutored, with her fiery hair and pale, translucent skin, had been like a flame in a long, cool glass. Since then she had achieved greatness, holding together her divided nation and restoring peace. But as he stood before her that final time, he could see the terrible cost of her greatness. She held his gaze only for an instant, then her eyes slid away.

'We are none of us getting any younger,' she had said. Then, 'It is only a temporary measure.'

Then she had died and been replaced by the posturing Scot. And with him all the religious strife had flared again. And he would have nothing to do with his predecessor's magician, who had once been counted the most learned man in Europe. He had not even replied to the Warden's letters. So with the death of his Queen had finally died the last of his hope.

The Warden pressed his fingers to his eyes. He must bathe them again, he thought. If his eyesight failed he would not be able to read.

Finally he could hear the uneven clump of Carter's footsteps as he dragged his bad leg behind him. He glanced towards the hidden doorway and, as the footsteps clumped closer, thought of disappearing into it again.

But Carter was no fool and the Warden did not want to risk the doorway being sealed off. So he waited until the footsteps paused, then flung open the door before Carter could knock.

'Are we ready then?' he said.

And without waiting for a reply from Carter, who stood breathing heavily and glaring balefully from his pink-rimmed eyes, the Warden swept past him along the corridor and down the stairs.

And back in his room, the tapestry bulged, then shifted to one side. The figure of a man dressed in black, with a pale oval face, short pointed beard and dark, dark eyes, looked round the panelled chamber as if well pleased. He took a step forward as though testing the floor, then turned neatly and looked towards the window, then the door. He looked at the instruments on the table, picked them up one by one and sniffed. He turned the pages of Dr Dee's journal and smiled to himself. Then he pulled back the rug, examining the pentagram that the Warden had painted on the floor, stood in the centre of it and disappeared.

3

Dr Dee returned to his room before anyone else could stop him. It had been a long, harrowing day. First all the nonsense at the Court Leet, where the ranting crowd had forced him to leave, then the woman outside, begging him to cure her children, whom, she claimed, were all possessed by devils.

'Everyone thinks that about their children,' he had told her, but she would not be shaken off and had finally been hauled away by the constables.

Then the evening meal which had followed the Court Leet had been every bit as trying as he had anticipated, for the radical Puritans of the Salford Hundred had been there, weeping aggravatingly as they ate their food. Their leader, Robert Downe, had been particularly unbearable. He wanted the chantry prayers to be abandoned, all services to be spoken, not sung, no meat or ale to be taken on a Sunday. There were to be services in the open fields for those who did not like the church, and the inns of Long Millgate would be closed.

Oliver Carter's face had darkened until it was the same colour as the wine in his goblet. 'Is that all?' he had said, and for once Dr Dee was in sympathy with him. Robert Downe spoke with the assurance of a man who has never once, in all his life, considered the possibility that he might be wrong. He would take no wine, only water, bread and a little cabbage. Only a young man, Dr Dee thought, as he climbed the stair to his room, could show such implacable confidence. One who had not lived through the reigns of six monarchs, each with differing views.

He reached his door and stopped. There, on the heavy oak, someone had scratched the numbers '666'.

Dr Dee stood for a long time, staring. One of the college boys, he supposed, although he wouldn't put it past the Fellows, even the curate. He reached out and touched the scratched marks with his finger. They were carved, not written – they wouldn't wash off. And if he made a fuss about it, it would draw attention to them even more, to the hostility in men's hearts that was less secret every day.

He closed his eyes and opened the door, feeling a great weariness wash over him. Lord what bullies and idiots men were, he told himself, and picking up his quill he wrote out a notice, *Do not disturb*, then tacked it to his door over the offending letters. Then he lit the candles and prepared to study. But he was so tired and distracted that he had lost the impulse to study. His eyes drooped and he kept having to press his fingers into them because the lettering on the page was blurred and superseded by the etching on his door. 666 – the number of the Beast.

That was the trouble with these people who thought of themselves as God's Appointed – they wore you out. All the petty squabbles and rivalries had eaten into his day and now, when he finally had some time, he could only sleep. Because sleep he must, if only for an hour. His head felt too heavy to support and he let it fall on to the leather pad on the surface of his desk.

Some hours later, he awoke with a violent start, staring into the dim light, for the candles had burnt low. He was immediately aware of a difference in the room. He could see very little in what remained of the light, but he felt a change in temperature, a sudden cold. What he could see of the room was undisturbed. With trembling fingers he lit the candle by the window. The waxy tip caught light slowly, the small flame curling up the wick. Dr Dee did not take his eyes from it. He was afraid, very afraid, of the preternatural stillness of the room.

He saw the draped folds of a robe first, unmoving as though carved in stone, and further down, feet sculpted in classical style, the second toe longer than the first, naked and muscular. *A statue*, he thought dazedly, but even as he thought this, the long toes flexed.

Dr Dee could not bring himself to look up. The candle in his hands shook so that a drop of wax fell on to his gown. 'Wh-who are you?' he managed to say.

'Do you not know me, John?' said a voice unmistakably angelic. There was music in it, and rushing wings. Yet it spoke to him in his own tongue, not Enochian, the language he had so painfully acquired.

At last the Warden forced himself to look up. Up and up his gaze travelled, past the carved folds and drapes of the angelic gown, the stone scroll held in the smooth stone hands. The angel's face was bent away from him in profile; he could see stone curls gathered on the carved neck.

The angel was much taller than him, he realized, and he was considered a tall man. But the presence of the angel filled the room, or rather it was as though the rest of the room had fallen away and he stood with the angel on a dark plane with no visible contours, somewhere outside the known universe, where time itself stood still.

Dr Dee could not hear the harshness of his own breathing, or the beating of his heart, though he knew it must be beating thick and fast.

It is the Angel of Death, he thought, and somewhere in the midst of his fear he felt relief, that the moment of death was, after all, so painless. But the next moment he was worrying about what was written on the scroll and whether everything he had been told about the Day of Judgement was true.

All this time the angel merely stood, not even as though waiting, but just there. Dr Dee thought he could detect an amused quality in the powerful silence. If he was doomed, he wanted the angel to look at him at least.

'You have come for me then,' he managed to say.

'I have,' said the angel, but Dr Dee could not see whether its lips were moving.

Then the angel lifted its great stone head, its eyes utterly blank. Dr Dee fought the impulse to close his own eyes as it turned towards him.

'Is that better?' it said, and Dr Dee wanted very much to say, 'No,' but he was speechless. From somewhere in all his reading he remembered a line: *calm and terrible are the faces of angels*, and he wished suddenly and foolishly that he could recall the writer's name. But what good was all his reading to him now?

The angel stood impassively with folded wings. Dr Dee was relieved; if they were suddenly unfolded, he thought, they would eclipse the universe, and for the first time ever he wished that he had not spent the greater part of his life trying to commune with angels. For now that one stood before him, Dr Dee had nothing to say.

'Have you nothing to say?' said the angel, as though reading his mind, and Dr Dee closed his eyes. Where were all his questions? Or perhaps the angel meant him to give an account of himself, if this was the Day of Judgement. But where to begin?

'Well?' said the angel, but Dr Dee still couldn't think.

'Wh-why are you here?' he said.

'That's better,' said the angel. 'Now. Open your eyes.'

'I c–cannot,' said the Warden, who genuinely found that he couldn't.

'Why not?'

'You – you are – it is – too terrible to look at you.'

This wasn't very polite, but it was the best he could do. There was a low rumble of what might have been amusement or wrath.

'Open them.'

With some difficulty, as though striving to awake from a great sleep, Dr Dee opened his eyes. The angel was still there, observing him with its own, sightless eyes, so that the Warden felt naked, as though his soul was exposed. He shrank back and considered falling to the floor, but his body wouldn't obey him.

'You do not like to look at me?' the angel said, and Dr Dee shook his head hopelessly. What answer could he give?

'Is this better?' asked the angel, and suddenly, without warning, a great wind whipped its hair and wings and robes, and before Dr Dee's amazed and horrified eyes, it was transforming into a lion, a calf, an eagle.

Now the Warden really did want to prostrate himself, for he feared that he was going mad. The wind whipped his cloak around him and fire and flames scorched his face. Yet he was powerless to do anything but look, as finally, from the phantom bestiary, a man's face emerged. The wind and flames died away and the Warden's room returned with the form and figure of a man in it. A youngish man in a dark suit, with a small pointed beard and a receding hairline, though his hair grew long and lank over the place where his ears should have been. Better than this, from Dr Dee's point of view, he had eyes that were recognizably human, large and heavy-lidded, except that when you looked into them, they were unfathomably dark.

Dr Dee stared at the figure that stood on the other side of his desk, wondering if he had indeed gone mad. He raised a trembling finger.

'K-Kelly?' he said eventually.

The figure walked round the table to meet him; nearer and nearer it came until Dr Dee was staring into the depths of its eyes, which were as blank and dark as the obsidian stone.

'Got it in one, John,' it said.

4

'It's been a long time, John,' said the angel, when the Warden failed to speak. 'Have you got nothing to say? To your old pal?'

Slowly, Dr Dee released the muscles of his jaw.

'Wh–what are you?'

The angel laughed. Dr Dee could see the blackened stumps of his teeth. The physical presence of his old partner was so real that all his memories came flooding back, very few of them pleasant. Edward Kelly had been both a reprobate and the best scryer Dr Dee had ever had. He had died a reprobate's death years ago, somewhere on the continent. But now he was here, tangibly, palpably real. Dr Dee could actually smell him. He lifted a finger and the figure shifted a little.

'No touching, John.'

Dr Dee pressed the fingers of his hand to his forehead, which was sweating.

'I – what are you doing here? What do you want with me?'

The angel gave another short laugh. 'One question at a time, John.'

Dr Dee looked straight into the obsidian eyes.

'Where – where have you come from?'

The eyes glowed. 'Where do you think?'

Dr Dee closed his own eyes. 'Do not play your tricks with me.'

'That's better, John. A spark of the old spirit.'

Dr Dee opened his eyes again. The angel, or Kelly, was still there. If it was a hallucination, it was the most powerful one he had ever had.

'Answer me,' he said.

'All in good time, John, all in good time.'

The apparition sat on the edge of Dr Dee's desk and sniffed in exactly the old, irritating way. Lank hair covered the place where its ears should be because Kelly's ears had been cut off years ago, the Warden remembered, for forgery. 'Not a bad room, this,' it said, looking around.

'You have come – all this way – to discuss the room?'

The spirit looked at him. 'I've come, John, to say that it's all true.'

Dr Dee's heart shifted. He licked his lips, but his tongue was dry.

'True?' he said, in a voice hardly louder than a whisper.

'All of it, John. Everything we ever worked for.'

'You mean –'

'I mean all of it – life after death, eternity, immortality, the whole package.'

About a hundred questions surged into Dr Dee's mind. He struggled to think.

'Heaven?' he said, finally. 'And – Hell?'

The spirit waved a dismissive hand. 'Old notions, John, old notions.' It got up and walked round the room, studying the tapestry and the portrait of Lady Margaret Beaufort on the wall.

'What do you mean, old notions?' Dr Dee asked faintly.

He felt as though the whole universe had suddenly turned a somersault. The spirit tapped its forehead.

'It's all in here, John. You mustn't restrict your thinking. Constrictive thinking – that's the trouble with the world today.'

'Look,' said Dr Dee, rubbing his fingers across his forehead again. What's this about? What do you want with me?'

'Isn't this about what you want with *me*?' said the spirit, suddenly very close again. 'Remember the old days, John?'

'No,' said Dr Dee, though he did, all too clearly.

'Do you remember the Queen, John?' the spirit went on as if he hadn't answered.

An image of Queen Elizabeth rose vividly in Dr Dee's mind – the way she was as a young girl: anxious, but spirited, eager for knowledge; the way she was at the end of her life, with her face ruined, lonely, but still with that enormous respect for learning, his learning.

'She called you her conjurer, her very own Magician. Them were the days, John. You could have had it all – beautiful women, riches . . .'

Dr Dee gathered his thoughts. 'Those were your desires, not mine.'

'Don't I know it,' said the spirit, with just a hint of exasperation. 'You didn't want any of the things a man might reasonably want, John. But I know what you did want.'

The dark, dark eyes were fixed on him now.

'Knowledge, John – that was all and everything to you. Knowledge that would lift a man above the angels. And you still do.'

Dr Dee felt a surge of yearning in him so powerful that

he thought his legs would give way. He groped for his chair and sat down in it.

'Yes, John,' whispered the spirit. 'That knowledge we're always being told we can't have – the reason Man was cast out of Eden. You've given up your life to it, John, and look where it's got you.'

The Warden mumbled something incoherent, but the spirit ignored him.

'A room that isn't yours, in a town you don't want to be in, and the people in it don't want you here either, do they?'

Slowly the Warden shook his head.

'And all because you stuck by the rules, John, that's all it is. You're getting old, John, and what happens then? What happens when them God-blasted Puritans take over, eh?'

As vividly as if it was all happening before him, Dr Dee saw himself old and outcast: a pauper without even a room to stay in and nowhere to keep his precious belongings. He was already poor, he had already had to sell some of his precious books.

'I'm talking about Hope, John,' the spirit said softly, and Dr Dee's heart leapt and hammered, but he said nothing.

'One thing about getting old, John,' the spirit said lightly. 'It means you don't have anything left to lose.'

The Warden pressed the fingers of both hands to his temples.

'Do not tempt me, spirit,' he said. 'You talk of rules – how many would you have me break? You broke them all – and I will not be like you – I cannot.'

The spirit looked vastly amused.

'Still such a stickler,' it said. 'Well, maybe you haven't got it in you after all.'

And when the Warden did not reply, it said, 'Oh, you

were all right when it came to books, yes. That much you could do – stick your nose in a book and hope the rest of the world'd go away. But when real things started happening, you didn't like it, did you? Things got a bit too real for you, oh yes.'

'I don't know what you mean,' said the Warden, but the spirit ignored him.

'And you're just the same now as you've always been – standing on the brink of something too big for you. You could reach out a hand and grasp it – but you won't dip your toes in the water, will you?'

Ludicrously, Dr Dee wanted to tell the spirit not to mix its metaphors.

'Call yourself a Magician,' the spirit went on, rolling its obsidian eyes. 'The great Dr Dee, feted in the courts of kings and queens around the world – you're nothing but a bookworm, a market juggler –'

'That's enough!' snapped Dr Dee. 'I don't know where you've come from and I don't know why you're here, but it's time you left. Begone!'

The spirit laughed again unpleasantly.

'You're forgetting one thing, John,' it said. 'You didn't summon me here, did you? And you can't make me leave.'

Dr Dee looked at the spirit, his face stricken. The spirit looked up and around.

'Maybe I will go,' it said, as if to itself. 'It's a bit boring round here. But I ain't finished yet, John. Not by a long chalk.' It looked at him once more with luminous eyes. 'I'll be back for another little chat, John, when you least expect it. But for now –' and suddenly the spirit was right next to him, though Dr Dee had not even seen it move – 'I'll be going – goodbye!'

And the spirit took Dr Dee's face in its hands, and before the Warden could cry out at the icy, burning touch, it planted a great kiss on his lips.

All his senses swam into a darkness so absolute, it was as though light had never existed. He struggled towards consciousness, as a drowning man struggles to break the surface of deep water. And when finally consciousness of his room, his desk and the window returned, the spirit had gone.

Dr Dee felt as though his stomach had turned to water, his mouth to ashes. He remained in his chair, incapable of movement or thought. He was drenched in a cold sweat. Finally he was able to grope for his handkerchief and press it to his face and neck, loosening his collar. He became aware once more of his breathing, harsh and ragged. *It was the food*, he told himself, *the wine*. But deeper than his disordered thoughts was the memory of his dream.

The Son of Darkness cometh, he thought.

5

When the spirit came again, Dr Dee was hardly even surprised, though it was a shock to wake suddenly in the middle of the night and find it sitting on the edge of his bed.

'Whence came you?' he said, pulling the sheet round himself.

The spirit smiled. 'You asked me that before, John,' it said.

'And you didn't answer.'

The spirit rolled its black eyes. 'Ain't it enough,' it said, 'that I've come in response to your wildest dreams?'

Dr Dee got up, reaching for his robe. The protective circle had failed him. All the candles were burning, but he would not ask how. 'When did you ever give something for nothing?' he said.

The spirit raised its palms, which were entirely smooth and without lines.

'Oh, now, John – is that fair? I come all this way to see you, and all you can think is that I'm after something. I put in months of work for you, John, without pay. Months,' it repeated with an edge to its voice. 'All that scrying, all that alchemy – useless for the most part; we might as well have scavenged for gold in the sewers. But did I complain? Not me. That man's a gent, Ned, I told myself. He's the real thing. He'll see you right in the end.'

Dr Dee felt fear licking upwards from the base of his spine. He didn't know what this thing was, angel or ghost, nor how it had got there, when the only incantations he had used were the ones appropriate to the Seven Spheres of Heaven. He had been most careful not to use any words or symbols that might encourage the darker side, yet here this being was, radiating evil, or so it seemed to him. And definitely wanting something from him. The Warden hardly dared ask, yet he had to. He licked his lips.

'What do you want?'

'That's better, John. Not exactly friendly, but not hostile. That's all it takes — a bit of "How are you?" "I'm fine, how's about yourself?" Never overlook the small talk, John — makes the world go round.'

Dr Dee wanted to tell the spirit to get on with it or get out, but he waited in silence while it stretched its arms and clasped its hands at the back of its head, apparently leaning back into empty space. But when it began humming, he felt forced to say, 'Well?'

The spirit broke off humming. 'Well what?'

'What do you want?'

The spirit looked at him. 'I want what you want, John,' it said softly.

Dr Dee turned to his desk, shuffling and stacking his papers with great energy.

'I want you to leave!' he said.

The spirit laughed. 'Now that's not quite true, John, is it?' it said. 'Not the whole truth, anyway. You can't fob your old friend off like that.'

Dr Dee stopped shuffling the papers. He shut his

eyes. It was one of those moments when he felt his age keenly, as though a great mantle of age had descended on him. He heard his own voice distantly. 'What can I do for you?'

'Much better, John, much. Now we're getting somewhere,' and when Dr Dee said nothing, it continued, 'I want what you want, John – life.'

Without opening his eyes, Dr Dee laughed, a harsh, eerie laugh.

'Life?' he said. 'Life? Why man – you are already dead!'

Suddenly the spirit was very close. Dr Dee could feel a creeping sensation on his shoulder and face. He kept his eyes shut and no longer felt like laughing.

'Very good, John,' the spirit murmured. '*Very* good.'

A thought so horrible that he could hardly bring himself to think it entered Dr Dee's mind. 'You speak in riddles,' he said, turning away from the spirit.

'I'll speak plainer then, shall I? Remember all that work we did in Prague?'

'You mean the necromancy,' Dr Dee said. 'That is a fool's game.'

'Fool's gold,' said the spirit promptly. 'That's all the alchemist's after. But what's the real end of alchemy?'

Dr Dee knew the answer to that one. 'The Philosopher's Stone,' he said wearily. 'The secret to eternal life.'

'Exactly, my old pal,' the spirit said, walking round to face him. 'The ultimate end to all our hard work and efforts. Eternal life.'

Dr Dee's heart began to thump unevenly. 'You mean – you know – how?'

'I do.'

Dr Dee turned away again. His fingers worked the fabric

of his gown. He struggled to gather his thoughts. 'What – ?' he said. 'How – ?'

'Well, not by all that fiddle-faddle you had going on,' the spirit said. 'All that filtering and distillation nonsense – what did that get you? Just a bad head and mercury poisoning. No. My way's a bit more direct.'

Dr Dee felt a chill along his spine.

'Direct – how?' he said in a low voice.

'Well – it's like the Bible says, old chum,' said the spirit, studying the books on the Warden's shelf. 'An eye for an eye, and all that. A life for a life.'

Dr Dee spun round and raised a shaking finger. 'Get thee behind me, Satan!'

The spirit didn't move.

'Now, let's not get into name-calling, John,' it said, lifting its hands. 'Keep your hair on. Anyone'd think it's your life I'm after.'

Dr Dee's face changed.

'You did, didn't you?' said the spirit. 'Gor blimey, John, give me a break. What would I want with yours? I mean – how old are you? You must be knocking on for eighty. On your way out. Give me some credit.'

Dr Dee's mouth worked strangely. 'You come here,' he said, 'to torment me – to remind me of things I cannot have –'

'I've come here,' the spirit interrupted, 'to offer us both the same golden opportunity. That thing, John, that all the alchemists and conjurers the world over are searching for in vain. That same thing you've spent your whole life looking for. A way out.'

Dr Dee sank into his chair. He felt worn down, frail. There was the familiar taste of ashes in his mouth.

'Course, I could've got it wrong,' the spirit went on. 'Could be that for all your grand talk and performances, all you ever really wanted was your books. A lifetime of studying and then – the long darkness. Is that it, John? Is that what you really want?'

Dr Dee didn't answer. The spirit sighed. Then it took something from the shelves.

'Well, look,' it said. 'Here's a book you haven't read yet.'

He placed it on the table in front of Dr Dee. It was a strange volume. The cover appeared to have been carved from wood and there was lettering on the front that Dr Dee didn't recognize. But as he looked, a flickering light passed over the letters, changing them into words he knew.

The Booke of Uncommon Knowledge, it read, and underneath: *The Booke of the Knowledge of Life and Death*

Dr Dee stared at it.

'That is not mine,' he said.

'Don't tell me you know all the books on your shelves,' the spirit said. 'Even you can't have read them all. Or if you have, you've led an even sadder life than I thought.'

It ran a finger round the lettering on the front, which smouldered.

'This is a special book, John,' it said, 'carved from the original tree in the Garden of Eden. Not the one we hear so much about – of good and evil – the other one. The one that God and all his angels were so anxious for man to know nothing about. Life and Death, John, Life and Death. Go on – open it.'

But before Dr Dee could touch it, the book opened itself, and on the first page the smouldering letters reorganized themselves. *Of Necromancy* they said, and unwillingly, hungrily, Dr Dee's gaze followed them along the page.

'Have I got it wrong, John?' the spirit breathed in his ear.

'No,' whispered Dr Dee. Then he tore his gaze away. 'Do not tempt me,' he said. 'Take it away!' He pressed his hands over his eyes.

'Oh, John,' the spirit said reproachfully. 'Don't tell me you're just like the rest of them – petty conjurers that don't have a clue what the real game is; don't tell me that, John. Why, you might as well go back to doing card tricks in the market. This is the real thing, John, The – Real – Thing. There's everything in these pages – everything you ever wanted to know. Don't turn your back on it – read it! The knowledge of angels and how their envy's kept man where he is – chained to his mortal coil. But you can break that coil, John – you can set yourself free!'

It was as if loud voices were clamouring in Dr Dee's head.

'No,' he said at last. 'No, no, no, no, *no*! You cannot come here like this!' he said, lifting his face to the spirit. 'Unlooked for – unsummoned; what gave you such power? I will not be tricked by you,' he said, standing now and his voice gaining strength. 'Do you hear me? I – will – not – be – tricked!'

For a moment he thought he saw an answering flare of anger in the spirit's blank eyes, but it was quickly gone.

'Well, it's up to you, John,' it said softly. 'I wouldn't want to get you in too deep if you're not up to it. Tell you what,' it said, before Dr Dee could answer. 'I'll leave the book with you for a while, shall I? You can't pass up the chance just to read it. Can't be any harm in that, can there? If you're going to turn your back on what I'm offering, John, and I sincerely hope you won't, then you ought to know what it is you're turning down, at least. There. I can't say any fairer than that.'

The Warden didn't answer. He kept his eyes closed, listening to his own breathing.

'Well,' said the spirit, and for the first time it sounded less than sure of itself. 'I'll be off, then. But I'll be back soon, just to see how you're getting on. Be seeing you, John.'

Dr Dee remained where he was, but he could tell without opening his eyes that the energy in the room had changed. When he finally looked, it was back to normal: the tapestry hung over the secret door, the papers were stacked on his desk, the red cloth covered the obsidian stone.

And there, before him, was the book.

6

Several hours later, the Warden sat in his study, reading the words he had once written in his diary.

At all times to be in readiness to leave this world, so that I might in spirit enjoy the bottomless fountayne of all wisdome . . .

'Long time ago, that, John,' came the spirit's voice. 'Before you were quite so near the grave yourself. Words are easy – it's looking over the lip of the pit that's hard.'

Unbidden, an image of his own grave came to the Warden. For a moment he seemed to stand dizzyingly on the verge of falling in.

'Puts it all in perspective, don't it?' whispered the voice.

The Warden stood, but the spirit was nowhere to be seen. He could hear the beating of blood in his ears.

'How is it,' he said, 'that you who are immortal, crave mortality?'

Silence.

'Answer me!' the Warden cried in a harsh voice. 'You are spirit now – what need have you of flesh?'

He thought he heard a faint sigh, but still he saw nothing.

'What is it like to be dead?' he said in a different tone.

'Would you like to find out?' said the voice.

'Where are you?' the Warden cried.

'In Hell, John, where should I be?'

The Warden's heart gave a great thump and seemed to go on falling.

'If – if you are in Hell,' he said with some difficulty, 'how can I see and hear you in this room?' And as he turned, he saw the spirit of Edward Kelly sitting on his chair, with his feet stretched out on the desk.

'Why, this is Hell,' the spirit said, staring, 'nor am I out of it.'

The Warden was about to speak, to ask the spirit if it was all true, the stories of fire and torment, but just then there was a tapping noise that came not from the door, but the secret panel. The spirit vanished, and Dr Dee looked round in alarm.

Uttering an oath under his breath, he recollected himself.

'Who is it?' he said, even though only one other person knew about the hidden door.

'Kit, sir,' said a voice. 'You said to come for my lesson.'

The Warden stared at his tapestry in confusion. Was it that time already? He was losing track of things and his study was a mess. He had been searching through his past papers to try to find some clue that would tell him which direction to take. Now he gathered them all up abruptly and searched for the special book given him by Kelly, but failing to find it, pushed back the tapestry, then tugged the rug back to hide the pentagram and opened the secret door.

A little warily, Kit came in. 'Is everything all right?' he asked. 'Are you – are you well?'

Dr Dee thought hard. In the last lesson they had made some progress in Astronomy, though not in Enochian, which the boy had seemed reluctant to learn. Perhaps they should continue the study of optics, but not through the telescope this time.

'Sir?' Kit said.

In the same moment, the Warden said, 'The mirrors,' in a definite tone. 'Today we will look in the mirrors.' And he brought them out from their secret place, wheeling the tallest one in front of Kit.

'Now boy,' he breathed, 'let us see what you can see.'

'I see myself,' Kit said dully.

'Keep looking,' the Warden said. 'Try to let your mind clear and your eyes relax. Let the mirror reveal to you its secrets.'

Kit glared at himself, pushing his hair back with his fingers. 'I see nothing,' he said.

The Warden stood behind Kit, placing his hands on the boy's shoulders. 'Look well into the glass,' he said, and stopped. His voice trailed away. For what he could see was not himself, standing behind Kit, but Kelly. He stood in exactly the same position as the Warden, with his hands on the shoulders of the mirrored boy.

Dr Dee tried to speak, but there was a rattle in his throat.

'Nice,' the spirit said, squeezing Kit's shoulders. 'A lovely young lad. Firm, pink flesh,' and in the mirror, he pinched Kit's cheek.

Kit rubbed his cheek. 'I still can't see anything,' he said, but Dr Dee could not reply.

'Ah, youth,' the spirit said. 'Bright eyes, high hopes, false expectations – and all that energy. Wasted on the young, they say – wasted.' In the mirror he ran his hands along Kit's arms and clasped his fingers, moving his arms about. Kit's reflection put up with all this as though lifeless, puppet-like. The real Kit lifted his arms once and then dropped them by his side.

'I don't know what I'm looking for,' he said.

'You could say that about a lot of people,' said Kelly. Finally the Warden found his voice.

'Can you see nothing in the glass?' he asked tremulously.

Kit shrugged his shoulders as Kelly squeezed them in the reflection. 'Nothing at all,' he said.

'Look at him breathing,' the spirit said, almost reverently. 'In – and – out,' it went on dreamily, as if entranced. 'In and out.'

'Get you gone!' said the Warden, in low, strangled tones.

'Pardon?' said Kit.

'Think of it, John,' said the spirit. 'What would it be like to have all that youthful energy now, at your time of life? Wisdom, youth and beauty too – now there's a combination! What couldn't we do together? What couldn't we accomplish? A clever mind, with years of study left in it, clear eyesight, keen hearing . . .'

As it spoke, it ran its hands over Kit's hair and face. Kit shook his head as though bemused. 'Have we finished now?' he asked.

'Not yet,' answered the spirit; it paused. 'There's something unusual about this boy,' it said.

'I said leave,' ordered the Warden hoarsely. Kit stepped away, looking warily at the Warden.

'Don't you want to know what it is?' the spirit said.

'What is it?' asked Kit, for the Warden had gone deathly pale.

'I can find out for you, if you like,' the spirit said, and it stepped from the glass into the room.

All at once the Warden seized a phial of holy water from his desk, opened it, then flung it at the spirit of Edward Kelly. The spirit's face contorted and it shot back into the glass. Water spattered over the surface.

'What is it?' Kit cried again. 'Did – did you see something?'

The Warden sat down in his chair, shaking.

'Are you all right?' Kit asked in a hushed voice.

The Warden covered his face briefly with his hands. 'It is nothing,' he said eventually. 'You had better go.

'Go,' he said again; then as Kit failed to move, he shouted angrily.

'I said GO!'

7

Robert Leigh the Choirmaster was taking the choir through the psalms.

'No, no *no!*' he said, rapping the lectern. 'E flat, then C. Start again.'

The Warden sat unnoticed in the shadows of the church. He had wanted to get away from his room, to sit quietly and think. Also he hoped that the demon, or whatever it was, would not be able to attack him here. The infernal book still lay on his desk unopened. He had not been able to bring himself to read it.

'Breathe from the diaphragm!' Robert Leigh shouted.

Spiritus, the Warden thought, for in Latin the word for spirit and the word for breath were one and the same. But how could something as substantial as Kelly's spirit be composed of air? He shuddered as he remembered how entranced the spirit had been with Kit's breathing. Why would a spirit composed of air require human breath? It was a conundrum and he couldn't solve it.

'Vowels, please – remember your vowels,' the Choirmaster complained. He stared despondently at them as they all finished at a different time.

'You sound like donkeys braying,' he said. 'What has got into you?'

The Warden knew that what had got into the choir was the fact that they might not be required to sing any more. If the Puritans had their way, there would be no choir. Their role in church services was steadily diminishing, and more and more of the services were spoken, not sung. And now the boys were tired after a long school day and merely going through the motions. None of them would mind, he thought, if they never had to sing again.

But he minded. And Robert Leigh, a small, neat, bristling man, also minded. They both craved the old days, when all the services were sung in Latin and there were virtuoso solo performances, intended to inspire the soul.

'Charles!' Robert Leigh snapped and his brother's eyes flew open. 'You could at least snore in tune!' and two of the choirboys sniggered, but Charles only responded with a shrug.

'The *Agnus Dei*,' Robert Leigh said. 'Kit will lead.'

The Warden watched Kit from his pew. He had an unusual voice, low and pure, unlike the usual tinny soprano. 'O Lamb of God,' he sang and heavily the others joined in.

The Warden sat back, thinking about the ritual of exorcism. Was it possible to perform it on oneself? Somewhere in all his books there was surely a rite of banishment that would rid him of Kelly's demon.

'Tak-est a-way the si-ins of the world,' said the Choirmaster, rapping out the beat. Remember the vowels and don't breathe after "away"!'

Kit started again.

Dr Dee heard the door of the church open softly. He looked round, but could see nothing from where he sat.

'Drone, drone, drone,' snapped the Choirmaster when

the choir had finished. For a moment it looked as though he would make them do it all again, but then he changed his mind.

'That will have to do,' he said, and waved a hand. 'Go on then, go,' he told them.

The boys all but ran out of the church. The Choirmaster sagged in the lectern and Dr Dee closed his eyes and pressed the tips of his fingers together. Ever since Kelly's last visit, he had felt in the grip of a nervous exhaustion that made it hard to concentrate. But he knew that somewhere he had read of a ritual that might work.

When he opened his eyes again, a woman was standing a little way from the Choirmaster, with a grown boy standing behind her. She was dressed, it seemed, in brightly coloured rags. She did not speak, but stood there hesitating until the Choirmaster looked up.

'Well?' he said.

The woman spoke in a low voice, with an odd accent.

'If you please, sir,' she said, 'I have brought my son to sing for you.'

The Choirmaster raised his eyebrows. 'To sing for me?' he said. 'Why?'

The woman didn't answer directly. She looked nervously around. Her son was staring upwards towards the ceiling. His mouth hung open. *An idiot*, the Warden thought.

'Will you hear him sing?' she said.

'This is not a theatre, Mistress,' the Choirmaster said, snapping his psalter shut. He stepped down from the lectern. The woman looked as if she didn't know what to say. Her hands twisted the rags of her skirt.

'Only hear him sing,' she said in a soft, pleading tone. But the Choirmaster turned away.

'Choir practice is over,' he said, stepping down from the lectern.

Dr Dee removed his hat. 'Let the boy sing,' he said, and both the Choirmaster and the woman looked startled. They had not realized he was there. The Choirmaster looked at him with dislike.

'We are not auditioning here,' he said.

'You are the Choirmaster, are you not?' said the Warden. Robert Leigh ignored him.

'I don't know why you are here, Mistress,' he said. 'I don't know what you have heard. But the choir is not open to auditions. All places are filled.'

'You think there is no room for improvement?' said the Warden, rising and stepping out of his pew. 'I have just listened to some of the worst singing I can remember hearing. Perhaps you should start again with new choristers.'

For a moment he thought the Choirmaster would tell him to mind his own business. But Dr Dee, in his capacity as Warden, still had powers. He could dismiss any of the school's officials if he chose. Robert Leigh opened, then shut his mouth. He sighed.

'What will the boy sing?' he said.

The boy was tapping his foot as though music was already playing.

'Simeon,' his mother warned. Then she said, 'He will sing the *Agnus Dei*.'

The Choirmaster looked from Simeon to his mother, then to the Warden. He raised his shoulders, then walked over to the organ. It was a new organ that the Warden had ordered in defiance of the new regulations. But before he could move a pedal to sound a note, the boy began to sing.

'I'll sing you one-oh,' he sang,

'Green grow the rushes-oh.'

The Choirmaster gave the Warden a look, but the boy went on singing.

'One is one and all alone and ever more shall be so.'

His voice was low and pure with a remarkable quality in it, the Warden thought.

'Simeon,' his mother pleaded, and there was an edge of desperation in her voice.

She touched his face to make him look at her, but the Warden raised his hand.

'Enough,' he said.

The Choirmaster had not even started to play. He sat at the organ and expelled a long breath. Then he stood down and came into the nave.

'Where did he learn to sing like that?' he said.

The boy's mother shook her head. 'He didn't learn.'

The Choirmaster looked taken aback. 'But – how does he follow the music?'

'He can always follow.'

'Wait a minute,' the Choirmaster said. He returned to the organ, pulled out a pedal and played a note. 'Sing it back to me,' he said, and the boy reproduced exactly the harsh sound of the organ.

'Simeon!' his mother said, and sang the note at him, then he sang it back to her. The Choirmaster began to play, simple phrases at first, which built in complexity, but each time the boy followed, and the notes he sang struck like arrows into the notes that Robert Leigh played, perfect and true. Higher and higher the notes climbed, until the whole of the church seemed lit by the final, quivering note. It was astonishing. The Warden had only once before heard anything like it, from the castrati who sang in the great cathedral in Rome. The Choirmaster stopped playing and sat back with an expression of painful yearning on his face and the boy's mother stood with her hand pressed to her mouth, tears pricking her eyelids. No one said a word.

'Well, I think we've established that the boy can sing,' the Warden said.

No one said anything to this. The Choirmaster stepped away from the organ and looked at the boy, who was still moving his fingers as though playing an invisible pipe. There was no doubt about it, the Warden thought, the boy was an idiot. And his mother a harlot. Yet such a gift! Not for the first time the Warden found himself questioning the mysterious ways of God. He shook his head, then addressed the woman.

'Perhaps you had better present him to the High Master,' he said, and the boy's mother, still with her fingers pressed to her mouth, her tears still unfallen, nodded.

'Now wait a minute,' the Choirmaster said. 'Just because the boy can sing does not mean that he can be admitted to the school.'

'Why not?' asked the Warden, though he knew as well as the Choirmaster that the High Master had no interest in music.

The Choirmaster stuttered a little, at a loss for words.

'It is a free school, is it not?' the Warden said.

'Yes, but –'

'But nothing. Go and fetch the man.'

Robert Leigh opened his mouth to speak, but thought better of it, then hurried out of the church. The Warden watched the woman with her son. She had caught his fluttering hands and pulled him down to sit by her. They gazed at one another as though communing silently. He wondered what had prompted her to bring the boy here. He cleared his throat.

'You serve in one of the inns of Long Millgate, do you not?'

Without looking at him, the woman nodded.

'Is that where you live?'

'It is, sir,' the woman said. 'But the inn has been closed by the Puritans.'

The Warden thought he understood. This woman had no further means of supporting her son. He had heard of the closing of the inn – yet another unwarranted action by the Puritan preacher – the same man who objected so violently to the music of the church. The Warden's lip curled a little. He himself was an absolute believer in music. Music was the point of intersection between the overlapping spheres of Heaven and earth, the one thing made by man that in its mathematical precision and purity, raised him to the celestial planes. But the Warden could see that to propose the boy for the school would provoke both the Fellows and the Puritans. He leant forward.

'How old is your son, Mistress?'

'Nearly thirteen,' the woman answered in her low voice that was also musical in its own way. The Warden thought of asking where her accent came from, but at that moment the High Master's voice could be heard.

'And I have already said that the school is not in need of new pupils!'

The mottled, bellicose face of George Stursaker, the High Master, appeared. He checked himself when he saw the Warden, then glared fiercely.

'What is all this?' he asked.

'We have a new pupil for you,' said the Warden. 'One who can sing,' he added.

The High Master's glare took in Simeon's open, empty face, his mother's clothes.

'There are no places,' he said.

The Warden raised an eyebrow. 'Since when?' he queried.

'Since funds ran low, that's when,' the High Master snapped.

'Every schoolmaster and usher,' the Warden quoted from the Deed to the school, 'shall teach freely and indifferently every child and scholar coming to the same school, without any money or other rewards.'

The High Master looked as though he would like to hit the Warden. 'No scholar pays to come to the school,' he said. 'On the other hand, the school is dependent on its wealthy benefactors. We cannot take indigents,' he said, pointedly.

'Will the angels play again?' the boy asked in a loud whisper, and the Warden glanced at him sharply, but then his mother pressed a finger to his lips.

'Two of the poorest scholars,' the Warden said, 'may be chosen by the High Master to keep the register and clean the school.'

The High Master ignored him. 'How old is the boy?' he asked, addressing the question to no one in particular.

The woman answered, 'He will be thirteen after Christmas.'

'Thirteen,' repeated the High Master. 'And can he read, or write? Perhaps he knows some Latin? No? Excellent.' he said. 'A boy of thirteen, already nearly too old for the school, who cannot yet read or write. And without any visible means of support. Splendid.'

'If – if you would but hear the boy sing,' the Choirmaster put in, but the High Master interrupted him.

'The boy is not required to sing,' he said. 'You know as well as I do that there is no place for virtuoso singing here.'

'Are you saying,' the Warden said, 'that you intend to ignore the school's Charter altogether?'

The High Master spoke in a low voice directly to the Warden.

'I am saying,' he said, 'that there is nothing to be gained by taking a boy of this kind into the school, whether or not he can sing. Nothing at all.'

The Warden softened his own voice.

'In the last instance,' he said, 'the decision is not yours.'

The High Master's face flushed a bright, angry red.

'Is it your job now?' he shouted. 'Perhaps you would like to take over my other duties as well? Why do you not take my robe – and my salary? Why not collect up orphans from the streets and dump them here? Why bother with a workhouse when you have a grammar school, eh?'

The Warden was amused by this outburst. 'Calm yourself,' he said.

'Calm myself? When my authority is undermined in this way? The Fellows shall hear of this,' spluttered the High Master.

'The Fellows can read the Charter as well as you,' said the Warden, unmoved. 'They know the extent of your duties even if you do not. And of mine,' he added in a softly threatening tone, for the High Master knew that the Warden could dismiss him if he chose.

The High Master nodded, breathing hard. He knew he was defeated. He lifted his arms and let them fall again by his side. 'Have it your own way,' he said, then added, 'we'll see what the Fellows have to say about this,' and he walked away, Robert Leigh hurrying after him.

All this time the boy's mother had sat with her arms round her son as though to protect him. Now the Warden turned to them. 'What is your name?' he asked.

The boy stared at him, wide-eyed.

'Simeon,' his mother said for him. 'Simeon Peploe.'

'Well, Simeon Peploe,' said the Warden. 'How would you like to start school here on Monday morning?'

Simeon shook his head, still staring.

'He will be here,' his mother said quickly. 'Thank you, sir,' and she caught the Warden's hand and kissed the ring on his finger.

'Well then,' the Warden said, slightly disconcerted, 'that is all. You may go,' and Simeon's mother rose quickly, leading her son out of the church.

8

Dr Dee slept badly and when he woke, Kelly's head was on the pillow next to him.

'Boo,' it said.

With a strangled cry, the Warden leapt from the bed.

'A little nervy, aren't we, John?' the head said.

'Get away from me!' the Warden cried. 'Get out of my room!'

Kelly's form took shape beneath the bedclothes, then he stepped out of the bed fully clothed.

'Why do you haunt me?' the Warden said.

'Just watching over you,' said the spirit. 'Like it says in the prayer, "May angels watch me as I sleep."'

Not angels like you, the Warden thought.

'Did you read the book, John?' the spirit asked, advancing towards his desk.

The Warden pursed his lips. 'I did,' he said, then burst out, 'it was foul – abominable!'

'Didn't you like it?' the spirit said in mock surprise. 'I brought it specially for you.'

The book flew open as the spirit reached for it.

'It is an abomination,' the Warden said, calmer now. 'A most unnatural, cruel and bloody book.'

'Strong words, John,' the spirit said. It pressed a grubby

finger to the page and began to read.

'Aloes, ambergris and storax, mixed with the blood of a goat, mole and bat. Four nails from the coffin of an executed criminal . . .' It looked up. 'Which bits didn't you like?'

The Warden pressed his lips together in a thin line, then he said, 'I did not like any of it and I will not read it again.'

'The horns of a goat, crushed to a fine powder,' the spirit went on as if it hadn't heard. 'The head of a black cat, fed on human flesh for five days . . .'

'*I will not read it!*' Dr Dee said again.

'Then I'll have to read it for you,' the spirit said, before continuing, 'the skull of a parricide . . .'

Dr Dee clamped his hands over his ears.

'Out, out, damned spirit!' he shouted, then to his horror, found that he could hear Kelly's voice inside his own head.

'Now, that's not very friendly,' the spirit said.

Dr Dee's breath trembled. He lowered his hands from his ears.

'Look,' he said. 'What the book speaks of is murder – foul, bloody murder. I cannot do it.'

The spirit's black eyes gleamed. 'Oh, but you can, John,' it said.

'I will not,' said Dr Dee. 'You cannot make me. It is not,' he went on, more beseechingly, 'what I do. You know that, Ned.'

'Ned, is it now?' the spirit said. 'That's better. And it's not what you've done until now.'

'No,' said the Warden, turning his back. The spirit sighed.

'Listen to me, John,' it said. 'We're talking about an orphan here, not someone anyone'd miss. Believe me, some orphan boys'd be better off – sleeping out under hedges till they're blue with cold, covered in sores and rags, never knowing where their next meal's coming from – if there is a next meal. What kind of life's that, eh?'

'Do not equivocate with me,' the Warden said.

The spirit laughed. 'There you go again with your long words. "Equivocate" – what's that? That's what you were good at – words. But there's a time for words and a time for action, John. I want my life back.'

Dr Dee felt as though the spirit's eyes were scorching him. He turned back towards it, taking a long, trembling breath, and felt his hands rise, then fall again helplessly.

'Then take me,' he said, nodding. 'Take me.'

The spirit seemed suddenly to swell to enormous proportions, filling the room, and his clothes flapped about as though in a great wind.

'*I don't want you!*' it roared. *Why would I want a clapped-out old fogey nearly eighty years old and already going senile? Ain't you heard anything I've said?*'

Dr Dee fell to the floor and crouched there trembling. Eventually the roaring noise subsided.

'Get up, John,' the spirit said in its usual tones. 'You'll wear a hole in the floor, dribbling like that.'

Slowly Dr Dee got up, clutching the desk to help him and wiping his eyes, which were watering freely. To his vast relief the spirit had returned to its normal size. It regarded him sorrowfully.

'There shouldn't be no need for things to get nasty,' it said. 'I hope I've made myself plain. What I want is a nice young body to replace the one that got took from me untimely. And healthy too – you can forget what I said about orphans under hedges. I'm not having any rickety old case covered in sores and smallpox. No. This orphan's got to be well nourished and strong, with a bit of a brain in his head.'

Briefly Dr Dee thought of Kit.

'That's what I want,' the spirit continued dreamily. 'My time over again. I want to breathe, John,' it said. 'I want to breathe.'

When the Warden did not answer, it said in a different tone, 'Who knows? If it all goes well, we might try it for you too. The pair of us could go on for all eternity – just you and me, John. Think of what we could learn – think of what we could do! We'd have the wisdom of Solomon – more than that; we'd make Solomon look like the village fool!'

'And lose our immortal souls,' the Warden said. A great weariness filled him. He wanted to sleep.

'Well, we wouldn't need them,' the spirit said. 'Why would we want souls when we could have bodies? Lots of lovely bodies – plump and sweet and young. You can keep your immortal souls,' the spirit said.

Dr Dee felt so tired, desperately tired, his head was almost nodding. It seemed that every time he encountered Kelly's spirit he felt a little more drained.

The spirit gave him a sidelong glance.

'You are a knackered old mule, aren't you?' it said, and Dr Dee was too tired even to take offence. 'I can see I'm wearing you out. And I don't want to do that, not just yet. I'll leave you, shall I? Let you get on with reading this book. And,' it said, suddenly very close, 'mind you do read it, John, eh? Word for word?'

Dr Dee managed to nod.

'That's a good wizard,' the spirit said, and for a moment Dr Dee felt almost as though it had pinched his cheek. 'I'll be back, John,' it said, its voice growing fainter. 'So – just – see – that – you – do,' and on the final syllable, the spirit that was Ned Kelly vanished.

Dr Dee sank down on his bed. He had his duties to attend to, letters to write, it was the day of the school inspection and he had the infernal book to read. But all he wanted to do was sleep. He couldn't even think about what was happening to him or what he might do about it. He lay down on the bed, pulling one edge of the coverlet over his trembling body, and closed his eyes.

9

The Warden dragged all his furniture to the sides of the room and pulled back the woven rug, revealing the great pentacle he had painted himself on the floor. It was inscribed all over with cabalistic letters spelling the names of forty-nine angels, seven in each of the different colours of the spectrum. Round the periphery was the Enochian alphabet, written backwards, and in the very centre were the seven hidden names of God.

'Doing a bit of spring cleaning, are we?' said the spirit in his ear.

Dr Dee ignored this. With trembling hands he fixed the censer so that it swung over the centre of the pentacle and filled it with incense.

'Having a bit of a sort out, John? That's good to see.'

Dr Dee paused, then picked up the phial of holy water. His head swam a little. He had been fasting all day, determined to get it right.

'Now what are you up to?' said the spirit. It was manifesting in the room behind him, but he was determined not to look. He was going to perform the rites of purification and exorcism according to all the secret doctrines he knew, Christian, Egyptian, Hebraic, Enochian. He would rid himself of the spirit or demon, or whatever it was, if it was the last thing he did.

'It won't work, you know,' the spirit said.

Dr Dee turned to the east and sprinkled a little of the holy water. He began to recite the names of the angels.

'Almalicl, Aldaria, Belhaziel, I know, I know,' the spirit said with him, but it stood to one side of the holy water. Dr Dee turned to the north and went on chanting.

The spirit sighed. 'How long's this going to take?' it said. 'Have you read the book?'

Dr Dee closed his eyes. Bright lights swam against his eyelids. He had to keep the full rite in mind and work it without distraction, or the ceremony would fail. He turned to the west, holding the phial out. The spirit nudged his elbow and the phial flew out of his hands. It hit the floor and rolled a little way, spilling drops of the precious water, but it didn't break.

'Oops,' the spirit said. Dr Dee scrabbled on the floor after the phial, picked it up and rose again.

'Jobladi, Jubladace,' he intoned.

'This is no way to treat an old mate,' the spirit said, standing in front of him.

Dr Dee turned away. The room seemed intolerably warm. He could feel sweat breaking out on his forehead beneath the skull cap and on his upper lip. But maybe this was a sign that the rite was working. He shook some drops of water into his palm and made the sign of the cross on himself.

'In the name of the Father,' he said, his voice quavering, 'the Son and –'

'Uncle Tom Cobley and all,' the spirit said, and it laid its hands over Dr Dee's, which were clasped round the phial.

'Now then, John,' it said. 'Give that to me.'

Dr Dee struggled, the sweat pouring freely down his face. He was forgetting the next stage of the rite.

'Get you gone!' he cried, clinging to the phial for all he was worth.

'John, John,' said the spirit, who appeared to be holding on without any effort at all. 'I can't do that.'

'Let go!' Dr Dee cried shrilly. 'Get off me!' and he tugged with a last, supreme effort.

At the same time, the spirit let go. Dr Dee staggered backwards, tripping over the hem of his robe. The glass phial flew across the room and shattered. Dr Dee struggled to his knees. From somewhere he felt a spark of pure rage.

'Begone!' he cried, in a terrible voice that had all its own strength. 'I – will – have – none – of – thee!'

'Tetchy,' the spirit said.

'Get back to whatever sphere of Hell you came from! Bother me no more! Stay in the corrupt grave and let the worms eat thee! Be bound for ever in torment and let all the devils of Hell gnaw thy bowels!'

Still on his knees, the Warden felt a great weight descend round his shoulders. The spirit was riding him, rocking him violently back and forth.

'That's the way, John!' it cried, bending over him. 'Now you're talking!'

Dr Dee gave a great cry and twisted round. He felt his fingers close on the shards of glass from the broken phial. With the last of his strength, he thrust the broken glass directly into the spirit's face.

There was a terrible sound, like the screeching of many demons. The spirit's face changed colour to a dreadful, obscene yellow and there was a foul, putrid smell. Dr Dee fell to the floor and lay choking. There was a buzzing noise in his ears, but for a few, peaceful moments, his mind became entirely blank.

When he opened his eyes again, the room was empty.

Slowly, the Warden got up. There was blood on his hands, and when he wiped his face, there was blood on that too. Where had it come from?

Dr Dee dragged himself over to his chair and rested his head on the cool wood of his desk. The ritual hadn't worked fully. It had not been powerful enough. Or he, John Dee, was not powerful enough. He was worried that the spirit would return.

Eventually, fearfully, he was able to look round the room. It was a mess. It looked – blasted somehow, but at least there was no sign of the dreaded spirit. He had, at whatever cost, expelled him for the moment and that gave him hope. He rubbed his knuckles against his forehead and tried to think clearly. 'Myrrh,' he muttered. He knew he had needed more myrrh for the incense. Then he could try the ritual again and permanently banish the spirit. He would have to get some more myrrh and candles.

Dr Dee did not often go out. He was well aware of the way that people looked at him in the town, with fear or suspicion or loathing. But the apothecary Josiah Fenwick had said that he could get some myrrh from a secret supplier in London. And right now he felt the need to get out of his room.

When he felt that his knees would not give way, he rose and splashed his face with water from the basin, then wiped it with a cloth. There was a little blood, not much. He put on his cloak, then the great hat over his skull cap that would hide any marks on his face, and opened the door, hoping fervently that he would not meet anyone he knew.

The sound of chanting followed him along the corridor, the chanting of the Catechism by the boys:

'Justice demands that sin is punished with the supreme penalty . . .'

He pulled open the heavy door at the entrance to the school and stepped outside into a world filled with a swirling yellow fog, that brushed against the college walls and windows. Dr Dee hadn't noticed any fog descending. The morning had been bright and damp. But now the fog seemed to be growing denser by the minute – he could hardly see the church. It twisted around him, insinuating itself into the folds of his cloak. There was a peculiar smell, like sulphur.

That was nonsense, Dr Dee told himself. He was just shaken by what had happened. He pulled his cloak round him, and for a moment thought he heard footsteps behind, but when he turned suddenly, no one was there.

Market Stead Lane was eerily quiet. Where was everyone? It was a working day, but no one was on the street and he could hear none of the usual noises from the workshops. Even the blacksmith's forge was silent.

Then as he approached the chandler's, Dr Dee thought he could hear a soft tread, *pit-pat, pit-pat*, behind him. He looked over his shoulder and believed for an instant that he could see a shadow, like a great dog, but when he looked again he could see nothing.

But there it was again, in the corner of his vision: a great, black dog. Its eyes glowed as Dr Dee hurried towards the shop door. The blacksmith's dog, he told himself, as he pushed the door open.

It was a relief to be inside the warm shop with its smell of wax and tallow. Two candles burnt on the counter, and behind it was the chandler, an old man with a harelip, who seemed half asleep. He did not look up as Dr Dee approached. The Warden glanced round nervously and there again was the shadow of a dog. He cleared his throat.

'I need six tall candles,' he said, and still without looking up, the old man shuffled into the back room, coughing noisily, and brought out the candles. He wrapped them in brown paper and Dr Dee noticed the warts and calluses on his hands.

'It is very quiet today,' he said, counting the money out, but the old man said nothing.

'Do you see a large, black dog?' he asked, and the old man coughed and spat.

'There's always dogs,' he said.

It was true, Dr Dee thought. There were always dogs on the streets of the town and in the churchyard. He had just been followed by one of them, that was all. He picked up the candles and tucked them into his cloak.

'It's quiet today,' the chandler said.

'What?' said Dr Dee.

'Quiet – on the streets.'

'Oh,' said Dr Dee. 'Yes.' He hesitated, wrapping his cloak around him, then turned to go out, feeling strangely nervous about leaving the shop.

'One will come,' the chandler said.

Dr Dee whipped round. 'What did you say?' he said.

For the first time the chandler raised his eyes. They were obsidian-black.

'*The Son of Darkness cometh,*' he said.

Dr Dee's throat constricted and his mouth felt too

dry to speak. He turned and fled into the street.

The apothecary's shop was at the top end of Market Stead Lane. Dr Dee panted with exertion as he hurried towards it, puffs of steam from his mouth vanished into the thickening fog, and he could hear another panting, snuffling noise that almost but not quite matched his own breath. Great paws padded behind him, but he dared not look round.

The window of the apothecary's shop was lit with lamps. Light from them spilt on to the coloured liquid in glass phials, the bottles filled with lozenges and the decorated pots full of herbs. As a little boy, Dr Dee had loved to look in the windows of apothecaries' shops. He pushed the door open and went inside.

There was a smell of sandalwood and aloes. The apothecary, a round-faced, jocular man, was dusting his shelves and he greeted Dr Dee cheerfully enough.

'One thing you can always be sure of in this world is dust,' he said.

The uneven beating of Dr Dee's heart slowed down.

'Yes, indeed,' he said. The apothecary wiped his hands on his apron.

'What can I do for you?' he said.

Dr Dee was so relieved to be spoken to normally that for a moment he forgot why he was there. He breathed in the warmth and light, the reassuring smells.

'Myrrh,' he said finally. 'I came to ask if my order had come.'

'Indeed it has,' said the apothecary, and he bent down beneath the counter, still talking.

'Now, I've put it here somewhere ...' he said, rummaging around. 'It's not something we get a great call for these days,' he went on, still looking. 'Do you mind if I ask what you're using it for?'

Normally, Dr Dee would not answer a question of this kind, but today was no normal day.

'It's for – the church,' he said.

'Ah, the church,' said the apothecary, who was now scrabbling around on his knees. 'Ashes to ashes, dust to dust, and so on. Sorrowing, bleeding, dying. Well, so long as it's for no unholy purpose,' he said, rising with a package in his hands.

Dr Dee looked straight into the pitch-black eyes of Edward Kelly.

'Not trafficking with demons, are you, John?' Kelly said.

Dr Dee gave a great cry and ran from the shop as fast as a man half his age. All the way down Market Stead Lane he ran, past the gates of the church and across the market square. He could hear the great, black beast loping behind him. He pushed open the heavy college doors and they swung shut behind him with an enormous clang. He stumbled up the stairs to his room, opened the door and leant against it, breathing hard. He did not need to open his eyes to know that Kelly was with him. He licked his lips once, twice.

'All right,' he said, when he could manage to speak. 'All right – I'll do it – whatever you want.'

He thought he heard a low, throaty chuckle.

'That's better, John,' the spirit said.

I O

Send for the boy, the spirit had told him, and now Kit was here, blinking owlishly at the Warden through the fug of smoke, for the Warden had burnt herbs in his room to disguise the terrible smell. Then he had gone to bed feeling unwell and had just got up, since he could not sleep and could not get a grip on his thoughts. He seemed to be looking at Kit down a long tunnel, and when he spoke, even to his own ears his voice seemed strange.

'Come,' he said. 'Let me look at you.'

When the boy reluctantly came closer, the Warden reached out and pressed Kit's chin upwards, looking into the clear, grey eyes, in which he saw, not fear, but uncertainty. After a moment Kit pulled away.

'I have not had much time –' he began.

'Never mind that now,' the Warden said, still in the same, hoarse voice. 'Tell me about yourself.'

'What?' said Kit.

The Warden sat down and indicated that the boy should do the same, but he remained standing. The Warden felt his throat constrict against his will. 'Your parents,' he said.

'My parents are dead, sir,' Kit said stiffly.

Somewhere inside the Warden felt himself observing

what was going on. He asked questions about the boy's background, establishing that he indeed had no family who might enquire about him, that he had been born into a Catholic family, and any property his family had owned was now in trust to the school. Kit answered the questions briefly, looking increasingly bewildered.

'Is that all, sir?' he said.

The Warden felt himself rise and walk round Kit one way, then the other. Involuntarily, it seemed, he lifted a lock of the boy's hair and sniffed.

'Do you know what the Great Rite is, Kit?' he murmured.

Kit backed away.

'I have to go,' he said.

'Oh, not yet,' the Warden's voice said.

Kit made a sudden movement, but the Warden stood in front of him. 'We've not finished yet, Kit' he said.

Sweat broke out on the boy's forehead as the Warden stepped closer to him, smiling.

'It is a ritual that has to be done at a certain time,' he said. 'Preferably at the dark of the moon. Do you know when that is, Kit?'

Suddenly the boy found his voice.

'I don't want to know about rituals! I've had enough! I don't want to come here any more.'

The Warden did not feel angered by this outburst. He felt strangely serene, as if it was all out of his hands. He stepped closer and suddenly he could tell what Kelly knew, that the boy was different and there was some great secret that he bore.

'Is there something you're not telling me, Kit?'

Kit stared at him.

'Some secret sorrow, perhaps,' the Warden murmured. 'A burden you cannot share.'

The boy's hand moved quickly, defensively, to his face.

'I can help you unlock that secret,' the Warden said, and he saw Kit's face change. 'We can work together, Kit. A sorrow shared is a sorrow halved. But you must work with me, Kit. I cannot work alone.'

'Yes,' Kit said, and the Warden could see that he had won. He turned away.

'The dark of the moon is next week,' he said. 'I will send for you and you will come to the church at midnight. Do you understand?'

'Yes,' Kit said again, and the Warden relaxed.

'That is all,' he said, half turning. 'You may go.'

And as the boy hurried away, the Warden felt something in him give. There was a weakness like water in his limbs and he barely made it to the bed before collapsing. He rolled over in the coverlet and lay, gazing at the ceiling. Then he fell into a deep, dreamless sleep.

Someone was calling him. He opened his eyes and stared round the room, bewildered. No one was there. Then he heard the voice again, feebly.

'Doctor,' it called. It was Kit's voice.

The Warden got up, fastening his robe and opened the door.

'Doctor,' Kit called again, more faintly this time, and the Warden could tell that he was at the bottom of the stairs. He hurried down the winding stair, and there was Kit, slumped over the lowest steps.

The Warden's heart thumped loudly in alarm. 'What – ?' he said, almost falling over his robe. Kit tried to raise his head, but it dropped forward, banging on the stone stair. The Warden felt even more alarmed as he hastened towards him.

'What has happened here?' he said, then gasped as he saw the blood.

Kit opened his eyes and groaned as the Warden leant over him. Dr Dee hesitated only for a moment. He was old now, but he had once been strong. He gathered Kit up, staggering slightly, then struggled back up the stairs. He put his weight against the door to open it, then dropped Kit, who slumped to the floor. The Warden sank back against the door, breathing with some difficulty. Then he opened the chest beneath the window, brought out a sheet and spread it on his bed. With a vast effort, he hauled Kit on to it, whereupon the boy lapsed into unconsciousness.

He had been stabbed, the Warden could see that much. He leant against the bedpost for a moment, then went to the boy and began unfastening his shirt.

Beneath Kit's shirt there was already a layer of bandages, tied in a rough knot, with the blood seeping through. The Warden stared at them for a moment, then began unfastening the knot. Kit made a feeble movement of protest.

'Keep still,' the Warden said, and Kit closed his eyes. The Warden pulled at the bandages, moving Kit's body this way and that. The different layers seemed stuck together, and some came off in a great clump, revealing the taut muscles of Kit's back, the prominent ribs and finally, as the Warden let Kit slip back on to his sheet, his shirt falling open, two small, but definitely female breasts.

Shadows

Manchester, Present Day

Kate let herself into the empty house. The emptiness and hollowness settled all around her, like dust. She stood in the hallway, unnerved by the silence.

It was not good for her to be alone, she thought. Her mind was playing tricks on her. She stood for a few seconds more, then went into the kitchen and picked up her father's address book, which he had left on the table.

Sitting down, she checked through every address in the book, but the names and numbers meant nothing to her. There was no one she could reasonably phone, apart from the police. But what would they do when they found out Kate was on her own in the house? Anyhow, her father might come back any minute.

But suppose he didn't come back?

This was the thought she had not allowed herself to think. She stared at her knuckles, thinking it now, and slowly opened her fingers. The nails were all bitten.

Kate stood up abruptly, pushing the chair back. It was mad to think of calling the police, she told herself. No way. She shouldn't even be wasting her time thinking about it. She should be getting her head together and thinking of a plan. She should be searching the house, looking for clues as to where he might have gone. And with any luck, before she'd finished, her father would come wandering back in, because this was all some terrible joke.

His bedroom – she would start with his bedroom. The least she could do was try to work out what he had taken with him, which might tell her how long he planned to be gone.

Kate made her way through the debris in her father's bedroom. As far as she could tell, most of his clothes were still in the wardrobe, which was some comfort, she supposed. She began gathering up the papers and books, looking for something, anything, that would give her a clue.

A file lay open on his bed. She glanced at it, then looked again. This was his book, his thesis into the mysteries of ageing, that he had started when he was still a medical researcher. It had never been published. *Eden Revisited*, it was called.

He had written it years ago, but obviously he had been looking at it again. She sat down on the bed and started to read.

Structural alterations and functional declines in body systems, with a consequent impairment of homeostasis . . .

Kate had no idea what that meant. She tried again.

The effects of ageing are a combination of genetically programmed processes and genetic alterations induced by exogenous and endogenous factors.

Then a bit she did understand.

Ageing might be viewed as the most widespread, late onset genetic disease affecting humans today. But it is not inevitable.

That was her father's research into the possibility of immortality. It had never sounded that attractive to her, but her father had said it was because she was still young.

Memories, impressions, images swarmed and flickered in

her mind. She saw the woman in the blue blanket crossing the square towards her and remembered the sensation like an electric jolt. It had been like watching a different channel on TV. *Or a different time*, she thought.

Kate remembered her father trying to explain to her about time.

'We are four-dimensional beings, Kate,' he had said, 'passing through a universe in which there are many dimensions.'

That was the kind of thing he was always saying – talking to her as if she was his student. Only that time she hadn't wanted to listen.

'Whatever,' she'd said, successfully diverting her father into a lecture about standards of speech. He didn't like her talking in that sloppy way, he'd said. Kate knew it. She did it mainly to irritate him.

But it hadn't worked for long. He had tried to get her to imagine a three-dimensional cone passing through a two-dimensional circle.

'If you were a two-dimensional being, living on that circle,' he had said, 'what would the cone look like? What would you see?'

Kate had given him the look she had perfected over the years, of deliberate obtuseness. She could still smell the drink on him from the previous night. He was talking himself out of his hangover as he had done many times before. She knew what he wanted from her – some sign that she was on the same wavelength as him, that they could communicate, but she wasn't giving it. She held his gaze and eventually he had sighed and picked up a piece of paper and a darning needle from the chair. He folded the paper several times, like a fan.

'Now look,' he'd said, 'suppose time doesn't go in a straight line, but in waves or folds, like this.' He pressed the point of the needle through one fold of the paper. 'If point A is the present moment and point B a moment four hundred years ago,' he'd said, 'then point A is actually nearer to point B,' he pushed the needle through the next fold, 'than to any moment before or since. You see?'

'No,' Kate had said. He had looked at her.

'What do you see?'

'What should I see?' Kate had said. 'A piece of paper, and a needle, innit?'

Her father had sighed, then carried on talking as though to himself.

'But what is it that connects the points?' he'd murmured, pushing the needle slowly through all the folds of the paper. 'Some force, energy or power, capable of bending light and time.'

Kate had felt her mind shutting down. She had stifled a yawn. 'Can I go now?' she'd said. But her father had already forgotten she was there.

That was her father. A genius. For all the good it did him. But for the first time Kate wished she had listened. It might explain something, anything about what was going on.

Tired and defeated, she lay down on her father's bed. Still holding the note he had written to her, she closed her eyes and fell at last into an uneasy sleep. And hours later, she began to dream.

Kate dreamt that she lay in bed in a strange room. There was a candle burning, casting a dim light and shadows. When she looked down, she could see her hand on the coverlet and it was pale, not brown. Someone was speaking to her.

'You could live with me as my daughter,' he said. 'We will tell no one. I will teach you everything I know.'

Revelations

I

October 1604

The Warden expelled a long breath.

'Oh dear, oh dear,' said the spirit, suddenly at his side. The Warden closed his eyes. Automatically he pulled Kit's shirt back across him. Her, he thought.

'This won't do. This won't do at all,' the spirit said.

All at once the Warden pulled himself together. Medical training came with the practice of magic. To most people they were the same thing. He went to a drawer in his desk and took out a packet of herbs.

'This puts a different sauce on the pudding, this does.'

Dr Dee ignored the spirit. He crossed to the window suddenly, flinging it wide. Though it was dark now, he could just make out the figure of the new boy hurrying across the courtyard. He leant out of the window and called him.

'You there!'

Simeon started, then stood absolutely still, as he would in the forest if there was danger.

'Up here,' the Warden called, and Simeon looked all around, without finding the direction of the voice. The Warden muttered a curse.

'Look up, damn you,' he cried, and the boy's eyes widened as he realized who was calling him.

'Come up here,' the Warden called, but Simeon looked as though he would turn and run.

'Your friend is here,' said the Warden, beginning to despair. 'He is badly hurt.'

In a moment Simeon was running up the stairs to the Warden's room. He stopped, aghast at what he saw, then pushed past the Warden to the bed, taking in Kit's pallor and the blood.

'He has been in a fight,' the Warden told him. 'Some schoolboy foolishness, no doubt.'

Simeon stepped back from the bed, still staring at Kit.

'We need water from the kitchen,' the Warden said, then, as Simeon turned to go, he had a sudden thought. 'Wait,' he commanded. Suppressing a sigh he put aside the tapestry that hung across the secret door. How many more people must know about it?

'No one must know,' he said to Simeon, and dumbly the boy shook his head. Dr Dee opened the door. 'Follow the stairway,' he said. 'It will bring you to a grid. Climb out through it and you will find yourself next to the scullery door. Fetch warm water in a basin and a clean cloth. Hurry.'

Simeon disappeared.

'Now what?' said the spirit. The Warden began grinding the herbs with a mortar and pestle.

The spirit began to pace. 'I knew there was something wrong with that boy,' it said. 'He's a girl!'

Dr Dee ground harder, breaking up the tiny leaves.

'I ain't coming back as no girl,' said the spirit. 'No way.'

Dr Dee said nothing, but took out a tin with some fatty substance inside and began mixing a small amount of it into the leaves with his finger.

'Well?' the spirit said.

'Well what?'

The spirit stood very close. 'We can't perform the Great Rite on a girl,' it said. 'It has to be a boy. A young boy.'

Dr Dee licked his lips. The mixture was almost ready. The spirit nudged his elbow. 'Did you hear me?' it said.

'I did.'

'Then – what?'

'Then we will not perform it,' the Warden said.

The spirit's face darkened, but at that moment Simeon reappeared, looking white and scared. He held a basin and cloth, which the Warden took from him.

'Kit – will get well?' he asked the Warden, but Dr Dee only dabbed at the wound with the cloth. It was clean and not too deep. Already the bleeding had slowed down. The Warden applied some of the ointment he had made, then tore the edge of the sheet into strips. As he bound Kit's chest again, he spoke curtly to Simeon.

'Tomorrow is Saturday,' he said. 'You will make some excuse for Kit tonight to the High Master – say he is sick and in his room. In the morning you will tell him that he is at choir practice and you will tell the Choirmaster that he has extra study with the Usher – do you understand?

Simeon nodded, staring.

'Kit will stay here in my room,' the Warden said. 'I do not think the other boys will give you away. We will see how he is by Sunday.'

He handed the bowl and the stained cloth back to Simeon.

'There is blood on the stairs – see if you can wash it out,' he said, opening the main door. 'Then take the bowl back to the kitchen and dispose of the cloth.'

Simeon didn't move.

'Well – go,' the Warden said.

But Simeon remained where he was. 'What is it?' demanded the Warden.

Simeon lifted a finger and pointed to the space beside the Warden. 'Who is that man?' he asked.

2

The Warden stared at Simeon. 'What man?' he asked, in a voice barely above a whisper.

Simeon could only look, appalled, at Kelly.

'Well, well, well,' said the spirit, and the door flew shut.

The Warden recovered himself. 'He is – a healer,' he said slowly. 'I – brought him in – to examine your friend.'

Simeon's expression did not change, but on the spirit's face there was a look of fierce exultation.

'He can see me!' he said.

'Be quiet!' the Warden snapped. He raised a shaking hand to his forehead. All this was too much, he thought, too much. 'You must go,' he said to Simeon.

'What for?' said the spirit.

Simeon didn't move. His gaze travelled slowly towards Kit.

'Your friend will be safe,' the Warden said. 'Go now, before the High Master begins to ask awkward questions.'

'Now wait a minute,' the spirit said. 'What's the rush? Where's the fire? I can't smell no smoke.'

He moved to the door so that he was standing between it and Simeon. The boy began shaking violently.

'Get out of the way,' the Warden said.

'Watch your manners,' said the spirit. 'Maybe our little

friend here can help us in our enterprise.'

'No,' said the Warden.

'No?' said the spirit. 'No what?'

'No, he will not be helping. And there is no enterprise.'

'Now, wait a minute.'

'Leave us,' the Warden said to Simeon.

Simeon looked at the door. The spirit smiled.

Heaving a sigh of absolute exasperation, Dr Dee walked towards the door. After a second's hesitation, he plunged his hand straight through the spirit to the handle of the door. The spirit hissed sharply and buckled. The room itself seemed to buckle momentarily and a look of agony crossed the Warden's face, but he tore the door open. 'Go!' he cried to Simeon.

Simeon stayed where he was, a look of agony on his face. 'Kit,' he whispered.

The Warden stared at him. Beads of sweat stood out on his forehead.

'I will take care of Kit,' he cried. 'Go and sort things out with the Master. Do it for Kit!'

Simeon fled and the door slammed shut behind him.

'Now that wasn't very nice, John,' the spirit said, recovering. It looked twisted with shock. 'What kind of game are you playing?'

'No game,' the Warden said evenly, though he was nursing his hand. 'I am not playing your game any more.'

'Not playing?' the spirit said, and there was an ugly expression on its face. 'We'll see about that.'

'You must leave,' the Warden said. He felt suddenly calm, as though a great mist had cleared from his head.

'I ain't going nowhere,' said the spirit, circling him. 'We've got an agreement, remember?'

'No,' said the Warden. He raised a hand. '*Vade,*' he commanded.

'Now just hold on –'

'*Procul este . . .*'

'You can't do this –'

'*Procul este,*' said the Warden again. He turned round slowly, following the spirit with his outstretched hand. The spirit's face looked contorted.

'John, John,' it said. 'You can't do this to me – to us.'

There was a new note of fear in its voice. The Warden hesitated for a moment and the spirit laughed. 'You can't do it,' it said. 'It's everything you've ever wanted.'

The Warden filled his lungs with air. '*Begone!*' he cried in a great voice.

All at once the room seemed to be spinning and the spirit with it. Round and round it spun, contorting horribly, then changing into the animal forms the Warden had seen before – the lion, the calf and the eagle – and as it changed there was a horrible howling shriek, as of all the souls in Hell.

'You – cannot – do – this!' it shrieked, and the room filled with a greenish, livid light. Dr Dee felt a searing pain in his arm and the spirit vanished. The room settled around him into a vast, calm emptiness.

Dr Dee felt his knees trembling. He made his way to the wooden seat beside his bed and sank down. He fumbled for his handkerchief, then pressed his face into it. Kelly was gone. It was, after all, possible to be free. All he had needed was to know, absolutely, his own mind. But he felt exhausted, drained of all power. He wiped his face with the handkerchief and slowly his breathing settled down.

A moan from the bed disturbed him. Kit was awake

and struggling to sit up. She clutched her side, her fingers exploring the unfamiliar strips of torn sheet that the Warden had used as a bandage. The look of dawning realization on her face changed to fear as she saw where she was. Then her eyes met the Warden's, and she gave a short gasp, sinking back. The Warden regarded her gravely.

'I think,' he said, 'that you have some explaining to do.'

3

Simeon ran into the courtyard and looked round wildly, gasping in clean, cold air. The light had gone and a few flakes of snow were floating down. Simeon had forgotten what he was supposed to do. He set off at a run towards the church, then stopped. He turned and ran instead towards the school, bumping violently into Master Gringold, the Usher.

The Usher gripped his shoulder violently.

'Look where you're going,' he said; 'what is it?'

Simeon looked at him as though he made no sense.

'What's the matter with you?' the Usher said. 'Where's Kit?'

'Kit,' the boy repeated stupidly.

The Usher shook his shoulder. 'Yes, Kit,' he said. 'Is he at supper?'

Slowly Simeon remembered what he was supposed to say. 'Pain in his side,' he stammered, touching his own stomach. 'He's – lying down.'

'In the sick room?'

Simeon nodded.

A look of fear crossed the Usher's face. Once illness started in the school it spread like fire. 'You have been with him?' he said, stepping back, and Simeon nodded again. His teeth chattered.

'Then you should be in your own bed. I will tell the High Master. Go at once!' He turned sharply towards the Great Hall.

Simeon's thoughts were whirling like the flakes of snow. *Kit*, he thought. Kit was his friend and Simeon had left him. He thought of the evil presence, both man and not man, in the Warden's room, and shuddered. He didn't know what to do. He thought about his mother. But that was tomorrow, not today. He would see his mother tomorrow and tell her, and she would know what to do.

4

In the Warden's room, Kit had been silent for a long time and the Warden said nothing. He had listened with his eyes closed and the tips of his fingers pressed together.

'So,' he said eventually, expelling a long breath. 'When your father was executed, before you were born, your mother believed that the only way to hold on to his lands and title was if he had an heir.'

'Yes,' Kit said, in a small, miserable voice.

'They had wanted a son more than anything and when you were born your mother called you Katherine, but soon began calling you Kit. As in Christopher.'

'Yes,' Kit said again.

'Yes,' the Warden murmured. Kit would have been the last of the Morley line; women could not inherit land and property. Or at least, if they did, they were quickly married off to someone who would take it from them. Queen Elizabeth would have seen that the girl was betrothed to someone Protestant and he would have been endowed with the Morley lands. Andrew Morley and his wife were passionate Catholics. They would have lived in hope, as so many did, that the Queen would marry a Catholic so that England would return to the true faith. Or that she would die so that a Catholic monarch could come to the throne.

'Then your mother died . . .'

'Before I was breeched, sir, yes.'

Before they were breeched, at six or thereabouts, girl and boy children were dressed identically.

The Great Hall, belonging to the Morleys, was isolated on the Lancashire moors, and after Andrew Morley's death, Kit's mother never went out. Already impoverished, apart from her home and lands, she had relied on the loyalty of one or two servants. When the Fellows came, they had royal permission to bring up Morley's heir in the Protestant faith.

It was an extraordinary story, extraordinary. The Warden thought of telling it to Oliver Carter, and almost laughed. Kit was the brightest scholar in the school, the one on whom they pinned their hopes.

Let your women keep silence in the churches, he thought. *1 Corinthians 14:34.*

'No one ever knew,' he said aloud.

Kit shrugged, trying to adjust her pillows so that the pain lessened. Until now, she had never been ill or injured. The boys never bathed, nor openly undressed. Kit had managed her changing body in secret, binding her small breasts. She had the muscles of a boy from all the swordplay and archery. She had learnt to sound like one, speaking and singing. It would never have occurred to anyone. Why would it? She could keep her secret indefinitely, go to Oxford, become a lawyer . . .

Except that now she had reached the age when boys' voices were breaking. She had tried, systematically, to lower her voice, but it was not the same. And each month she had another problem. She had managed, tearing an old shirt into cloths, but had begun to feel a resistance to so much deception. She had wanted someone to know and now the Warden did. She leant back, and ran her fingers through her hair, wondering why she didn't feel any better. She felt horribly exposed, as if she had turned into something unnatural beneath the Warden's gaze. But there was nothing further she could do. She closed her eyes.

The Warden looked at Kit. There was nothing female about her. Even the way she lay in bed and ran her fingers through her hair was like a boy, not a young woman. He could envisage no kind of future at all for Kit as a woman. What would the Fellows do if they knew? They would expel her. She could be tried for blasphemy. Or maybe even silenced to avoid the scandal. What they would never do was return her property and wealth. What might Kit hope to do as a young, penniless woman?

'You could work for me,' he said, and Kit opened her eyes. 'You could live with me, as my daughter. We will tell no one. I will teach you everything I know of magic, healing, mathematics, astronomy. That way, after I am gone, you might live and work alone.'

He felt a surge of excitement as he said this. It was what he had always wanted, to pass on his knowledge, so that his work might carry on after him. Kit stared at him appalled. *Live with the Warden?*

It was not what she had expected him to say, but she did not know what she had expected. It was madness, an insane plan, and the Fellows would never allow it.

'We would go away, of course,' the Warden went on. He was not looking at Kit, but at some distant point, as though staring into the future. 'I have a house in Mortlake, where we can work. I will train you as a magician.'

Kit did not want to train as a magician. She shifted

restlessly in the bed, but the Warden ignored her. 'You can help me in my Great Work,' he murmured.

Kit felt a nervous sickness in her stomach. 'But what will the Fellows say?' she asked. 'What will you tell them?'

'I do not know yet,' said the Warden, looking at her at last. 'Are you not curious, about the Great Work?'

Kit shifted again. The discomfort in her side was growing. 'What is it?' she asked.

The Warden rose and began to pace round the room. 'The Great Work,' he said, 'is the pursuit of immortality. That is the ultimate end of all science, alchemy and religion. To live forever.'

Kit thought of her father, who had given up his life for his faith. Then she thought of the heroes she had read about every day: Achilles and Hector, or Arthur and his knights.

'What?' the Warden said, catching the expression on her face.

Kit tried to think clearly. 'That is not a noble aim,' she said at last. 'The hero – must be prepared to sacrifice his life.'

And so they all died, the Warden thought. How many heroes lived beyond thirty?

'We do not live in heroic times,' he said.

Kit did not know what to say to that. She was still grappling with the problem of her future. But the Warden leant forward, gazing at her earnestly.

'You do not want to live with me?' he said.

'I do not know,' said Kit, watching him warily, but he did not seem angry.

'I will treat you well,' he said.

'I know – but –'

'What do you want?'

Kit did not know that, either. She had learnt that she could not have what she wanted, to have known her father, to have carried on living with her mother. She wished that her mother had not died, that she could have had some kind of normal family life. But what was normal life for a girl? To live at home, to be married by Kit's age into another noble family. Kit had spent so long as a boy that she could not begin to imagine life as a girl.

The Warden was waiting for her answer. Kit turned her face away, overcome by the futility of all her wishes.

'I wish,' she said, and paused.

The Warden leant closer.

'Yes?' he said.

Kit sighed. 'I wish I could be born again,' she said, 'into a different life.'

The Warden nodded, looking away from her.

'So do we all,' he said.

5

Simeon began to fear, feverishly, that he would not see his mother again, but tomorrow was Saturday, the day he would meet her by the church gates. He had asked everyone that day, to make sure he got it right, and they had replied with varying degrees of patience that yes, it was Saturday, and yes, there was a half-day free of school. He lay in his narrow bed, and waited for the night to pass.

Somewhere out there, his mother was sleeping. If he closed his eyes, he could feel himself joined to her by an invisible cord. He could match the rhythm of his breathing to hers. The younger boys came in, but he did not stir. Joseph Pryor whimpered in his sleep, but Simeon did not go to him. He had learnt that lesson, at least. He lay in his narrow cot in the room that stank of piss and the breathing of boys, and let his mind fill with the scent of her, the scent of forest and field.

Beyond the chaotic mumble of the boys' dreams in the beds that surrounded him, he could hear the murmur of the town, the barking of a dog, and the lap, lap of the river. He could see the glitter of small fishes breaking water to escape the larger fishes swimming after them; and in the fields beyond the river, mice creeping among the grass, moles working the earth and the night hawks hunting them silently.

He dreamt that his mother was beckoning him into the forest.

'Simeon, wake up,' she said, then something was shaking him.

'Wake up – come on – wake!'

In the darkness, Chubb's face was leaning over him. 'Where is Kit?' he asked. Simeon recoiled, scrambling away from him.

'Where is he?' Chubb repeated.

Kit, Simeon thought, and the events of the previous day flooded back. His heart thudded once and seemed to sink. He stared at Chubb. The older boy's face was not jeering, but worried.

'I will not hurt you,' he said, 'but you must tell me where he is. Is he all right?'

Dumbly, Simeon nodded.

Relief flooded Chubb's face. 'Where is he?'

'The Warden –'

'The Warden?' Chubb stared. 'Not with that Black Wizard?'

Simeon nodded again. He dared not tell Chubb what he had seen – the evil presence that was also there, with Kit. He rubbed his forehead, as though trying to rub the memory from his mind.

'But he is coming back,' Chubb said, 'today?'

Simeon shook his head. 'Tomorrow.'

'But he will be expected today – in church.'

Simeon tried to remember what the Warden had said. Today was Saturday – half-day. They would say their prayers in church and practise for Sunday's service. He had to say that Kit was with the Usher.

He told Chubb this, stumbling over the message. The

293

older boy stared at the wall, thinking hard.

'It will be all right,' he said at last. 'The nurse will come soon. We will say that Kit is better and has already gone to practice.'

Chubb worked out his plan. Sometimes Kit did practise early, alone. He would get the other boys to back up his story. All day they would cover for Kit. They would say he was doing his sword practice, then his Greek.

'But he must come back tomorrow,' Chubb said.

Simeon nodded, yes.

Chubb fumbled with the cuff of his sleeve. 'The Warden – will not hurt him?'

Simeon shook his head, his eyes wide.

Chubb nodded slowly. 'You will see him?'

'I don't know.'

'Yes – go to him. Tell him – tell him I'm sorry.'

Simeon bowed his head. He didn't trust Chubb. When he looked again, the older boy was slipping out of the room.

The rest of the morning passed in a blur. Simeon ate breakfast without tasting it, listening as Chubb explained to the High Master that Kit had already gone to church. He was a much better liar than Simeon and the Master seemed relieved. Then they all went to church for morning prayer, and one by one the boys fell silent as Simeon's voice soared. Then the Choirmaster made him stay behind to practise his solo. He did this in an abstracted way, making several mistakes, and the Choirmaster made him sing it several times.

'*Ave, ave, verum corpus . . .*'

'What ails you today?' he asked. 'All right, that will do. Let us hope it is better tomorrow.'

Simeon could only think of his mother. When he saw her, he would tell her that he was never going back to the school. He would never leave her again. As soon as he was released from practice he ran out of the church. Several women were passing on their way to market, none of them his mother. Simeon stood tense as a spring by the church gates, searching for her face.

6

Marie awoke from a strange, powerful dream. Rosa, Queen of the Gypsies, held out the scarf decorated with many bright coins that she had once given to Marie.

'Marisa,' Rosa said, using the name she had always called her. 'These are the coins of your heart. One for Tobin,' she named her son, 'one for your father, one for your sister . . .' As she spoke she let each coin drop into a glass of water and before it touched the water, each coin turned into a tear, then dissolved. 'One for me,' she added, smiling. 'One for each of the men you have known –' Several coins dropped like tears into the glass. 'This one,' she said, holding up a coin that was dull, like lead, 'is the colour of a man you know now. It is the last coin you will ever spend. Use it well.'

Marie's head ached dully as she woke and tried to shake off her dream. A feeling of dread weighed her down. Black Jack's arm lay across her and she pushed it off. They were lying in the hayloft of one of the new barns on Dean's Gate. Rising to her feet, she shook the straw from her skirt, which was the same one Rosa had given her all those years ago. She raised a hand to her hair, but the scarf with its many coins had long since gone.

She needed money for Simeon, that was all the dream was telling her. But she couldn't help remembering that the people named in the dream were dead. They were all people she had loved, who had died.

But not Simeon, she told herself, fighting down a feeling of panic. Simeon was safe and well at school. Receiving an education that she, Marie, had to pay for.

She'd had a letter from the school. Susan had taken it to the mercer's wife, who had read it for her. Simeon needed money, it said, for books and uniform, quills and sheets. He had to pay a penny each morning for his name to be registered in the book.

Marie's gaze travelled over Black Jack's sleeping form. His jacket and breeches were black, but it was a shabby black, dulled to a soft grey, like lead. There were silver threads in his black hair, and on his belt, next to the short dagger he always carried, there was a leather pouch, full of money. Marie closed her eyes. Almost involuntarily, she moved towards the pouch.

And when she opened her eyes, Black Jack was looking at her. He smiled. 'What are you up to?' he said.

'Nothing,' Marie told him, withdrawing her hand. 'I'm going to work.'

'So soon?'

'Not soon enough,' she said, with a forced lightness in her voice. 'I'm late.'

Black Jack sat up, dusting himself off. 'Suit yourself,' he said.

Marie turned to go. She had sworn she would never ask this man for help, yet some impulse made her say, 'I need money,' in a low voice.

'Oh aye,' Black Jack said. 'We all do.'

'No,' Marie said, turning back to him. 'I need money for Simeon.'

He stood up, straightening his doublet. 'Best get to work, then,' he said.

'Jack,' she said softly, 'if you could see your way to lending me some ...'

Black Jack's eyes turned canny. 'What would I do that for?' he asked. He slapped her backside. 'A pretty woman like you can always earn money,' he said, winking.

'But Simeon needs money now, for the school,' Marie persisted. 'For books and clothes –'

Black Jack stood behind her and put his arm round her.

'Why don't you come away with me?' he said. 'We could go travelling – anywhere you like. You wouldn't need money ever again.'

Marie shook her head. 'Simeon –' she began.

'Forget the lad,' Black Jack said. 'He's old enough to take care of himself.'

He kissed the back of her neck, but Marie twisted away. 'I cannot leave him,' she said. 'All I need is a little money, until I get paid.'

'If I gave money to every pretty lass who asked me,' Black Jack said, 'I wouldn't have any left now, would I?'

Marie's face hardened. Then she turned and kissed him suddenly. Black Jack kissed her back and she bit his lip. He laughed, and kissed her again, hungrily. They stood together for a long moment, then she pulled away.

'I must go to work,' she said, descending the ladder rapidly.

Black Jack watched her, smiling. Then he turned to pick up his sword. Only as he fitted it back into his belt did he realize that the leather pouch had gone. His face darkened and he swore under his breath. He swung himself down the ladder and ran to the door of the barn, looking along the street. But she had already gone.

7

Marie called at the Wagon Inn to say that she had finished her work there, and would not be returning. With a great show of unwillingness, the landlord counted out coins into her hand.

Marie looked at him.

'That's all,' he said. 'Think yourself lucky. I don't pay my serving maids to let me down.'

Marie bit her lip. It was on the tip of her tongue to utter the curse she had learnt from Rosa long ago.

'Well, go on, then, be off with you,' the landlord said. He turned away and reluctantly Marie left. She looked fearfully along the street before stepping out and the anxiety in her stomach tightened to a knot of dread. She should never have taken Black Jack's purse, he would come after her for sure. She would have to disappear from the town. But she had promised Simeon that she would never leave him. And she had to get the money to him.

She wrapped her blanket round her in the freezing drizzle that was turning to sleet. It was Saturday and she had said that she would meet Simeon by the church gates. She would have to make him see that she had to leave, just for a little while. Her face ached with worry. He would never understand.

She walked past wagoners unloading barrels on Long Millgate, boys playing knucklebones in the street. It was the noisiest part of the day, with people coming to and from the market, dogs barking, donkeys braying, and already there were drunken men reeling home singing. Marie dodged and weaved, wrapped in her thoughts, on her way to the market to buy some food for herself and Simeon.

She should never have got involved with Black Jack in the first place, but he was a persistent man, not used to being refused. And something about him reminded her of Tobin. It was not in the features or the colouring, but in a look, once in a while, and in his recklessness. Tobin had been only fifteen when he died. She had sometimes wondered whether he would have been like Black Jack if he had grown up.

But it was only a fugitive resemblance. Something in Black Jack had turned corrupt, like browning fruit, and then hardened. He had boasted to her that he would slash one man's cattle, then be paid by that man to slash another man's cattle in turn. She had told him she thought it a poor way to earn a living.

'As good as any,' he had said.

Now she had taken his purse and could not go back to the inn. She had made everything a hundred times worse. Briefly she wondered what he would do if she took it back to him. She held the blanket tightly, shivering as the wind cut into her. It was unseasonably cold.

In the market square she stopped short. Someone had pinned a notice to the whipping post. She couldn't read it, but she could make out the sign for ten guineas. She stopped a wagoner who had pulled up his cart.

'What does it say?' she asked.

'That?' he replied. 'It's only a notice about some criminal.'

'"REWARD: ten golden guineas for information leading to the capture of the notorious villain, Black Jack of Ancoats,"' he read, then looked at her closely.

'Why – do you know him?'

Marie licked her lips, which were very dry.

'No,' she said.

'Because if you do and you don't tell the Beadle, you'll be whipped yourself. Have your ears docked.'

He made a slashing movement to the side of her face, then flicked at the horse with the reins and moved slowly away, pulling up his collar against the sleet. Marie stood for a while, staring at the notice. She knew where Black Jack would be that evening. He would be visiting Ralph Hulme's cattle again. She did not like what he did, but to turn him in was a terrible thing. And yet, it would solve all her problems. It would stop him coming after her, which would mean that she could stay with Simeon. And ten guineas would pay Simeon's debts to the school for as long as he stayed there.

She could not do it, she told herself, and turned to go. Yet she had only taken a few steps across the square when she turned back and, pulling the notice from the post, hurried towards the Beadle's house on Long Millgate.

Almost as she reached it, she was grabbed from behind. A hand clamped over her mouth and she was pushed into an alleyway.

'My money, sweetheart,' Black Jack said. He twisted her wrist and the notice fell from her hand.

'What's this?' he said.

Marie couldn't speak as he snatched up the notice and

read it. The tip of his sword pricked her so that she fell back against a wall.

'Well, well, well,' he said. He looked towards the Beadle's house, which was only a few yards away.

'Would you betray me, Witch?' he said softly.

'No!' said Marie. 'I took it down.'

Black Jack looked at her through narrowed eyes, then seized her hair and pulled her along the alley. It ended in a little courtyard, surrounded on each side with tumbledown buildings.

'I do not have your money,' she cried, 'but I will pay you back!'

'The lady says she will pay,' Black Jack said. He yanked her head backwards so that she was staring up at him. 'The last man who stole money from me,' he murmured, 'I slit open from his throat to his crotch. But you are a woman,' he went on, winding a strand of her hair round his finger. 'What should I do with you?'

Marie looked straight into his eyes. 'Let me go,' she whispered.

'Can't do that,' Black Jack replied. He dragged her again to the other side of the courtyard, to a rough path that ended in bushes. Marie felt a pulse hammering softly in her forehead.

'Jack,' she said, managing a smile. 'I would not be false to you. We are good together, you and I . . .'

Black Jack's eyes hardened, but behind them there was something else. She spoke to this.

'Simeon —' she began, but his eyes flared savagely.

'You took my money to keep your halfwit son in school!' he shouted in her face. 'Didn't you! Didn't you!'

He seemed beside himself, spittle flying from his mouth.

Marie stared at him, at this man she hardly knew, and suddenly she saw Rosa's face, mouthing at her silently. *It is come*, she thought.

'What are you staring at, Witch?' Black Jack demanded, and he drew his arm back. The next moment, Marie felt a terrible pain in her side.

'Jack,' she said.

'No man cheats me, Mistress,' he said, calm again. 'Nor woman neither.'

He tugged his sword free and Marie stumbled to her knees, retching. Black Jack stepped forward, thrusting the sword in again, and a third time. Marie lifted a hand towards him, but all she could hear were his footsteps retreating.

In her eyes there was a gathering darkness. It gathered until there was only a point of light at the end of what seemed like a long tunnel. At the end of the tunnel there was Simeon, an infant just learning to walk.

'Come to me, Simeon,' she called, and he stumbled forward in a tottering run, the look of anxiety on his face changing to pride as he fell into her arms. Marie could smell him, damp and warm in the summer rain, the fine baby hair barely covering his scalp. In that moment she knew that the finest thing in her life had been loving him; the greatest gift was being able to see, even for an instant, the world through his astonishing eyes.

Voices

Manchester, Present Day

Kate woke into darkness and did not know where she was. Slowly she adjusted. She had fallen asleep in her father's room. She was freezing, though she still had all her clothes on. What time is it? she thought; then she remembered. *Dad?* She looked at the clock – 7 a.m. Surely she couldn't have slept that long?

She sneezed as she got out of bed, and her eyes started to run. She began switching on lights: in the bedroom, on the landing. 'Dad?' she called. 'Dad?'

No answer. Her heart gave a hollow thud and her stomach twisted as she went from room to room. Where was he?

She went into the kitchen and gazed at the mess. In a short while she would be due at the cathedral.

Kate groaned aloud. She didn't want to go to the cathedral at all. But she couldn't afford to miss a session and be reported. She had to carry on as normal.

Her stomach felt funny. Maybe she could go to the phonebox and call Babs, tell her she wasn't feeling too well. But if she did that, Babs might come round to see how she was.

There was a pile of clothes in the basket by the washing machine. She should put a wash on – none of her clothes were clean. But distracted, she made herself a cup of tea first and sat at the table, reading her father's note again.

What was she supposed to do?

Babs wouldn't be in any doubt. She would have phoned the police by now. If he didn't come back, Kate would have to tell them sometime. And they would want to know when he had first disappeared. She should tell them now. She stared round at the untidy kitchen. Perhaps she should clear it up first. Then it would look less like she wasn't coping.

Kate started to pull the clothes from the wash basket. The washing machine wasn't working properly – it made a huge racket because the bearings had gone and she had to stand by it to make sure that it didn't get stuck on the rinse cycle. She began to load it, automatically going through the pockets in the clothing. She pulled out a few coins and tissues, an old bus ticket and a pen from her father's trousers. No clues there. She started the washing machine and stuck two slices of bread under the grill.

While she was waiting, the sun rose, huge and brilliant, showing up the stains on the window. Kate glanced outside. All the cars were frosted over. Ali from the shop was scraping the frost off his windscreen. She went into the lounge. Despite the sun it was freezing since the gas had been cut off. It was supposed to be switched back on when her father paid the bill. But he hadn't paid the bill yet, and if he carried on drinking, the electric would be next.

The lounge needed hoovering. That was one of the things she had meant to do this half-term – get to grips with the housework. But now she had to spend all her time at this stupid project.

There was a photo of her father on the bureau, receiving a sponsorship award for his research. *What happened to all that money, eh, Dad?* Kate thought bitterly. Her father looked so pleased and proud. She stared at the photo for a moment, then went to the bureau and opened it.

The usual clutter fell out – old bills, newspaper clippings, receipts. They didn't tell her anything. But at the back of the bureau there was a locked compartment, where he stored stuff that he didn't want her to see. She opened all the drawers, looking for the key, and was only interrupted by the smell of burning toast.

Kate munched the toast anyway, then kicked the washing machine to start it again. She began to shift the greasy pots in the sink and had to unblock the plughole. She got so distracted by the housework that she lost track of time and swore softly when the bells of St George's struck nine. Now she would be late again. She stuck her feet in her trainers, zipped up her jacket and opened the door to a blast of freezing air.

The cathedral was busy. Some volunteers were showing visitors around. She made her way towards where Karin was standing, but was blocked by a group of visitors standing to the left of the choir screen.

'Nobody knows how old it is,' the volunteer was saying. 'Some people date it from the eighth century, when a much smaller church stood on this site. The lettering is Anglo-Saxon. The words mean "Into thy hands, O Lord, I commend my spirit."'

Kate peered over the shoulders of the woman in front of her. She was looking at an oblong stone, covered by a glass panel.

'It's always been known as the Angel Stone,' the man said, and Kate could see that there was a rough carving of an angel on the stone. 'Originally it would have been over the entrance to the church, then, when the church was rebuilt, it was placed here, over the crypt. It survived the loss of the old church and bombing of the later building. Some say that while the Angel Stone is here, the church will always be protected. Even the Second World War didn't totally destroy the building.'

The group moved on and Kate walked slowly up to the stone. The bottom edge of it had crumbled away and the sculpting itself was blunted by age, so that the head of the angel was misshapen and it was not possible to see any features. But the figure seemed to be sideways on, possibly kneeling, its wings jutting out at odd angles. It held a scroll, almost as big as itself, and the lettering on the scroll looked like runes.

Kate pressed her hand against the glass panel. The figure was small enough for her to cover it with her open hand.

'What you doing, you?' said Babs, behind her. Abruptly Kate dropped her hand.

'Nothing,' she said.

'Well, you're late and you should be doing something,' Babs said. 'We've all been given our parts. I'm going to sing a solo!'

Kate followed Babs across the nave to Karin.

'Ah, the late Miss Morley,' Karin said. 'Good of you to join us.'

Kate said nothing, but tried to slouch behind Babs and Nolly, which wasn't easy, since she was a good six inches taller.

'I'm afraid you've got some catching up to do,' Karin said. 'You've actually missed quite a lot.'

She paused and Kate knew she was waiting for an apology. 'Yeah, well,' she mumbled.

'Sorry?' said Karin, cupping her ear. 'What was that?'

'I said I'm here now, innit?'

For a moment Karin's pleasant face changed and Kate thought she was going to lose it right there in front of them all. Then she drew a breath and gave them a lecture on the importance of timekeeping.

'And I don't know why you find it so amusing, Lee Kenyon,' she said. 'You were late as well.'

'Lee's always late, Miss,' one of his friends piped up. 'It's that bed-wetting problem.'

There was general amusement and Karin held up her hand.

'All right, all right,' she said. 'Everybody get into their groups, please.'

'Kate?' said Danny, as she hung back. 'Are you with us?'

She stared at him.

'We're nearly ready to film,' he said. 'I'm just going to show you how the lighting works.'

Kate followed her group to the back of the church, where Danny showed them the control panel that worked all the lights of the cathedral.

'We've rigged up some studio lights so that they can be operated from here as well,' he said. They followed him back up the aisle where there was a stone slab with a ring in it in the floor in front of the Angel Stone.

'And this,' he said, 'is where we'll be doing our filming.'

He knelt down and tugged, and the stone slab moved. Everyone clustered round.

'Manchester doesn't have a proper crypt any more,' he said. 'The original passages were built by the Romans, but because of flooding they fell into disuse, or were bricked up. At one time there would have been an extensive crypt for all the rich families who were buried here. But now we only have access to part of it. You can see steps leading down and the remains of a tomb. The rest of it's been walled off.'

He shone a torch into the open crypt. Everyone could see a kind of scaffolding down there, rigged with lights.

'Creepy,' muttered Nolly,.

'You've got to be joking,' Danielle said.

'Is this a horror film, then?' asked Stefan.

'In a way,' said Danny. 'I thought we could call it *Voices from the Crypt*.'

Everyone laughed except Kate. She felt a strange reluctance to go down into the small stone room.

'Come on, you,' Babs said, tugging her down.

'The main point about the crypt,' Danny said, 'is that there's no natural light. So it's perfect for studio lighting. I want the effect of people talking from their own time, in candlelight, with just the stone walls as background.'

Two of the lights stood on tripods and could be wheeled around. They were floodlights, one blue and one white, and both dazzling. Danny said they were about 10,000 watts each.

'Obviously, we're not going to use them at full strength,' he said, 'or we'll all be blinded,' and he showed them the long cable that connected the lights to the computerized panel to one side of the church. They left the crypt and practised turning the lights on and dimming them. There was a key light to be focused on the subject's face and a backlight for atmosphere. These could be operated from the crypt itself.

'Now for the sound,' he said.

Back in the crypt, there was a digital recorder and a couple of microphones. These were plugged into a mixer about the size of a large radio, and the mixer had five grooves on the front with switches that could be moved up and down. Danny showed them how to position the microphones to minimize extra sounds, and how to move the switches, so that no one sound predominated over the others. He handed Kate a pair of headphones. Kate put them on and heard a rushing, clinking noise.

'Hear that?' Danny said. 'That's called ambient sound.'

He pressed a button and his voice spoke from the machine. 'Ambient sound,' it said.

'I'll be showing you how to get rid of that later,' he said. 'Stefan and Lorna can have a go at working the lights, Danielle and Nolly are on sound. Kate, why don't you try filming?'

He held out the camcorder to Kate and showed her where to look.

'Now just keep it tilted, so,' he said. 'Keep your finger here.'

Babs beamed into the camera at Kate. Then she draped herself in a shawl that covered her hair and shoulders. Danny adjusted the lens for Kate and the microphone in front of Babs.

'Babs is going to read a script that is based on the diary of a man called Martyn Rigby,' he told them all. 'Martyn was a tanner by trade and he managed to escape from the town at the height of the plague. He returned, years later, to take over his master's business, and later still he wrote an account in his diary of what happened in that fateful year. He tells us he only learnt to write in his fortieth year, when one of his sons went to school. This is not his story, so much as a dramatized account of what happened to someone he knew.'

He adjusted the microphone again, then went up the steps to give Stefan the signal for the lights.

This was Babs's moment. She arranged herself gracefully on the stool and Kate stood in front of her, holding the camera.

'Ready?' said Danny from the top step. 'Go.'

A floodlight shone directly on to Babs's face and she began to speak.

'"My name is Susan Barlow," she said. "I work at one of the inns on Long Millgate . . ."'

Danny guided Kate round to one side, then the other of Babs, as she told the story of how Susan had been promised in marriage to a man who had not yet finished his apprenticeship, and whose master was too mean to let him marry. Then, when the first cases of plague had been diagnosed, early in 1605, all the inns and shops had shut and the market had closed down.

'"The rich left fast, like rats from a sinking ship,"' Babs said. '"Then word came from the King that the rest of us could not leave and a guard was posted round all the exits of the town. You couldn't buy food anywhere. No malt for brewing, no salt for preserving. And the Lord's oven closed down so that no one could bake bread. People were starving in their own homes. There was rioting in the streets and the shops were looted. Gangs of men captured the cattle of those that had left, and slaughtered them, distributing the meat to those that had none, and making great smoking pyres of the bodies in the abandoned gardens. They moved into the houses of the rich and slept in their beds and drank wine from golden goblets.

'"Everyone blamed the Warden,"' Babs said, staring into the camera at Kate. '"For the Warden of this parish was a notorious Black Magician called Dr Dee, who had left the town early, and people said he'd known what was coming.

Some even said he'd brought it on the town by magic. And they broke into his room in the college and burnt everything they could find there: all his books and fine cloths and his tapestry – thousands of pounds' worth, they said. But what use was money to us now?

'"All that spring the rains fell, until the river burst its banks and streamed into the streets of the town and the half-built houses on the bank were washed away. Crops rotted in the fields and the graveyard was covered by the streaming brown tide. The dead were piled into a common grave in Angel Meadow, but as more and more rain fell, churning the earth, the black and bloated bodies rose to the surface and bobbed about in the mud. Then Oliver Carter gave orders for a new pit to be dug on higher ground and quicklime poured in to dissolve the bodies. Everyone who was infected was left in cabins on Collyhurst Common to die.

'"One morning Martyn came to me, and said his master had fled, and he was no longer bound to him. We could escape as well, through the old tunnels, he told me, for he had found a way that was only partly flooded. He would come for me that night, he said. We would be married in the church in his mother's village.

'"At last, I thought. But later that day, I started to feel unwell and feverish. *Just a cold coming on*, I told myself. Then I felt the lump, under my right armpit.

'"I sat on the bed in my room and stared at the wall. Out there, the sky was blue and the birds chittering in the trees, or scratching about for food. *Not much of a life*, I thought, *but all we have*.

'"When Martyn came, I wouldn't open the door.

'"*Martyn*, I said through it, *I can't go with you. I'm staying here*.

'"Martyn argued, of course. He said I'd been on at him for three years to get married. In the end I had to open the door a little so that he could see me, and his face changed.

'"*Don't touch me*, I said, thinking that he would try to hold me. *Not now, eh? Best not.*

'"I managed a smile, but he stepped back in horror.

'"*Susan*, he said, then I watched him as he turned and ran."'

'Blue light, Stefan,' Danny called, and there was complete silence as the blue light shone eerily on to Babs's face. Kate lowered the camera, and Danny said, 'Well, I think that's going to be really effective.'

Babs bounced up from her stool 'Can we see it?' she said.

They all crowded round the monitor, to see how the film had turned out. Danny knew what he was doing. The backlight created shadows round Babs's head, just as though she was speaking by candlelight, then the blue light changed her features and the colour of her flesh.

'I look – dead,' Babs said, and Danny said that was the idea.

'All these people died of the plague, remember,' he told them. 'Now, we'll record the song for the soundtrack and I'll show you how to get rid of the ambient sound.'

He moved the microphone even closer to Babs and she began to sing.

'I'll sing you one-oh,

'Green grow the rushes-oh.'

Babs had a good, husky voice, and the acoustics were excellent. The tune sounded wistful and haunting. The anxious, eerie feeling that had disappeared when Kate was concentrating on filming Babs, returned powerfully as she sang.

When she had finished Danny showed them how an extra microphone got rid of the ambient sound in a process he called 'phase reversal' and they listened to the song again, without background noise.

'How did I do?' Babs whispered and Kate stuck her thumb up.

'Now we've got to edit one or two bits,' he said to Babs, 'and add more of the soundtrack. Tomorrow we'll do some more filming. But that about wraps it up for today. Good work.'

Released at last, Kate hurried up the steps.

'It's going to look fantastic!' Babs said, catching up with her. 'I can't wait!'

'It's going to look fantastic,' Lorna said, walking past with Danielle. 'She can't wait.'

'Hey, Lorna,' Babs said. 'How d'you get your make-up on that thick?'

Kate smiled to herself as they left the cathedral.

'You look terrible,' Babs said.

'Thanks,' said Kate.

'You sure you're not coming down with something?'

Kate sniffed. She did seem to have a cold.

'I didn't sleep too well,' she said. Babs took her arm and for once Kate didn't shake it off.

'You got to take care of yourself, girl,' she said. 'Why don't you come round to my place?'

Kate hesitated. 'Don't know,' she said. 'I've got stuff to do.'

'What stuff?'

Waiting for my father to come home, Kate thought.

'You never come round any more,' Babs said.

It was true, Kate thought. And she never invited Babs round

either. Seemed like her life had just got too complicated.

'You coming to the shops?' Babs said, as people filtered past them.

Kate shook her head. She didn't have any money for shopping. They walked towards the grassed area that led to Victoria Station.

In 1605, Karin had said, Manchester was little bigger than this. There had been a marketplace, and courthouse, and the street running alongside the college, Long Millgate, had been full of inns. Now the area was landscaped, with stone benches leading down to the fountain, where jets of water rose unevenly in a row. There was a couple entwined on one stone slab, a group of students drinking beer on another and a mother giving her son a sandwich on a third. The sun was low on the horizon and dazzling. The light had that pristine, rinsed quality that made solid objects appear unreal. Kate squinted into it . . . and saw the woman, wrapped in her blue blanket, hurrying past the sign that read *Long Millgate*.

'*Hoy!*' Kate cried and began to sprint after the woman, bounding over one of the stone slabs, to the surprise of the couple entwined on it.

'Wait for me!' Babs called behind her, but Kate didn't stop. Then just as she reached the sign, with the woman still ahead of her, it was as if the whole scene had been suddenly snuffed out –

Kate stared round wildly at the printworks and Urbis and ahead towards Victoria Station, but the woman had gone.

'What's going on?' panted Babs as she finally caught up.

'Did you see that woman?' asked Kate, squinting again in the glare of the sun.

'Well, there's about a thousand women here,' Babs said crossly. 'Could you be a bit more specific?'

'She had a blue blanket wrapped round her,' Kate said. 'Long red hair . . .'

Her voice trailed off as she realized Babs didn't have a clue what she was talking about. *Maybe I'm going mad*, she thought, and a little pulse began hammering in her throat.

'Sounds like a homeless person,' Babs said. 'No need to go haring off like Paula Radcliffe.'

Kate didn't say anything, but pushed her hair back with her fingers. She was remembering that all round the woman it had not been sunny, but dark. She could have sworn she had seen flakes of snow.

'You're such a cliché, girl,' Babs said, taking her arm. 'People always expect black girls to be able to run.'

This was a sore point with Babs, who couldn't see why anyone would want to.

'What about you, J-Lo?' Kate said automatically.

'Jamelia, if you don't mind,' said Babs, steering her back towards the shops of the Triangle. They sparred in the old manner, all the way back to Kate's bus stop, where it looked as though Babs might follow her home. But Kate put her off by promising to shop with her the next day. Then the bus arrived and Kate got on it, and as soon as Babs disappeared, all her anxiety returned.

Why did she keep seeing the woman, she thought as the bus pulled away, and who was she, anyway?

The Dark of the Moon

I

October 1604

Simeon was very cold. The cold bit through his woollen clothes and hurt his chest when he breathed. It made his nose run. He did not know what to do. The only other place his mother might go was to the market for supplies. He hesitated, hopping from one foot to the other in anxiety, then hurried along Smithy Door to the market square. It was thronged with women, none of them his mother. The wind whipped their long skirts. Simeon stood by the water pump and waited.

The minstrels came and performed the song that his mother had sung in the inn.

'I'll sing you one-oh,

'Green grow the rushes-oh.'

The song reminded him so sharply of his mother that tears gathered in his eyes.

A row broke out between two people who were haggling for cloth, and in no time at all they were fighting and Simeon had to jump back. He began approaching those who came to draw water.

'Have you seen my mother?' he asked, but most looked at him blankly, as though he had lost his mind. As the light started to fade, the guard at the pump told him to clear off. The Beadle came by, ringing his bell, and Simeon backed away. He began to run, not knowing clearly where he was going. He passed the church gates again, but no one was waiting. Then, despite what his mother had told him, he ran to the inn where she now worked, but a rough man told him she was no longer employed there.

'And good riddance!' he said.

Without another word, Simeon turned and ran all the way to the wash house. He couldn't see Susan at first, for all the steam. Then he saw her, her arms pink and naked, plunged up above her elbows in a big tub. She caught sight of him and stepped forward, wiping her hands on her apron.

'Simeon!' she cried, catching hold of his hands. 'You've grown already! And you're frozen through!'

Simeon couldn't speak for the chattering of his teeth. 'M–M–Mother,' he stuttered.

'She's not here,' Susan said. Then seeing the look on his face, she added, 'but I dare say she will be soon. Come in and get warm.'

Simeon followed Susan to the fire. 'Well?' she said, sitting him down on a bench.

'Do you like school?'

'No,' Simeon said. 'It's horrible!'

'What, and you've only been there a week?' Susan said.

Simeon tried to remember all the horrible things about it, but he had already forgotten. He could only think that he was warm now, in this crowded, steamy room with the piles of clean washing, and that his mother would be there soon. Susan fussed round Simeon, taking the wet jerkin from him and bringing him a blanket from the pile that awaited washing.

Mistress Lowther passed and gave them a look.

'He'll be on his way in a minute, all right?' Susan said. Mistress Lowther, a hatchet-faced woman in an enormous apron, with arms so huge that the mottled flesh hung over the elbows, looked as if it was anything but all right, but Susan ignored her. She chattered to Simeon in the old, cheerful way, and when Mistress Lowther left the room, she brought him a bowl of soup.

'I've heard from Mistress Butterworth and she's doing fine. She expects to be back after Christmas, and the inn'll reopen – things'll be back to normal at last. Your mother can stop working at that dive – the landlord runs a den of thieves, they say.'

'She's not there,' Simeon said, and he told her what the man had said. Susan seemed taken aback by this, but soon recovered.

'Well, that'll be what's happened, then,' she said. 'If she's lost her job there, she'll have had to get another one – and maybe she couldn't get off work.'

Simeon didn't look convinced. 'She said she'd meet me,' he protested.

'Well, but you know what some folks are like,' said Susan. 'Mean as flint. Wouldn't give you the skin off the milk. If she's got a new job, she wouldn't get time off to see you. She'll have had to work.'

'She didn't tell me,' Simeon said. He felt like lead, weighed down with misery. The soup tasted of nothing in his mouth and he pushed the bowl away.

'Happen she's not had chance,' said Susan, pushing it back.

'But she comes here?' Simeon said, looking round as if he expected to see her emerging suddenly from the steam.

'Well, only when she can,' Susan said, and paused. She

didn't like to tell Simeon that lately his mother had been staying with Black Jack. 'But she'll most likely call in today – I know she will. And when she does, I'll say, "Where've you been, Madam?" I'll say. "Leaving your big, handsome lad out waiting for you in the cold. And him so fine now, in his school clothes, and doing so well – like a real gentleman!"'

Susan babbled on, and slowly Simeon began to feel better. Warmth from the fire and the soup seeped into his flesh. His mother must have found some other work quickly; she would not have been able to let him know. But she would be at church tomorrow. Everyone had to go to church. He looked up.

'I sing the solo tomorrow,' he said.

'Well, there you are, then,' said Susan. 'She'll not miss that – not for a barrelful of monkeys. What – miss her boy singing? Never!' Susan cried. 'She'll be that proud!'

Simeon hung on to what Susan said. He would see his mother tomorrow. She would be there to hear him sing.

Susan talked on, folding sheets. Mistress Butterworth's niece had just given birth to three baby boys. 'Triplets!' she said. 'Three babies all at once! Think of that!'

He helped her to stretch out the washing on a long beam that hung over the fire, and then yawned hugely.

'You must be worn out,' Susan said. 'And here's me babbling on. You need a good night's rest, you do. Big day tomorrow.'

When Simeon didn't move, she handed him his jerkin.

'You get back to the school now. You'll see your mother in the morning.'

Simeon looked at her with eyes full of doubt. 'She will be there?'

'Of course she will,' said Susan, fastening the jacket. 'And if she's not, I'll come with you myself and find her. There! That's a promise.'

Simeon started to leave.

'Here, take this with you,' Susan said, and she pressed a little sugared cake into his hands. 'You make sure you sing your heart out for her tomorrow.'

'Yes,' said Simeon, and stood still, looking into her face.

'Now, where are you going?'

'To school.'

'That's a good boy. Go straight back, mind.'

Susan waved after him as he left, a look of anxiety replacing the cheerful look she had assumed for him. She dared not tell him the thought that had crossed her mind, that his mother had run off somewhere with Black Jack. *She wouldn't,* she told herself as she went back into the wash house. *Surely not.* Marie loved her boy, that much Susan knew. And Simeon would never survive without her.

Susan dropped a neat pile of white linen on to the table. She would start asking about Black Jack, she thought. She would go to the inns after work and ask if anyone knew where he was.

Simeon passed by the church gates twice, still hoping that by some wild chance his mother would be there. *Simeon,* she would say, reproachfully, and he would fall upon her neck and bury his face in her hair.

He crossed the market square again, but it was empty now, and sleet had turned the remains of vegetables and meat to a slippery slush. He walked slowly back to the gates, then down the steep banks of the river, watching the birds fly over it like arrows from a crossbow.

Simeon watched them, mesmerized. Across the river,

the sky looked like the butter his mother churned for the alehouse. His breath came out like steam in the wash house. He could hardly bear the thought of going back to the school, but eventually, mindful of his promise to Susan, he turned away.

His steps dragged. He was afraid to listen to the knocking of his heart. He would see his mother tomorrow, he told himself. Susan said. But as he passed the church gates one more time, he felt a terrific pang and he stood still, letting others push past or round him. His own heart pounding, he listened for his mother's heart, but all he could hear was silence. He lifted his hand in the direction of that silence, as though following a thread, then slowly, hesitantly, began to walk towards Long Millgate.

Dr Dee sat in the church. He had come here to think, leaving Kit asleep in his room. In the morning, the Sunday services would begin, but for now he was here, alone.

He preferred the church when it was empty. It was cool and dark, and even though it was empty he could smell the peasants who gathered there, a smell of horse piss and rain and rotted straw. Rain fell through the roof with a steady, persistent sound that rose in echo like a flapping wing, for it was one of the many complaints made against him, that he did not attend to the repairs of the church.

Dr Dee shivered in the draught from the windows. His chest hurt, and he had coughed so much while trying to sleep in his chair, in spite of the sage leaves from the apothecary that he had brewed into a tea, that eventually he had got up, without disturbing Kit, and locked the door behind him.

His bones ached. Four winters ago, when the weather

was particularly harsh, he had caught a terrible cold that he had thought would kill him. He did not know if he could withstand another one. He was four winters older and more fragile. Already he had outlived most people in his generation, but he didn't know whether that could be attributed to his life's work, or to a skill with herbs. Had he in fact achieved immortality, like Tithonus, without youth?

Kit, he reminded himself. He must think about Kit. Here in the quiet church, the full enormity of Kit's situation came to him. How could they keep up this pretence? They would have to leave and soon. Kit was expected in church the next day. But even if Kit agreed to go with him, could he pass on his arcane knowledge to a girl?

As he sat, wrapped in thought, he heard a rustling, snuffling noise. He ignored it at first, thinking it was some beast that had crept in from the fields, but as the noise came again, he thought that the beast might be hurt and rose stiffly, carrying his candle, to look.

The echoes were deceptive. The noise did not come from the altar. Dr Dee followed it into the Lady Chapel. The candle threw long shadows on to the altar, and illuminated the image of the Virgin with her child on the window, the window that Robert Downe particularly wanted to remove. The Warden shifted the candle into his other hand.

'Who is there?' he said, and heard a whimper that was not like the whimpering of a beast.

'Speak!' he said, suppressing a qualm of fear. He saw the curtain round the altar move.

Dr Dee did not lack courage, but his heart shook. He took two or three steps forward. 'Show yourself,' he said in a husky voice.

Nothing happened. Dr Dee closed his eyes briefly, then strode towards the cover draped over the altar and drew it aside. There was a scrabbling noise and another whimper, and as the Warden bent down, he realized he was looking at the new boy Simeon.

'Boy?' he said, nearly dropping his candle in surprise. 'What are you doing here?'

No answer. The boy was filthy, wrapped in a stained blanket. His limbs were folded in preposterous angles that looked somehow beastlike. There were leaves, twigs and grass in his hair, and the blanket, the Warden now realized, was stained not with mud, but blood. He stared at the boy in horror.

'Are you hurt?' he managed to say.

No answer. But there was a look in his eyes that the Warden recognized – the look of a rabbit that is about to be killed by a hawk, a look beyond fear – shock, and a kind of hopeless knowledge.

'You – you cannot stay there,' he said, and extended a hand under the table. At first there was no movement, then suddenly his hand was caught by a filthy claw and gripped tightly. Dr Dee pulled, hauling the boy out. He would not stand, but crouched, clutching the Warden's cloak, burying his face in the Warden's knees.

The Warden stared down at him hopelessly. Another problem for him to solve. How long had he been there?

'Get up,' he said, but the boy didn't move. Sighing vehemently, the Warden lowered himself into a crouching position, hearing the click of his knees as they bent. *I am too old for all this,* he thought, suppressing his breathing, for the boy stank like a sewer. He put the candle down and eased the boy's face upwards. Now the black eyes looked beseeching.

'What is it?' said the Warden. 'What has happened?'

For answer, the boy let go of the Warden's cloak, and held up the blood-stained blanket he was clutching. The Warden recoiled slightly at the smell, but the boy mouthed something he couldn't hear.

'What?' he said, and the boy gave one harsh sob.

'Where did you get this cloth?' said the Warden.

'Mmmmu−' said the boy. 'Mmmu-mmmu−'

It was like the sound made by a beast in pain, and the boy went on making it, the echoes magnifying the noise.

Dr Dee shook him slightly. 'Answer me!' he said.

'Mmmu-mu-mu−' Simeon moaned, and suddenly the Warden remembered the boy's mother, who had come into church with him the first time he had sung.

'Mother?' he said, shaking him again, and the boy stopped moaning on a sudden breath, his face full of pain.

'Where is she? Is she hurt?'

Simeon seized the Warden's cloak again and buried his face. Dry, racking sobs burst from him and all his muscles clenched in agony.

The Warden licked his dry lips with a dry tongue. Was the boy trying to tell him that his mother was dead?

'What about your mother?' he said faintly. The boy began to shudder violently, uncontrollably. The Warden took his face in his hands. 'Simeon?' he said, remembering. 'It is Simeon, isn't it?'

There was the faintest acknowledgement in the boy's eyes.

'Simeon, what is it? Something has happened to your mother?' he asked, holding firm as the boy made a sudden movement away. 'Tell me. Is she − dead?'

Another harsh sob, but the boy's eyes were dry. The

Warden closed his own eyes, his fingers pressing lightly into the boy's skull, as if he could extract his story from it. 'Have you told anyone?'

But he knew the answer to that one. The boy had come here, to him.

'You have come here,' he said, speaking slowly and with some difficulty, 'to me. Why?'

The boy reached out his grubby hand again and the Warden winced as he touched his face.

'Bring – her – back,' he whispered. He had to say this three times before the Warden understood.

'Bring her back?' he repeated, staring at Simeon. 'From the dead?'

The boy nodded.

Inwardly, the Warden groaned. This was what his reputation had done. He reached out a quivering hand and gripped a wooden seat, hauling himself and the boy upwards. He sat down on it and the boy sat next to him, gazing earnestly into his face.

The Warden shook his head. He felt bent, and tired. This was what Kelly wanted, he thought suddenly. Necromancy. Not his thing.

'I cannot bring people back from the dead, boy,' he said, thinking that if he could, he would not be here now in this backwater. But the boy was looking at him as though he did not understand.

'Look,' he said. 'The dead are – gone. Gone on their final journey. With the Ferryman. Over the river Styx. Into Hades.' He was babbling now, trying to find words that the boy would understand. This was not what he was supposed to say at all. 'Into Heaven,' he added. 'Or Hell. They do not return.'

As he spoke he saw an image of Kelly and quickly suppressed it. The boy was saying something.

'I – will go,' he said.

'Go?' repeated the Warden foolishly. He sounded like the boy. What could he mean?

'Go where?' he asked, but the boy only looked at him with that appeal in his eyes, and Dr Dee suddenly realized what he meant. His heart began to pound uncomfortably. He thought suddenly of Dante's *Inferno*. Dante had gone into Hell and come out again. But how would the boy know that?

'Like Dante?' he said, and the boy looked blankly at him.

'Yes,' said the Warden, thinking aloud. 'Like Dante. Orpheus. Persephone. But those are just stories. They are only books.'

As he spoke he felt that his whole life's work was falling around him lightly, like dust. 'Only books,' he repeated, and found, astonishingly, that he didn't even care.

But the boy was clutching his cloak again.

'Send me,' he said, and the Warden felt a sudden lurch in his stomach as he realized what the boy was asking.

'What are you saying?' he whispered. He looked round nervously, as though at any minute, one of the Fellows would arrive.

Simeon tugged again at his cloak. 'Send me,' he repeated.

The Warden passed a hand over his forehead. He had felt a sudden pressure there.

'Calm yourself,' he said. 'You do not know what you are asking.'

Simeon's eyes seemed to be burning into him.

'I cannot *send* you,' he said. 'How would I send you? And how would you return. No one returns.'

The feeling of pressure swelled in his head.

'Look,' he said. 'The dead do not return. I cannot bring them back. And the living cannot go after them.'

O yes they can, said a voice in his head.

The Warden flinched, then continued, ignoring it. 'Something has happened to your mother,' he said, pulling his thoughts together. 'It is not me you should be telling, but the Beadle, or the Borough Reeve.'

The boy shook his head violently.

'What do you want from me?'

'Mother,' the boy said. Simple. It was as simple as that. The Warden looked at him in disbelief.

'Are you asking me to – to *kill* you?'

The boy's great, dark eyes continued to burn into his. About a thousand thoughts, words and explanations swarmed into the Warden's mind. He started to speak, then stopped, then tried again.

'I cannot help you,' he said. It was pointless trying to explain. 'It is not what I do. I am not a murderer, boy,' he said, and his voice rose a little in anger at the injustice of all those who had defamed him. 'I am not a murderer,' he said again, 'and I do not understand the mysteries of life and death.'

There, he had said it. The simple truth, that all his life's work had been for nothing.

'I do not know where your mother is now in death and I cannot send you after her. I do not know how to. I cannot help.'

O yes you can, old son, said the voice.

Dr Dee shouted suddenly, 'Will you begone!'

His voice rang round the church. The boy started at the noise, but went on gazing at the Warden. As though he *knew*.

'I saw him,' he said. 'The man – in your room.'

Horrified, the Warden remembered that Simeon had seen Kelly.

'He will take me,' he said.

The Warden gasped as though all the air had been punched out of him. At the same time he felt a swirling darkness behind his eyes. He pressed the heels of his hands into them and saw flickering lights. For a moment he thought he would faint, or run screaming from the church. Then he knew he had to stay calm.

'I want nothing to do with him,' he said.

Well, that's nice, the spirit said. *That's gratitude for you.*

Slowly the Warden lifted his face. He would not respond. He would not look round, in case he saw something. He had to think. The Fellows, he thought. They would be coming to the church soon.

'You cannot stay here,' he said, thinking aloud. But where could the boy go? Not to his room. He already had Kit there. What would it look like if the Fellows discovered both students in his room?

Suddenly he remembered the hidden chambers in the church. The crypt. He shivered. Not the nicest place to hide, but maybe it would put the boy off following the dead. And it would give the Warden time to think.

'Someone is coming,' he said. 'You have to hide.'

Fearfully, in case he saw Kelly, the Warden stood up and left the Lady Chapel, walking towards the main altar. He would not look behind, or to the side.

'There is a hidden room – here,' he said, as he found the

335

iron ring embedded in the floor. He forced himself to turn round. Relief flooded him as he realized he could only see Simeon. 'It is a crypt. I am sorry about that, but it is the best I can do. Have you eaten? If you wait for me down there, I will bring you food. Do you understand?'

He tugged the trapdoor open, revealing a flight of steps.

The boy didn't move.

The Warden sighed. 'Look,' he said. 'I will think about what you have said to me. I will consult my books, I promise. But for now you must hide. It is not a pleasant place, but it is safe and with any luck it will cure you of your desire to be with the dead. Do you understand?'

Slowly, the boy nodded. He crept towards the Warden, looking at him with those eyes that seemed to see right through him. But it was the Warden who shivered as Simeon began to step down through the trapdoor.

That's the ticket, said the familiar voice in his ear.

The Warden's throat constricted. 'It will not be for long,' he said, and his voice echoed strangely. 'Here,' he said, passing the boy his candle. The boy stood at the foot of the stairs, looking up, his face lit eerily by candlelight.

Suddenly it seemed to the Warden that he was looking at him down a long, dark tunnel.

Dark of the moon, the spirit said. *You got the boy, you got the crypt. Leave the rest to me.*

At the same time the Warden felt a surge of power so immense that he forgot all about his weariness and age. Everything seemed possible. Darkness welled, swirling into his mind. The muscles of his throat worked strangely.

'If you really want to do this,' he said hoarsely, 'I may be able to help.'

And without waiting for an answer, he lowered the trapdoor and it fell, with an echoing clang.

Once more, Kate let herself into the empty house. The hallway still needed hoovering, the kitchen was still in a mess. She had forgotten to take the clothes out of the washing machine.

In the lounge the bureau was still open, just as she'd left it, all the papers scattered over the floor. She picked them up and stacked them, then stood still, distracted by the silence.

Her glance fell on the secret compartment. She hesitated for a moment, remembering all the times her father had told her that it was strictly private, then went into the kitchen and returned with two screwdrivers and a hammer.

She tried at first to twist the small screwdriver into the keyhole to unlock it, and when that didn't work, used the large screwdriver as a chisel, wedging it into the gap round the wood and knocking it in with the hammer.

It made a mess. Her father would be furious. But eventually the lock broke, and then the hinge, and she was staring at an old book, bound in leather. She took it out and opened it.

She didn't know what she had expected. A box full of money, maybe. Or a map telling her where her father was. Not this.

On crumbling yellow paper, as thick as parchment, there was a strange script, set out in tables. Kate turned the pages carefully. There were ninety-eight tables altogether, numbered and filled with strange flourishes and symbols. Kate couldn't make head or tail of them. They seemed to be some kind of code. Kate stared at the symbols, and there was a vague stirring in the depths of her memory. But she couldn't remember where she had seen them before.

Then, on the last page, there was a scribbled drawing. Kate recognized it immediately from the cathedral. It was a drawing of the Angel Stone.

Kate's heart gave a great thud against her ribs. It looked as if someone had traced the stone itself, then transferred it into the book. There was the angel's incomplete head, its sideways stance, the peculiar angles of its wings, and the scroll. All round the drawing there were symbols of the moon: in its first and last quarter, then full; Kate could recognize that much. But at the top of the sketch was a round, black circle, which she supposed must mean the dark of the moon, and the letters *12 a.m.*

Kate's heart thudded again unevenly.

Twelve a.m. was midnight, wasn't it?

And the Angel Stone was in the cathedral.

Did her father intend to go to the cathedral at midnight during the dark of the moon?

Why?

She reminded herself that she didn't know when the note had been written, or what day it referred to. But if that symbol did mean the dark of the moon . . .

Kate went back into the kitchen. She found the calendar stuffed in the drawer. Her father always kept a calendar that showed the phases of the moon. Yes, there it was. Saturday 31 October, coincidentally or not, the dark of the moon.

There was a terrific knocking on the door. Kit started awake, heart pounding. For a moment she did not know where she was, then her memory rushed back to her. She was in the Warden's room.

The pounding on the door began again.

'Doctor?' said the Usher's voice. 'Open the door!'

Where was the Warden? Kit thought, looking stupidly round the room.

'I know you are in there,' the Usher said. 'You must open this door at once.'

Kit half rose from the bed as the Usher rattled the handle then, to her vast relief, realized that the Warden had locked the door. She did not feel up to offering explanations.

The Usher rapped so fiercely on the door that she feared for his knuckles.

'There are two boys missing from the school –' he said.

Two? thought Kit dazedly.

'Master Morley and the other idiot boy!'

Simeon? thought Kit.

'We know that you have had Kit Morley in your room. It did not take much questioning to prise the full story from the boys. If you do not let me in,' he said, 'I will send for the High Master and the Fellows, and we will break down the door.'

Kit clutched at her shirt, twisting it anxiously, but the Usher only banged on the door one more time, then retreated, muttering, 'Very well.'

Kit stayed where she was, staring at the door. She was locked in, that much seemed plain. But what time was it? And where was the Warden?

Kit pushed the sheet back and stood up warily, conscious of the pain like a severe stitch in her side. There were the rest of her clothes on the back of the chair, still stained with blood. Her old clothes, from her old life as a boy.

Kit limped over to the tapestry and pushed it aside. Even walking felt strange, as though now she was a girl she didn't know how to move, or even think. She checked with her fingers that she could still find the secret panel. Good. At least she wasn't trapped. She didn't like the idea of being locked in the Warden's room. And she might need to use the passage if the Fellows came back.

Even as she stood by the secret panel, Kit heard the sound of footsteps on the corridor. Her heart leapt. Instinctively, she pushed the hidden door open and paused, half in and half out of the secret passage.

This time Chubb's voice came through the door. 'Kit?' he said. 'Kit – are you in there?'

'Kit,' he said again, 'The Master's going mad. That fool Hewitt forgot his story. We all got back from the taverns, drunk as usual, and the Usher was waiting. He asked Hewitt where you were and like an idiot he said 'with the Usher.' And now the Usher's gone to fetch the Fellows and anyone else he can find. They'll have the door broken down in minutes. If you're in there, you'd best let me in.'

Kit said nothing, swallowing nervously. Her throat was very dry.

'I hope the old wizard's not experimenting on you in there,' said Chubb, raising his voice a little and rattling the handle. Kit stepped back into the secret passage, even though she knew there was no way Chubb could open the door alone.

'I'm sorry, all right?' he said. 'I wanted to tell you I'm sorry. Let me in, please.'

Kit stepped back again and knocked her elbow against something. She almost cried out, then realized it was one of the Warden's mirrors. She steadied it, propping it back up against the wall. There was a long pause, and then Chubb said, 'Suit yourself,' and she heard his footsteps retreating.

Kit expelled a long, shaking breath. What was she

supposed to do? She couldn't keep on hiding in here. But neither did she feel like facing them all in school. She didn't care whether Chubb was sorry or not. Everything had changed.

And yet, she could do it. Put her school clothes back on, resume her disguise, let them take her back to the school. But she could not imagine living her old life now. There could be no going back.

But what had the Warden said? That she could live with him as his daughter and train as a magician. Anything would be better than that.

Kit stood for so long that her side began to ache. Cautiously she stepped back into the room. One thing she could do was to dress, then at least she was prepared. She couldn't run through the streets in her shirt.

Kit pulled on her stained clothing. Everything felt unfamiliar, as if she was moving into a different world. It was almost as though she was being pursued by the ghost of her other self, a little girl growing older, into brocaded dresses with wide skirts, her long hair tumbling down her back. Her mother had been married by the time she was Kit's age. Kit could just about imagine her past as a girl, but the future remained a horrifying blank, like a door opening on to nowhere.

She needed to speak to the Warden, and soon. He was the one person who knew who she was. Maybe he had gone to the church, she thought. That would be somewhere she could go, using the secret passage.

Kit wondered if the Warden had left some note for her, some indication as to where he had gone. She looked briefly round the room. Everything seemed as normal. Nothing had been touched. There were some papers on the Warden's desk and an open book, the pages filled with his handwriting. Kit glanced down at the strange script.

Enochian.

It seemed a long time since Kit had been set to learn that onerous language. She had given up on it as soon as she could. She turned the pages slowly, looking for some kind of message, but each of the ninety-eight tables was as incomprehensible as before.

Kit closed the book and looked round the room, but there were no further clues. How long would it be before the Warden returned? And what had happened to Simeon?

Perhaps he had run away, she thought suddenly. Back to his mother and the woods. She felt a pang of something almost like envy. At least Simeon knew where he wanted to go.

She fastened her jacket and paused, feeling a sudden fear at the thought of being seen. She wondered crazily for a moment whether she still looked like a boy, then remembered the mirrors. She went back to the secret door and hauled one out. It was the tallest one that stood on its own stand, the one in which Kit had fought with herself as though with an opponent.

She pulled the mirror across the rug, so that it stood close to where the single candle remained burning. Then she drew off the cover.

It was as if the world had shaken suddenly, then reassembled itself. Kit stumbled and almost fell. There in the mirror was the image of a girl Kit had never seen before. A girl so strange that Kit hardly understood what she was looking at. Kit had flung her hand out to prevent a fall, and the figure in the mirror had stretched her own arm out towards Kit. She had bronze skin and wild black hair, and the blackest eyes Kit had ever seen. She wore strange, outlandish clothing, so that it was hardly possible to tell that she was a girl, yet Kit knew.

She felt a rushing noise in her ears, the sensation of water shooting upwards from her stomach to her throat, causing her to step backwards suddenly. The surface of the mirror shone blank and cool. The image was gone. Kit grasped the cloth and threw it back over the mirror. She felt her knees giving way, and clutched the back of the chair.

It was nothing, she told herself. *A trick of the light. Or one of the Warden's demons,* she thought, but she wouldn't allow herself to dwell on that.

One thing was certain. She couldn't stay in this room any longer. The Fellows were coming and who knew what other witchcraft and sorcery was trapped here? There was nowhere in the town she could go apart from the church. *The Warden,* she thought. She had to find the Warden, and he had to help her work out what she could do.

Kit picked up her sword. It felt reassuringly familiar. Shakily she made her way back to the secret door. She felt an intense qualm as she looked into the darkness beyond. The other mirrors were there and who knew what they contained? But it was her only way out of the room. She stepped forward, making sure that the tapestry fell back in place behind her and, muttering a prayer beneath her breath, entered the darkness of the secret passage.

Hulme, after eleven o'clock at night, was not the place to be. Kate dressed in a dark grey hoodie and joggers. She was tall enough and thin enough to look like a boy with the hood up, though she wasn't sure how much of an advantage that was. She stood in front of the mirror, examining herself, then reached forward and tilted it to get rid of the peculiar lights and shadows obscuring her reflection. For a moment, she thought she saw something strange, but when she put her hand up to the mirror, the image was gone. *Seeing things again*, she told herself, then bent down to tie her laces. She always wore trainers, in case she had to run. She was faster, harder and stronger than anyone else in her class.

Across the square some young lads were shaking up cans of lager, and firing the foam at one another. Kate walked past them, head down, but one of them detached himself from the group.

'Where yuh goin'? Hey, you – where yuh goin'?'

Kate ignored him, thrusting her hands into her pockets. He was close enough for her to make out the fuzzy down on his upper lip, and to smell the greasy, lager-soaked odour of his clothes. When she ignored him he dropped back, making a comment to the others, and there was a shout of laughter.

On the main road, an old woman stood in front of a boarded-up church. There was a poster on the side of the church with the message, *Brush up on your Bible, avoid truth decay*. The woman wore a cardigan buttoned over an army coat. She was barrel-shaped and stuck her chin out aggressively.

'Are you judging me?' she called out to anyone who passed. 'Are you judging me?'

Fortunately a bus was already approaching and Kate flagged it down. But the bus wasn't much better. At the next stop a man got on waving a can of lager and lurched from one seat to another along the aisle, spilling the lager as he went.

'Ooops,' he said several times. Kate ducked in her seat

as he went past. She fingered the contents of the small rucksack she had brought with her. She had packed a flick knife, just in case, and a torch.

Then a man with a bulldog got on and talked loudly to the driver all the way.

'You got a dog, mate? Bulldogs are the best. I had a bulldog called Sarah once. Looked just like the wife.'

Kate stared out of the window at the streaming lights, the flashing green crosses of pharmacies, the metal grilles and shutters at shop windows.

The pavements were packed with people leaving pubs and bars. The night was windy and wet, but not overly cold. The Triangle in front of the cathedral was brightly illuminated. Urbis glowed green against the night sky, neon lights flashed from the Arndale Centre, and above the expensive shops, Jigsaw and East. If it was the dark of the moon, Kate couldn't tell because of the permanent electric glow.

'Spare us some change, love,' a man said, appearing in front of her suddenly, but Kate slipped round him without a word.

Now that she was here, she wasn't sure what to do. She walked all the way round the cathedral, but there was no sign of her father, and no sign of anyone who might be waiting for him, apart from Kate. She hunched her shoulders and stood near the main entrance, which was closed, of course.

She couldn't meet her father inside, if the cathedral was closed.

The rain began to penetrate her hoodie. Kate shivered and dug her hands further into her pockets. She set off walking once more round the periphery of the cathedral.

At the north side she paused, gazing at a small dark

doorway she hadn't seen before. She looked round quickly, then back. It was still there, seeming to open on to darkness.

She was sure that it hadn't been there before or that, if it had, it wasn't open. Maybe this was it – her father was meeting someone inside the cathedral. The thought made her breathing quicken and the blood thrum in her ears. This was it, she thought. It was her father and she had to go. Without giving herself time to think, she slipped in through the darkness of the open doorway, fumbling for her torch.

Darkness and silence. All sense of the outside world fell away. Kate switched on the torch. Its thin beam didn't travel very far. She had to walk further into the nave.

It took her a few moments to realize what she was looking at. The cathedral was as they had left it that morning. There were the studio lamps standing by the open crypt, ready to be used. There was the video monitor for the PowerPoint Presentation. Kate swung her torch round. There was the Fire Window, put in after the bombing of the church in the Second World War.

Kate stood where she was, not knowing what to do. What was going on? The air in the cathedral was cold and there was an aura of emptiness. She wanted to go, but she couldn't just leave.

'Dad?' she said uncertainly and her voice seemed unnaturally loud. There was no answer – she had hardly expected one. But she didn't know whether she was relieved or frightened.

'Dad?' she said again and by her side, the video monitor turned itself on.

Kate felt as though she had leapt several feet into the air.

There was a click and the screen was covered in a grainy fizz. The tape was running.

'Ambient sound,' said Danny's voice and Kate backed away from the monitor as a face appeared. She didn't recognize it at first, then she realized who it was. There was a picture of him in her notes, she thought, then it dawned on her that there was, in fact, no picture. Yet she knew who he was. Dr Dee.

He stared at Kate and Kate stared back at him. It seemed as though he was looking at her directly from the screen. When he spoke, all her nerves jumped at once.

'When I first knew him, he was called Edward Kelly,' he said.

Kate leapt forward and pressed the Off button. The screen switched rapidly to fizz, then cleared and the face of the Warden appeared again.

'When I first knew him, he was called Edward Kelly,' he said.

With a stifled cry, Kate grabbed the cable leading from the monitor to the wall socket. It was still plugged in. *Danny*, she thought. He must have done a piece on the Warden for the PowerPoint Presentation. She yanked the plug out and the screen dissolved into fizz again. Then, to her horror, the fizz cleared and the face of the Warden filled it once more.

'When I first knew him, he was called Edward Kelly,' he said.

Kate backed away from the monitor, her hand pressed to her mouth.

'That was not his real name, even then,' the old man went on. 'But it was the name by which I knew him.'

Kate bumped into a stone pillar and stood still, her heart thumping so that she could hardly hear.

347

'He was a thief and a forger, but the best scryer I ever had. That means he could see angels, you know,' the Warden said, looking at Kate. 'He gave me certain proofs of that and I never doubted his ability.'

'Stop!' Kate said in a strangled voice and the face on the screen stopped talking.

Kate closed her eyes and felt the stone pressing into her shoulders.

'I don't know who you are,' she said, 'or why you're talking to me. But it's got to stop. Now.'

Silence. She should leave, Kate thought. She should get out now, while she still could. Yet she remained where she was, and after a moment, the voice went on.

'He said, "the trouble with the Bible is, it's all written from a certain point of view,"' the monitor explained, and Kate's eyes flew open again, for the voice had changed. But it was still the Warden's face filling the screen, looking at Kate.

'"All that Adam and Eve stuff about being thrown out of the Garden,"' he went on in the voice that was not his own. '"And for what? Because the woman wanted wisdom. You read the Bible again, old son, and see what it says. It says that in the middle of the Garden, there was the Tree of Life, and the Tree of the Knowledge of Good and Evil. And God said, *You must not eat from the Tree that is in the middle of the Garden – touch it and you will die.*"'

Kate wanted to stop him, but she couldn't move.

'"Put it like that and what else was there to do? Serpent says to Eve, *Eve, old girl, why d'you think God doesn't want you to touch that tree? Because He knows that when you do touch it, and you will, your eyes will be opened, and you'll be just like God, knowing Good and Evil. So, go on then, have a go.*'

'"Oh, I can't, says Eve. Course you can, says he. No, no, I really mustn't, says she, and so it went on. But then the Serpent said, *What kind of a God is it that doesn't want His children to grow? What kind of a parent doesn't want his children to be fully grown, just like him? Maybe*, he says, *he's just testing your initiative.* So, in the end, of course, she takes it, and all Hell breaks loose. In a manner of speaking."'

Kate shook her head. What did all this have to do with her father? Or with her? But the Warden hadn't finished.

'"The man blames the woman, the woman blames the Serpent. But it all comes to the same thing in the end. They're all thrown out of the Garden. And God puts an angel with a fiery sword on the East side, and he says to that angel, *Man is now like one of us, knowing Good and Evil. He must not now be allowed to take also from the Tree of Life, so that he might live for ever."'*

Kate thought of her father's research.

'"But just supposing,"' the Warden went on, '"just supposing that the only way forward for Man is back – back to that other Tree. After all, he's already eaten the first fruit, hasn't he? Can't do anything about that now. Suppose that the only way to put things right is to get to that other fruit?"'

The Warden finished speaking and looked at Kate. Then he returned to his own voice. 'So he spoke to me and I listened.' His face was gentle, melancholy.

Kate found her voice.

'I don't understand,' she said.

'Listen to me,' said the Warden. 'Ever since Man began he has tried to conquer the Darkness. Your generation knows nothing of the dark. Do you know why people are afraid of the dark?' he enquired conversationally.

Kate wasn't going to respond to this. In any case, he didn't seem to require an answer.

'It is because only in the Darkness – the absolute dark, mind you, not the half light from the moon and stars, or any man-made light – do we find out who we really are.'

Kate started to ask what that had to do with anything, but the Warden went on.

'The human race has not managed to conquer the ultimate Darkness yet. In every generation there are those who believe that eternal life is the one way forward for humankind. The being that was Edward Kelly works through such people. But he only wants immortality for himself. Immortality of the flesh, not the spirit. And for that he needs a body.'

'A body?' Kate echoed.

'It is not a simple thing,' the Warden said. 'He has tried many times and failed. He does not just want any body – it must be young. And it cannot happen anywhere – it has to happen here.'

Kate felt as though she had wandered into some bizarre universe in which nothing made sense. 'Why?' she said, meaning why here, in the middle of Manchester.

For answer the Warden turned his head. Kate followed his gaze. He was looking towards the Angel Stone above the crypt.

'The Angel Stone,' he said reverently. 'The symbol of Man himself – eternal spirit trapped in mortal clay. It is older than the church, far older. No one knows how old it really is.'

Kate could barely see the outline of the angel. It carried a scroll, not a sword, she remembered.

'"Into thy hands, O Lord, I commend my spirit,"' the Warden said. 'That's what the words mean. The act of incarnation and the act of death. Life and Death.'

'I don't know what you mean,' Kate said desperately.

'It was here all the time!' the Warden said almost gaily. 'And we did not know it. For the ritual to work, it must be performed in the presence of the angel. So that the occupation of the body may be made permanent – eternal flame into mortal clay. The ultimate mystery.'

The Warden looked at Kate once more. She felt as though she was trying to wake up from a dream.

'But – how?' she said, and when the Warden was silent, she cried, 'What am I supposed to do?'

'You are supposed to be there,' the Warden said. Then the picture on the screen changed once more into fizz and simply went out. Kate was staring at a blank monitor.

Kate badly wanted to leave, but she had found nothing. She was no further on in her search for her father. She couldn't leave now, there were too many questions to ask. But the cathedral was empty. There was no one there.

Then she heard a slight movement behind her and spun round. A flickering light came from the crypt and she could hear a voice chanting. She turned back sharply, but the video screen was still blank. Kate was alone with the flickering light and the chanting that streamed upwards from the entrance to the crypt.

As soon as she entered the church, Kit could hear the Warden's voice, but she couldn't work out where it was coming from. At first she followed the sound rather than the words, but then the words struck her and she paused for a moment to listen.

'"One side of the rocky citadel had been hollowed out to form a vast cavern, into which led a hundred broad shafts, a hundred mouths, from which streamed as many voices."'

Kit recognized the passage at once. It was from the book in *The Aeneid* in which Aeneas travels into the Underworld. The boys were not supposed to read it because of its portrayal of the Afterlife, but they all had anyway. Even so, Kit was shocked to hear it being read aloud in the church. She crept closer, following the sound of the Warden's voice, though it wasn't easy, since the echoes reverberated like the hundred voices of the sibyl.

'"Now is the time to ask your destinies . . ."'

Kit noticed a dim light that seemed to be coming from the floor. She quivered suddenly as she realized that the entrance to the crypt was open. Was this where the Warden practised his Black Arts?

Involuntarily, Kit's hand went to her sword. She crouched first, then lay flat on her stomach, creeping towards the open crypt.

'"The sibyl stood before them, her wild heart bursting with ecstasy. The more she tried to shake the great god, the harder he strained upon her foaming mouth, until the hundred huge mouths of her house gave her answer to the winds . . ."'

Kit hooked her fingers around the open hatch and pulled herself forward a final few inches. What she saw made her heart lurch and her flesh crawl.

The Warden stood chanting over the body of Simeon, who lay on the tomb, wrapped in a bloodstained cloth. Four candles burnt around him – at his head and feet, and to the right and left of his body. He did not move and Kit felt her stomach turn.

He's dead, she thought, *the Warden has killed him,* and a sick bile rose in her throat. She should run for help, she knew, yet she could not move. The scene seemed to be imprinted on her eyes. She saw with horror that there were dead animals in the crypt. A cockerel hanging upside down, its blood dripping slowly to the floor, and the carcass of a cat. Was that the blood on Simeon's blanket? Was he actually dead and if so, why was the Warden chanting over him?

'"No man may enter the hidden places of the earth before plucking the golden foliage . . ."' the Warden said, and he laid a flowering branch on Simeon's breast, then seemed to be forcing something into his mouth.

Do something, Kit told herself, and she clutched the stone floor so hard that her knuckles turned white. The Warden raised his head and Kit pressed herself down in alarm. He was wearing ceremonial robes, she could see that much, like no robes Kit had ever seen before.

'"It is easy to go down to the birdless lake,"' he intoned, and he lifted something in his left hand. Kit tried to see, but it wasn't easy pressed flat to the floor.

'"Then the earth bellowed underfoot, the wooded ridges quaked and dogs could be heard howling in the darkness,"' the Warden moaned. '"Here begins the road that leads to the boiling waters of Acheron . . ."'

And Kit saw that the object in his hand was a knife.

She leapt to her feet, drawing her sword in a single smooth motion. This was it. The time had come for her to find out whether she was a hero or a coward.

'Doctor!' she cried in her loudest voice. 'What are you doing?'

The Warden stared up at her as she ran down the steps, waving her sword. His eyes were entirely black, like the obsidian stone. For a moment they stared at one another, appalled, but before Kit could speak, the crypt was filled with a terrifying light.

Kate stared all round, but she could no longer see the Warden. The only light came from the crypt. She was not going into the crypt, she thought. No way.

'"Hidden in a dark tree there is a golden bough,"' the chanting voice said. '"No man may enter the hidden places of the earth before plucking the golden foliage from this tree . . ."'

No way, Kate thought again. She started to back away from the crypt. She didn't know what was going on down there and she didn't care. She should get out now, she told herself, and tell the police.

'"Then the earth bellowed underfoot, the wooded ridges quaked, and dogs could be heard howling in the darkness . . ."'

It was like a mass, Kate thought, or the Last Rites. Some terrible ceremony for the dead. She stepped back once more and almost cried aloud when she bumped into something hard.

'"*It is easy to go down into the birdless lake,*"' *the voice intoned.*

The thing she had bumped into was the computerized panel from which all the lights of the cathedral could be operated.

'"Here begins the road that leads to the boiling waters of Acheron,"' moaned the voice, but another voice spoke urgently in Kate's ear, making her jump violently.

'Kate,' it said. 'Your generation knows nothing of Darkness, but mine knows nothing of Light.'

Kate wheeled round, trying desperately to see where the voice was coming from, but she could only hear that other voice chanting in the crypt. And suddenly she knew that the two voices were the same. The Warden was down there, chanting, and at the same time he was up here, speaking to Kate.

Kate's thoughts reeled. But before she could make any sense of what was happening, a third voice cried loudly, 'Doctor – what are you doing?'

And the voice that she heard was her own.

The shock propelled Kate into action. She pushed back the wooden cover, her fingers clawing at the switches in the panel.

Instantly the cathedral filled with light. She turned the switches that operated the floodlights full on, and twenty thousand watts of blue light blazed upwards from the crypt. Armoured by the light, Kate ran towards the stone steps.

In the intense blue blaze Kate could only see outlines, almost like negatives. There was a figure on the tomb, and behind him Kate could just make out the figure of the Warden, writhing and cowering in the glare.

'What have you done?' she cried, running down the steps. But the Warden only moaned, sinking to his knees.

Kate's foot kicked something as she ran. She stooped and picked it up, brandishing it at the Warden who cried aloud in terror.

'Forgive me!' he cried, his arm flung over his face. 'Do not judge me,' he begged. Tell me what I must do!'

Kate raised the sword over the motionless figure of the boy.

'No!' screamed the Warden. 'Mercy!'

Kate felt calm, and terrible. 'What have you done to him?' she demanded.

'Forgive me!' the Warden gasped. He appeared to be clutching his chest. 'I – was not myself. Help me –' He reached out to her, but Kate towered over him, tall and stern. 'Help me to put it right!'

'How?' said Kate, still towering over him with the sword.

'Anything,' gabbled the Warden. 'I'll do anything. Tell me what to do.'

And from nowhere the words came into Kate's mouth.

'You must go after him,' she said.

The Warden's head wobbled foolishly. He seemed to be trying to speak. Then, with one hand still outstretched towards her, and the other clutching his chest, he toppled forward on to the floor . . .

And in that moment, everything vanished. The Warden, the boy on the tomb and the tomb itself vanished into darkness and Kate stood alone. She felt dizzy, shaken and her mouth was dry as dust.

Where am I now? she thought. *When am I*?

As if in answer there came the sound of a slow handclap.

'Oh, well done, well done,' said a terrible voice that buzzed like a swarm of insects into her ears, or like the radio when it is not properly tuned. 'That was quite a show you put on.'

Kate gave a loud cry and fumbled for the light switch.

'I think you'll find it's gone,' the voice said.

Kate groped wildly, but she could feel nothing. The walls of the crypt itself were gone. She seemed to be standing in a darkness without contours, that was as absolute as though light had never been. Where was the Warden?

'That old fool thinks you're the Angel of Death,' said the voice.

Kate closed her eyes. It made no difference to the darkness. She opened them and made herself look.

He was no taller than she was. He had a large, pale face, with lank hair hanging to his shoulders. He was dressed in black with a white lace collar and he had a sword at his side. He was outlined in darkness, as though projected on to a black screen. Kate wished she still had the sword she had picked up, but it had gone, along with everything else.

'Kelly,' she whispered, and the man, or spirit, or whatever it was, shrugged.

'Some call me by that name,' it said.

'Wh-what have you done with my father?' said Kate.

'Me?' said the spirit. 'Nothing at all. Never touched him.'

'Where is he?' Kate demanded.

'Well, he ain't here, is he?' said the spirit, giving her a look that crawled over the flesh of her face. 'There's no one here but you and me.'

The spirit stepped forward and Kate stepped back.

'Stay away from me,' she said.

There was a sudden movement and a light began to glow. Kate looked down. There between her and the spirit, was the tomb from the crypt, with four lighted candles, one on each side. Between the candles was the space where the boy's body had lain. He was not there now.

'Dark of the moon,' the spirit said. 'It won't work till then. There're always these tedious rituals to observe. Bit of goat's blood here, nails from a coffin there – I ask you.'

Kate moved away from the tomb, or thought she had, but she was only facing a different edge.

'You'll be pleased to hear that we don't need all that nonsense,' the spirit said. 'Just the dark of the moon and that stone up there. And you and me, of course.'

Kate looked up and saw the Angel Stone, suspended in

darkness. Gradually the dimensions of the crypt returned: the walls and the steps leading to the cathedral nave. The Angel Stone was in the wall above the crypt. When she looked down at the tomb again, the spirit lay between the candles, exactly as the boy had lain.

'What's going on?' she asked faintly.

'Well, you're a bright girl, Kate,' the spirit said. 'I'd've thought you could work it out.'

It hoisted itself towards her on the stone slab, picking up a candle on the way. Its short, thick legs swung over the edge of the tomb.

'See this?' it said, and it tilted its head backwards, attempting to balance the candle on its forehead, then catching it as it fell over. 'Used to be able to do that,' it said, with a faintly regretful smile. Kate could hear her heart thumping, but she couldn't hear herself think. It was as though there was a buzzing noise inside her head.

'What are you?' she asked, trying once more to step away, but succeeding only in moving along the edges of the tomb. The spirit watched her, propped up on its elbows.

'Perhaps you should be asking what *you* are, Kate – or should I call you Kit?' it said.

Kate ignored this. 'Where's the boy – where's Simeon?' she asked, suddenly remembering the name. 'What happened to him?'

'Well, that was a bit unfortunate,' the spirit said, without taking its eyes from her face. 'You might say he got lost.'

'Lost – where?' Kate said stupidly, and the spirit smiled.

'Now if we knew that, he'd hardly be lost, would he?' it said.

Kate shook her head, as though trying to shake the buzzing noise out of it.

'I don't understand,' she said.

'No, well, you don't need to. Suffice it to say that things should've turned out a bit different. My learned friend should've performed the ritual at the appointed time, sent the boy's consciousness off into the beyond and bingo – I'd've occupied his body until it got too knackered and the next one came along. The perfect plan. Only it got interrupted.'

And the spirit stared at Kate until the hairs on the back of her neck stood on end.

'But – the Warden,' she stammered.

'He got lost too. In fact we all did, with the ritual interrupted in that untimely way. The whole lot of us, blasted into limbo. Or whatever you'd like to call it.'

The spirit was leaning on one elbow now, but still gazing at Kate. 'With the ritual interrupted,' it said, 'none of us could find our way back.'

Kate swallowed in horror.

'I don't know what you're talking about,' she said.

'Ain't you been listening?' the spirit said, sitting up again. 'Who was it interrupted us? Just when we got it all going? Who was it blasted us through the wormhole of time? Wormhole,' it went on, scratching its head. 'That's a good one.'

The buzzing noise increased in Kate's ears. She pressed her fingers to her forehead. 'I – don't understand,' she said faintly.

'No? Well, let me put it a different way,' said the spirit, rising from the tomb.

> 'There was once a young lady called Kit,
> Whose mum took a terrible fit,
> Dressed her up as a boy,
> Told her not to be coy,
> And keep shtum or she'd never inherit.

'Something like that. The Warden was always more of a one for poetry than me. And he took to you, Kit, oh yes. Wanted to leave you his legacy. And in a funny kind of way, you could say he has.'

A series of images flickered through Kate's mind, too rapidly for her to make sense of them.

'Either way you look at it, it's the same story really,' the spirit went on. 'Child looking for father, father looking for child, the quest for immortality. Except that the father can only get what he wants by giving the child up.'

'My father didn't give me up,' Kate said faintly, and the spirit looked at her with exaggerated surprise.

'No?' it said. 'Well, what are you doing here, then?'

Kate couldn't speak. *I'm so sorry. I love you, Your father,* his note had said.

'What do you want?' she managed to say. 'What do you want with me?'

'Well, let's find out, shall we?' said the spirit, patting the empty space on the tomb. 'Why don't you take the weight off your feet.'

Kate backed away. 'Don't touch me,' she said. She thought she had shouted, but hardly any sound had come out.

The spirit smiled. 'Oh, I hope there won't be no need for any of that,' it said. 'That strong-arm stuff never was my style. I thought you'd just lie down easy of your own accord.'

Kate almost laughed. 'You're dreaming,' she said, and she backed away further as it drew near. 'Stay away from me!' she shouted. She thought she had turned away from the spirit, towards the steps, but found herself pressed up against the tomb, the cold stone digging into the back of her thighs.

'Kate, Kate,' the spirit said. 'What have you got to live for, really?'

Kate gasped in horror. The spirit stood in front of her, blocking her way. She could feel sweat breaking out on her forehead.

'Dad!' she called suddenly. 'Dad – Dad!'

The spirit laughed and she had a sudden, unpleasant view of its teeth.

'I told you before, there's no one here,' it said. 'Your dad left the note because he knew you'd come. That was part of the deal.'

'No!' Kate cried, but the next moment she was stumbling backwards on to the tomb. The spirit was leaning over her, pressing down.

'Used to think I wouldn't want a girl,' it said. 'Just shows you how times change, eh?'

'Get away from me!' Kate shouted, and she pushed at the spirit, but it was like pushing at a concentrated field of force.

'All that lovely breath,' it murmured, and it placed a finger on her lips. Kate felt a prickling sensation like an electric current as he rubbed it back and forth. 'In and out,' it murmured dreamily. 'In and out.'

Kate twisted away, but the spirit lifted her chin and leant forward smiling with its terrible, blank eyes. And its kiss burnt her lips like ice. Kate screwed her eyes shut, holding her breath, and felt herself falling backwards into darkness. And at the same time, the cathedral bells began to ring.

She could see and hear nothing, yet she felt she was moving towards some vast abyss. Everything that had ever existed, that had lived or died, was simultaneously hurtling towards that same abyss, at a speed impossibly beyond all motion. Round the edges of that abyss, like a great waterfall, streamed a thousand, thousand souls, like points of light, so that light itself and time, seemed to be pouring over the edge.

Kate knew that if she fell over that edge, her consciousness would erupt into light and dust. But a thought came to her, as though shaping itself into the contours of what might once have been her mind. It was: *Breathe*.

Breath was the thing she possessed that the spirit did not.

Breathe, the voice said.

And Kate breathed out into the spirit's cold lips, then she breathed in deeply and it was like breathing ashes into her soul.

A judder ran through the spirit, as though of surprise, then it was as though they were both spinning round into a vortex.

Deeper and deeper Kate breathed, so that all the spaces and cavities and hollows behind her flesh filled with air, and the alveoli of her lungs flowered and swelled. Shifting images appeared in her internal vision – of her father and Simeon and the Warden, and her life going on simultaneously in two different schools. They flickered past so rapidly that she could not hold on to them or make any sense of what she saw. But she reached up and found the sides of the spirit's face, where its ears should have been, and breathed into its lips the burning air that charged all the particles and processes of her body. And she felt the substance of its face crumple in her hands and when she released her hold, finally, the being that was Kelly hurtled backwards into the abyss.

Then from the centre of that abyss came a great motion, a bursting energy, as though it had turned into a vast generator. The being that was Edward Kelly opened its mouth as though to scream, but no sound came, and the next moment it was enveloped in light. For a moment its outline flickered, black and writhing in the glare. Light streamed from its eyes and mouth. Then it was gone, vanished simply as though it had never been.

And Kate followed, tumbling over and over into what appeared to be a tunnel of light.

The shifting images returned, of crowds of people, towering buildings, armies marching, chariots of steel and flame. Then all at once she seemed to be travelling at great speed through a market square. All round the square there were buildings, black and white like Tudor houses. The woman with the auburn hair and the blanket stood in front of a wooden post. She seemed to be reading a notice roughly tacked to it. There was a man, leading his horse and cart away from her.

Kate saw the woman turn away from the notice and take a few steps, then turn and hurry back towards it, holding out her hand. Kate could do nothing about the impossible speed at which she was travelling. She flung out an arm as though to catch hold of the post as she passed.

'No!' she cried with the full force of her lungs. She just had time to see the woman look at her aghast. Her hand flew to her mouth and she turned and ran as Kate hurtled past. Then she was hurtling forward again, into the tunnel of light.

Simeon stood by the gates, waiting for his mother. He had begun to fear, feverishly, that he would not see her again, but now at last it was time for the Saturday half-day, when she had said she would meet him. When he saw her, he would tell her that he was never going back to the school. He would never leave her again.

Several women were passing on their way to market, none of them his mother. Simeon stood, tense as a spring by the church gates, searching for her face.

He began to get very cold. There was a fading yellow light and the first few snowflakes of the year were falling. The cold bit through his woollen clothes and hurt his chest when he breathed. It made his nose run.

Simeon did not know what to do. The hollowness of waiting had numbed his mind. The only other place his mother might have gone was to the market for supplies. He hesitated, shifting from one foot to the other in case he missed her, then turned suddenly and set off towards Smithy Door.

But before he reached it he heard her voice calling him.

'Simeon!' she called out. 'Simeon!'

And at last he saw her, hurrying towards him round the corner of the church. He ran to her and hugged her and held on until she broke free, laughing.

'Simeon, you will crack my ribs,' she said, and she held his face in her hands. Simeon was breathless from running and from the need to make her understand.

'Take me with you,' he said in their own language, and his mother's face softened. He could see his face in her eyes. She hesitated a long moment, then nodded.

'Yes,' she said. 'We do not belong here.'

Simeon felt that his heart would burst with joy. He buried his face in her neck. He had thought that he would never see her again, but now she was here with him. They would not be parted again. He could feel her breath shaking and he looked at her in surprise. She seemed suddenly older and more frail, the lines of her face more drawn.

'Simeon,' she said. 'I have done so many things wrong. I have made so many mistakes –'

'No,' he said, lifting her face. She closed her eyes and for a moment he thought that she would fall.

'I do not know where we will go, or what we will do,' she said, and a shudder ran through her. 'We have nowhere to go,' she said.

Simeon touched her eyes. 'You are here, in my eyes,' he said.

She looked at him. 'I am so tired,' she said, and all at once Simeon saw the image of the fallen bird and he felt a great pang.

'I know,' he whispered. Then he said, 'I will find us somewhere to go.'

And his mother nodded, pressing her forehead into Simeon's.

'I have bought food,' she said, showing him the bundle beneath her blanket, and for the first time he noticed the leather purse, but did not ask where it had come from.

'We must go now,' she said with sudden urgency and he nodded. He took the blue blanket from her shoulders and wrapped it round them both. Then he looked up one more time at the church. It seemed to him to glow suddenly with an orange light, and they paused for a moment, watching. Then they turned together, walking on the path that led away from the church, towards the bridge across the river.

Slowly the spinning sensation stopped and the darkness returned. Kate could feel tiles beneath her feet and smell a cold, night smell. Where was she now? she thought. *When* was she?

She seemed to be sitting on a wooden bench. When she

groped along the bench her fingers closed round something metallic. The torch.

Kate switched it on. Its pale beam fell on the Angel Stone with its sand-coloured carving. She took a deep breath. She was here again, back in the cathedral, just as if nothing had happened. There was the choir screen, there the video monitor. The door to the crypt lay closed and still. What was she supposed to do now?

I'm here, all right? she said silently. *What happens now?*

Here, Now

Manchester, Present Day

'It's all here,' she said aloud, wonderingly. 'All of it, here, now.'

'Indeed,' the Warden said.

So many questions rushed into Kate's mind that she could hardly separate them out.

'How – where am I now?' she asked. 'Who am I – I mean . . .' She faltered and stood, simply staring at him. *How can you be here, talking to me?* she thought. But the Warden only smiled and inclined his head. Kate followed the direction of his gaze and saw the woman with the blue blanket, holding on to a boy a little taller than she was, pressing her forehead into his.

'Simeon,' Kate whispered and the Warden nodded. 'But – *how*?' she asked.

But the Warden was looking at Simeon and his mother, not at Kate.

'She has kept her appointment,' he said, 'because of you.'

And vividly Kate remembered crossing the square towards the woman and the wooden post. '*No!*' she had cried, and the woman's eyes had widened with fear and she had hurried away, while the wagoner had carried on leading his horse as though he hadn't seen her at all.

Now the boy took the blanket from his mother's shoulders and wrapped it round them both, and for a moment the two of them looked towards the church.

'You have changed it, Kit,' the Warden said. 'You.'

Kate looked back towards Simeon and his mother. Her heart quickened as they stared in her direction. Did his mother remember Kate, hurtling towards her through the square, or had her memory already closed over that impossible encounter, like water covering a hole? Would they see her now?

But they were gazing up past Kate and their faces were full of light. Kate turned to see what they were looking at and saw the tower of the cathedral, lit by an electric glow. She turned again in time to see them walking away from her, still holding on to one another.

'They are leaving now,' the Warden said. 'They escape the plague.'

Kate felt a fierce pain as she watched them walking away. They seemed so close, as though wherever they went it would not matter, as long as they were together. She turned back to the Warden, her mind brimming with questions.

'What happened – in the crypt?' she said.

The Warden was looking at her with a peculiar expression on his face.

'You sent me after him,' he said. 'Do you not remember, Kit? You sent me after the boy.'

Kate gasped. She was looking at the Warden, but she could see her father in his eyes. She jerked her arm away.

'Don't play your tricks on me,' she said. 'Where's my father? I want to know where my father is.'

Then the Warden spoke to her in her father's voice.

'I was one of those people,' he said, 'who shine a light in

a single direction, who sacrifice everything in pursuit of their vision. I was one of those people who set out to conquer the Darkness without realizing that it is the Darkness and the Mystery that matter. It has taken me all this time, all these hundreds of years, to find out that I do not need to know more after all. Do you understand?'

Kate shook her head. She couldn't speak.

'No, how could you,' he said. 'We never do see the full picture.'

Kate still said nothing. Her voice seemed trapped in her throat.

'If the boy's mother had not died,' the Warden went on in the voice that was both his own and her father's, 'the boy would never have come to me. And I would never have been possessed by the demon. I would have defeated it when I banished it from my room. As it was, I needed help. An intervention.'

Kate stepped forward, gripping the Warden's arms. 'Dad, this is me, Kate,' she said, shaking him.

'I know who you are, Kit,' her father said.

'Stop calling me that!' Kate cried. She shook him again hopelessly, and then her arms fell to her side. She stared at the Warden's face. 'I want my father,' she said. Her voice sounded like a child's and she looked away, afraid that she would cry.

'Kate,' her father said, and she looked up and he was there. It was his face looking down at her. She clutched him and he held her tightly.

'Dad – Dad,' she sobbed, and he stroked her hair. She buried her face in his shoulder and wept. She could feel the rough wool of his jacket and smell the familiar smell of him through his clothes. This was her father, who had tried to teach her so many things that she hadn't wanted to know.

When she looked at him again he was smiling at her, a wounded, painful smile. She could see herself reflected in his eyes.

'Dad,' she whispered. He was trying to tell her something, but she couldn't hear. He took hold of her hand and opened the fingers one by one. Then he began tracing a pattern on her palm with his fingers. She said nothing, watching the pattern of his fingers on her palm, then looking at her reflection in his eyes. She felt as though he was telling her the story of her life. She had lost her father before she was born, then she had been taken away from her mother. She had gone to the school to be brought up in a different faith. Then she had met the Warden and he had asked her if she wanted to live with him as his daughter.

Suddenly she understood with a shock like an electric jolt. He had tried to be a father to her – this father, with his strange moods and sudden absences, his drinking.

But he never had been a father to her.

What was I? she asked him with her eyes. *Was I the sacrifice?*

Now his lips were moving as well. 'I'm sorry,' they said.

Kate felt a pang of fear. 'Don't go,' she whispered, but she knew he had to. He had never fully belonged in this world.

He touched her face. 'You are in my eyes,' he said. And he touched her eyelids so that she had to close them, and she sensed him change, then disappear. When she opened them again, the Warden was looking back at her with the same painful, wounded expression. She breathed in and her breath was shaking.

'Who am I then,' she said, 'Kit – or Kate?'

'Yes,' the Warden said.

She gazed at him. So many memories were returning from two different lives. But the Warden was speaking again.

'You sent me on a journey, remember, to undo the wrong I had done. But I took you with me, as my daughter Kate. There was no place for you in that time.'

'Who was it blasted us through the wormhole of time?' the spirit had said.

And it all came together in Kate's mind: the ritual she had interrupted in the crypt, the tunnel of light, her missing father. She shook her head. She didn't understand anything at all.

'But *how*?' she said. 'How could you take me with you?'

The Warden sighed. 'Don't you remember me talking to you about time,' he said, and vividly Kate recalled her father pushing a needle through a piece of paper.

If point A is the present moment, he had said, *and point B a moment four hundred years ago, then point A is actually nearer to point B than to any other moment before or since* . . . and he had pushed the needle through the paper, connecting the folds. *But what is it that connects the points?* he had continued. *Some force, energy or power, capable of bending light and time* . . .

The Warden was watching her closely.

'It was the power of the ritual,' he said. 'And the Angel Stone.'

So many questions flooded into Kate's mind that her thoughts jammed.

'We passed through a loophole into a different time,' he said, 'a different world. But we took with us what was essentially ours. My obsession with immortality, my intellect and learning. You –'

'I was an outsider,' Kate said faintly. She was both people,

373

Kit and Kate. Dr Dee was also her father. She couldn't understand it, but there it was. The mystery.

'You took with you your courage,' the Warden said. 'And now you have a choice.'

'Choice?' said Kate. 'What choice?'

The Warden inclined his head and she followed his gaze. There were the two worlds, laid out before her.

'You have a choice, Kit,' the Warden said. 'You can choose the time in which you live.'

Kate stared at him and he looked back at her with glittering eyes. She could hardly comprehend the implications of what he was saying. *Choose the time in which you live?*

Kate could not imagine going back to Kit's old life at the school, pretending to be a boy. There was no place for her there. But there was no place for the Warden either. 'What will you do?' she asked.

The Warden shook his head slowly, looking into the different worlds.

'I have caused enough damage,' he said. 'I will return to my house in Mortlake and lead a quiet life, for what time I have left.'

He looked at her. 'You could come with me, Kit,' he said softly. 'The offer still stands. You can live and work with me, as my daughter. I will leave you everything I have. Not,' he added with an ironic smile, 'that I have much left to leave.'

He would give it all up, she thought, staring at him. The chance to lead another life as a much younger man, whose research into immortality might actually bear fruit. He would not live in this later time as her father.

The choice came to her vividly. She could return to the earlier century, with its prejudices and limitations, or remain in the later one, with its different set of prejudices and limitations, against race and poverty. Either way, it seemed, she would live as a girl.

She closed her eyes briefly. In this century she would not suffer religious persecution. And there were more opportunities for women. She could work hard, make the most of her education, as her father had always implored her to do.

Her father. But there would be no father now. Already her memories of him were slipping away, like sand through an hourglass, and with them the pain subsided, though there was still fear. She would be on her own, and poor, suffering a different kind of prejudice. What would happen to her? How would she live in that house alone? The Social Services would come for her, she thought.

The Warden was still waiting for her to answer, watching her with those dark, dark eyes. 'Each road has its dangers, Kit,' he said.

And in that moment she made her choice.

'If it's all the same to you,' she said, 'I think I'll stay.'

The Warden drew in his breath sharply and closed his eyes. 'You know what that means,' he said. 'It will not be easy.'

'I'll take my chances,' Kate said. She felt lightened, suddenly, by her choice. There was no future for her in that other world, at least, none that she wanted. Here there was some possibility and potential. 'I'll be all right,' she said.

The Warden was looking at her strangely. There was emotion in his face and something else, like admiration. He tipped his hat to her in an old-fashioned gesture.

'Yes,' he said. 'I dare say you will.'

Kate started to say something, to question him, but he only pressed a finger to his lips. 'Have I not told you,' he said, 'that it is only the mystery that matters?'

Then he touched his hat to her once more and smiled and her vision blurred momentarily, and when she blinked he had gone, along with all the inns of Long Millgate. The buildings of Chetham's school and Victoria Station glowed in the electric light, traffic rumbled by on Deansgate. She stared into the distance for a moment, as though still looking for that unseen world, then turned and walked slowly away from the cathedral.

And as she passed the gates, Kate thought that she could hear, like a distant echo, different footsteps fading into their time, as her feet went on walking into hers.

Author's Note

I have taken considerable liberties with the story of Dr John Dee (1527–1608) the Elizabethan scientist and philosopher, known as the 'Queen's Conjurer'.

Dee was a brilliant scientist and mathematician, the first to apply Euclidean geometry to navigation and to devise instruments which enabled the navy to apply this knowledge. He translated Euclid and wrote the famous *Mathematical Preface* to Euclid's treatise, which was considered to be the definitive work of its time. He trained the first great navigators and developed the maps charting the North East and North West Passages. He had the greatest library in England – estimates vary between 4,000 and 10,000 books, and was instrumental in developing new approaches to both architecture and the theatrical arts.

In those days, science and magic were closely intertwined. Dr Dee was an alchemist and cabalist, an adept in esoteric and occult lore. Early in his career, he was imprisoned by Queen Mary for producing an unfavourable horoscope for her, and later made the dangerous move of predicting the coronation of Queen Elizabeth I. He also predicted the death of Mary, Queen of Scots and the invasion of the Spanish Armada. He is said to have put a curse on the Spanish Armada, which is why there was bad weather and the English won. His reputation as a magician grew. Shakespeare depicted him as Prospero and Christopher Marlowe as Faust.

He is recognized today as one of the greatest thinkers of the Renaissance, but some say that his genius led him to become deranged and deluded. Others attribute his downfall to his association with Edward Kelly, (1555–93/95/97?), a lawyer who had been convicted of forging land deals, fraud and coining.

Dee and Kelly met around 1579, at which point Kelly convinced Dee that he could turn lead into gold, and that he could relay messages from angels using a technique known as 'scrying' – gazing into a crystal ball or the reflective surface of an obsidian stone.

In 1583, Kelly and Dee produced the *Book of Enoch* in the special language they called Enochian, which was dictated to Kelly by angels and transcribed by Dee. This language, Kelly claimed, contained the perfect truth of God.

In 1584, however, Kelly became convinced that Queen Elizabeth's spymaster, Sir Francis Walsingham, was watching them, and they fled to Poland and then to the court of the Holy Roman Emperor Rudolph II.

More travels ensued, but in 1589 Dee and Kelly parted company. Kelly returned to the court of Rudolph II and was kept there on the promise of revealing the secrets of the Philosopher's Stone. This was the ultimate goal of alchemy. It enabled the transmutation of base metals into gold and was also the key to eternal life. Kelly was imprisoned in Prague, apparently for failing to produce either gold or immortality. The exact circumstances of his death are uncertain and the year given variously as 1593, 1595 or 1597, but most sources agree that he died in an attempt to escape from prison using a rope made of twisted bed linen.

Meanwhile, Dr Dee returned to England. He was granted a licence to practise alchemy by Queen Elizabeth I, but had no official position until she made him Warden of the Collegiate Church in Manchester (now the cathedral). This was a deeply unpopular appointment. There was a growing fear of witchcraft and the occult, and Manchester, at that time, was a town deeply divided by religious strife. On one side of the river there were the radical Puritans of the Salford Hundred, while despite persecution, powerful Catholic families still remained in Lancashire. Increasingly, in the rural areas outside the town, witchcraft was practised. Meanwhile, the Fellows of the Collegiate Church tried to establish and maintain the rule of the Church of England, with its different prayers, vestments and services, all still relatively new. Dr Dee's reputation had preceded him – a reputation that associated him with necromancy (invoking the dead), spiritualism and witchcraft. He was thought to be in league with the Devil.

Few things cling so well as a reputation, however unjust, and the appointment of Dr Dee as Warden of the church was unpopular with all factions. Although few records remain of his time in Manchester, it does not seem to have gone well. At one point his magnificent library and laboratory were destroyed by a mob, and when a great plague struck Manchester in 1605, he left under mysterious circumstances, later dying in poverty in Mortlake, in 1608.

John Dee had a wife, who died in the plague, and eight children, none of whom are mentioned in this book. He coined the word Britannia, and was the founder of the Rosicrucian Order, which was a Protestant response to the Jesuits, and the Enochian keys are still used by Occultists today.

While Simeon and his mother are fictitious characters, the gypsies were indeed slaughtered in Scotland after being promised a land of their own.

Livi Michael

The Whispering Roads

Wherever you go, the past will follow . . .

'*Vivid and powerful*' – *Funday Times*

'*A powerful and quite extraordinary novel*'
– *Berlie Doherty*

Annie is strange – she has visions, hears voices in her head.

Her brother, Joe, just longs for freedom.

They're on the run. The question is, where? Because it's hard to feed yourself on whispers and lies, and the road ahead is a long and dangerous one . . .

puffin.co.uk

A country in turmoil. A family at war.
Can one boy and a blood red horse
save the throne of England?

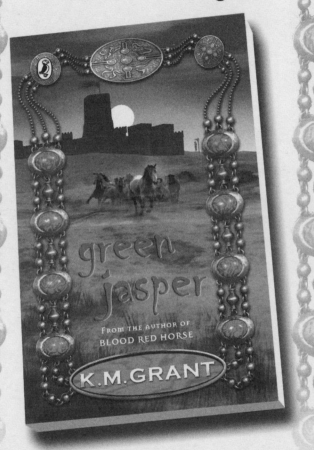

THE HEARTBREAKING
SEQUEL TO K. M. GRANT'S
BRILLIANT DEBUT NOVEL,
BLOOD RED HORSE

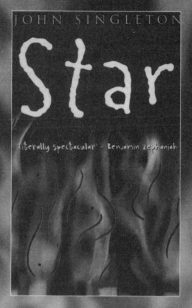